C000301600

Published by Ennay Publishing

Contact: nevillejarmstrong@gmail.com

Printed in Great Britain

Although every precaution has been taken in the preparation of this book, the publisher and author assume no responsibility for errors or omissions. Neither is any liability assumed for damages resulting from the use of the information contained herein.

ISBN 978-0-9572731-3-9

Foreword

Guy of Warwick is one of Briton's greatest literary heroes whose past fame rivalled that of the legendary King Arthur.

Within the Middle Ages, his popular renown placed him as a member of the assembly of the 'Nine Worthies'. This would put him alongside King Arthur and Charlemagne as the three Christian princes that exemplified chivalry, valour, and virtue.

The stories of Guy of Warwick became one of the first printed books, alongside 'The Canterbury Tales', 'Robin Hood' and 'Le Morte d'Arthur' and one of the first chapbooks printed for the common people. The adventure and moral instruction that surrounded Guy lasted until the Victorian Era but has since been forgotten in the literature of the modern age. The stories of Guy have varied in their telling, and over the centuries they have seen numerous changes in their characters and adventures. But the essence of a low born man rising through the social ranks with courageous and chivalrous deeds to win the hand of an Earl's daughter have stayed fundamental to the tales.

This book is the first in a series, which tells the story of Guy's early years.

Chapter One

The rank smell both disgusted and excited the young girl as she escaped from her guards. She lifted her dress from the dry brown dust that sprang up from her light steps as she ran down the well-trodden path of the narrow alley. The rough, stone and daubed timber walls of the buildings stretched up on both sides of the alley, providing some limited shade. But the oppressing glare of the overhead sun still reached down past the rough thatch of the overhanging roofs to bring a sting of perspiration to her brow.

She was a pretty girl in her twelfth year, with a light rosy complexion and shiny straw hair that was neatly tied in braids. She wore a long thin ivory satin dress that draped to the ground, beneath a light but heavily embroidered red cape that hung down her back to her waist. Her blue eyes shone bright with a keen intellect that took an intense interest in her surroundings.

She slowed to a halt and looked down to shake the powdered dirt from the expensive thin leather slippers. She had never worn the shoes before that day, and she raised her eyebrows at the dark stains that would need to be washed out. That task, however, would not fall to the girl but would be unnoticeably carried out by one of the many handmaidens that served her needs.

The girl had only just managed to escape her entourage, to explore the depths of the town that she regularly travelled through. She had never seen past the rich facades of the buildings that lined the main roads that surrounded her home. The busy thoroughfares both led to, and past, the magnificent castle fortress that dominated her life and she had a determination to see more of the town. She was fully aware of the grandeur and splendour of Warwick Castle, as she heard it emphasised from every guest that visited her father. But she knew of no other world, and was accustomed to its security and extravagance, although her parents had raised her to appreciate the indulgent personal care and service that she received due to her privileged position.

But now she wanted to take stock of her situation and compare her life to that of others. To do this properly, she would need to be without the presence of guards and servants that would alter the reality of the experience of observing how common people lived.

This day was the town's annual Pageant, and the streets were full of Warwick's townsfolk, as well as a large number of visitors and peddlers, who had come to the town especially for the occasion. The event had slowed her small procession of carriages and mounted horse guards, as she knew it would, and she had planned on being quickly hidden amongst the festive crowds when she slipped away.

She had waited until the attention of her guards and maids were diverted by an opportune disturbance. This was provided by a large woman, who worked in the inn, who was loudly quarrelling with some pedlar, who had picked on the wrong person to make a quick profit.

The shouts of the woman and the laughter of the crowd that had gathered to witness the entertainment had now faded as the girl moved quickly through the small maze of alleys. The high enclosed passageway echoed with the dull hum from the ever-present swarm of flies, broken only by the rhythmic sound of her heavy breathing, brought about by the exertion and thrill of her adventure.

The light danced brightly around her in smooth strokes, as the thin translucent washing, which hung on lines that stretched between the alley walls, billowed lightly in the breeze. A dog barked close by and a baby, awoken by the noise, cried for attention, as the girl walked slowly on. She constantly looked around to capture all the details of this new environment and she smiled to herself at the success of her scheme.

She had watched and waited for this moment during the regular trips to the town's mighty church from the castle where she lived, always alert for such an opportunity. When, moments before, the chance had presented itself, she executed her escape with surprising ease, which she attributed to a superior cunning that both delighted and satisfied her. She knew she would not have long to explore the town before her guards discovered her and she knew she would have to face the consequences of running away. But at that moment, she put that concern aside, as the thrill of the new experience commanded her attention.

She had to watch her steps carefully to avoid the dark murky patches that stained the path ahead. These dark damp patches also stained the timber and mud walls on both sides of the alley and in some places flowed down in sticky fingers from the roughly cut windows before sullying the edge of the path. It was these effluent dumps that created the smell that assailed the girl's senses and although the odour was a common backdrop to the town, she had never experienced it so strong.

She continued along the alley and as she turned a tight corner, she entered a small courtyard and disturbed a dog who was foraging amongst some waste, behind an empty wicker basket. The dog looked up and growled at the girl and then ignored her as it bit into a discarded bone. The girl paid little attention to the scruffy animal and looked ahead down a larger street, which stretched several yards back towards the main road, which seemed a mass of activity compared to the empty alleyways around her. She recognised the main road as Warwick's High Parade, and this would be alive with

5

guards and servants searching for her. So, she looked around for another exit to the courtyard, as she was not ready to be found yet.

There were other alleys in each side direction, as the courtyard was a crossroads to several paths. Some of the paths were narrow and dark from the shade of the thick thatched roofs and they seemed dank and unwelcoming, so she chose the left-hand alley for no other reason than it being lighter. But as she moved towards the alley, she was suddenly faced by a small band of young boys who walked out in front of her.

Their eager chatter ceased, as she caught their attention, and they stopped to stare at her before looking towards a larger boy who stood at the head of the group. The boys were dressed in similar clothes, with dirty baggy shifts, of the same dull shades of brown, and trousers that ended mid-calf. On their feet, they wore either leather slippers or ankle shoes that were tied with string. Some of them, even though it was a warm day, had cloth hats on their heads which barely covered their long untidy hair.

The larger boy, who was the leader of the small gang, became aware of the group's attention and that the others looked to him for a response. He stood forward and smiled at the girl, as he looked over the finery of her attire.

"Well, what have we here?" he said slowly, with a threatening undertone. "A lost rich girl in need of direction. That will cost her a penny or two," he continued and then turned to smile at his friends.

Although the boys were generally bigger than the girl, she thought that they were of similar age and as she looked across them, they all smirked back as they understood the head boy's intentions. They all thought that this young rich girl would provide them with some sport.

The girl was not overly intimidated by the boys, as they were just examples of the town's poor urchins that lived in a different and poorer world than hers. This was the world that she wanted to experience and the reason why she had escaped her escort.

"I am not lost," she said with an air of confidence.

"Perhaps she is not lost, but looking for someone to play with," one of the boys said moving around to the girl's side. Another boy moved deliberately to her other side to pen her in.

"Hinder me and you will be sorry," she responded, slowly looking around at the boys.

The boys all whooped their derision at her threat.

She thought about mentioning her father, who was the Lord and benefactor of these louts, but she felt it would be cowardice to hide behind his name, and the girl was not a coward.

"What are you going to do?" one of them called out with a sneer.

"What I am going to do is none of your business," she replied, raising her eyebrows. "But what you will do is get out of my way and let me move on," she continued with the air of authority and superiority that was inbred into her being.

The head boy lifted the short wooden staff that he was carrying and pointed it at the girl as he stepped towards her.

He pressed the end of the staff into the girl's shoulder and pushed slightly to force her back a step.

"You are not in your rich house now, with your rich belongings provided by your rich parents and we are not your servants to order around," the boy said, aggressively. "You are a stranger here and we will decide who can pass. We are the masters, and you will pay us toll to pass through, or we will take what is owed."

The boys all laughed in anticipation of what might come.

"I have no money, so I cannot pay you," she responded firmly. "But if you give me your names, I will make sure that you receive your dues and get what you deserve." Now it was the girl's turn to sound threatening.

The head boy's smile disappeared, and he reddened as his anger rose.

"You have rings on your fingers and at least one necklace that I can see, and probably other treasures that I cannot see. You have a rich dress and expensive shoes, and they will all raise a fair price. These I will take, and I may leave you a couple of bruises as a receipt of payment."

The boy, with an air of arrogance, poked her shoulder again with his staff, pushing her back another step.

The boy then suddenly crumpled and rolled over onto the floor as another staff hit him heavily across the side of his head from behind.

The blow was struck by a new boy, who had suddenly joined the group and he stepped forward with staff in hand to stand in front of the girl. He bowed his head slightly towards her in acknowledgement, and then smiled mischievously.

"My lady," the boy said, with a happy tone to his voice, "I hope these idiots were not bothering you."

The girl looked at the boy and smiled. She did not mean to smile, as the situation did not warrant any form of humour, but the boy's demeanour was amusing.

He was shorter than the other boys, which made him look younger, but he also seemed more heavily built and had a more assured and confident manner which, then again, made him look older.

He had a rounded face and bright blue eyes that lit up when he smiled back at her. His long straw-coloured, unkempt hair hung down straight to his shoulders with a fringe that was cut straight just above his eyebrows to frame his face. He seemed to be totally at ease and entertained by what was going on.

He unslung a small narrow bow from his shoulder and passed it over to the girl, along with a grubby linen basket that was full of arrows, which he unhooked from his waist. He smiled again at her before turning quickly around to face the gang's leader as he rose from the ground.

"Not very brave, Tom, to attack an unarmed girl," the boy said with an air of assurance.

"Bloody hell, Guy!" the gang's leader responded, rubbing the side of his head to alleviate the pain from the staff's blow.

"And was it brave to hit me from behind?" Tom then said, holding up his staff.

"I am not behind you now Tom, if you want to take it further," Guy replied, raising his own staff in an offensive gesture.

Tom slowly looked around at his companions and then smiled at Guy.

"There are five of us and only one of you," Tom finally said. "Not good odds for you, I think."

"I think you will find that there are two of us," the girl said from behind Guy. "But there is only one who has an arrow nocked."

Guy slowly looked behind to see the girl with his bow drawn and an arrow aimed over Guy's shoulder directly at Tom. Guy raised his eyebrows at the girl and then slowly looked back at the other boys who were now slowly backing away towards the alley from which they came.

Then suddenly, the relative quiet of the courtyard was shattered by the thunderous noise of horses pushing in from the alleyway that led towards the town's main road. The horse's hoofs thudded on the hard surface and their breathing was laboured as their riders forced their mounts through the narrow path. A small number of foot soldiers, who followed behind, then added to the din as they shouted at the boys. But the gang of youths had now turned to run back along the narrow dark alley and away from the men.

Clouds of dust exploded into the air from the horses as they were turned tightly within the courtyard and Guy and the girl had to turn their heads away to allow themselves to breathe within the maelstrom.

Guy did not run but turned to the girl and casually raised his hand to take back his bow. The girl relaxed the pull of the string and unhooked the arrow.

Returning the arrow to the bag, she passed the bow back to Guy. But as he reached out, he was suddenly sent sprawling to the ground as one of the riders kicked him heavily on the shoulder with the heel of his boot. The bow fell to the floor and Guy instinctively reached for it, so that it would not be damaged by the horse's hoofs. The clear ringing sound of a sword being withdrawn from its scabbard then pierced the air followed by a cry from the girl in protest.

"Sir Roderick. Stop!" the girl quickly shouted over the noise as she held up both of her arms towards the horseman to bar his way. "He is a friend."

The two horses were quickly reigned in, and the three men of arms calmed themselves. The men then stood quietly against the wall on the far side of the courtyard, keeping out of the way of the riders. The noise in the courtyard gradually dropped until only the abrasive snorts of the horse's panting could be heard.

"Are you hurt, Felice?" Sir Roderick enquired with a heavy tone of arrogance and superiority, as he looked down at the girl.

"No, not at all," Felice said calmly regaining her composure. "But I may have been if it was not for this brave boy who came to my aid."

Guy rose to his knees. Without taking his eyes from his assailant, he slowly dusted himself down and analysed his situation. He then slowly rose to his feet and rubbed his shoulder which would be bruised in the morning.

Sir Roderick was a tall thin man who sat very upright on his horse. He was dressed in his finest ceremonial armour with a bright polished helmet from where within his dark narrow eyes peered out. He had a thin pointed nose that stretched down in line with the helmet's hinged side plates, and he sported a wide, but thin, oiled moustache that stretched over a tight-lipped mouth.

Sir Roderick looked down on the boy with disgust.

Guy looked over the man's outfit. He wore a black surcoat over his polished chain mail with a large white symbol that Guy did not recognise. He also spawned a large plume of white feathers that were fixed to the back of a gleaming eagle figure that was fixed to the top of his helmet. Guy assumed by the rider's grandeur that he was a trained and high-born knight.

The other rider was also dressed in full dress armour, but he sat more relaxed on his horse behind Sir Roderick. He had removed his helmet and was wiping the sweat from his brow. He had short light brown coloured hair and ruddy cheeks and a friendlier demeanour. Even wearing his armour, the rider still looked broad and stocky and sat in sharp contrast to the slight build of the other horseman. The man was older than Sir Roderick and appeared, in his nature, more approachable. He wore a bright red surcoat bearing the standing black bear clawing at a ragged staff, which was the familiar livery of the Earl of Warwick. His horse was much larger than Roderick's and Guy instantly recognised the great grey destrier as a horse from the castle that his father; the town's blacksmith and farrier, had regularly shoed.

Guy quickly looked back at the knight and then recognised Sir Harold of Arden, the owner of the horse. "And why are you here, my lady? Did you get lost?" the older knight said, looking around Roderick at Felice, with a knowing smile.

"Oh yes, Sir Harold. I got lost," Felice replied, looking down at her shoes. "I went to look at some pretty coloured ribbon and then I must have wandered off in the wrong direction."

"Ah, pretty ribbon," Sir Harold answered with amusement. "You have such a passion for pretty ribbon," he stated more than asked, knowing full well that the girl had little interest in such trivia. He then slowly dismounted, keeping tight hold of the horse's reins.

"Who were those ruffians?" Sir Roderick asked sharply of Guy.

"I don't know," Guy answered, shrugging his shoulders. "They must be strangers from out of town, not used to our ways," Guy lied. "But I am sure that they were only messing around and did not recognise Lady Felice."

"And you do recognise her?" Sir Roderick asked sternly.

Guy turned to look at Felice. "I do now," he said smiling at her.

"And you faced several of them all on your own?" Sir Harold asked, quickly leading his horse around Roderick's to prevent his companion from hitting Guy again. He then stood and faced the boy.

Guy bowed his head towards the knight as a sign of respect.

"I know how to handle myself and I was not the only one facing them," he said glancing at Felice.

"So, my archery lessons paid off, my lady?" Sir Harold then asked Felice without expecting an answer. "Can I see the bow, my lad?" He then asked Guy.

Guy handed it over to the knight.

Sir Harold took the bow and released the horse's reins. He drew the bow's weight a couple of times, before handing it back to Guy.

"A lot stronger than your usual bow, my lady, but you managed to draw it back well enough," Sir Harold said.

12

"It must be the inner strength that you have instilled in my body, Sir Harold, brought about from your training," Felice said as she breathed in to expand her chest. She then heavily patted her stomach to mimic her tutor's actions that he demonstrated constantly during her weekly lessons.

The knight smiled warmly at Felice.

"And how well can you use this bow?" Sir Harold enquired of Guy.

Guy looked over and then nodded towards Roderick.

"I could bring him down at two hundred paces in most weathers; four out of five times."

Sir Harold raised his eyebrows.

"And what of a target my size?" Sir Harold asked again lightly.

Guy looked Sir Harold up and down. "Five out of Five," Guy responded.

Sir Harold laughed heartily.

"And you are?" Sir Harold asked of Guy.

"I am Guy. The smith's son," Guy replied. "And a friend of Galahad."

Guy moved forward as he spoke and reached up to stroke the horse's flank above its foreleg. The horse snorted affectionately.

Guy was then knocked forwards and smashed his face into the horse's neck before bouncing off the hard flesh and falling to the floor. Roderick had once again kicked out at the boy from above.

Galahad reared slightly from the impact and nickered in agitation.

"How dare you!" Sir Roderick yelled furiously at Guy. "I should have you thrashed for your impudence."

"Calm yourself, Roderick!" Sir Harold interceded angrily, before taking a deep breath to compose himself. "If this boy is, as he says, a master archer, a friend of Galahad and the protector of Lady Felice, then we owe him some respect." He then turned to Guy.

"Although my lad, you should know your place, and not behave with such familiarity."

Sir Harold looked up and glared at Roderick, clearly showing his displeasure at his unwarranted and excessive treatment of a boy, who did not know any better.

Sir Harold then looked back at Guy and puffed his chest out with exaggerated authority. "I could have you killed for your insolence," but there was a tone of heavy mocking behind his threat.

He then offered Guy his hand to pull him up.

"And is your father not also the town reeve, and as the reeve's son you should know better on how to conduct yourself."

Guy took the knight's hand and pulled himself back to his feet. He looked up at Roderick and slowly brushed himself down with an air of defiance.

"My humble apologies, my lord. I must be dazed from the blow to the head," Guy answered looking directly at Sir Harold.

The knight laughed again at Guy's reply.

"Apologies accepted," Sir Harold said. "And now it's time to return Lady Felice to the castle. Her father is expected to return later, and she will be required to attend him."

Sir Harold handed the longbow back towards Guy.

"You have my thanks, Guy, the reeve's son for coming to the aid of Lady Felice," he said warmly. "If I had a coin, I would reward you."

"The lady's wellbeing is reward enough, my lord," Guy said taking the bow with slight apprehension.

Sir Harold laughed again and regained Galahad's reins. "You see Roderick, chivalry stretches even to the gutters," he said and then turned to wink at Guy.

Sir Harold then reached out his arm to beckon Felice to walk alongside him.

Felice paused as she passed Guy and slowly turned to him. "You also have my thanks, Guy. You showed both courage and valour in saving me," Felice said with an air of formality and with a slight nod of her head. She then presented Guy with his bag of arrows and walked away with Sir Harold.

Roderick glared down at Guy before he turned his horse sharply, pushing Guy roughly to the side with the horse's flank and then kicked his horse to follow Sir Harold and Felice.

The men at arms then moved away from the shadows and followed quietly behind, almost unnoticed.

Guy watched them go before brushing himself down more thoroughly. He then rubbed his shoulder to ease the pain before tying his arrow bag to his waist. It was then that he noticed a pale cloth hanging down and was surprised to find a small cream satin kerchief wrapped around one of the arrows.

Guy looked at the delicate piece of cloth and saw the elaborate light green clover leaves that were embroidered into the satin, which were only highlighted when angled into the sunlight.

'A lady's token.' Guy thought with a strange mix of amusement and pride. He stood tall, as he walked away back down the alley towards his home, whistling happily to himself.

Chapter Two

Guy pulled down on the forge bellows while his father pushed a red-hot metal strip into the glowing charcoals. Sparks danced up as the coals were pushed around to cover the newly formed gate hinge.

Guy and been working with his father in the forge for most of the morning and his face was already streaked with black dust, hardened in the sweat caused by the fire's heat and smoke. The forge was a grim place to work.

The heat from the fire radiated out across both Sigard and Guy, with the fire's smoke drifting up to the wide hole in the thatch roof and out into the outside air. Some of the smoke, however, remained inside the forge and curled across the roof's black tarred thatched surface before sinking slowly down towards the floor, creating the dark and engulfing atmosphere that they worked in. Although Guy enjoyed working with his father, he was impatient for this more mundane work to end, so that his father could then spend some time teaching him some of the more intricate skills of a blacksmith. This was especially in the forging of the sword that they were working on together, which was as a reward for Guy in dutifully carrying out the daily monotonous work.

Guy's father only spent a brief time in the day, forging the sword with Guy. He knew that that the sword was a good incentive to keep Guy's interest and commitment in the everyday work, so he had to plan his schedule carefully and time the jobs accordingly.

"Sigard, are you there?" A man's commanding voice called out from the street outside.

Guy's father quickly turned around at the calling of his name, to see two riders, mounted on their horses, waiting in front of the forge's entrance.

Sigard quickly pulled the red-hot hinge from the coals of the furnace and went outside to greet his visitors. He ducked his head under the overhanging thatch of the low roof and wiped his hands on his leather apron as the light of the day stung his eyes.

He recognised the man immediately and quickly bowed his head in respect.

"Sir Harold," Sigard said, with deference.

Guy's father then looked at the young girl next to him who was sitting side-saddle on a small brown pony.

"My lady," Sigard said bowing his head to the girl.

The girl, as she had been schooled, did not respond, and looked past the blacksmith.

"Greetings Sigard, and how are you on this fine day?" Sir Harold asked in obvious good spirits.

"I am well, my lord," Sigard replied. "How can I be of service?"

Sir Harold was wearing light riding clothes with long boots, and he swung his right leg over the horse and lightly dismounted to the ground. He then moved across to hold the girl's reins.

"May I introduce Lady Felice, daughter of Earl Rohand?" Sir Harold replied. "Whose pony needs its shoes examined."

Sir Harold took Felice's hand and supported her as she gracefully slipped down the saddle to the ground.

"At once, my lord," Sigard said, again wiping his hands down the front of his apron.

"Perhaps your lad can look to it," Sir Harold said, as he gestured towards Guy, who was standing in the shadows looking out at them. "As I would like to discuss a proposition with you in private."

Sigard looked closely at Sir Harold, trying to work out what the revered knight could want to discuss with him. Sigard regularly provided services for the Earl of Warwick and his large entourage, but rarely saw anyone of a higher rank than a squire. The exception was when Galahad needed shoeing and Sir Harold nearly always brought the horse himself.

"Of course, my lord," Sigard replied and then called for Guy to come forward. "Attend to the lady's pony, Guy," he told his son. "And be sure to mind your manners," he then whispered to Guy as he passed.

Sigard then gestured for Sir Harold to enter the building towards a rough bench where his customers would sit if they wanted to wait for him to finish any work.

Guy acknowledged Sir Harold with a nod as he passed and then walked out of the forge and into the daylight. He wiped his hands down the front of his apron and then bowed his head to the girl.

"My lady," Guy said in greeting Felice and moved towards the front of the pony to stoke its muzzle. He paused.

"May I?" he then asked, remembering his lowly position.

"Of course," Felice answered.

"Have you recovered from yesterday's trouble?" Guy asked with a genuine concern.

"Facing my father was more of a trial," Felice answered and stood alongside Guy to rub the pony's neck. "He is very protective and does not like me to be out of the castle without a guard," she smiled. "Sir Roderick could not wait to inform him of my so-called ordeal and painted himself in a greater picture than truth warranted, but Sir Harold covered for my indiscretion and made light of it. And Sir Harold's opinion carries more weight than Roderick's; thank the Lord."

"Sir Roderick wanted to ride out to the surrounding villages," she continued, "to search out the ruffians and punish them for their misdemeanours. But I suspect a simple inquiry to the blacksmith's son on the whereabouts of Tom and his friends would have probably sufficed."

Guy glimpsed Felice's smile as she spoke, and he also smiled.

"No friends of mine, my lady," Guy responded, "and I doubt if they would have harmed you. It was all bluster and empty words."

"I would, however, still like to thank you for coming to my aid. I have never been rescued before."

Guy laughed.

"I think it was the arrow that you pointed at them that did the rescuing, my lady," Guy said. "Did you see their faces?"

"They were surprised," Felice answered smiling. "But I do not know what my next move would have been if Sir Harold had not shown up."

"It would have been interesting," Guy replied walking slowly around the pony looking it up and down. "But they will think twice before threatening a pretty girl again."

Guy caught his breath at his indiscretion, although Felice held her hand to her mouth and giggled lightly.

"I apologise, my lady, for my rudeness. I am not used to behaving properly with people of your rank."

"Apology accepted Guy, although a part of me does not want to receive apologies for being called pretty," Felice said. "Especially as it happens rarely."

"I doubt that my lady," Guy said and then screwed up his face as he repeated his imprudence.

He then took a deep breath and concentrated on what was required of him.

"What is wrong with your mount, my lady?" Guy then asked as he stood back to look at the pony.

"Oh, nothing Guy. It was just an excuse for me to come to see you and offer my gratitude. The pony was Sir Harold's idea."

Guy smiled at Felice.

"It was my honour, my lady," Guy said warmly. "You do not often get damsels in distress around these parts."

Guy stepped back towards Felice to stroke the pony again.

They were then suddenly interrupted by a boy, who ran from around the side of the forge. He stopped as he turned the corner and was taken aback at the presence of Guy and Felice on the roadside.

Felice held the pony's reins, as it stepped back nervously at the sudden arrival of the boy. She recognised him at once as a member of the gang from the alley that assailed her the day before, but she remained casual and said nothing as she looked on in interest.

The boy looked around to see if there was anyone else in earshot.

"I have not spoken with you Guy," the boy said quickly in a hushed tone. "But take care of your pits. Tom is out to pay you back."

The boy then quickly turned and hurried back in the direction from where he came.

Guy was instantly agitated as he considered the boy's words and their meaning.

"Is there trouble?" Felice asked with concern, not understanding the meaning of the warning, but seeing Guy's unease.

"Probably, my lady," He replied. "It looks like Tom is either going to wreak the charcoal pits up in the Budbrooke woods, or he is devising a trap for me to get his revenge for yesterday. I hit him fairly hard, and he won't forget that in a hurry." He then paused and looked towards his father. "But either will mean trouble."

"What is the more likely?" Felice asked with a hint of excitement.

"Probably the trap, my lady. Even Tom would not be so stupid to ruin the coal pits. My father would not be happy." Guy squeezed his fingers into the palms of his hands. "I need to act," Guy continued. "But I do not wish to do you the discourtesy of leaving you here unattended."

"Sir Harold!" Felice called out aloud.

The knight came out from the forge immediately.

"Is there a problem, my lady?" He asked looking at Guy.

"Not with me," Felice answered. "But I think we need to go. Are you disposed to leave your discussions with Guy's father until later?"

A smile crossed Sir Harold's face, as it always did when Felice acted in that manner. Her training and education had given her the air and sophistication of a Lady of the court, but there was also a natural bearing to her character. She had inherited this from her father, which made her appear far more mature than her age. It provided Sir Harold with constant amusement, although it was accompanied by a great deal of pride.

"I think our business is done, my lady. I have left the smith with something to think about."

He turned to Guy's father who was standing in the shadows.

"I will take your leave Sigard, but I will return tomorrow for your answer."

"Thank you, my lord. I am much indebted," Sigard replied, bowing his head.

Sir Harold stood back quickly as Guy brushed past him, as he ran back into the forge to retrieve his bow and a bag of arrows that were leaning against the rear wall of the building. Guy then quickly ran through the back doorway and into the street beyond without any acknowledgement to Felice or Sir Harold.

Sir Harold looked sideward at Felice with interest. She was now climbing back onto the pony with considerably less grace than when she dismounted and not waiting for any assistance to mount.

"I think we need to hurry," Felice said, glaring at Sir Harold to indicate her intent.

"At once, my lady?" Sir Harold said quickly placing his foot into a stirrup and pulling himself into Galahad's saddle.

Guy ran up the Hampton Road towards the woods near the village of Budbrooke, which was situated a couple of miles to the west of Warwick. This was a familiar route for Guy, as he attended the charcoal pits daily, but he left his usual route and diverted down a small dirt track as soon as he crossed the Gog brook. He then followed the stream around the low hills and into the denser trees that made up the immense Forest of Arden that stretched for many miles to the north and west of Warwick.

Guy was familiar with the local forest and knew its tracks and paths well. It was in these woods that he regularly honed his archery skills, which helped him put food on the family table, and then sell the surplus for profit. But on this day, it also enabled him to approach the charcoal piles with the stealth and guile of a hunter and from the opposite direction that Tom and his gang, would be expecting.

The trees thinned out as he approached the charcoal piles, as the birch, alder and other trees in the local area had been regularly coppiced to supply the wood for the production of the charcoal. The piles themselves were built in a line that stretched across the side of a small meadow clearing at the edge of the forest.

Guy's father leased this area of forest from the Earl of Warwick, which was equivalent to the land measurement of a hide, within which he managed the trees for the charcoal to power the forge. The lease was negotiated in respect of reduced rates for the Earl to maintain his soldier's arms and to provide farrier services for his many horses. But there was also a loose understanding of the hunting and foraging rights within Sigard's forest lease which allowed Guy free rein to roam, trap, and hunt within the Budbrooke woods. Guy had taken advantage of these rights and was intimate with all the paths and hidden dells in the local vicinity.

The four charcoal piles were large six-foot-high cones that contained wood logs piled on their ends and covered in turf and mud, which Guy regularly kept moist. These turf covers removed the oxygen from the smouldering wood inside the pile to prohibit them from catching fully alight. Guy took pride in manipulating the piles so that they were neither extinguished nor fully lit by flames. He controlled the piles by manipulating the air through the conical structures by systematically lifting areas of turf to create drafts, but in a controlled manner to keep the process alive. Guy had spent years carrying out this task and had become very adept in the process.

The piles were all intact.

Guy sighed and smiled to himself in relief. Guy's biggest worry had been the destruction or damage to these piles as their loss would have had a great impact on his father's income. Although their destruction would not have been directly his fault, he would have still been blamed for not maintaining them.

Guy sank to his haunches and caught his breath as he considered the situation at hand. He knew that it must be a trap and Tom and his gang would be located somewhere south of the small meadow within which the piles were built. There was a tall boundary hazel hedgerow that stretched along the bottom of the meadow and several aspen coppices, which were evenly spaced back towards the town. These trees reduced in their number and size as they gave way to the rough ploughed fields and grazing areas for cattle and sheep.

Guy crept forward to the edge of the meadow and unslung his bow and placed it carefully on the ground. He then lay his arrow bag alongside it before slowly settling himself among the clumps of hazel and fern, with the minimal amount of noise or movement. The greenery stretched up in front of him hiding him from the meadow and beyond.

He carefully scanned the green pasture and the hedgerows that surrounded it, looking for anything that was out of place, but he saw nothing.

The Budbrooke meadow was a strange place and showed obvious signs of a previous settlement. Regular ditches spread out like fingers across the grass with remnants of building materials, such as rough bricks and timbers. The old walls and roofs of the demolished buildings had, over the years, been gradually taken and reused within the town, farms, and other local villages. Several sheep grazed in the meadow that kept the grass well cropped, and they seemed unaware of any disturbance or threat. Clumps of thistle and nettle were dotted around the meadow along with the occasional hawthorn bush which offered shelter to the sheep.

From the meadow, Guy could look down over the town and the castle fortifications that were built across Aethelflaed's mound. The castle was built upon a sandstone outcrop, and could easily be seen above the trees, as could the large tower of the town's church in the centre of Warwick. Aethelflaed's mound had been built recently and marked Warwick as an Anglo-Saxon burh, which was a fortified town that had been constructed in defence against the Danes. The town's people and the local garrison could retreat into the fortification and defend themselves from behind the large palisade walls if the Danes ever attacked. Warwick was one of the larger burhs in the Anglo-Saxon kingdoms and rivalled Winchester, Stafford and Tamworth in its size and importance.

Guy slowly crossed his legs beneath him on the ground and relaxed his posture for what might be a considerable length of time. Waiting in silence was an attribute of a good hunter and Guy had developed that skill to an art. He listened to the chirping of the birds and the buzzing of the insects as he sat at ease. He was not at all afraid at the prospect of Tom's revenge, but he was excited at what might occur, and his mind was engaged with the planning for all eventualities. To Guy, it was all a game, and he would enjoy trying to outwit his opponents.

It took around thirty minutes before anything unusual occurred. A reverberating scream of a pheasant called out from the far side of the meadow and Guy carefully focused on the direction of the noise. He saw movement in between the trees and watched as figures moved towards the meadow between clumps of bracken and thorn. He recognised the path into the meadow as the main route from the town and realised that the movement was situated on both sides of the track.

Guy smiled at how obvious the trap was and wondered if he should have approached the meadow from that side, to put himself closer to Tom's gang.

Then Guy suddenly stiffened, as he heard the distinctive crack of a breaking twig directly behind him. He instantly realised that it was caused by a heavy footfall and that he was in full view from that direction. While still in control of his reactions, he kept calm and did not look around, as he did not want to make any sharp movements that might expose him further. He sighed and then cursed in his mind for not protecting himself better and felt foolish that Tom might have got the better of him by anticipating Guy's response to his trap.

Guy slowly and carefully reached down and grasped his bow with his left hand, while simultaneously, and just as carefully, selecting one of his blunt practice arrows from his bag with his right hand. Guy had made these arrows especially for his own use and they allowed him to disable prey without cutting any flesh. The arrows were weighted the same as a bodkin arrow, but they had a broad, rounded tip that would not pierce anything of significance but would easily incapacitate a rabbit or bird. They also produced a significant bruise when fired at any adversary.

Guy gradually notched the arrow to the string in front of him with the bow lying flat on his lap and then in a sudden movement fell quickly backwards while turning to face into the forest. While falling, he drew the bow across his body and over his face as he lay prone with his back to the ground.

Guy fired at the legs of the person approaching and at twenty paces he was unlikely to miss.

The man cried out in pain as his leg buckled beneath him and he tumbled heavily to the ground. Another man, who was walking behind the first, moved quickly sideward to take cover behind a large tree.

Guy suddenly blanched at the sight of the grown man on the floor, who was holding his thigh and cursing. This was not Tom or any of his cronies. This was no longer a game and Guy wondered what trouble he was now in. Guy waited as the other man carefully peered from around the tree and then waved at Guy to put his bow down.

"Hold your fire young lad," he said, "it is me, Sir Harold." Guy closed his eyes and like the man rolling around on the ground in front of him, he cursed, but unlike the man it was quiet and under his breath.

Sir Harold stepped slowly out from behind his cover and, ignoring his companion, picked up the arrow which was lying on the ground. He examined its blunt point.

"Stop your moaning Alfred, I thought I asked for stealth," Sir Harold said smiling, as he lightly kicked his companion as he walked past.

However, Sir Harold stopped in his stride, and the smile was gone, as Guy pulled out another arrow and stood up drawing his bow again.

But it was not Sir Harold that was the threat, as Guy had heard a noise from behind him as Tom and his gang, who were shouting raucously, were running across the meadow towards them. They had not missed the commotion that had just engulfed Guy and they had seen him hiding in the ferns.

The sheep scattered as the boys ran through them and Guy turned and let loose the arrow. He then watched Tom cry out as the arrow hit home and bounced off his thigh. Tom dropped the staff he was carrying and toppled over to the ground holding his leg with both hands.

Guy pulled another arrow from his bag, but then heard the ringing sound of a sword being drawn from its scabbard, as Sir Harold walked past him and out of the cover of the forest.

Sir Harold screamed a loud war cry and raised his sword high as he ran towards the boys.

The sight of the knight charging towards them with sword raised stopped the boys in their tracks and they instantly turned and fled. Only one of them stopped to help Tom get off the ground, allowing him to painfully scamper behind them with a strange limping hop.

Sir Harold had only stepped a few paces into the meadow before he stopped and turned back towards Guy, smiling broadly.

"If only all skirmishes were that easy," he said as he sheathed his sword.

"On your feet Alfred," Sir Harold bellowed at the man, who was now sitting up and rubbing his thigh.

"You won't need armour. That's what you said," Alfred moaned quietly. "It's only boys. That's what you said, and now I am crippled."

"You should be grateful that the lad aimed for your thigh and not your knee," Sir Harold replied.

"How do you know what he was targeting, Sir Harold?" Alfred said. "He might have been aiming at my head."

"Were you Guy?" Sir Harold asked of the boy.

"The thigh, Sir Harold," Guy answered. "A headshot would have killed him at that short distance."

"And you know this?"

"It has killed animals with harder heads than his," Guy replied.

Sir Harold laughed again.

"I doubt if any animal has a harder head than Alfred's."

"I am sorry to have shot at you, "Guy said calmly, "but you caught me by surprise. I have never seen any castle folk in these woods before. You usually hunt in the southern woods."

Sir Harold looked down at Guy with raised eyebrows.

Guy looked back and the silence hung around them for several moments before Guy, recognising the look from their previous meeting, understood Sir Harold's request with slight embarrassment.

"My lord," Guy stated as his shoulders slumped.

"Manners and respect are important in our lives, Guy, and my position, and hopefully my actions, require your respect. Your new life will demand manners, so you must learn and learn quickly."

"But you are right," Sir Harold continued, "although I am Sir Harold of Arden, I am not intimate with this part of the forest, and we rarely come here when hunting." He then stood up straight in a noble stance. "But shooting at a Knight of the Realm, who is a sworn oath man of the Earl of Warwick, and also the King of Wessex and Mercia, has serious consequences."

"Hang him; here and now," Alfred said standing up, cautiously putting his weight on his injured leg."

"But with all the noise that this oaf made, you had every right to fire on us and are therefore pardoned. But we were sent on a mission of mercy by Lady Felice to watch over you," Sir Harold replied and smiled. "Well, I was sent on a mission, but Alfred here, one of my accomplished retainers and supposedly a skilled huntsman, said he knew the area. I therefore brought him along, as I thought that he would be an asset in tracking you."

"Why on earth the lady would care for such a scruffy peasant like him, I don't know," Alfred replied.

"I believe she feels responsible for getting him into this fight with this dangerous gang of troublemakers," Sir Harold said. "Out of town strangers, I think you said, Guy?"

Sir Harold tilted his head and gave Guy a questioning look.

"I suspect so, my lord," Guy replied bashfully.

"And Lady Felice will therefore be amused at the outcome," Sir Harold said.

"Yes, my lord," Guy answered.

"Well, if the Lady is happy, then the Earl is happy and therefore I am happy."

"Yes, my lord. But what did you mean by 'my new life requiring manners'?" Guy asked picking up on Sir Harold's earlier comment.

"Oh, that," Sir Harold answered. "I have just offered your father the new position of Steward to the Earl," he continued, looking back across the meadow. "And if he accepts, then he will be required to lodge within the castle walls. You and the rest of your family will have to accompany him."

He then looked down at Guy.

"Your manners will therefore have to improve if you live in the castle and are surrounded by people who will expect and demand your respect," he then added.

Guy looked away from Sir Harold as he tried to take in what was just said.

Sir Harold also looked away, understanding Guy's anxiety at the sudden announcement of his father's potential appointment. He knew the impact that it will potentially have on the boy's life, along with all the changes that it will incorporate. Sir Harold tried to visualise Guy's concerns and thought that whatever he was thinking, it will not be half of what will face him.

"Well, my lad," Sir Harold said. "Let me have a look at one of those arrows," and reached out his hand for Guy's bow.

Guy handed it over.

"I will give you two minutes head start, Alfred," Sir Harold said, "to stretch your legs across the field and we will see how well this arrow flies."

Sir Harold smiled at Guy and playfully raised his eyebrows.

Chapter Three

Guy avoided the straight thrust with a downward vertical parry, before swivelling around to arc his sword across his opponents back.

His opponent dived forward and rolled over his shoulder before then crouching, with his own sword brought back into a defensive pose to face Guy.

Guy, however, had followed the outward swing of the weapon and once again twisted his body against the sword's momentum. The manoeuvre brought him to the left of his opponent, and it opened up the right side of their body to the final stroke.

The blow was hard, but it was not executed with any real force and the heavy padding of his opponent's jacket prevented any injury. However, it still hurt and left Guy's opponent rolled up on the ground, slightly winded.

Guy leant on his heavy wooden training sword, panting heavily to regain his breath, before offering his hand to his opponent. The young man, who was now lying on his back, clasped Guy's wrist and pulled himself up, slapping Guy on the shoulder.

"Are you hurt, Terold?" Guy asked of his opponent, with concern.

Although the swords were wooden, Guy had fixed iron strips to the sides of both Terold's and his own blades. The modifications were, not just to match the weight of a normal broad sword but to be heavier so that it would increase their strength. He also had to effect a metal collar to the sword's pommel to balance out the weight, but these were the benefits of his blacksmith training.

"Only in body and pride," Terold said smiling. "That was a neat move, though," Terold continued, as he stretched his back, grimacing with the pain.

"Well practised, that is all," Guy answered, "and I know you so well now that I can predict your moves."

Terold was a couple of years older than Guy and they were like brothers. He was taller and broader than Guy and had short black hair and a growth of dark stubble on his face, that he always tried to present as a beard, much to the amusement of his elders.

Terold was the first of Sir Harold's pages who had recognised Guy's capabilities when he first turned up to his first practise session at the castle. Guy entered the training field as a scruffy ruffian who looked completely out of place, but with a weapon in his hand, he showed a level of raw skill and courage. Terold liked Guy straight away and quickly befriended the lost and lonely new arrival. The other pages and squires mocked and abused Guy because of his age, size, and background. But the bullying slackened when Guy first fired at the archery range, and instantly proved himself the best archer of the group. But archery was a commoner's skill and Guy's total inexperience in swordsmanship and tournament skills left him isolated from the other rich sons of Warwick nobles. Terold however saw the drive and intelligence of the young boy. He also recognised the subtle attention that Sir Harold paid him. Sir Harold had not overly signalled him out for any special attention but always discreetly watched over him. Sir Harold was the 'Master of Arms' for the Earl and was responsible for the training of the young pages and squires. Terold thought it would be good to keep on his good side by befriending Guy.

Terold was then knocked forward slightly as a hand slapped down on his shoulder from behind.

"Well done, young Terold. In fact, well done to the pair of you," Sir Harold said as came alongside them.

"Although, Terold, you may have to now stop holding back with Guy and apply some of your strength," he continued.

"I tried that several weeks ago, Sir Harold," Terold replied, "but he just turns it against me."

"Guy is fast," Sir Harold stated.

"Practise, Sir Harold," Guy responded, "from all of that running away."

Sir Harold looked down at them in thought.

"Well, I think I will now need to see how quick you both are when weighed down with armour," Sir Harold eventually said.

"Really!" both boys said in unison and with the same level of excitement, suddenly reacting with unbridled glee, playfully pushing each other like the children they were.

Sir Harold smiled at their exuberance, recognising the advancement this presented to the boys.

"And once you can both dance and tumble with full chainmail, I may then consider getting some proper horses for you to ride, instead of those child's ponies that you currently play with."

The boys jumped up with joy. This was a major development for them, as it represented a move from the status of a page to a position of a squire and a growth into manhood.

"I think that will even things up, young Terold. He may be faster than you, but he is not stronger," Sir Harold said as he again patted Terold on the shoulder and turned away back towards the castle keep.

"Go and see the armourer and get measured for your chainmail. I have already given my approval," Sir Harold shouted as he walked away.

The boys instantly ran past their fighting tutor and up towards the armoury in a race to get there first.

"Halt!" Sir Harold called out to them.

The boys stopped and stood up straight, awaiting Sir Harold.

"You do not get away with it that lightly," Sir Harold said as he drew level. "You will also need to increase your skills by learning some household tasks. I think that I would like you to perform as Cup Bearers at the Easter feast that the Earl has planned. The Earl and his family will be returning from Court for the spring, while the King is in France, and he will be hosting several important guests."

The boys lost some of the excitement.

They were used to serving the requirements of the Earl's retainers and senior castle staff, where they enjoyed the raucous and drunken atmosphere in the castle canteen. It also often meant that they would have more than their fair share of leftover food and ale. This made up for the relentless verbal and physical abuse, although good-natured in its intent, which was liberally handed out by the men to the young boys.

But a formal feast in front of the Earl was a different matter altogether.

"And your performance will reflect my tutoring," Sir Harold continued, "so I expect the same level of commitment and application that you give to your weapons training."

"So once, you have gathered your armour, you will then report to the steward for instructions, which will include getting fitted out for Cup Bearer's outfits," Sir Harold said. He then smiled as he saw their lack of enthusiasm for wearing ceremonial uniforms. "I like my trainees to look pretty," he then said as he stopped in front of Terold and made a show of straightening his jacket. He then laughed as he walked on.

It suddenly dawned on Guy, why his father had not been around very often, and why he was distracted when he was. This feast will require a lot of planning and work, as well as a big worry for him.

"No tumbling or rolling around necessary for this task, Guy," Sir Harold said as he strolled away from them.

"Just good manners and correct etiquette," he continued, laughing. "Just down your street."

Guy and his parents had moved into lodgings within the castle, following Sir Harold's offer, four years ago. The old steward had died from a sudden illness and the Earl had to find a replacement quickly.

The Earl first sought to find a suitable candidate from within his British estates, but Sir Harold had recommended Sigard, due to his effective organisation of the town and local farmlands.

As Reeve of Warwick, Sigard ensured that all taxes were paid to the Earl and in return, the merchants and peasantry were lawfully protected. Sigard's role included the management of any disputes, which he did with efficient common sense and compromise. But beyond his role, Sigard also provided a level of social care within the bounds of the area of his responsibility. He always made sure that families were protected from paying taxes if they suffered any illness or loss that was no fault of their own.

The role of reeve should have compensated Sigard from working elsewhere, as the job was seen as demanding of time and effort. But Sigard still worked the forge as much as he could, to support the contingency money needed to finance the town's welfare fund. It also helped to provide a trade for his son that would give him a decent future. All this added to the respect that Sigard had gained throughout the local area. This respect eased the amount of work in carrying out his reeve duties, which in turn allowed him more time to work with Guy in the smithy.

Although the Earl had not recognised Sigard's capabilities, Sir Harold had.

Sir Harold regularly had to investigate why Warwick and the local villages had virtually no disputes or grievances compared to other of the Earl's estates across the country. But it was found to be just down to efficiency, integrity, social justice, and general region-wide respect for the reeve. This was a mirror for how Sir Harold saw his own behaviour and attitude. He, therefore, had no doubts in recommending Sigard to take over as Steward to the Earl.

But Sigard had his own doubts and concerns over the role.

When Sir Harold first offered it, he was unsure that he could carry out the required obligations of the position, as he had no experience in the role and would receive no formal handover. But Sigard was a very conscientious man and recognised the benefits that he had already received from being a vassal under the care of the Earl of Warwick. So, he accepted that he had a duty to his liege lord and if Earl Rohand required his service, and had decided that he was capable, then who was Sigard to disagree.

But he also recognised that this promotion would accord to both himself and his family a substantially increased income and living standard, along with a significant elevation in social status.

Sigard could therefore do no other than accept the position.

Guy also had concerns about the change. But this worry was replaced with excitement when his father reported back from a meeting at the castle that Guy would be apprenticed as a page to the Earl of Warwick. Such an apprenticeship was standard for the family of the Earl's retainers and was fitting for the son of his steward. He would also be under the instruction of Sir Harold of Arden.

Guy had quickly grasped what his father's advancement had meant to him personally. A page or squire was just a steppingstone to becoming a knight and being a knight was everything that Guy had, up until that time, dreamt about. But dreams were all they had been, as they were out of reach of a peasant. But now, as the son of the steward, the dreams were within his grasp.

Guy's anticipation, however, was tempered by his father, who continually counselled him on the difficulties that faced him. Not with the physical training, in which Sigard had no doubts of his son's abilities, but because of the gulf in social class and breeding that would exist between Guy and the other boys. But his father could only warn of what might be expected, as he could not provide any real instruction because he was equally ignorant to court behaviour and protocol.

Sir Harold, however, as well as being an experienced trainer, was worldly wise, and fully understood Guy's position. He had gently introduced him into the chores and classes, taking care to mentor or provide a mentor that groomed the social aspects of Guy's new role as well as the physical. But after a few weeks, Sir Harold was more concerned at how more capable Guy was at the physical elements of his training, compared to his peers. He did not know how he could integrate Guy without creating jealousy and victimisation, due to his superior capabilities but inferior rank.

The answer came with Terold's early attention to Guy.

Terold was already popular among the other pages and Sir Harold encouraged the friendship when he allocated training pairings or household tasks.

As a favour to Sigard, Sir Harold also maintained Guy's blacksmith apprenticeship, under the guidance of Warwick's new blacksmith. However, Sir Harold recognised other advantages in keeping Guy at the forge. He thought that as well as bringing on Guy's strength it would also retain an element of grounding for the boy, who might otherwise be overwhelmed by his new status. He would also expect to get a good service when he required Galahad to be reshod.

It was not only Sir Harold who paid a guarded interest in Guy. Lady Felice could often be seen on the battlements or at a window looking down onto the training field. She would often ask Sir Harold about the boy and took a certain pride in his achievements.

Sir Harold initially had Guy help in Felice's archery lessons, but it was too much of a distraction for the young girl. It also allowed too much familiarity for Guy in his interactions with the Earl's daughter, as they constantly fed off each other in playing games and creating childish enjoyment.

Sir Harold appreciated their young age and was happy that when they were together, they acted more like the children they were.

They played and joked with each other, and Felice lost the serious demeanour that she exhibited when she was with her parents. But she was the Earl's daughter, and he was the steward's low born son, and he tactfully brought the lessons to an end with the excuse of the girl's age, as she was now approaching womanhood.

Guy would look out for Felice whenever he had time alone in the castle grounds, but there was seldom an opportunity that either he or Felice would be unaccompanied.

She was also away from the castle for long periods when she went to stay with relatives or make appearances with her parents at the Royal Court. Her absence always affected Guy, as the castle and the castle life seemed so much more oppressive when he knew she was not around.

But he had a friend in Terold, and he could focus on his tasks and training with an air of near obsession. Guy, like his father, recognised the need to be better in their performance than their newly acquired associates, to allow for their inferiority of their birth.

Guy looked across the top tables of the Great Hall to see if there was any cup or glass that needed filling. He was aware that there was a couple of sizable tankards that were not there originally and had been placed on the table by guests from the lower tables in hope of getting a draft of the best drinks. No one, however, seemed in need of his attention and the chatter was flowing freely, as well as the wine. He looked over at Terold, who was at the other side of the hall but also serving the top tables. Terold nodded in acknowledgement when he met Guy's eye, but he also scanned the tables in earnest.

"Over here, lad," a large man with a ruddy face dressed in a gaudy green and gold tunic shouted at Guy, lifting his tankard for a refill.

Guy looked to the rear of the hall where his father was watching over affairs and caught his attention. Guy raised the large jug that he was carrying and then gestured to the man who was still waving his tankard. His father, in his role as steward, instantly understood and beckoned another servant to attend the man.

The man was not a guest of the top table.

Guy again looked down his allocated tables, conscious of performing his duties well. The Earl was generous with his fare. But the wine that Guy provided was of superior quality to the drink that the rest of the hall received and had to be distributed to only the special guests of the Earl. These guests were on the three large tables that were in a line at the top of the hall and seated around thirty people.

Earl Rohand was in the centre of the middle table listening carefully to the bishop who sat alongside him to his right. The Earl had to lean close to the Bishop to hear above the loud clamour within the hall. Guy could not hear any of the conversations around him; just the incessant loud growl of noise from the gathered guests that reverberated around the room. The noise, loud as it was, lulled him into a drowsy reverie, and he had to keep constantly take deep breaths to keep alert. He focused on each of the top table's guests, ready to react when he was summoned for more drink.

Sir Harold sat to the left of the Earl and slowly sipped his wine. Guy had noticed that Sir Harold often sipped his wine, but his glass rarely needed filling. Guy suspected that the knight was also on duty in safeguarding the Earl, although Guy could not think of how the Earl could be threatened within these surroundings.

There were no ladies at this particular feast, as they had a more private gathering in their private hall within another part of the castle. But several serving maids were the butt of many jokes to the back of the hall. The top tables, however, were only attended by the Earl's most senior and trusted staff and the two young cupbearers.

Guy was dressed in a plush red tunic with long sleeves that were edged with gold coloured material, over a plain white shirt. The tunic sleeves were bunched up at the elbow and tied with a gold tassel. He had short trousers and long socks which came up past his knees. He also wore a ceremonial short sword that hung in a decorated scabbard from a wide black leather belt. The sword was a symbol of his position as a squire, but this blade had to be returned after he completed his duty as a cupbearer. Guy was pleased to be armed with this blade, to show off his status, but although the sword was decorated, he recognised its poor quality.

Guy liked to be armed with a sword, as it was something he never owned before he came to the castle. Terold, from his privileged background, already possessed his own sword, but Guy was still making his own. His father had offered to purchase one for him, but Guy was adamant that he would forge his own weapon and that it would be the finest blade ever made. His thoughts then drifted to the sword as he stood there waiting to serve. He shook his head slightly as he realised that he was daydreaming and returned his attention back to the guests and then across to Terold.

Like Guy, Terold was also too hot in wearing the many layers of his dress costume indoors within the crowded hall and Guy could tell he was uncomfortable. Guy also felt restricted in the tight-fitting garments, but he was determined to look and act the part and constantly watched Terold and imitated how he stood and walked.

Guy looked again across the tables and noticed a man on the nearest table holding his glass up and looking around for more wine. Guy walked quickly along the back of the seated guests to serve the man from behind as he was instructed. But as he leant over him with the jug, another man on the right, in conversation with another guest, swung his arm around in an extravagant gesture. The man's elbow caught Guy's arm and jerked the jug upwards, splashing wine over the table and onto Guy, as well as the nearby guests.

"Idiot!" the man who knocked Guy's arm shouted, as he jumped up to his feet to avoid the mess.

With a sudden rage, he swung his arm out again in an attempt to strike Guy around his head.

Guy was attempting to keep the spilt wine on the table and away from dribbling onto the other man's lap when he sensed the attack. Guy swiftly swung his head backwards and away from the blow.

The man's hand flew past the side of Guy's face. The momentum then caused him to fall sideward onto the table, knocking over another goblet and spilling more wine in the process.

The man to Guy's left, who had been sitting there laughing at his predicament, now stood up. With an outstretched arm, he pushed Guy carefully backwards behind him, as he also stepped back and away from the table.

Guy backed into the tapestry that hung from the wall and clutched the jug to his chest. The room suddenly went quiet.

"Trouble, Sir Roderick?" Sir Harold asked, as he suddenly stepped into the middle of the affray.

"That idiot threw wine over me," Sir Roderick said with rage through gritted teeth, as he straightened himself up.

Guy started to reply, but Sir Harold shot him a stern glance and Guy remained silent.

"I think that the boy was inadvertently barged as he served me," the man that Guy was serving calmly stated. "It was not his fault, Sir Harold. It was a pure accident. And swimming in such fine wine cannot be such a bad thing," he then chuckled.

The noise in the room picked up again as the situation appeared to be diffused.

"Are you saying that it was my fault?" Sir Roderick then said angrily.

"Oh, accidents happen, Sir Roderick," the man replied again with an assured calm. "It need not be anyone's fault."

"I will see you flogged," Sir Roderick continued, turning his head, and directing his threat at Guy.

The amusement seemed to drain out of the other man, and he stared at Sir Roderick with steely eyes.

"Sir Roderick," Sir Harold quickly intervened, as he noticed the change in the other man's manner, "can we speak alone?" he continued, staring directly at Sir Roderick, and holding out his arm as a forceful gesture to invite him away from the table.

Roderick took a moment to calm himself before moving past the others and away in the direction that Sir Harold had indicated.

Sir Harold sighed and raised his eyebrows at the other man before following Roderick out of the hall.

"Can I be of assistance, my lord?" Guy's father said from in front of the table, his passive face masking any concern.

"No, No," the man said, "the boy was coping quite adequately."

The man then reached across and picked up his glass and held it towards Guy.

Guy instantly stepped forward and filled the glass.

"Thank you, my lord," Guy said.

"No, thank you, young lad," the man replied. "A bit of excitement is always welcome."

The man was dressed in plain but clean clothes and showed no sign of any livery to indicate who he was or where he was from. Guy looked into the man's face and the man looked back at him. He was neither young nor old and his face, although not particularly handsome, was not marked by any disfigurement or scarring. His eyes however were intense and bore into Guy and although his gaze was not threatening, it made Guy feel vulnerable.

"Cupbearer!" Someone shouted to Guy's right.

Guy turned to see the Earl standing up and holding his gilt goblet aloft towards Guy.

Guy took a deep breath and hurried over to the Earl, suddenly nervous at what the Earl might have to say to him.

Guy stood before his liege lord and poured wine into the goblet from the jug, staring at the cup and not the Earl, focusing on not spilling any.

The Earl slowly and deliberately moved the goblet slightly back and forwards in all four directions as Guy poured. He watched the boy intently. Guy aligned the jug with the movements of the cup and eventually lowered the jug as the Earl's Goblet was replenished.

Guy backed off a pace and bowed his head.

"Thank you, Guy," the Earl said, "now show me your hand!"

Astonished that the Earl knew his name, Guy held out his right hand towards the Earl.

The Earl took hold of his wrist and brought it towards him so that Guy's arm was stretched out straight in front of him. He then turned Guy's hand face down and then let go.

"Keep it still, Guy!" The Earl said and observed it closely.

"There you are, Sir Hector!" The Earl said loudly to the guest that Guy had just served. "Not a tremor. We breed them tough here," the Earl continued happily.

"You also breed them fast, my lord," Sir Hector replied. "He was quick to avoid Sir Roderick's blow, while graciously and courageously holding on to the jug of wine."

Sir Hector held up his glass as a toast, "Praise to the lad's awareness and priorities."

"Quite right. Sir Hector!" The Earl said laughing, "Now away with you boy, and get about your business."

Sir Harold held both Guy and Terold back after the feast.

"Tell me all, Guy?" Sir Harold asked. "What happened with Sir Roderick?"

"Sir Roderick knocked my arm as I was pouring it into Sir Hector's cup and spilt wine everywhere," Guy answered.

"No, not with the wine boy, afterwards!" Sir Harold asked impatiently.

"The Earl wanted more wine and called me over to serve," Guy replied, slightly confused at what was being asked.

"Terold!" Sir Harold then commanded with an air of impatience, "What happened this night?"

"Sir Roderick lost his temper with Guy, who was defended by Sir Hector, my lord," Terold answered.

"Sir Roderick did not recognise Sir Hector and made the mistake of being boorish with him."

"And?" Sir Harold asked.

"You took Sir Roderick away before it worsened to the detriment of Sir Roderick."

"And Earl Rohand?" Sir Harold continued.

"He wanted to demonstrate that Guy was not affected by the incident."

"Why?" Sir Harold continued.

"To show Sir Hector, the quality of his squires and how well you train us, my lord."

"Well said, young man," Sir Harold said laughing, "All in all, what could have been a nasty situation turned out quite well."

"I don't understand," Guy said bewildered

Sir Harold dropped his shoulders and sighed.

"I don't understand, my lord," Guy said regaining his composure.

"Sir Roderick, as we know can be...." Sir Harold paused. "Impetuous," and then smiled at Terold.

"But if he realised that he had angered Sir Hector, then he would have been more circumspect with his actions."

"Who is Sir Hector, my lord?" Guy asked.

"Who is Sir Hector?" Sir Harold said with raised eyebrows, "I will let Terold tell you who Sir Hector is. But you will get to meet him again tomorrow, as he has just asked if he can assist me in the delivery of your daily lessons," Sir Harold replied.

Terold whooped in excitement.

"And what was that?" Sir Harold asked with a stern face.

"Just happy that you are training us in person, my lord," Terold replied, suddenly serious.

Sir Harold laughed and patted Terold on his shoulder as he walked past them.

"To bed with you boys," Sir Harold said, "You will need your wits about you tomorrow."

Guy however could not wait to interrogate Terold over Sir Hector and pulled him up when they left the hall.

Terold knew of Sir Hector from reputation only, but he told Guy all that he knew about him. Sir Hector, Guy learned, was a renowned tournament champion from across the known world, especially with the sword, and represented both royalty and nobility as a hired champion in disputes of honour. It was said that Sir Hector protected the righteous and that he was an agent of God. Terold laughed at this and said that the righteous were often determined by the highest bidder and validated by victory and victory, in itself, was by the grace of God. But an agent of God or a hired killer, Guy thought, was only determined by whose side of the dispute you supported.

Terold told Guy of all the stories that he had heard from his father's mixed society, with suitable adolescent elaboration, as Sir Hector was a hero of Terold and a source of inspiration. Guy, however, was not so sure.

Guy had grown up with stories of King Arthur and his gallant knights where heroic deeds were carried out in defence of the land. These deeds were to fulfil an oath, in the protection of the weak or for the love of a fair lady. Paid mercenaries did not fit well within the stories of King Arthur and did not sit comfortably with Guy.

But Guy, however, liked Sir Hector and his actions had rescued him from at least an embarrassing rebuke in front of the guests in the Great Hall. It may have also saved him from a beating if Roderick had forgotten his place, which had looked more than likely.

Sir Roderick was the son of the Earl of Stafford and a constant guest at Warwick, although Guy knew that he was not popular with Earl Rohand or any other member of the castle nobles. His visits corresponded with Lady Felice's presence, and he thought himself an appropriate suitor of the Warwick heiress.

But Guy had paid little heed to Sir Roderick in those first two years. In the early months when he spent time with Felice, she made it very apparent of her dislike of Roderick. Guy would watch her attitude switch to tedium when he fawned over her or irritation at his constant arrogance. But generally, she just displayed boredom whenever he entered her company.

Guy rarely saw him when Felice was not around, but Guy had never forgotten Sir Roderick's treatment of him when they first met in the alleys of Warwick when he was a boy.

Chapter Four

The next morning saw clear skies with a low sun which cast a crisp brightness that spread long shadows across the castle grounds. Although there was a chill in the breeze, it was pleasantly warm for the time of year. All the Earl's pages and squires were gathered in the castle courtyard under the instruction of Sir Harold. They would normally have been put through their exercises in the training field, outside of the castle palisades, but for this day's display, they were brought into the courtyard at the request of the Earl. All the boys and young men were keen and eager in their workouts, and they practised their fight sequences with more vigour than usual.

The squires were dressed in the bright red tabard of Warwick, with the emblem of the bear and ragged staff, which they wore over light body mail and a large, padded gambeson that protected their arms. Their helmets were polished pieces of thick leather brought together over the skull with metal cross braces. The helmets had a long metal nose guard and leather neck guards and a leather thong that tied around the chin to secure the helmet in place. They had the usual heavy wooden training swords, of an appropriate length, and weight, and the smack of the wood as they cut and parried, echoed out within the walls of the castle. For that morning's session, they were instructed to participate in sword training only, and having no shields or spears to worry about suited Guy fine.

Although Guy was skilled with most weapons, along with the use of the defensive shield, he much preferred fighting with just the sword. To Guy, the sword had more prestige and more in the manner of King Arthur and his knights.

The pages were separated from the squires, and they wore simple green shirts and brown trousers beneath a simple leather tunic. They also wore padded jackets with leather arm protectors and grieves to protect them from the strikes of the wooden swords.

Sir Harold watched them closely, as he was very aware of the increased force that they put into their swordsmanship, and he knew that even with the light training swords that they could severely hurt someone. "Pull your strokes," Sir Harold shouted to no one in particular. "I want to see control, not injury."

He then walked across to the front of the group and looked over Guy and Terold who he had purposely put together. There was no worry about these two not being in control. They always fought hard in their bouts of fighting, and today was no different. They did not fight against each other so much as fight with each other, as they seamlessly timed their attack and defence sequences, pausing slightly after each exchange to catch their breath.

Sir Harold was never bored in watching them, as they always looked like they were dancing and not fighting, and the enjoyment was plain to see on their faces.

Sir Harold was both pleased and proud at their skills and smiled to himself as he walked away to instruct the other of his charges.

There was a sudden murmur above the noise of the fighting. Sir Harold looked around to see Earl Rohand with an entourage of dignitaries and other guests walking towards them.

Sir Harold recognised Sir Hector on the Earl's right, who was now dressed in light chainmail armour and wearing a bright blue tunic underneath. Sir Roderick, who was also dressed in armour, accompanied the Earl, and walked slightly behind Sir Hector. The Lady Felice was also there and casually strolled a few paces behind the others. She wore a large heavy green cape with the hood drawn down, allowing her golden hair to gleam in the early morning sunlight.

She was accompanied by a priest, who was dressed in a full-length grey woollen robe with the large hood also folded down over his shoulders. He was clean-shaven with a round earnest face, and he had small eyes that were overshadowed by large eyebrows that seemed out of place with his short, tonsured hair. His hands were clasped around his waist in front of him and tucked within the large open sleeves of his robe. Guy did not recognise him, but he did not recognise many of the clergymen that were ever-present in the castle. Guy had always thought it strange that there were far more priests worshipping God within the confines of the castle than there were in the town.

Sir Harold groaned to himself when he saw Sir Roderick. He, like his trainees, was looking forward to the participation of Sir Hector, but Sir Roderick's presence always marred any event.

"Sir Harold," the Earl said out aloud, as he strode forward in front of his party. "They are all looking the part."

"Thank you, my lord," Sir Harold replied. "As always, they are keen and eager to do their duty."

"May I address them?" Then Earl asked in enthusiasm. Sir Harold just moved aside and bowed.

"My good men," the Earl shouted above the noise, which instantly ceased as the boys all stopped their exercises and faced the Earl.

"We are fortunate today that in our presence we have one of the most esteemed knights of our age," the Earl stretched his arm out and beckoned at Sir Hector.

The knight approached the Earl and bowed towards the group of trainees.

"Sir Hector has fought in many tournaments across Britain, Francia and in many less chivalrous surroundings, with courage, skill, renown and success."

"He has faced many threats and dangers and he has overcome all challenges that the best fighters of the world have brought against him. But he now wants to test himself further, against the terriers of Warwick," the Earl spread his arms and smiled broadly. The boys in front of him whooped and raised their swords.

The Earl drew back and clasped Sir Hector on the shoulder.

"Sir Harold," the Earl then said. "Please continue."

Sir Harold strode forward and held out his hand to Sir Hector.

The two knights shook hands warmly.

"What can we show you?" Sir Harold asked.

"Just continue with their exercises and with your leave I will walk through them and observe," Sir Hector replied. "And perhaps offer the occasional advice, but I am sure they need little instruction from me."

"Any tips that you might offer will be like golden nuggets to them," Sir Harold replied and smiled warmly.

"Continue," Sir Harold shouted to his trainees.

"Please," he then said to Sir Hector, holding out his arm towards the boys.

Sir Harold walked back and stood alongside the Earl.

"Has he agreed to attend your Easter tournament, my lord?" Sir Harold asked quietly.

"He has not committed, but he is here now and that is a good sign," the Earl replied.

Sir Harold looked around and glanced over at Sir Roderick, who was standing on the other side of Felice to the priest and was instructing her in some of the aspects of the training. Felice just looked ahead, and her lack of interest in the words of her would-be tutor was obvious.

Sir Harold and the Earl then stood in silence and watched Sir Hector walk around among the young lads, who were now exhibiting their skills with both precision and show. Both men thought of the esteem that Sir

Hector's appearance at the tournament would bring. His attendance would attract other famous knights and assure a royal presence, which in turn will add to the Earl's reputation and position within the country's nobles.

"Perhaps, my lord, I can also help?" Sir Roderick then suddenly asked from behind them.

The two men moved aside and gestured him through, although both showed little enthusiasm.

"If you want," the Earl said without any real eagerness.

"But please do not obstruct Sir Hector," Sir Harold added. "The boys are excited at his presence."

Sir Roderick lightly snorted and walked out into the mass of moving bodies.

Earl Rohand sighed as he watched him go.

By this time, Sir Hector had reached Guy and Terold and he stood a couple of paces away from them. He watched them closely, slowly stroking his chin in concentration.

The two boys, aware of Sir Hector's presence, increased the intensity of their swordplay, and with it, they both enhanced their enjoyment in the contest.

Guy kept his guard high and slightly to the left, leaving his right side open. Terold, aware of Guy's feint would not take the bait, keeping his attacks high and vertical and waited for Guy to come underneath so that he, in turn, could parry and sweep around. Guy accepted the challenge but bounced off the parry to twist around and try and expose Terold's back. Terold felt the lack of force in Guy's attack and knew that he would use the sword weight to swivel around. So, he quickly stepped sideward and away from Guy. They paused facing each other, with swords raised in defence and smiled as they caught their breath.

Sir Hector watched silently and smiled.

"Get up boy," came a sudden call from Sir Hector's right and he glanced around to see Roderick standing over an older boy, who was sitting on the floor holding his shoulder.

"Where was your defence?" Sir Roderick then said, kicking out at the boy's leg before resuming his guard position.

"Come on then, get up and show more effort."

The boy tentatively stood up and faced Sir Roderick, grimacing at the pain in his shoulder. Although the swords were the standard wooden training swords, they were still a dangerous weapon when swung with force; as Sir Roderick was demonstrating.

The boy held his sword up so that the tip was in line with his opponent's.

Roderick pushed out his sword and quickly turned his wrist to bring his sword down on top of the boy who responded with an upward parry. Sir Roderick quickly circled the blade under the parry and twisted his body to sweep the blade up and around the boy's guard to bring it down over the boy's back and across his injured shoulder.

"Too slow," Sir Roderick said harshly.

"Sir Roderick," Sir Hector called across to Roderick. "Perhaps you can help me here in instructing these two young squires."

Guy and Terold stopped their fighting and lowered their swords. They glanced at each other with a sense of unease.

Sir Roderick turned towards Sir Hector and walked across with a strut.

Sir Hector then looked around at Sir Harold and Earl Rohand, who were both watching the two knights. Sir Hector raised his eyebrows with an expression that sought approval.

The Earl lightly shrugged his shoulders but Sir Harold, with a serious expression, nodded his head.

"Guy," Sir Hector said as he turned back towards the two boys. "Can you please benefit me with your company?"

Guy walked quickly over and stood alongside Sir Hector.

"Sir Roderick," Sir Hector continued, "can you please engage this lad with light sparring?"

Sir Roderick nodded at Hector and strolled over to stand in front of Terold. He looked around the castle courtyard and across the faces of the company of pages and squires who had all stopped their training to watch the unfolding events with interest. He then looked toward Felice and slowly nodded his head as if competing in the final of a tournament. Felice remained impassive.

Then, with a quick strike, Sir Roderick swept his sword in a tight arc across Terold's side.

Terold, as he had been trained, was watching Sir Roderick carefully and was not caught off-guard. He just stepped lightly backwards to allow the sword to sweep past him but did not counter.

"I do not think Sir Roderick understands the concept of light sparring," Sir Hector said with a hushed voice, so that only Guy heard.

Sir Roderick took guard again and then conducted a compound attack with a series of lateral left and right strokes that forced Terold backwards as he parried the attacks.

Roderick then stopped and walked back to his original position and stood on guard, awaiting Terold to also return. Terold obliged and Sir Roderick repeated his attack with an initial hard thrust followed by a different set of strokes.

"How is your friend performing?" Sir Hector asked of Guy, as the sword bout continued.

"He is only defending and not countering, my lord,"

"Is that usual? Does he prefer defence?"

"No," Guy answered, "He feints in attack for at least two sequences, prefers to riposte, and likes to parry with the point high."

"So why does he defend?"

"Because he is afraid to attack because he would not want to cause any affront to Sir Roderick, my lord."

"Even during training," Sir Hector responded.

Guy shrugged. "We have not been instructed in how to fight a knight and what liberties we are allowed to take."

"Training is where we experiment Guy. It is where we try things out and where we then hone our skills to perfection. Reputations are designed during training and there should be no desire for success or fear of failure, and definitely no apprehension of affronting an opponent," Sir Hector grunted lightly in amusement. "I have suffered and still suffer embarrassment and miserable failure in the training field. But with that failure, I learn knowledge and I succeed when it matters. So, in my mind, anything goes in training and no offence should be taken by any participant."

Guy nodded in agreement.

"Stop!" Sir Hector ordered loudly.

Roderick halted his attack and he looked over at Sir Hector with an air of impatience

"Can you please demonstrate to the boy how you would defend an attack, Sir Roderick?"

Roderick returned to his guard position and waved his hand slightly for Terold to attack him. Terold obliged and conducted a series of sweeping strokes, bouncing off Roderick's parries but using little force. Roderick stepped back elegantly with each stroke but then suddenly stepped forward and moved to strike Terold with the sword's pommel. Terold, surprised by Sir Roderick's unexpected counter, stepped quickly backwards, and stumbled slightly in the process.

"Defence, Sir Roderick'," Sir Hector repeated with frustration. Roderick shrugged his shoulder and waved his hand at Terold to attack him again.

"And Sir Roderick's performance?" Sir Hector asked.

"Apart from the overconfidence, my lord?" Guy answered.

Sir Hector smiled. "Yes, apart from the overconfidence."

"He is using his height and weight advantage and mainly cutting from above."

"And the counter?"

"A late prime parry and then an elbow to his face as his weight brings him forward, my lord."

Sir Hector looked down at Guy with a feigned stern look.

"A late prime parry, right crouch and a flick upward thrust," Guy said in response.

Sir Hector continued looking at Guy as he pictured the manoeuvre.

"Using my height advantage," Guy continued.

"Stop!" Sir Hector commanded again.

"Can you now show this boy how it is done, Sir Roderick?"

Sir Hector gestured for Guy to go and face Sir Roderick.

"This is a training session Guy," Sir Hector said quietly to Guy. "I do not recognise reputations, only ingenuity and application."

"Full duel, Sir Roderick," Sir Hector then stated aloud.

"If you insist," Sir Roderick answered smiling broadly and sweeping his arm across his body as he bowed low in a gesture of mockery in respect of Sir Hector's instructions.

Sir Harold looked hard at Sir Hector.

"Enjoyable as that was, Sir Hector," Sir Harold said. "I believe you have made young Guy an enemy of Roderick. I suspect that there will be nothing but trouble for the boy in the future."

"Even under the blanket of your protection?" Sir Hector asked, smiling at Sir Harold warmly.

"I am not always there."

"I am sorry, Sir Harold, I did not mean to create a problem for you," Sir Hector said contritely. "But it is good that young Guy learns how to deal with enemies," he continued and gave Sir Harold a friendly slap on the arm. "We have not got where we are today without having enemies."

"And I think lessons were learned on both sides." He then continued in a more serious tone.

"Of that, I doubt," Sir Harold replied with a rueful smile.

"The boy is good, my lord," Sir Hector then said to Earl Rohand, who was still standing alongside Sir Harold. "I look forward to seeing him again when I attend your tournament. I may even be brave enough to take him on myself."

"Thank you, Sir Hector," the Earl replied.

The knight nodded in respect to the Earl and then bowed his head at Felice, who smiled back warmly. He then walked away back towards the main hall. There was a bounce to his stride; he was obviously pleased with himself.

"Please give young Guy some additional training and get him on a horse. I want to see him fighting in tournaments, and even in the mounted melee," Earl Rohand said quietly to Sir Harold, who did not miss the command in its undertone.

The Earl then sighed as he considered Sir Roderick.

"Guy should have the honour of serving on the ladies tonight and not participate in the Great Hall," Earl Rohand said, emphasising the word 'honour'.

"Keeping away from Sir Roderick, my lord," Sir Harold stated.

"It is an honour to both serve and protect the ladies," Earl Rohand repeated the emphasis. "Suitable reward for his performance in front of Sir Hector, don't you think."

Earl Rohand turned and gestured to Felice to walk beside him and followed by the priest, they strolled back across the Courtyard.

"Watch over him, Sir Harold," Earl Rohand said as he turned and walked away.

Chapter Five

"It is an honour, Guy!" Sir Harold said slowly and tersely.

He had expected Guy's disappointment at being given this task at the night's feast, but he wanted it to be presented in the best possible way, and not let it diminish his achievements of the day. Guy's skills had shone a light on both Earl Rohand and Sir Harold, and they were rewarded with a more eminent tournament in the Easter, thanks to Sir Hector's support.

"You will be one of the few of the Earl's retainers who will be armed, and you are expected to assist if there is any danger to the ladies or their maids. It is an honour, Guy."

Guy was not convinced. Up until the wine spilling, Guy had enjoyed the raucous atmosphere of the Great Hall with all the banter and drunken revelry, and he had low expectations of a similar air within the lady's hall.

"The Earl asked for you to perform the honour specifically," Sir Harold continued.

Guy remained unmoved and looked straight ahead.

"It is also your duty," he finally stated as to close the discussion, although Guy had not offered any dialogue.

"I recall that you have already stood in and protected Lady Felice in the past, so this should be familiar ground," Sir Harold then said more warmly.

And with that, Guy's demeanour changed. He still had the lady's kerchief stored away in his trunk. A token that Lady Felice had given him when he had protected her from a gang of boys that threatened her.

Sir Harold recognised his change of demeanour and slapped him on the shoulder.

"Off to your father and receive your duties," he said and turned to leave the boy. "You can tell me all about it tomorrow."

"And don't spill wine down any of their dresses," he continued, as he walked through the door.

"Sir Roderick's anger will pale in comparison if you soil any of their gowns."

"You must be alert tonight, Guy," Terold spoke up with great pomp after Sir Harold was out of earshot. He had been standing a few strides behind Guy and listened to all that Sir Harold said. "You must protect Lady Felice from the great dangers that face her. I have heard that chicken bones can be devilish if caught in the throat." He then grabbed his throat with both hands in terror and then laughed.

"Is this punishment for Sir Roderick?" Guy asked, ignoring the sarcasm. "I only did what I was told."

During the training, Guy had performed his counterattack on Sir Roderick just as he described to Sir Hector but then rolled forward to slice his sword across the back of Roderick's legs bringing him to the ground.

This caused a roar of approval from his fellow pages and squires, but Sir Roderick was furious and had to be restrained by Sir Harold and Sir Hector before limping away with embarrassment.

"Nah," Terold answered. "Probably keeping him away from you. You know what he is like, and the Earl will not want a repeat of his bad behaviour from last night or this morning. I suspect it caused him quite a bit of embarrassment to the Earl, especially in front of Sir Hector."

"I think Sir Hector quite enjoyed it," Guy replied.

"He seemed happy enough, but I would not want to cross him," Terold then said.

"Anyway, I do not want to think about Sir Roderick. Had you known that Lady Felice was back?" Guy then asked.

"She came back with her father, but I had not seen her out until this morning, and it has been several months since I last saw her," Terold said, and then smiled mischievously. "I did not get a good look at her at training, but it seems that she has changed a lot since she was last here. It may well be, that she no longer resembles a troll."

"And she would no longer be mistaken for your twin," Guy replied laughing, knowing that Terold was teasing him.

"Her presence may, however, make tonight more bearable," Guy continued. "But I envy you, Terold." "Sir Roderick or no Sir Roderick."

"You like her, don't you?" Terold asked.

"Yes, I do," Guy replied. "She is courageous, and she was generous to me when I was a simple peasant."

"Was?" Terold said, in feint earnest. "You are still a peasant."

"Yes, my lord," Guy said, bowing low to his friend. He then leapt at Terold and grasped him around the chest in a bear hug and with his momentum, pushed him over and they fell to the floor in a heap. Terold laughed and rolled away when Guy released his hold.

"She will have forgotten you by now," Terold said more seriously.

"Probably," Guy replied with equal earnest. "I am only a peasant."

Guy still felt awkward as he stood up straight, dressed in his finery, in front of the attractive young woman. Guy's father had brought in one of the serving girls from the Warwick Inn, to make sure Guy was adequately groomed to serve the ladies of the castle. Sally, who had already given Guy a close shave and washed his long hair, was now tying it neatly into a ponytail, which hung a couple of inches down the back of his neck. His mother, who would usually have helped to get Guy ready, was busy in the castle kitchens, helping with the preparations for the feast.

The girl laughed and made the most of Guy's unease, and Guy, although slightly embarrassed, was enjoying the experience.

Sally was a couple of years older than Guy and he knew her quite well from his previous life in the town when he worked with his father at the forge. She often helped the Inn's stable hand, in bringing the guests horses to the smithy and Guy would talk with her as his father fitted their shoes. Since moving to the castle, he had not seen her as often as he had in the past. But she always made sure that Guy did not wait long for any jug of ale whenever he visited the inn.

"This is equal, if not more important, to yesterday's feast in the Great Hall. You must behave properly if you want to impress the ladies," Guy's father said as he hurried into the room to check on Guy's progress. "They have more influence than you can imagine and if you let yourself down then it will reflect badly on you."

Sigard placed Guy's dress sword on top of the small side table and hurried back out of the room again.

"You impress me, my lovely," the girl said softly as she flirted with Guy. "And I think you could let yourself down on me."

"I think my father said 'ladies'," Guy responded with a smile, although he struggled to hide his blushes.

The girl lightly cuffed him around the side of the head.

"Now look what I have done. I will have to start all over again," she said with an alluring and well-practised purr in her voice, as she undid the tie and then roughly ran the comb back through his hair.

"Give me a break, Sally," Guy said grimacing, as the girl pulled the comb hard through his hair, "I was only joking. You are a true effigy of a lady."

Guy was pleased that his vocabulary had vastly increased through knowing Terold, and now he used it as a tool to impress the uneducated girl.

"My oh my," Sally replied. "Aren't you a nob with your fancy language and here's me not knowing if I should be flattered or not?" Sally again pulled down hard through Guy's hair. "Probably not," she continued, "as we both know that I am not a lady."

Guy again winched at the pain. "Don't be silly Sally," he said. "You will always be a lady in my eyes."

"There you go, young Guy," she purred. "Impressing me again."

Guy waited at the side of the top table as the ladies entered the hall.

The hall was smaller and lighter than the castle's main hall, with many more candles on the tables and torches fastened to the walls. There were white linen table clothes draped over the long-benched tables, which reflected the light onto the colourful tapestries that hung from the walls.

A small group of musicians were positioned in the far corner of the hall, directly opposite the entrance, and they played a soft ballad as the ladies strolled calmly to their allotted places.

Lady Elaine, the wife of Earl Rohand and mistress of the castle, led the way, with several ladies-in-waiting following closely behind. Lady Felice came next with her smaller entourage and then the other guests and prominent women of the county followed.

When Guy saw Felice that morning, she was dressed in a heavy cape that hid her features, but now, without the cloak, he looked upon her with wonder. She was the most beautiful thing that he had ever laid eyes upon.

She elegantly walked up to the top table and took her seat and Guy found it hard not to stare. She had not noticed him, as he stood in the shadows, as his position of 'Cupbearer' required.

The role of 'Cupbearer' was ceremonial and like the previous night, his duties were in personally serving wine from a special barrel to the most privileged guests. Guy had already tasted the wine and passed it for service, but he did this with the aid of his father, as Guy could not tell a good wine from bad. This, historically, was not only to prevent any attempts to poison the host or guests, but to allow only the best wine to be served to the most important guests. If the wine was not poisoned and Guy stayed alive, then all he needed to do was watch over the wine and serve it on request to the selected few.

Guy carefully held the large silver flagon, which he only half-filled from the barrel as it was heavy to carry. When the guests at the top table had settled, he moved forward and filled the array of silver cups that were set out in front of them.

Guy was on his best behaviour, and although he wanted to look at Felice, he kept his attention on all the senior ladies and the task at hand. When he was not serving, he stood still against a wall, with a tapestry behind him, just as his father had instructed. Sigard had repeated to him repeatedly that a good Cupbearer should remain unnoticed.

After replenishing each cup, Guy would slowly return to his standing position as he felt that it was then acceptable to freely look along the table to see if he was needed again. In doing so, his eyes always lingered towards Felice.

The change in her was striking and Guy thought that he might not have recognised her in passing. She was now very much the young woman and she looked around the room with an air of solemnity that befitted her noble position. Guy could not imagine this girl pulling a bow or playfully punching a young boy in jest. In his mind, he could no longer visualise her skipping along as she walked or the innocent and exuberant smile that revealed her unbridled joy in life. Memories of her incessant chatter, which had no relevance or purpose, also faded. All he saw now was this new elegant, reserved, and sophisticated woman and to Guy she was beautiful.

"Cupbearer," the Earl's wife called out, waking Guy from his thoughts.

Guy walked forward slowly with a straight back and stood in front of the lady. He carefully poured wine into her cup as she held it towards him.

"Well, young Guy," she said, smiling warmly at the squire. "I have heard that you performed admirably this morning, and in doing so, have provided us with some amusement."

Once again, Guy was taken back with the familiarity of the castle nobility, who felt happy to acknowledge him by his name.

"Guy. Is that you?" Felice suddenly said, leaning forward excitedly and looking across from her seat further down the table.

Guy looked back and forward at both women, not knowing what to say and then straightened and bowed slightly to the Earl's wife.

"Thank you, my lady. I do not know how I have amused you, but I am gladdened by it," Guy said and then turned and bowed to Felice.

"It is me, my lady," he said. "But I am in disguise." He gestured his hand across his ceremonial dress clothes. He then smiled at her and bowed again before backing off to return to his position.

"Not so quick, young man," the Earl's wife said. "We need to hear a first-hand account of your exploits, as we cannot believe that how you, a simple squire, bested Sir Roderick so easily."

"There is not much to tell, my lady," Guy replied and stepped back up in front of the lady. "I was fortunate to be under the guidance of Sir Hector, and instructions from such a great knight carried the fight."

Guy smiled to himself as he suddenly recognised the confidence in himself as he spoke. What he heard coming from his mouth was not Guy, the Blacksmith's son, but a strange likeness of Terold, with his educated vocabulary and noble upbringing.

"That's not what Sir Hector told me," she replied. "Come on, Guy, false modesty will not do. We want to know."

"Yes, come on Guy. You never used to be shy in telling a story," Felice added. Her face had suddenly come to life.

"You know this man?" a woman in-between Felice and the Earl's wife asked.

"Oh yes, Aunt," Felice replied. "Guy saved my life from a bunch of ruffians when I was a young girl."

"And he is quite a favourite of Sir Harold," the Earl's wife added.

"Really, who's his family," Felice's aunt asked.

"He is the son of Rohand's Steward," the Earl's wife replied, "and my husband quite depends on him."

"Oh!" The elderly Lady said dismissively.

"So, Guy. Tell us all about it," Felice added, laying her arms on the edge of the table in front of her and crossing her fingers

"There is not much to tell, my lady," Guy replied. "I had time to observe Sir Roderick while he was fighting Terold and with Sir Hector's encouragement, I took note of his weaknesses so that I could take advantage of them." He then paused. "One of those weaknesses was that he underestimated the ability of the Earl's terriers."

The Earl's wife laughed lightly.

"Rohand will love that. But I think your abilities are more down to Sir Harold's training."

"I don't know why Sir Harold spends so much of his time training the boys when he could promote himself so much better elsewhere," the elderly Lady said. "We hardly ever see him at court anymore or at any tournaments. He used to be quite dashing."

Felice giggled behind her hand.

"Really! Mildred. I did not know you had eyes for Sir Harold," the Earl's wife stated affectionately.

"Oh yes, and not just Sir Harold. There were many handsome knights on the circuit that caught my attention. But I thought Sir Harold was both brave and gallant and he always commented on the brightness of my eyes."

"What do you think, young man?" Mildred asked of Guy.

"I think your eyes are quite captivating, my lady," Guy responded lightly. "They light the room like a summer's morning."

The Earl's wife and Felice laughed out aloud.

"Really! Young man. I was talking about Sir Harold."

"Well, my lady," Guy said with a coyness in his tone. "I find his eyes strangely dark, and sometimes quite sinister." Guy then lowered his head and looked at the floor in a theatrical gesture of embarrassment.

The ladies sitting at the table, who were all listening in on the conversation, were now also laughing at Guy's response.

"I meant Sir Harold's gallantry," Lady Mildred answered impatiently, before realising that Guy already knew that, and that the young squire was playing with her.

Lady Mildred snorted and then joined in with the levity. The ladies continued to question him throughout the evening, whenever he approached to fill their cups, and they seemed interested in his replies. The Lady Felice called on him more than the other women, and his stomach tightened whenever she brought him forward.

Their conversations, although often, were however only brief and superficial in their content, and at the end of the night, when the feast had finished, Guy was left feeling empty. He felt as if an abyss had been opened and could now only be filled with the full knowledge of Felice's thoughts, views, and opinions.

The emptiness was still there the next morning when he walked into Warwick town to carry on with his blacksmith apprenticeship. His sullen mood was detected by the new town blacksmith who tried to chivvy him on, but Guy could not break away from his reflections of the previous evening.

It was both reassuring, yet strange that he was working in the same forge as his father had owned. Things had changed so drastically for Guy over the last few years, that his previous life seemed to have belonged to someone else. But here he was, still using the same tools as he did with his father when he carried out the same mundane tasks.

He managed to raise more enthusiasm when he finished the day's routine work and then focused on balancing the blade of his new short sword. The sword was nearly complete. He had finished most of the laborious work of hammering and tempering the metals of the blade to fuse into a hard edge but with a flexible core. He had also drawn it out into its correct length, with a single tailored fuller that was perfectly mirrored on both sides. And although it was laborious, Guy knew that this work was the heart of the sword, and he applied all his effort and application into assuring that it was done correctly and with care.

The sword had a substantial tang that supported the cross-guard, grip and heavy pommel and was constructed to balance the blade to Guy's preference.

Guy was always tempted to decorate parts of the hilt like other squires at the castle, but it was only a passing thought. A small but elaborate initial that was etched on the tang, sides of the guard and the pommel would be good enough to identify it. The rest of its design was purely for operational efficiency.

Guy understood that the sword was first and foremost a tool, but he also recognised that it was a tool that decided life and death, both his own and that of his enemies. The sword, therefore, demanded respect, honour, care, and pride, so he would name it when the time was right, and that name would be personal to him.

"Guy, get out here now," a voice bellowed from outside of the forge.

Guy instantly recognised the tone of Sir Harold, and quickly placed the sword on the workbench before hurrying outside.

"Yes, my lord," he said quickly, not knowing what brought Sir Harold out of the castle so early to seek him out.

"I need you to get your arse back to the castle straight away and get dressed in full livery," he said impatiently. "You were, reportedly, such a success last night that Lady Elaine has asked for your attendance this morning. And to make it worse, I have to accompany you." He wiped a hand down his face and stroked his chin with his fingers, trying to control his frustration. "How I am supposed to get you ready for the tournament if we are gallivanting around the county in attendance of the senior ladies." He sighed and then turned back towards the castle, gesturing for Guy to go ahead of him up the road.

"One moment, my lord," Guy said and hurried back into the forge to collect his sword, without asking for permission. In the mood Sir Harold's was in, Guy thought that he may have refused it.

He rushed back out and ran after Sir Harold, who had now turned and was marching back towards the castle.

"What's happening, my lord?" Guy asked guardedly, as he came alongside Sir Harold.

"Lady Elaine is to visit Prince Athelstan's sister, who is visiting her parents to the east of the region.

It is a good day's ride, but she wants to stay over at Coventry. They are preparing to leave at this very moment." Sir Harold replied. "Why she suddenly demanded your presence, only the devil knows, and why I have to attend, only the good Lord knows."

"And," he went on determined to continue his rant. "I had to come and fetch you in person because you are that important. And I have yet to prepare for the trip and unlike you, who can just throw all their worldly belongings into a small backpack and leave at a moment's notice, I have responsibilities to attend to. I have tasks to delegate, and horses to get ready, and then somehow pack for my own needs.

"I am sure that there will be inns on the way, my lord," Guy replied mischievously.

"I hope that you are not belittling the sustenance requirements of a Knight of the Realm," Sir Harold replied in a stern tone but with a slight smile. "Because it is obvious that your manners and deportment have improved so much as to greatly impress the nobility that you would not think of showing me such disrespect."

"Of course not, my lord," he answered quickly. "Will we need our dress clothes?"

"Have I not taught you anything?" Sir Harold answered, still frustrated. "We have to be prepared for all eventualities and I expect that your 'Cupbearing' skills will be required," there was heavy sarcasm in his tone.

"I can prepare the horses if you require?" Guy then offered.

Sir Harold thought about it for a while. There were already castle grooms that looked after Galahad and his other horses, on top of their other stable tasks and he also employed a squire who attended him personally, and whom he trusted explicitly. But he thought that having Guy more attached to him may be good for both of them. He also liked Guy's company, as he was more grounded than the other squires, who were from privileged backgrounds and were used to mixing with nobility. Guy's ignorance of the correct protocol was refreshing which was accompanied by a dry wit that always amused Sir Harold.

"Find Walter, my squire, and tell him that I need you to ready Galahad for a fortnight's journey, and to include light armour."

"A fortnight!" Guy suddenly exclaimed. "I have to be away for that long? Does my father know?"

"Yes."

"Will he be coming with us?"

"No."

Guy suddenly became concerned, as he thought about his own needs.

He had never been on a long journey before. The farthest that he had ever travelled was to Stratford upon Avon to watch a travelling fair with his father, and that was only a distance of around ten miles. He started to panic about how he was going to eat and sleep, or how he will be able to clean his clothes. He needed to talk with his father immediately to take advice on what was needed.

Sir Harold looked at Guy's worried expression and realised the boy's anxiety about the trip away.

"You will work alongside Walter on this journey and act as my second squire," Sir Harold said. "I will then compensate you with food, accommodation, and a small allowance for the duration of the trip. Walter will assist you in all your needs."

"Thank you, my lord," Guy then said with sincere gratitude.

"Oh, no need to thank me, Guy. You will be working hard for your upkeep." He then paused. "But it will also be good training for you. I have lots of demands and expect high standards," Sir Harold said more warmly. "But I suspect the ladies will require other duties from you or why would they have asked for you."

The reference to the plural suddenly caught Guy's attention.

"Will Lady Felice be accompanying the Countess?" Guy asked.

"Of course," Sir Harold replied.

Guy's mood was suddenly lifted as a sudden wave of excitement and anticipation washed over him.

"As well as Lady Mildred, and all their ladies-in-waiting and a fair few other maids and servants," Sir Harold continued, his tone nearly developing into another rant.

"I like Lady Mildred," Guy said casually, as the anxiety had disappeared as quickly as it had come. "Do you not think that she has the most beautiful eyes?" Guy asked innocently.

Sir Harold looked down at him in confusion.

Guy smiled inwardly.

Chapter Six

The procession left the castle and slowly moved through the town's Eastgate and then weaved north past Woodloes Park towards the village of Wootton. The townsfolk lined the streets and waved and cheered with real joy and enthusiasm as the party passed by.

Guy rode at the front of the convoy alongside Walter, directly behind Sir Harold who, seated on Galahad, formed the vanguard. He carried the pennant standard of the Earl that rippled from a stout polished wooden pole with a gleaming silver cap. The pole sat in a leather holder strapped to the side of Sir Harold's saddle and supported by the knight's outstretched arm.

Sir Harold and his two squires were dressed in their finest uniforms. They sat detached and official on their mounts and did not acknowledge the crowd. This was the first time that Guy had formally carried his shield, which was painted red with the usual black bear emblem of Warwick emblazed at its centre. The shield was strapped over his left arm as he rode, but he found it cumbersome to both carry it and ride at the same time, as he had to keep repositioning it to support its weight.

Behind the squires were members of the household guard, who smiled and waved to the crowd as they rode past, occasionally calling out to friends or relatives.

Guy looked straight ahead as he rode and felt both honour and pride in performing his role. He had been in such a crowd on many occasions throughout his childhood and had cheered at the Earl or his party whenever they formally left the town or returned. He understood the warmth and affection that the crowd was demonstrating towards the Earl and his family, because he had felt it himself.

The people of Warwick were very aware that they were indebted to the protection and grace of the Earl, and they liked to express their regard with a celebratory joy whenever the occasion arose.

As a child, Guy had dreamed of riding in such a procession. He would be dressed in a knight's armour, carrying his sword in service of the Earl, but he never thought that one day it would come true. And here he was, although still only a squire, parading through the town on horseback and presenting himself to the crowd like a knight.

Behind the small vanguard, the ladies travelled in horse-drawn covered carts that were decorated with rich embroidered garlands wrapped around the wooden frames. Light muslin curtains were pulled back and tied to the cart's posts so the crowd could see the magnificence of the women. Behind the ladies, there was another cart with a handful of priests, who sat opposite each other. They had their hoods drawn over their heads which were bowed in an act of reverence.

Following the lady's carts came the luggage waggons, store wagons, spare horses, servants and finally, the rear guard of soldiers.

The procession continued along the perimeter of the grounds of Saint Sepulchre's Priory, and then past St Dubricious's Chantry. The small chapel, which was dedicated to Mary Magdalene, was hidden behind a corpse of dark bare yew trees and rich green holly bushes. Stone gate posts, however, showed the path that led to the oratory which was built on a rock promontory overlooking the river.

The wide dirt road then ran north above the west bank of the river, and as the procession passed Warwick's boundaries, the crowd diminished. There was only the occasional farmhand, traveller, or pedlar to hail their passing.

Guy was struck by how the landscape suddenly changed from the brown, earth colours of the town and its people, to the fresh green of the country. He looked around over the fields and meadows that swept down from the low wooded hills to his left and down to the river which was banked with large willows. Their bare branches hung down in tendrils to dip into the water's surface and were interlaced with low hawthorn bushes that were white in blossom.

Guy became anxious when they approached the lower slopes of Blacklow Hill, on the outskirts of Wootton, and he crossed himself to ward off any evil spirits. The hill bore the remains of mysterious structures that capped its summit. The structures were said to be ancient temples where long-dead tribes worshipped their pagan gods in ages past. Guy could remember the ghost stories that were told throughout his childhood. Tales that were whispered in the dark nights around log fires and he now felt an air of malevolence that seeped from the hill as he rode past. The sense of evil also affected his mount, who startled at the slightest noise or movement.

But those feelings were just as quickly forgotten, as they travelled on towards Coventry. The skies were blue, and the sun shone brightly in the late morning, warming the procession.

The peace of the country however was spoiled by the background noise of the party as the carts creaked and groaned as they were pulled along by the horses. Their hoofs thumped over the firm ground and their iron tack rattled as they slowly meandered along.

But other noises caught Guy's attention as ducks splashed and cried out noisily from the river, as they fought and squabbled in their forceful courtships. Corncrakes cackled from between the tall grasses of the meadow and Dippers chirped excitedly from the branches that overhung the river, as the wildlife welcomed the change in weather and the hint of spring. All these sharp, shrill noises were unfamiliar to Guy, who was more used to the soothing and melodic song of woodland birds, and he constantly sought out the source of the calls.

The road turned away from the River Avon, as they passed the village of Stoneleigh. It then followed the River Sowe towards Coventry, through another small village called Bagot. Metal hammering from the village smith rang out across the quiet surroundings as they passed, providing a lead melody to the base noise of Lady Elaine's convoy.

They eventually entered Coventry through the town walls and came to a halt at the residence of the Abbess. The senior nun was in sole charge of the convent of the religious order of Saint Osburh, who was the pious mother of Alfred the Great and whose body rested in the convent's grounds.

Coventry was not as big or as affluent as Warwick, as it lacked the direct patronage of the castle and the castle's inhabitants. But it was a welcoming town and its townsfolk crowded around the convoy as it travelled down the main street.

Sir Harold, Walter, and Guy, accompanied by Earl's Rohand's constable, organised the stabling of the horses and the lodgings for the men. The ladies rested in the Abbess's rooms while the priests hurried off to find their own sleeping quarters within the lodgings of the local clergy.

The ladies paid homage to the Saint Osburh and then ate with the nuns, while Sir Harold, Walter and Guy sought out the nearest tavern.

"Where exactly are we going, Sir Harold?" Guy asked across the rough wooden table.

The tavern was dark and filled with smoke from the evening fire and from the poorly distributed, cheap tallow candles that flickered in the corners of the room. There were local tradesmen in the tavern, who continually leant forward and whispered to each other while eyeing Sir Harold's party with suspicion. This was not surprising, considering that they were still dressed in their light mail and wore swords to their sides.

Sir Harold took a large swig from his wooden tankard before answering.

"We are going to visit Lady Edith, who, as you should know is the sister to Prince Athelstan."

Guy didn't know.

"Her family resides in Polesworth, which is five or six miles south of Tamworth," Sir Harold then said and took another sip of his ale. "Does that help, Guy, and have you ever been to Tamworth?"

"No, my lord, but I have heard of it," Guy answered. "I have been told that it is bigger than Warwick."

"That is not true, but they like to think they are, as in the past they often played host to our beloved Lady Aethelflaed, and it is in Tamworth where she sadly passed away. It is however rougher and more dangerous than Warwick," Sir Harold answered. "That is because Danes frequently visit the town and not just traders; there are often small bands of Viking warriors who spend time at the town. And the Danes like to drink, fight and cause trouble."

"Why are there Dane's there?" Guy continued as he rarely had an opportunity to ask questions of Sir Harold.

"Because the peace with the Danes still holds and Tamworth is on the Saxon frontier of Danelaw and traders like to trade and warriors like to drink and fight."

"And whore," Walter added.

Sir Harold looked down at Walter for a few moments before returning his attention to Guy.

"Hopefully, the Tamworth militia will be prepared for our visit and provide us with a suitable guard, as the land is not as safe, or as civil, as we are used to in Warwick."

"Hopefully?" Guy questioned.

"The visit was not planned until the Earl heard of Edith's presence in Polesworth, and the Earl thought it an opportunity for Lady Felice to continue to engage with royalty. The lady is of marriageable age, and the Earl would like a good, if not royal, union."

Guy felt suddenly disheartened. Arranged marriages were commonplace, especially with nobility, to secure or increase the power or wealth of a family. The status of the Earl of Warwick's daughter and heir to his large estates within Mercia was extremely high, so it was not surprising that the Earl looked towards royalty for a suitable match.

The Earl, trying to secure a good marriage for his daughter was no surprise to Guy. But having to face the prospect of Felice's future away from Warwick, and away from him, made him depressed.

"But a visit at such short notice does not fill me with confidence in their ability to organise sufficient security in time," Sir Harold continued. "Messengers have been sent to inform the Tamworth reeve of our intentions, but we did not have time to wait for a reply."

"Sir Roderick was not happy," Walter again cut in, smiling.

"I think the whole castle heard of Roderick's displeasure," Sir Harold responded also smiling.

"What was up with Sir Roderick?" Guy asked

"Roderick decided that last night was the most appropriate time for him to lay forth his legitimacy to court Lady Felice," Sir Harold replied. "And he petitioned the Earl with his intentions and his credentials. The Earl, however, made it clear that they were not good enough for his daughter's hand."

"He made it quite clear," Walter emphasised. "Sir Roderick was not happy."

"Sir Roderick left the castle in the early morning before our departure," Sir Harold continued. "And a few bridges were burned in the process."

"Quite a few bridges," Walter again added. "He was not happy."

"Although I believe that Lady Felice was not too disappointed," Sir Harold said. "She seemed in good spirits this morning."

"Proper party mood," Walter stated dryly.

The ladies were up early the next morning to attend the Morning Prayer with their priests and the local nuns, followed afterwards by a leisurely breakfast in their own company. The men had also risen early and had prepared the wagons. They then awaited the lady's readiness within the courtyard of the convent. Guy had already eaten with Walter in the stables, as they prepared the horses and they shared a loaf of bread, with cheese and dried beef. This was accompanied by cups of watered-down ale to swill the food down. Guy, however, drank sparingly, as his stomach churned with acidity from the previous night's drink. His head was also heavy, but he ignored the discomfort and worked hard to fulfil his tasks.

The ladies eventually appeared and took their places in the wagons and said their farewell to the Abbess. The cavalcade then pulled away and slowly left the convent. As was commonplace, the ladies distributed alms to the poor at the gates of the convent, before the party moved northwards away from Coventry, heading towards the small village of Atherstone.

It took most of the morning and afternoon for the wagons to reach Watling Street. The Roman road was well kept and stretched across the east and north of the Earl of Warwick's estate. The party paused near the old settlement of Mancetter, where they halted the convoy alongside the wide road to feed and water the horses.

A nearby meadow was chosen for the privacy of the ladies, where the servants prepared the ground and raised the tents. Guy was told to escort the ladies across the short distance to the tents and then watch over them.

Guy pulled his wooden shield from the armoury wagon, as well as his bow and a bag of arrows. The bow was unnecessary for his guard duty, but he thought that some fresh meat would not go amiss if the opportunity to hunt presented itself. He strung the bow and stretched it across his back, clipped his arrow bag to his waist belt and hooked his arms into the leather lops of the shield. With his helmet and chainmail vest, Guy felt every part a warrior.

Guy led the ladies over a small wooden bridge across a small but fast-flowing river, which was only wide enough to let a small cart pass over it. A couple of priests hurried behind them and Guy recognised one of them as the priest he had previously seen with Felice. The castle staff had already swept the bridge clean of mud and cattle excrement to allow the ladies to cross without sullying their shoes and a short path was cleared in the meadow beyond. One of the castle guards, who accompanied Guy, remained on the bridge and Guy took up his guard position at the far side of the tents.

The day had remained fair throughout, and Guy basked in the late afternoon sun which shone in a watery haze across the early spring sky. There was a slight breeze in Guy's face as he scanned the edge of the field for any sign of a rabbit, pheasant or small dear. He realised that the noise of the party would keep any game undercover, but they were downwind, so there was still a slight chance of some animal showing itself.

Guy then stiffened as he sensed someone approaching from behind, and he turned to see Lady Felice walking towards him.

"Hello, Guy," she said as she neared. "It is a fine afternoon, considering the time of year."

She then turned to the priest that followed her and held her hand up to stop him from coming any further. He remained standing several paces away and watched Felice.

"My lady," Guy replied as he formally bowed his head in respect. "And the afternoon is all the finer for seeing you," he then said.

"Really, Guy," she responded laughing, "you never used to be so flattering, I am not sure that I know you."

"You have a friend, my lady," Guy asked, curious of the priest.

"Ah, Father Cuthbert," Felice said. "The protector of my soul and my constant chaperone." She then smiled. "My father believes that I am now of an age where I require a moral and religious guardian, hence my instructor and my shadow," she said and gestured towards Father Cuthbert. "But he is a courteous and kind man, unlike other priests who have been involved in my upbringing."

Felice then stepped alongside Guy and looked out across the field. Guy turned to stand next to her and face the same direction.

"Any threat?" She said mockingly.

"Only for supper, my lady," Guy replied. "I was hoping to prod a rabbit or two, but they are keeping their heads down."

He then looked across slyly at Felice.

"There is a pigeon, my lady, sitting on a bough of that solitary tree in the hedgerow to our left, which I was leaving in case no other quarry comes along. If you would you like to try out the bow again then it would provide a challenging target."

Felice laughed.

"They were good times," she said. "But such enjoyable pursuits are now regarded as not becoming of a lady and have been taken away from me."

"And can you not see the lady that I have become, Guy?" She then said as she swept both her arms across her body in an exaggerated gesture.

"And you are very becoming, my lady," Guy then said and then grimaced at his over-familiarity.

"And have a trail of suitors, I hear," Guy then quickly said to try and cover up his rudeness and grimaced again. "Not that it is any of my business, my lady," he added, trying to again correct his manners.

Felice smiled at Guy's embarrassment.

"Sir Harold sometimes despairs at your lack of propriety, but I believe when in the company of friends, we can be less formal and discuss things more openly."

"Thank you, my lady," he replied warmly.

"But you must always be on your guard with etiquette, Guy. It may make or break you."

"Yes, my lady."

"And you can start by calling me by my name, as I think we are friends. But only when we are in our own company. It would not be befitting for a squire to refer to an Earl's daughter by name," she said smiling. "And Father Cuthbert will be on to you straight away to correct your manners and familiarity."

"Yes, Felice," Guy said quietly.

"A trail of suitors for the daughter of an Earl is unavoidable," Felice then continued with a sigh as she stared out into the meadow. "I have a responsibility to my father and to my family that will have to be met."

"Which, I hear, did not stretch as far as Sir Roderick," Guy said.

Felice laughed out loud at this.

"I would like to feel sorry for Sir Roderick, who spent so much time trying to secure me. But his arrogance made him ignore all the hints and advice of his unsuitability, from more than one source, so I cannot feel that sorry for him." Her smile faded as she became more serious. "And there was not the slightest display of love, affection, or respect in his courting. There was only a grasp for power," she said solemnly. "But perhaps, for me, that is all that I can expect; a grasp for power, and I will have to make the best of it that I can."

They both looked onwards, lost in their individual thoughts, when a screeching racket brought, them back to reality. A brace of pheasants had flown out in panic from a coppice at the far side of the open field. The disturbance was followed by a band of strangers who stepped quickly out of the cover of the trees. They were all dressed in battle gear and had their shields, axes and swords raised, ready to attack. The score of men walked slowly into the field until all the band was present. They then lined up to face Guy and with a loud cry of encouragement, ran forward with their weapons raised, shouting their war cries.

The attackers were around two hundred paces away from them and Guy quickly assessed his position.

"Get back now, my lady," he said pushing Felice behind him with an outstretched arm. "Raise the alert to your mother and the rest of the ladies and get over the bridge as quickly as possible." Felice paused and looked across at the raiding soldiers. "Quickly Felice," Guy said with urgency as he dropped his shield to the ground and then opened his bag of arrows. He then pulled his bow from over his shoulder. "Crossing the bridge will make a safe harbour. Do you understand?"

Felice suddenly did understand, and she turned and ran back to the tents, calling out to the other ladies and their maids. Father Cuthbert picked up the hem of his robe and hurried at her heels.

Guy nocked an arrow into the string and pulled the bow, so the arrow's feather fletching brushed his right ear. He had never shot a real arrow at a man before and he anxiously swallowed at what the consequence would be. He looked at the men running towards him. The men in the centre of the group were running ahead of the rest of the attackers and they had bunched up into a tighter group four or five abreast. Guy then did not hesitate and sent the first arrow into the leading man's knee, who instantly fell over and brought the following raider down as he tripped over the thrashing body. The next arrow was quickly removed from the bag and onto the bowstring. Guy, just as quickly, sent it flying through the air and into the shoulder of the man on their left flank. The next arrow went into the left thigh of the man on the right flank. There were now screams amongst the attackers as some of the men rolled around the ground in pain, the rest however roared in anger, jumped over their fallen comrades, and ran on ever closer towards Guy.

Guy then picked his shield and ran a dozen paces back toward the ladies' camp.

"Hurry," he screamed towards the ladies as they were quickly leaving their tents in panic and running back towards the road. He looked out for Felice as he ran and saw her shepherding her mother and aunt across the bridge.

Guy stopped and turned again towards the attackers, lowered his shield to the ground and repeated his salvo. The next three arrows went into the group, in the same pattern, and more bodies fell to the ground, either with an arrow impaled in them, or from tripping over the injured men in front of them.

Guy nodded, measured the distance to the maddened assailants and withdrew again, allowing one more occasion to stop and shoot off another three arrows.

This time Guy fired them straight into the attacker's chests with little or no elevation to the aim of his bow. Because of their close range, they thudded into the attacking men with deadly force, ripping through the metal chain of their armour and deep into flesh and bone.

He then sprinted back to the bridge with the attackers in axe throw distance away from him.

As he reached the bridge, he was met by Sir Harold, Walter, and several guards, who were waiting for Guy to cross. The ladies of the party had all got over the bridge and were now running towards the wagons.

"Shields ready!" Sir Harold cried out and stepped forward to stand at the centre of the bridge, with his shield in front of him. Guy instantly threw his bow and arrows away onto the grass on the far side of the river. He then drew his sword and hooked his arm into the straps of his shield. He ran back into the middle of the bridge and pushed his way to stand to the left of Sir Harold. He then placed his shield alongside Sir Harold's, overlapping the edge to present no gaps and form a wall. Walter had repeated this manoeuvre on Sir Harold's right side and the castle guards had overlapped their shields on top of the shields below. They now leant over the three men in front, who were now crouching with bent knees to await the attack. Other soldiers from the Earl's party also came onto the bridge to support the wall and add weight to it from behind.

Guy heard the attacker's heavy boots stomp on the wooden floor planks of the bridge and then braced himself for the impact, as shields clashed onto shields and axes came down from above.

Guy's arm trembled as the force shot up to his shoulder from the direct impact on his shield. The shield above then smacked down onto his helmet as an axe blow hit into it. The shield wall, however, was well organised and held firm against the momentum of the charging assailants.

"Push!" Sir Harold called out and Guy and the others threw their weight hard forward into their shields. They pushed the attackers back a stride or two and then shuffled their feet into the gained space to maintain their impetus and pushed again. An opponent lost his balance and fell backwards, his foot coming under Sir Harold's shield. Sir Harold stamped heavily onto it and called to push again. The shield wall moved forward, and Sir Harold then stamped on the man's groin before the man was pulled back, screaming, into his own body of men.

Then an axe wrapped around Guy's shield from his unprotected side and pulled quickly back in an attempt to open a gap into Guy. Guy knew that an enemy sword would be ready to stab into him and he pulled frantically to hold the shield in place. But the force was too much, and Guy felt the shield being twisted away from his body. Then his shield smacked back into his body as the pressure was suddenly released and he staggered slightly backwards.

"Push," the call from Sir Harold came again.

Guy then understood why he had regained control of his shield, as the body of the assailant facing him toppled over the bridge side and splashed heavily into the river with an arrow protruding from his neck. Guy quickly glanced back to see Felice standing proud on the bank of the river on Guy's left, still holding her archer's stance with his bow in her hands.

Guy pushed and gained more assurance from his pressure. He then heard horse's hoofs from behind him as the Earl's cavalry pushed forward adding their weight to the fray. They had now gained the far end of the bridge when the opposing wall collapsed as their attackers turned and fled. Guy and the other front row of the shield wall stumbled forward as the resistance to their shields was suddenly released. The horses then came through the centre and galloped after the fleeing men.

Guy stood up quickly and moved to his left to allow the horses through and sensed the axe before he fully saw it and swayed to his right. He felt the wind of the axe as it arced past his face. The axe came straight back towards him in another heavy swing and Guy parried it with his shield, but the force sent him staggering backwards, his arm reverberating with the shock and pain. Guy nearly fell, but he remained crouched on his ankles as he regained his balance, but his enemy had once again raised his weapon. The axe was now directly over his head, to be brought straight down in a killing stroke. Guy, seizing his opportunity, leapt upwards and forwards to thrust the point of his sword past the rim of his enemy's shield and straight into his armpit, where Guy had seen a gap in his armour.

The axe dropped to the ground and the man staggered backwards, his arm hanging limply from his side with blood running down its length to drip off his outstretched fingers and onto the green tufts of grass below. Guy was suddenly hypnotised by the contrast of the deep red blood staining the lush greenness of the meadow.

Guy was then woken from his trance as another arrow shot into the man's chest. The warrior was knocked back a pace from the force of the blow, as the arrow bounced off the tight links of his chain mail. He then roared in defiance as he dropped his shield and stepped forward to pick up his axe with his good hand.

Guy took up a defensive stance with his sword pointing forwards, as his assailant recovered the axe and quickly swung it from side to side as he came forward. He smoothly raised it high and brought it down, aiming to hack into Guy's shoulder. Guy watched it arc down and then parried it away as he rolled forward over his right shoulder. He quickly regained his feet and swung the sword around, in one smooth motion, to cut the blade across the back of the man's neck, slicing into flesh and arteries.

The attacker dropped the axe and crumpled to his knees with blood spurting from the wound in his neck. He held himself up with the last strength in his uninjured arm and managed one sideways look at Guy before another arrow thumped straight into his side. The arrow, this time, pierced his armour, forcing him to topple heavily to the ground.

"Felice!" Sir Harold bellowed. "Get back to the Wagons. Now."

Guy looked over at Felice, who had not moved from her position on the river's bank. Father Cuthbert was tugging at her arm in panic, although he did not have the strength or will to move her. Guy watched her look first at Sir Harold and then back towards him. She smiled at Guy and lowered the bow to the ground. She then turned to walk slowly and elegantly away towards her mother, who was also calling her name to get her out of harm's way.

Guy then looked down at the man, who was now lying on his back, flat to the ground. His hand grasped around the wound to his neck, trying to stem the flow of blood, but to no avail, as it gushed through his fingers. Guy had seen many a dead body on the streets of Warwick, the results of a tavern brawl or just through illness, but he had never seen a man in the process of dying. Blood ran down his hand in streams onto the grass and bubbled from his mouth into his beard. But his eyes were fixed on Guy.

Guy just stared back; he felt no elation or remorse, there was just a calm assurance that he had fought his first battle and he was still alive.

The dying man then quickly lowered his good arm and swept it back and forth across the ground with an urgent panic. Guy looked at the man and his attire. He had a big bushy beard and heavy black eyebrows, which did not disguise his badly broken nose. He wore a light fur cloak over his chainmail body armour which was now sodden with blood and a brightly polished decorated helmet. There were silver and gold amulets hanging from around his neck and silver rings around his injured arm. Guy then suddenly realised that the dying man was a Dane and instantly knew what he was reaching for. Guy stepped to his side and bent down to pick up his opponent's war axe, which had fallen outside of his grasp. He then sank to his knees to carefully place the leather grip into the Danish Warrior's hand, which was red and sticky with blood. The Dane kept his eyes on Guy and with a slight nod of his head, closed his eyes with one last inhale of breath, shuddered and died. Guy had sent him to his afterlife as a warrior with his weapon in his hand and had given him honour in his death. But Guy did not know why he did it, as the man had been intent on killing him.

Guy then looked around to see how the rest of the fight was going and it was obvious that it had finished, and all the attackers had been either killed or captured.

"Bloody Danes," Sir Harold said quietly to Guy, as he kicked a dead body, in the middle of the field, which had been run down by a spear from one of the Earl's horsemen. Sir Harold and Guy were strolling around the field, calming themselves after the brief, but ferocious, battle, examining the remaining bodies and gathering fallen weapons.

"But I do not understand what they are doing so far from their border. They are too few for a war band, but too many for opportunists," Sir Harold added.

Guy looked at a corpse. It was heavily bearded and had long plaited hair, but the face was no different to any other stranger that he might have met on the street.

"We will take the captives to Tamworth and get a translator to find out what this was all about," Sir Harold continued.

Walter walked over to meet them and placed a handful of gold and silver jewellery into Guy's hand.

"Your reward, from that big bastard you killed," Walter said.

Guy looked down at the blood-stained chains and rings. "I can't take these," Guy said, feeling disgusted at the thought of taking a dead man's processions; it felt dishonourable and a lot like theft.

"If you don't then someone else will," Walter replied. "And anyway, you deserve them."

Guy looked at Sir Harold for direction, who just shrugged his shoulders. Sir Harold reached into his tunic and brought out a gold torque.

"A souvenir from an ambitious young Dane who thought that he could beat an old man with a sword in single combat. He was very insulting and uncourteous," Sir Harold said. "I will look back at this trophy with fond memories, remembering how I proved him wrong. Take your trophies and do the same, Guy, as you fought well today," He then placed his hand onto Guy's shoulder. "I am proud of you."

"Although," he then said. "I am mainly proud of how well I have trained you." He then punched Guy lightly on the arm.

"I think Lady Felice might have helped," Walter said in a matter-of-fact tone, as he chewed casually on a long stem of grass. "I saw the body in the river with an arrow in his neck. It was lucky she did not hit you, Guy."

"She would not have had the chance, if Guy had not got her across the bridge," Sir Harold answered sternly.

"However," Sir Harold continued with a smile returning to his face. "I think you will find that I also provided Lady Felice with archery lessons." He then punched Walter lightly on the arm. "I have trained you all well."

Guy just listened without any real emotion. He felt numb and drained of energy.

He had just experienced his first real fight and he had long thought of how he would react to it. It did not scare him like he thought it might. It did not panic him like he worried it would. It had strangely and unexpectantly exhilarated him.

He was aware of his skills and capabilities, developed through his training and he realised that this small fight did not get anywhere near the limits of his performance, and that surprised him. His only weakness, he thought, was in his lack of physical strength compared to the men who attacked him that day, in a situation where he could not apply his greater agility.

When he thought of that attack, he could not help but also think of Lady Felice and her actions during the fight. He could still picture her with his bow in her hand, killing the man on the bridge and saving his life. His heart warmed when he considered the extent to the limits of her own strength.

The rest of the journey proved to be uneventful, but Sir Harold, with Walter's help, had been constantly busy supervising the prisoners. They had also gathered a collection of the plunder, which had been taken from their attackers, both alive and dead, including their armour and weapons. This would all be given to the Earl to distribute accordingly. They also had to sort out the local reeves and make sure the legal requirements concerning the attack were covered. The deaths had to be reported and arrangements made for their bodies to be taken away and buried. They then had to provide enhanced security for the lady's convoy, in case of further attacks, as it continued on its way.

Guy was left to vanguard the party alone, which he did with little effort or concern.

The following day found Guy standing in front of Lady Elaine and the other ladies in the gardens of Lady Edith's hall.

The sun was tepid in the cold grey sky, but the birds were chirping happily in the neatly trimmed hedges and borders.

"Well, Guy," Elaine said. "You acquitted yourself very well yesterday from what I saw, and also from what I have heard from both my daughter and Sir Harold."

"Thank you, my lady," Guy replied formally. "But it is my duty to serve, and I am well trained to perform that duty."

"Yes, yes. That is all well and good. But it was you who got us over the bridge to save us," Lady Mildred cut in. "You deserve a heavy reward."

"Your safety and wellbeing are rewards enough, my lady," Guy again replied formally.

"No Guy. That is not good enough," Lady Elaine then said. "We recognise your outstanding courage, and we would like to reward you." She then held out a velvet money purse which jingled in the motion.

Guy reddened and looked aghast at the purse.

"No, my lady. I do not seek reward for my actions. I am here as a squire due to the benevolence of your family, and that is rewarding enough. I truly am rewarded by being of service."

"I told you that you would embarrass him," Felice interjected sternly. "Guy lives by his duty and service. Lancelot, Galahad, or any of the Knights of the Round Table would not have been rewarded with monies."

Lady Felice was sitting behind the other ladies with crochet needles in her hands and balls of wool on her lap.

"What do you know of duty Felice?" Elaine said firmly, without looking at her. "Your duty was to protect yourself and the family honour. Not to parade around with a bow and arrows, lowering yourself to that of a common soldier and then actually killing people."

Felice put her tongue out at her mother from behind her back and then sternly shook her head at Guy as he started to speak in her defence.

"We would like Lady Felice's involvement in yesterday's affair to be forgotten," Elaine then said. "As it was not seemly for a lady of her stature to behave in such a fashion. I understand that she is accomplished in archery, and heaven knows what else, which was not my doing, but yesterday's carry on was not the actions of a lady."

"I cannot forget Lady Felice's actions yesterday, my lady, as she undoubtingly saved my life on the bridge," Guy replied. "But for my part, I will speak no more about it."

"Thank you, Guy," Elaine said and then rose from her chair to leave.

"Please attend me, Felice," Elaine said and walked towards the hall.

Felice also rose, nodded an acknowledgement to Guy and then followed her mother.

"So, Guy," Lady Mildred continued playfully. "What do you think of Felice's actions? Was it her place to fight the Danes?"

"Aethelflaed, the Lady of Mercia, fought the Danes and no one doubts her place in society, my lady. She was a queen."

"But did she put an arrow in any of them?" Mildred said.

"Probably not, my lady. But I would like to think that she would have liked to and, if she had been trained by Sir Harold, then she might well have."

"Yes, we must not forget Sir Harold in all of this. I must offer him my respect and commendations. He performed most efficiently."

"And with quite a bit of gallantry, I thought," Guy added.

"Most definitely, young man. You would learn a lot from Sir Harold."

"I already have, my lady, and I am sure that there is plenty more for him to teach me."

"I will ask him to provide your services at our meal tonight. I am sure Edith will not mind and I would so much like to hear your versions of events," Mildred said and then looked at him with narrowed eyes. "And what did Felice do?" She asked haughtily.

Guy looked back at Mildred and took a moment before speaking.

"Lady Felice was calm and collected, my lady and she made sure that her family were safe before she thought of her own security." Guy then smiled slightly. "And during the fighting, she prayed to our Lord for a righteous outcome and her prayers were answered in our deliverance."

"Quite right, young man. Now away with you," Mildred said.

"The Danes were mercenaries," Sir Harold spoke aloud as he entered the stables where Guy and Walter were wiping down the horses with straw.

"Who hired them, my lord?" Walter asked. "Is it anybody we know?"

"We have not found out yet, as it appears that we killed their leader, who carried out the negotiations. But they were targeting our party specifically and they somehow knew our itinerary. But they were told not to harm the ladies."

"Why would someone want to attack us?" Guy asked.

"Probably for the ransom," Sir Harold answered

"Not sure about that, my lord," Walter replied. "Something does not smell right, and I have a nose for funny business."

"You certainly have a nose, Walter my lad, and you are usually surrounded by funny smells."

Sir Harold was still lively and in good spirits following the Battle of Anker Bridge, as they now called it. The skirmish would unlikely make the annals of English history, but it was still an unexpected adventure for Sir Harold, along with a resounding victory, and his charges had performed well. Sir Harold was quite pleased with himself.

"And the ladies would like you to attend their dinner tonight," he said poking Guy in the arm with his finger. "And you have been given instructions. So, make sure you behave."

Guy moved around the other side of the horse, muttering aloud as he wiped.

"Nobody says anything about me facing down a marauding army of Vikings, with just a bow. Or standing in the front line of a Shield Wall for the first time. Or fighting a massive War Lord with a giant axe. But when there is a dinner to attend, in front of ladies, then it's; 'make sure you behave', 'mind your manners', 'remember your instructions'."

Guy was smiling at his light-hearted rant. "It's not fair." He then added.

"And: It's not fair what?" Sir Harold asked, recognising the good humour in Guy's tone of voice.

"It's not fair, my lord."

"Another life lesson, Guy," Sir Harold replied laughing. "Ask Walter about it. He is an expert in life not being fair."

"That's not fair, my lord," Walter cut in.

"That's the spirit," Sir Harold replied laughing, and then walked away.

Chapter Seven

Earl Rohand had greatly reinforced the guards and an edict went out to Jarl Sitric Caech, who was the self-proclaimed head of Danelaw, to explain the attack on Lady Elaine's party. It took five days for the Danish Jarl to respond, in which he stated his dismay at the attack and gave assurance that he knew nothing of it. He was to leave for Tamworth immediately to investigate the incident in person, and he arrived a day after his messenger. The Jarl immediately requested an audience with the Earl's wife to offer his apologies for any affront caused to her dignity and safety, and to personally assure her of his innocence.

The Jarl Sitric was a massive opposing figure, and he attended the meeting with Lady Edith and Lady Elaine with only a small personal guard. He arrived dressed in fur, chainmail, and leather, which he did not remove for the meeting. He did not look uncomfortable wearing the excessive clothing and armour, and he portrayed an impressive figure. Sitric had a stern face that was skewed by a scar that stretched from his brow to his upper right cheek, although his sight was not damaged. But even with the scar, he was not an unattractive man. Sir Harold and the newly arrived captains of Earl Rohand's household guard attended the meeting, and Guy was also invited at Lady Elaine's request. The Reeve of Tamworth, who accompanied Sitric, was also present.

Guy was surprised at the politeness and apparent mildness of the Danish leader. He immediately swore an oath on his Gods and for some reason, on the Christian God, that he had no knowledge of the attack. He promised that he would leave no stone unturned in finding out who was responsible and why. He then assured Edith that the peace between the Danes and the English would hold and that the ladies should not be anxious over their safety. Guy watched the Dane closely, and, for some reason, instantly believed him.

His English was good, and he needed no translator, although his Norse accent required concentration to fully understand his words.

Sitric was given quarters in Tamworth and after interrogating the prisoners the Jarl sent out messengers to the towns of Nottingham, Northampton, and Leicester.

A few days later, Sitric returned to Polesworth, where he requested a meeting with Sir Harold and his two squires.

Sir Harold, Guy and Walter went to the main hall on the invite of Lady Edith, and they were surprised to find only the Danish Earl present when they walked into the room.

"I welcome you as my guests," the Jarl said. "Please sit."

Sitric waved his arm to indicate the four cushioned chairs that were positioned around the large window that overlooked the garden.

The Jarl, who was standing at the fireplace, walked across to the window, and looked out over the garden. The three guests sat down on the chairs.

"Where I am from, the scenery is beautiful," Sitric said. "It is massive, wild, aggressive, and powerful. It reflects my Gods." He paused and looked across the garden. "In your country, the scenery is also beautiful, but it is small and comforting; it embraces you with warmth and fertility. It is like a mother, and I think it reflects your old Gods. In time it may even dilute this new Christian 'one God'."

The three men also looked out of the window and felt the heresy behind his words. Christianity had been engrained for decades since the rule of King Alfred and the church doctrine had removed any reference to the old Gods from much of the English culture.

Sitric then looked down at them.

"I understand the offence that I may cause in speaking of other Gods, but I am not the same as you, so please excuse me. I am not Christian, and, in my culture, I am allowed to consider other Gods. I can work out for myself what provides the best explanation to who I am, where I come from and where I am going. The Christian God, however, is a jealous god and demands obedience at all times and at all costs, from which it seeks to make servants of us all." Sitric paused before continuing. "It is hard for me to understand the Christian culture, but it does not make it wrong."

Sir Harold, Guy and Walter waited in silence, unsure where this conversation was leading.

"The Saxon culture is all about serving," Sitric continued. "Your peasants serve their lords, the lords serve their earls, the earls serve their king, and the king supposedly serves his people. And yet you all fight to maintain this existence of servitude."

"You boy!" he said calmly to Guy. "You risked your life fighting a Danish warrior." He paused again and looked at Guy closely. "Yes, he was a mercenary, but he was still a Viking Warlord and fundamentally all the Danes that are here in your country are mercenaries. They are rewarded for taking this country's wealth, by Jarls such as me, and risk their lives doing so. But I am interested lad, for one so young, what was your motive in risking your life? You accepted no reward. Was it purely in the service of your Earl?"

Guy remained silent and looked at Sir Harold, who then spoke out formally.

"I think that you can speak openly, Guy. There are no enemies here."

"It is not that I do not want to speak openly," Guy said. "But rather it is difficult to answer the Jarl Sitric when I have no easy answer at hand," Guy said.

Guy thought for a few more moments.

"I consider it as my duty, my lord," Guy continued, looking directly at Sitric. "But my duties cover lots of tasks and those duties do not hold the same desire as I felt when fighting our attackers. I think that my actions are best described as both duty and honour. I fought your countryman because that was my duty, but I fulfilled that duty to achieve honour." Guy struggled to find the words to fully explain what he wanted to portray. "But it was to achieve honour, not for myself and not for duty to my Lord, but for a belief."

Walter stared at Guy with an open mouth. But Sir Harold just nodded.

"And that belief is your God?" Sitric asked.

"No, not exactly," Guy replied. "I do not want to sound fanciful, but my belief is in an ideal that is represented by a famous past legend named King Arthur and his achievements. Those ideals have been passed down through stories across generations."

Guy looked at Sir Harold.

"My father told me these stories when I was young, and they influenced my ambitions to what I wanted to become."

Sir Harold continued to look at Sitric but nodded acknowledgement to Guy.

"Is King Arthur your God?" Sitric then asked of Guy.

"No," Guy answered firmly. "My God is the Christian God and King Arthur was a tool of my God. But he also represented values such as love of your fellow man, chivalry, social justice, and national pride. I think that Arthur is the heart of Britain and I think it is for his honour that I carry out my duty, and through him, God's plan."

Guy paused, as he considered his words.

"I risked my life fighting the Danish Warrior, primarily, to protect the welfare of defenceless women that were under threat. All other duties fell beneath that."

Guy paused and smiled at Sitric. "I give thanks for my life to God, but I fight for duty, honour and the principles of a past legend that epitomises the person I want to be."

"Even in my country, we have heard of your King Arthur, and I know of his knights," Sitric replied. He then paused for thought. "I think it is naive that you believe all men can treat each other equally, especially people with power. But I understand how it can inspire the less fortunate."

"It is not in treating others equally, my lord," Sir Harold intervened. "It is treating others in a way that they want to be treated themselves. People are not the same, so they can never be equal. But if we accept our positions and are content in that social justice, then we will all fight to maintain it, no matter who we serve."

"And you serve Earl Roland?" Sitric asked.

"Yes, and he treats me with respect and courtesy," Sir Harold answered. "He treats me how I want to be treated and I serve him because of it."

"So, you would die for your Earl?" Sitric asked.

"Yes," Sir Harold replied.

"And you Guy. Would you die for your Earl?"

"Yes," Guy answered without hesitation. "It would be an honour."

"And would your Earl die for you?"

"Earl Rohand would do his duty and if that meant forsaking his life for ours, then I believe he would gladly do it," Sir Harold answered.

"Jesus Christ died on the cross to save all our lives," Walter cut in.

Taken aback by his interruption, they all looked at Walter

"We all serve," Walter then said, embarrassed at the attention.

"Well, I serve only my own desires and pleasures," Sitric said with amusement and moved the empty chair around to face them. He sat down, stretching out his legs in front of him.

"And it was not my desire to attack your party," he continued.

"But I have been making enquires. Your attackers were Danes, and they came from within my lands, but were not acting under my, or any other, Danish orders."

He placed his hands on his lap and interlocked his fingers.

"They were mercenaries from Leicester and led by a Viking warrior called Sven Signudson." He then looked at Guy. "This was the Dane that you killed in battle, and he was a renowned warrior, known as Sven Blackheart." Sitric then pulled a large silver ring from his arm and threw it at Guy. "This is a token of respect in recognition of your courage and your victory and also in respect to Sven."

"This we were told by the prisoners, my lord," Sir Harold said.

"And it was probably all that they knew," Sitric responded.

"But searching out their Leicester haunts, I have discovered that they were hired by a Saxon noble."

Sir Harold straightened.

"Who was this Saxon?"

"Average height, slim build, narrow face, thin moustache, and a short beard. That is all I can tell you. He was a stranger to the establishment."

"Sir Roderick," Walter said immediately.

"Several people could fit that description," Sir Harold quickly responded, looking hard at Walter to silence his allegations.

"How do you know the Saxon was of noble birth?" Sir Harold then asked.

"Shiny sword, clean polished leather and arrogant," Sitric said and then laughed.

"And he did not smell of shit," he continued and laughed again.

"He also had a couple of guards who referred to him as 'Lord'," he finally said in a more serious tone.

"I will make further enquiries, but perhaps you can also find out which of your people were in the area on that day. I do not think, however, that this noble would have risked going into Leicester. The town is not overly friendly towards Saxons and your people are infrequent visitors, apart from the occasional trader. However, it was known that Sven may have visited a village called Stoney Stanton, but I do not know when or why."

"I will inform the local reeve and he will also make enquiries," Sir Harold replied.

"Sir Roderick could have easily travelled to this area. It is well within a day's travel from Warwick," Walter again cut in.

"You do not like this Sir Roderick?" Sitric asked Walter. Walter just shrugged his shoulders.

"I do not think Sir Roderick has the motive, courage or stupidity to initiate such an affront to the Earl of Warwick," Sir Harold continued. "But we will investigate."

"I sincerely hope you find out who was behind this attack and that I am cleared from the blame," Sitric then said rising to his feet.

The others also stood up and recognising their dismissal, went to leave.

"It has been interesting talking to you, Sir Harold. I wish you well."

"You have my regards and my thanks, my lord. I hope the peace lasts."

"As I do, Sir Harold. I would not like to face your warriors in battle, especially if your squires are all the same quality as young 'Guy of Warwick'," Sitric replied laughing as he walked the men to the door.

Terold fingered the silver arm ring, with amazement and envy. The two squires had finished their morning chores and were sitting together in the castle mess hall, after eating their mid-day meal.

"Sven Blackheart," Terold said. "You killed Sven Blackheart."

"I think an arrow in the side finally killed him," Guy answered. "But I did get a sword thrust through his mail and a slice across his neck."

Guy hunched his shoulders and imitated the stroke towards Terold.

"Sven Blackheart," Terold said again, lightly whistling.

"Do you know of him?" Guy asked, placing his elbows on his knees, and looking up towards his friend.

"Not at all," Terold answered, "I have never heard of him in my life. But what a name."

Terold then quickly leant forward and pushed Guy to the ground.

"Lord, I wish I had been there. Reputations are made on killing people called Sven Blackheart," Terold said.

Guy quickly rolled over and stood to his feet and casually brushed the light dust from his tunic.

"Perhaps I can find a Dane for you to fight," Guy said. "Someone who has a name worthy of your reputation. Perhaps the renowned 'Ivor Sheepsbladder'."

Terold flicked the arm ring back to Guy and as he caught it, Terold stepped quickly forward and pushed Guy again, laughing as Guy hopped backwards to regain his balance.

"Some people have all the luck."

They then walked out of the canteen in silence.

"Didn't get much training in though," Guy then said. "Walter did not seem up for it and Sir Harold was always too busy."

"However, I rode a lot, which was a bonus." He continued.

"More than I did," Terold responded. "It's been boring since you all left."

"Tell me about Sir Roderick?" Terold then asked excitedly.

"Nothing to tell," Guy answered. "Walter thinks it was Sir Roderick who hired the Danes and is happily spreading the gossip. But there is no evidence that he did."

"But no evidence that he didn't," Terold said smiling.

"You are as bad as Walter," Guy said, laughing.

"Anyway, let's go and practise swordplay. I am in desperate need of training. The summer tournament is only weeks away," Guy said, pushing Terold out of the guardhouse and onto the castle bridge. "I can pretend to be Ivor," Guy then said laughing.

"Where are you two going?" Sir Harold bellowed from above as he leant over the gate's parapet.

"Sword practise, my lord," Guy answered.

"Not today boys. Get back in here," he ordered.

The boys walked back through the gatehouse and awaited Sir Harold at the foot of the stairs leading up to the rampart's walkway.

"You will be fighting in a melee today, first on horseback and then on foot," Sir Harold said, walking slowly down the steps.

Guy and Terold both smiled broadly in delight and enthusiasm.

"However, it will not be against your peers."

The smile left their faces.

"It will be against the best of the Earl's guards and the elite of the Warwick militia."

Guy and Terold looked at each other with surprise and trepidation.

"It will be with sword and shield," Sir Harold continued, and then smiled as he walked past the boys to walk into the courtyard.

The boys turned and hurried to catch up with him.

"But it will be with training swords only."

"The Earl's soldiers have not been as well-schooled in swordcraft and single combat as you pair. Therefore, you will have an advantage." Sir Harold then suddenly stopped and turned around to face them.

"They are however killers and trained in the art of war," he said sternly, before turning and walking away again. The boys trailed behind again.

"They are also stronger, and more malicious than you and do not recognise chivalry, so they are not above a bit of underhand skulduggery. You will have to be prepared to defend yourselves against them and even match their aggression." He then stopped and looked up to the sky for no apparent reason. "They have been told to give you no quarter," he said and then walked on again.

"I do not expect you to last long in the melee, but I do expect you to show courage and some level of capability. I will not be happy if either of you is the first to fall or suffer any serious injury."

"So, get yourselves dressed and collect your weapons and I will see you on the training field. Your horses will be there waiting."

"What's up lads?" Sir Harold then said, "Cat got your tongues,"

"Ur, no. Ur yes, my lord," they both replied in a state of anxious confusion.

Sir Harold laughed and waved them away.

They then turned into each other and after a bit of jostling, ran away to their quarters.

"Whoa!" Sir Harold called after them, and the boys pulled up and turned back to face Sir Harold.

"And make yourself presentable, there may be spectators."

Sir Harold smiled broadly and turned to walk towards the rear gate of the courtyard with large purposeful strides.

Guy and Terold walked on the training field together and looked on at the spectacle in front of them.

A dozen horses and their grooms were lined up to their left and a couple of tents were pitched on their right, with cushioned benches placed in front of them. Earl Rohand was standing in front of his wife and Lady Felice, who were seated together on one of the benches. Although the weather was not cold, the ladies wore long hooded capes with the hoods left down, allowing their hair to shine bright in the sun.

The ladies-in-waiting and other servants were either seated or were mulling around, seeing to the needs of the Earl's party. Father Cuthbert, maintaining his constant presence, stood to attention toward the rear of the ladies and quietly looked on.

In front of the tents, there were several yards of open space before the boundary markings of the circular melee arena. Several household guards stood on each side of the Earl's party to provide protection, as spectators had been known to get hurt from runaway horses, or flying debris.

Sir Harold was standing straight ahead, and he smiled at the two squires as they walked up and stood before him.

"At least you look the part," Sir Harold said and checked the tightness of the leather pauldrons that protected their shoulders and the leather cuirass's that guarded their chests. As he removed his fingertips from the inside of the collar of Guy's cuirass, a small piece of cream satin cloth was pulled out.

Sir Harold gave it a small tug, but it was tied to one of the metal buckles.

"Is that a token, Guy?" Sir Harold asked smiling.

"For luck, my lord," Guy said and reddened with embarrassment.

"Then wear it for show, Guy," Sir Harold said as he carefully straightened and flattened the small square of cloth down over the front of his chest guard.

"Although I do not think you want it resting over your heart, Guy," he then said and twisted it around the cuirass strap. "It presents too good a target."

At that moment, Earl Rohand appeared from behind Sir Harold.

"Well met, Guy and Terold," the Earl said warmly. "This must be a treat for you."

"Yes, my lord," they replied together.

"And Guy, I understand that I am indebted to you for protecting my family."

"It is my duty and honour, my lord," Guy said quietly.

"Yes, Sir Harold was telling me of your duty and honour. It was enlightening," the Earl responded. "So, I thought, as a reward, I would create a 'round table' for you to melee in."

Guy's eyes widened in surprise at the formality of a 'round table' arena being arranged just for them.

"I was also telling the Earl how much you both like pain and aspire to the odd broken bone," Sir Harold then added. "He was gracious enough to pit you with his best, to satisfy your desires."

Sir Rohand chuckled, as both men enjoyed themselves in the banter.

"So, you will both be fighting against us, my lords," Terold replied with a tone of sincerity.

"Oh, well said young Terold," Earl Rohand said, happily. "Although I am sure that Sir Harold would enjoy the encounter, for my part I would rather watch. But there was a time when you would have not kept me away from such a challenge. To judge yourself in contests such as these open a window to your soul," he then said with a touch of solemnity. "And I am sure that for you lads, the experience will be edifying?"

"Come," the Earl said enthusiastically, and waved the boys towards the tents. "My wife would like to wish you both well."

They then strolled over to the group of ladies and stood before them. Guy and Terold bowed their heads towards the ladies to show their respect.

"You both seem very young to fight in a melee," Lady Elaine stated more than asked.

"Youth will allow them to heal quicker," Earl Rohand said and then patted Guy on his shoulder and laughed.

"Don't jest, my lord," Elaine said with light amusement. "They must be frightened enough."

"My terriers are not frightened, my dear," Earl Rohand replied.

"They are excited. Is that not so Guy?"

"My hands shake only because of the eager anticipation, my lord," Guy replied formally.

Both the Earl and his wife laughed at Guy's reply.

There was a noise to Guy's right, and they all looked to see a group of the Earl's household guard marching informally onto the field, followed by a less orderly group of soldiers.

"Excellent," the Earl said. "Please excuse me as I sort out the two sides."

The Earl then strolled away with a keenness to his stride.

"My husband has been looking forward to this all morning," Elaine said smiling. "It has been a welcome relief from the concerns he had over our safety when we were away."

She then looked them up and down.

"Well, you both look like warriors," Elaine said.

She then noticed the cloth that stood out on the front of Guy.

"What is that cloth on your tunic, Guy?" Elaine then asked, as she sat up and looked at the satin kerchief wrapped around his shoulder strap. "Is it possible that you are gathering tokens of a lady's affection already?"

Felice also sat up and leant across towards her mother to get a closer look. She recognised the kerchief immediately and then relaxed back into her seat, trying to appear uninterested, but she could not disguise the reddening in her cheeks.

Guy also blushed.

"It is a token of luck, my lady," Guy replied. "It has brought me good luck for many years and protected my life on several occasions."

"Did you have it with you at Polesworth?" The Lady asked in a more serious tone. Tokens were important in society, and good luck tokens required a level of respect.

"It was with me on Anker Bridge," Guy replied with equal gravity.

"Then Guy, you should wear it at all times. As that incident proved, you never know when you might need such good fortune."

Guy swallowed.

"Yes, my lady. I hold it most dear," he said.

He then instantly regretted saying it.

"So, what are your chances, Terold?" Elaine then asked Terold, not wanting to exclude him from her attention.

"I believe we will exceed Sir Harold's expectations, my lady," Terold said smiling.

"That is good," she replied warmly.

"Not really, my lady. If only one other person falls before Guy or me then Sir Harold's expectations will have been met."

Both Elaine and Felice smiled.

"You must not believe Sir Harold," Felice said, who had been listening intently.

"I have seen the monies that have been wagered around the castle on the outcome of this melee and they do not reflect your view of Sir Harold's expectations."

Earl Rohand then returned smiling and rubbing his hands together.

"I have also wagered a few coins on the outcome," he said genially as he overheard Felice's comment. "But I will not tell which way I have bet; however, my household guards are very good."

He then looked around him and waited until all the participants had gathered in the vicinity.

He then held out his arms to gain their attention.

"Welcome all," the Earl shouted out aloud as the crowd fell silent. "And may I thank you for attending in this impromptu little sport, as a treat for two of our squires and I hope that you will enjoy it."

"However, I will remind you that it is only a sport," he then said smiling.

"The rules of the day are:" The Earl then said across the gathering.

"Two teams; evenly split across the castle companies. One wearing red sashes the other blue."

"We will start on horseback and score up until a single rider remains. That man will then dismount, and we will score again until there is only one final man standing. A standing man will not be scored until the last rider has dismounted."

"A rider will not attack a standing man, and a standing man will not attack a rider. There will be disqualification from the contest for any breach of these rules."

"Only sword and shield will be used within the melee, and these will be provided by the judges. Only wooden training swords will be used for obvious reasons. Any other weapons used will disqualify the man using them and may be followed by a trip to the gallows," The Earl smiled broadly, to emphasise his joke.

The crowd shouted out in a jovial but mixed response.

"There will be four judges with their supporters, who will be wearing yellow sashes. Any melee participant who attacks a supporter will be disqualified. Any participant on foot that is put to the ground will remain on the ground until pulled away by the supporters. Any rider who is dismounted can get to their feet only from that first fall off their mount. Any person judged as unable to continue or in breach of rules will be pulled away by the supporters."

"Are we all clear?" Earl Rohan shouted out and the crowd acknowledged him heartily.

"There will be a winner on horseback, who will be the last man riding and a winner on foot who will be the last man standing. There will be an overall winner between the two, depending on their performance."

"The two squires will be split between the two teams, but they will not face each other unless they are the last two in the melee."

A large mocking cry went up across the crowd.

"Additional points will be awarded across a team for the longer they keep their squire in the melee. Hopefully, each team might consider it appropriate to protect their own team's squire."

"There will be refreshments served at the end of the contest for all those still able to participate." The Earl smiled broadly again.

There was another roar of approval.

Rohan turned to his wife.

"I do not think I have seen them this boisterous for a long time," he said excitedly. "Or so vehement."

"Oh, stop it, my lord. I think the boys are nervous enough," Elaine said.

"To your mounts, my terriers. And lay into them," he then said warmly to both Guy and Terold, gesturing them away to their horses.

Chapter Eight

Terold and Guy lay flat on two low beds. They were lying next to each other in the specially prepared recovery ward, which was only a cleaned-out storeroom positioned to the side of the kitchen.

Terold kept moaning for effect, although he was in considerable pain from his injuries. Guy looked over at him slowly from his one good eye.

"I do not know if I should laugh or cry," Terold said.

"Laugh, I think. At least we are alive," Guy answered through swollen lips.

"What did you say?" Terold said, laughing. "I did not understand a word you said."

Guy chuckled, but then grimaced in pain. Then they both laughed and moaned together.

Their injuries, although superficial, were many. Both squires were prime targets for all the other competitors in the melee, and often got hit from behind when facing other opponents.

"Well, well, my boys. It is good to see you alive," Sir Harold called out in good humour as he walked into the room. His smile was bright in the darkened room, but neither Guy nor Terold looked up.

"I don't think we are, my lord," Terold replied.

"Nonsense," Sir Harold said. "You both managed to eventually walk away from the round table."

"How did we do, my lord?" Guy asked again with some difficulty.

"Good grief," Sir Harold said to Terold, after looking at Guy. "Is that some kind of monstrous troll? It both looks and sounds like a troll." Sir Harold and Terold then both chuckled aloud.

Guy just groaned.

Sir Harold took out a leather purse and jangled it in front of them.

"You did very well," he then said, the metallic clink from the purse indicating quite a few coins.

"At one point in the contest, you were fighting with more men outside the arena than inside, so you managed to participate well into the second half of the contest where all riders had dismounted." He then chuckled again. "You did however come off your horses very early on in the fight, although the Earl did comment on Terold's spectacular dismount."

"The horse just stopped by itself," Terold answered indignantly.

"Did it. That's a shame. The Earl thought that you deliberately and bravely threw yourself at that other rider to take him down," Sir Harold said and then paused. "Although you did hit him arse first and facing up to the sky."

"I believe you managed to floor the horse with your shield as well as knocking out the rider," he continued in high spirits.

"A judge wanted to disqualify you, but the Earl suggested that they gave you double points for ingenuity."

He chuckled again.

"But you did well, boys, and if you feel up to it, I will buy you both drinks in the Inn tonight. I suspect that there will be a few men there who will want to shake your hands."

Sir Harold, again shook his purse at the two boys and left, whistling to himself in the process.

"Did I hear him correctly, Guy?" Terold said. "Did he offer to buy us a drink?"

Guy slowly pushed himself to sit up and then twisted his legs off the bed and onto the floor. He grimaced at the pain and then chuckled to himself.

"I do not think it has ever been heard of before," Guy answered smiling wide at Terold. "The only explanation I can think of to his extravagant offer, is that he does not expect us to show up."

"But we the Earl's terriers," Terold continued, also getting up from the bed and whimpering.

"And we will not let a few broken bones deter us from a free drink from Sir Harold."

"I will meet you at the gatehouse in two hours," Guy said and limped out of the storeroom to go home and find his father to get some attention for his face and sore body.

Guy's father was elated when Guy walked through the door and barely noticed his injuries, until Guy pointed them out.

Sigard quickly shouted down a servant and sent him off to get some healing balm and clean bandages. He then set about boiling water for Guy to bathe and soothe away some of the aches. Sigard always swore by bathing, and as a blacksmith, he had the luxury of owning large wooden sealed tubs which he used for cooling and tempering swords, large plates of armour and other worked objects. Sigard's body had often been coated in grime from the forge and he regularly ached from the heavy lifting and hammering at the anvil. So, to alleviate his discomfort, he had a spare tub made, which he kept in the Smithy and always used as a bath. He was loathed to leave it behind, when he became Steward to the Earl, so he brought it with him when he moved to the castle. Sigard valued the soaking ritual and ensured that Guy also bathed frequently. Guy however found it a chore to get the bath ready, but when he eventually did bathe, he always enjoyed the experience.

"I think you need some Chamomile added to your bath," his father said, busily trying to find the herbs on a shelf.

"That will take away the aches and pains. Oh, and I think that I have some St John's Wort leftover as well. I will add a pinch just to make sure."

"You did me proud today, my lad," Sigard then said. "The Earl sought me out especially to tell me of your endeavours and how well you fought."

"Really," Guy said. "It all seemed a blur."

"The Earl said you grounded two men in one prolongation. Whatever that means."

Guy gingerly sat down into a tattered but soft cushioned chair, and slowly shuffled himself into its high back.

"It just means that once I sliced across one opponent, I continued moving my bodyweight to line up another one. That allows me to then bring my sword across that next opponent in what looks like one continuous movement," Guy answered. "I generally do it with a single or even double turn of the body depending on where the opponent is positioned. There was one manoeuvre that I think I can remember, as it was very clean, but I am sure that there were many others as there was always more than one opponent in front of me." Guy stretched his back. "Or behind me if it comes to that."

"You still seem to have been hit a lot."

"I would like to think that I was hit hard, rather more than a lot," Guy joked. "It seems both Terold and I were the main targets."

"You lasted longer than Terold," Sigard said with pride.

"Yes, but he remained on his horse longer."

"Ha. Did you see him fall off?"

"No Father, I had other things to watch out for. But Sir Harold has already described it."

"Was he happy with you?" Sigard then asked.

"I think so, as he has invited Terold and me for a drink at the Inn. As his reward for fighting well."

"Really. He is not usually generous."

"I think he made quite a bit of money today."

Sigard smiled sheepishly. He then pulled his purse from the inside of his shirt and shook it at Guy. Like Sir Harold's, it jangled opulently.

"Ha!" Guy laughed. "Profiting from your son's pain."

"You should come along and buy me a drink as well," Guy continued.

Sigard jangled his purse again.

"But I first need to be in a fit state to get to the Inn," Guy then said.

"Do not worry," Sigard replied. "A bath will work wonders for the body. But I am not sure about your face though."

Guy grimaced as he ran his fingers over the swollen contours of his cheeks.

"And Lady Felice also stopped me," Sigard then said as he suddenly remembered the meeting.

"What did she say?" Guy asked immediately, as he sat up straight and then winced at the pain.

"Nothing of importance!" Sigard said, who was suddenly taken aback by Guy's impatient tone. "She was concerned about your injuries and wanted to make sure that you were not too badly hurt. She also wanted me to tell you that she was glad your luck held," he continued as he checked the boiling water on the fire.

Guy smiled and leant back into the chair, wondering if it was a reference to her satin token.

"I suppose I was lucky. It could have been a lot worse."

Terold was still full of himself on the next morning and would not stop commenting on the proceedings from the night before.

They were sitting on the soil and stone bank that was piled up to support the thick wooden poles that made up the northern side of the castle that adjoined Aethelflaed's great mound.

Guy felt heavy headed and slightly nauseous and Terold's constant chatter was grating on him. He had been given quite a few ales by quite a few of the castle staff and militia and he was now paying penance for it. A lot of the soldiers who fought in the melee were there and a lot of them looked equally as battered as Guy and Terold. But they were all in high spirits and rallied round the two squires, treating them as if they were one of their own.

Sir Harold was also in a good mood which lasted throughout the night, and he constantly patted the squires on their backs whenever he had the opportunity. Although the gesture was appreciated by the squires, the pain made them wince, which Sir Harold found amusing.

There were several tavern girls in the inn, who constantly served the men with ale, fawning over both Terold and Guy as they passed. Terold enjoyed all the attention, but Guy was more reserved. Even though the Warwick Inn was dark and shadowy, he was conscious of his facial injuries.

He did, however, spend a lot of the night talking to a young man called Harry, who was a member of the castle Household Guard. He was the man who put Guy to the ground in the melee, although Harry only remained in the affray for a few minutes longer, before the eventual winner sent him sprawling to the ground.

Harry, like Guy, also supported a swollen and closed eye, but it was also accompanied by a broken nose. They looked a strange pair as they sat on a bench against the wall; Harry with his red and swollen left eye, Guy with his red and swollen right eye.

Their drinking companions would constantly turn and raise their tankards to the two of them and shout: "Aye, Aye," and everyone, including Harry and Guy, would down their jug of ale. This was the main reason that Guy was so hung-over.

The two squires were now cleaning their leather and chainmail armour from the day before with Guy having the harder task, as his armour was stained with his blood. Their shields and swords were resting on the ground next to them awaiting their treatment. The cleaning would take most of the morning and Guy was glad that in his condition, there was nothing more physical to exert him. Guy was also amused that Terold would fall silent whenever anyone walked past as he casually awaited a word of greeting or acknowledgement, which occurred, to Guy's surprise, far more often than had ever happened before. People in the castle now seemed to know who they were.

"Good morning boys," Sir Harold called out as he came up to them. Guy and Terold stood up gingerly and nodded their respect.

"Good morning, my lord," they both said together

"How are you feeling today?" Sir Harold then asked. "You are not looking so good, Guy."

Guy gently touched his inflamed eye and winced. The eye was still heavily swollen and now darkening. He could still not see out of it.

"My father says that I will be back to normal in a couple of weeks, my lord," Guy replied.

"Your father, as competent as he is, is not however as knowledgeable as me, and I say that you will be back to normal in a couple of days," Sir Harold smiled at Guy and then threw him a small clay jar, which, after fumbling around with it due to his impaired vision, Guy eventually caught hold of.

Sir Harold screwed up his face at Guy's attempt to catch it.

"To rub on your eye to reduce the swelling and bring out the bruising." He then said. "Use it liberally. It used to work wonders for me on the rare occasion that I ever got hit."

"And you Terold?" He then asked.

"I will be back to normal in a couple of days, my lord."

"That's the spirit," Sir Harold said with good humour.

"I need you fighting fit as soon as possible as the Warwick Tournament is only a few weeks away, and Earl Rohand has plans for you."

"Plans, my lord?" Guy quickly asked.

"Nothing to bother yourselves with now. But you need to be back training as soon as possible."

"Oh, and Guy, Lady Elaine requested you to attend them tonight, but I declined their invitation on your behalf saying that your injuries prevented your service. Although what I meant was that your looks would scare them."

"Thank you, my lord," Guy said with a sigh of gratitude.

"Carry on then," Sir Harold said and walked back to the hall.

Guy looked across at Terold who like Guy was wondering what the Earl's plans were.

It took two days before the swelling went down around Guy's eye, allowing him to see out of it well enough to go and practise swordplay with Terold and recover his coordination. All other aches and bruises were just uncomfortable and not restricting. His split lip had also started to heal and there was no damage to his jaw or teeth. Terold had also recovered, and the two squires went about their routines at the upper edge of the training field, under the shade of a large, tall maple tree. The ground was dry and well-trodden, and dust flicked up from around their feet as they shuffled in circles in front of each other, armed with their training swords.

Terold paused in his manoeuvre and stood up from his defensive crouch. He held up his hand to stop Guy from carrying out any further attack. He then removed his helmet and waited as two young pages ran up towards them from the castle. Guy also stood up straight and turned to see what caught Terold's attention and also watched the young boys as they struggled to carry two heavy shields.

They pulled up in next to Guy and Terold and leant on the upright shields as they stood them on their rims in front of them.

"Sir Harold told us to tell you: 'About time'," one of the pages said with some difficulty, as he tried to talk and catch his breath at the same time.

"And he said that he does not want you practising swordplay without shields," The other page then said.

The two pages were only eight or nine years of age, and their faces were bright with youthful keenness.

"So, he got us to bring you these," the first page said, and then patted the shield in front of him.

Guy and Terold looked over their shoulders towards the castle, but Sir Harold could not be seen.

"He also wants you to prepare your horses, and to be ready outside of the stables, to accompany a hunting party at noon. He wants you to dress and behave as formal squires, as the Earl will have important guests within the party," the first page then said.

"And we are to attend any tasks that you have, to help you prepare," the second page added.

Guy and Terold turned their heads in unison as they looked at each page in turn, as they alternated their messages.

"And if we forget to tell you anything, then it will be your fault as much as ours," the first page said.

"Because we are just young pages who do not know any better," he then continued, looking at Guy and then at Terold.

"Sir Harold told you that?" Terold then asked, agitated.

The two boys nodded together.

"And you will feel his wrath if you are not prepared properly," one of them said smiling.

"Have you forgotten to tell us anything?" Guy asked.

The boys looked at each other thoughtfully.

"Because if you have, then you will feel our wrath," Terold said.

The boys then thought some more before one just shrugged his shoulders at Guy.

Terold looked at Guy, who raised an eyebrow. The months and months of regimented training and scheduled chores had now, within the last few days, been suddenly replaced with a series of new, unplanned and unexpected exploits and adventures. And on top of that, they were suddenly no longer the dog's bodies of the castle, but now had young pages who they were responsible for.

"Well then," Terold said smiling. "We need our horses walked, fed and watered and tacked up ready for the hunt."

The two boy's faces changed to horror at the prospect of preparing the two large horses that Terold and Guy now rode. Terold knew very well that these tasks were well beyond their capabilities and training.

"And then we will need our clothes to be brushed down and laid out," Terold continued.

Terold then paused and thought for a few seconds.

"Oh, and an early lunch would be needed, so you will need to get some bread and cold meat from the kitchens. Oh!" Terold then exclaimed as he thought of something else. "And get a couple of slices of the cook's game pie ready for us in the canteen."

The pages were dumbstruck at the requests. They did not know anything about the two squire's personal attire, but they were fully aware of the personal danger of asking the cook for food outside of mealtimes. There was also the increased risk in requesting specific food items, especially pieces of her pies.

Guy smiled. He knew that Terold was only playing with the pages.

"What are your names?" Guy asked

"Edward," one answered straight away.

"James," the other one then said.

"All we need at the moment, Edward and James," Guy said. "Is some more shield practise," and he took the shields from the boys and passed one to Terold.

He then tossed his sword to James, who was the nearest and then assumed a defensive stance facing the young page, with his shield raised.

Terold laughed and did the same with Edward.

Edward and James looked at each other and then swung the swords in large arcs towards the two squires. Guy and Terold easily defended the blows on their shields, but they backed away step by step in the process to encourage the pages forward.

The two pages struggled with the saddle's girth strap that stretched around the barrel of Guy's horse, and then eagerly ran around the horse inserting their fingers in between the strap and the horse's flesh.

"Wait until the horse breaths out before you check the tightness," Guy instructed. "And because the horse will be exerted during the hunt, the chest will be expanding more than usual, so you need to have less tension and therefore slightly more give."

The pages pulled at the buckle some more and the horse whinnied and shuffled its feet in agitation.

Guy stood up and pushed two crossed fingers under the strap.

"That should be fine," Guy said nodding. "But you need to find your own measure and remember it for next time."

"But if the saddle slips, and I fall off, then there will be all hell to pay," Guy then said, poking Edward lightly, and pushing him into James.

The two boys laughed and shoved Guy in retaliation. Guy grabbed James in a loose headlock, while Edward jumped on Guy's back and wrapped his arms around Guy's neck.

"What's going on here?" Sir Harold's voice suddenly called out loudly as he entered the stables and walked past Guy and the two pages, as they quickly untangled themselves. He strode to the front of the horse to stroke its cheek and muzzle.

"Guy is teaching us how to saddle a horse, Sir Harold," James said quickly as he stood to attention.

"And you do that from on top of Guy's back?" Sir Harold said, not looking at them as he continued to stroke the horse.

"No, Sir Harold," Edward answered quickly.

Sir Harold then stoked the horse down its shoulder and chest and quickly put his fingers under the strap to check the tightness. He then patted the horse's shoulder and turned to face them.

"That's enough for today, you two," he said to the pages. "You can get off to the canteen."

The two pages nodded their respect and ran off.

"As for you," Sir Harold said, turning towards Guy. "You, along with Terold, will be joining me to participate in the Earl's hunt this afternoon, and we will be eating in the field."

Sir Harold looked around the stables.

"Where is Terold?" He asked.

"Getting our formal attire, my lord."

"Good," Sir Harold said. "Which reminds me. You need to increase your wardrobe, and the Earl has provided funds to your father for that purpose. Terold also needs to acquire some additional clothes and armour to match, but he has enough family funds to support him."

"I have provided your father with instructions, but you will need time to get measured up and get it all made. So, make sure you address this tomorrow."

"Yes, my lord. Thank you."

"No thanks required Guy. This is just a reward for your recent behaviour and achievements." Sir Harold slapped Guy on the shoulder. "More rewards will no doubt be due if you continue at your present improvement. The Earl pays particular attention to your development and achievements."

Guy nodded.

"Thank you, my lord."

"But, as it's a beautiful spring day, the Earl has decided to arrange a hunt for this afternoon, in honour of an important guest. You are to once again attend the ladies which, as we all know, you are very accomplished at. But this time you will be supported by Terold," Sir Harold said. "Walter will also be with us as well as will your friend Harry, from the Household Guard, who you seem to get on with well enough."

"And will you be there, my lord?"

"Of course. My hunting skills and legendary," Sir Harold replied. "And for this outing, I will be hunting, and therefore not performing any guarding duties. Which is why I am bringing you two."

"And what will you be hunting, my lord?" Guy asked.

"We will be in the southern estate, so probably deer, but I am hoping for an unfriendly boar."

"And who will be in the party, my lord?"

"As well as the Earl, there will be Lord Athelstan, who is the son of the King and the brother of Edith, who you know from Polesworth." Sir Harold paused. "I am not sure if we call him 'Prince' or not." He paused again for a few moments, while he considered this further "I will find out," he continued. "But he will also have many supporters and guards."

"Lady Edith, who is visiting the Earl to meet up with her brother, asked specifically to accompany him on the hunt and the Earl thought it good manners that his wife and daughter joined her," Sir Harold said and then sighed.

"Which meant that the hunt had to be arranged for this afternoon, which was better for the ladies, and not for early tomorrow morning, which is better to hunt game."

"And, of course, all their entourages will also be attending, so stealth will not be needed to find the game, as is usual for a hunt. The plan is to first wake them from their midday sleep with the noise of our revelry. Then when they come to see the cause of the celebrations, they will feel the urge to come and join the gaiety and we will then spear them."

Sir Harold sighed again.

"The master of the hunt will of course be there, along with the Earls' hounds and a contingency of the castle guard to protect the party."

Sir Harold looked at Guy and awaited any further questions. But Guy remained silent, happy in the knowledge that Felice will be there.

"I understand that there will also be a picnic, fit for a prince. If, of course, he is a prince. But I am not sure you are included, so make sure you have your own provisions before we leave."

"You and Terold are to be ready at noon and you will gather in the courtyard, to line up with Walter and Harry," Sir Harold finally said, and then walked away back towards the castle.

The skies were a crisp blue, above the castle walls, with hardly a cloud in sight and the sun was creating an unseasonal warmth in the brightness of the spring day. Guy and Terold had been sitting on their mounts for about half an hour, dressed in their full squire's uniform, which included light armour, while they waited for the Earl and his guests. The full heat of the sun bore down on them and with no cooling breeze, they both felt tired and uncomfortable. The horses were also uneasy and wanted to find shade. The riders were constantly calming them by stroking their necks as they shuffled on their feet and shook their heads in agitation.

There were also several horses without riders that also awaited the Earl's party. They were all neatly brushed and adorned with woven blankets of the Earl's livery spread across the horses back, beneath polished saddles and bridles. They were held patiently in a straight line by individual grooms, alongside wooden platforms to allow the riders to easily mount.

Guy had his shield strapped down the right side of the horse, positioned outside of his stirrup which kept rubbing against his leg, but the long leather boots protected him from any abrasion. He had his sword buckled to his belt hanging down his right side, which also bagged against him with the horse's gait. None of it felt comfortable and Guy planned to investigate it later to see if he could arrange it better.

Although Guy was wearing his light armour, he was allowed to remove his helmet and store it in the cart. He had placed it alongside his bow and arrows, which, after his trip to Polesworth, he thought prudent to bring along.

The Earl and his party eventually came out of the Great Hall and went to their mounts. Most of the senior ladies were riding, and some were accompanied by their ladies-in-waiting, who also rode. The others travelled by cart. All the men rode on horseback, apart from Father Cuthbert, who travelled in the cart with the maids. It took several minutes to get all the hunting party settled, and once the Earl was assured that all was in place they were eventually led off by the Master of the Hunt and his pack of hounds.

Guy rode alongside Terold, behind the group of ladies. Walter and Harry rode in front of the ladies but directly behind Earl Rohand, Prince Athelstan, and Sir Harold. The carts followed behind, along with a small contingency of castle guards that were distributed evenly across both flanks of the group.

They quickly rode through the castle walls and then through the town, before crossing the old stone bridge over the River Avon.

The green grazing land on the far bank of the river suddenly gave away to woodland and the party left the bright sunshine and entered the shade of the trees. The fresh crispness of the open-air changed to a more earthy smell as they entered the wood. Guy noticed the more oppressive atmosphere straight away, but it was something that he was used to, and it did not bother him. He was aware, however, of the increased risk of an ambush, because of the proximity of the trees and he looked closely to each side for any signs of unnatural colours or unexpected movements.

They travelled along the main road for a mile or two, before turning off along a narrow farm track. The track was obviously in common use as the carts moved easily along it without hitting too many old ruts. But some of the group had to reduce their spacing, as the path's width only allowed the riders to travel two abreast. They were now in dappled shade, as large trees reached over them with large, rounded boughs and well-spaced branches that dropped down like fingers, laden with large, newly formed, broad leaves. The wood itself was well coppiced with ample space between the tree trunks along with a cleared ground cover. Cut branches were piled together at regular intervals to support the forest wildlife. The woodland canopy provided a cool dampness to the riders, but it regularly broke to let in the daylight and allow the heat of the sun to wash over them, before closing again into a vivid green hue.

After another hour, the woodland suddenly cleared into a small meadow, which had a couple of wooden huts and various shelters spewed across the open area. Wooden trestles were sited around the huts, with various sized, newly split, tree trunks and large trimmed branches scattered about them. Clumps of fern, bracken and nettles grew in isolated bunches around the field and up against the walls of the rough buildings.

The head of the castle guard brought the party to a halt, where the Earl and his male guests quickly dismounted to stretch their legs.

Guy and Terold rode forward and pulled alongside the ladies. The two squires quickly dismounted and tied their horses to a wooden frame before moving back to secure the ladies horses. Guy went straight to the Earl's wife, whereas Terold attended Lady Edith.

Other guards also attended the ladies and held the horses as a large wooden step was brought from the cart and placed to the side of Lady Edith. Terold then supported her as she dismounted.

"Bless you," Edith said as she moved off the step and past Terold, brushing her dress straight with her hands. The step was then moved to Lady Elaine was also dismounted.

Guy moved back to Lady Felice, who was waiting patiently.

"My lady," Guy said and turned to wait for the step.

"Your hand Guy," Felice said and held her hand down to Guy.

Guy smiled and reached up to gently take her hand as she elegantly slid off the horse and onto the ground. Guy used his other hand to support her elbow as she landed. Felice placed her other hand on Guy's shoulder, as she lightly fell against him. She remained in contact with him as she regained her balance, and he felt a wisp of her breath caress his face.

She slowly moved her head away from him to allow her to focus on his face, as his injuries were more apparent close-up.

"Oh Guy," she said and carefully touched the bruising around his eye. "That must be painful,"

Guy felt a sudden energy surge through him at her light caress and reddened. There was no pain, just pleasure.

"Not really, my lady," Guy answered warmly as she stepped back away from him, and he released her elbow.

"But it is something that I am getting used to," he continued.

"I thought you fought very bravely," she then said.

"Thank you, my lady," he replied.

Father Cuthbert then hurried up and stood in front of her.

"Are you alright, my dear?" Cuthbert said.

"Yes Father, Guy was here to help," Felice replied.

"Young Guy always seems to be at hand to help you," he then said pointedly.

"Or so it seems, Father," Felice said, in a matter-of-fact tone.

She then turned slowly and started to walk towards her mother, as a guard led her horse away. Guy walked with her, leaving Father Cuthbert to follow behind.

"Are you hunting today, my lady?" Guy asked.

"I would if I could," she replied quietly. "But in the present company, I think it would be highly unlikely."

"Do you have to, my dear?" Lady Elaine said with slight scorn, as Felice approached. "There was a step at hand."

"Oh Mother, I am totally at ease un-mounting a horse."

"But it could have been done with a bit more elegance," Lady Elaine replied. "Thank you for your support, Guy," she then added kindly to Guy. "It would have been a fine site if she had fallen to the ground."

"Oh, Mother! That was never going to happen," Felice cut in.

The two ladies then walked away, towards Lady Edith. Guy bowed his respect and moved away from them, back towards Terold to help him unpack the cart.

It did not take the castle staff long to raise a couple of large pavilions and smaller tents along with a large canvas awning. The large sail was held aloft by an intricate arrangement of poles and ropes to provide shelter for the party.

Blankets were laid on the ground underneath the canopies and provisions were unpacked. Guy and Terold then supported the castle staff in serving refreshments to the hunting party and their guests.

Walter and Harry looked after the men's horses while the hounds were driven past them to the edge of the clearing and then tied in a group to a small tree. There were half a dozen large dogs that barked vigorously, leaping on each other in excitement and anticipation of their participation in the hunt. Their hunt master was wading in between them with a long thin stick, whipping them across their sides to try and calm them, so that he could untangle their leashes.

It was not until the end of the picnic that Guy was relieved from serving the ladies, allowing him to retire to his other duties.

The Earl, Athelstan and Sir Harold had also left the ladies and were now checking on their horses and assessing the weight of a selection of boar spears. The men were now keen to get the hunt underway.

The ladies would not be joining the actual hunt and they were to remain in this clearing, with several guards and servants to attend them, including the squires.

One of the ladies-in-waiting had left the group and walked over to Guy, who was busy checking over his horse's tack. He was examining the reins and saddle arrangement to look for a better way to carry his equipment. She carried a silver platter with a piece of a pie in one hand and a cup of ale in the other.

"The Lady Felice sends her compliments," the young lady said as she passed the food and drink to him.

"Thank you," Guy said as he balanced the cup on the platter and took a bite of pie.

The lady-in-waiting was of similar age to Felice and had shiny black hair that crept out from beneath a long white linen headscarf. The scarf was draped over the top of her head and then wrapped in a spiral around her hair before trailing down her back, held in place with a thin leather strap around her forehead. She had large brown eyes and like Felice, she had fair, unmarked skin.

"My name is Janette," she said. "I am Lady Felice's companion and I have been her friend since we were children. I serve as her lady-in-waiting."

She scrutinised Guy closely while he took another mouthful.

Guy, noticing her stare, felt embarrassed at her attention and casually wiped his mouth with the back of his hand while he looked at her cautiously.

He slowly chewed the contents of the pie and waited until he had emptied his mouth of the food before nodding at Janette.

"You are fortunate," he said. "Will you pass on my thanks to Lady Felice?"

"I think that you would be very handsome if your face was not so battered and bruised," she then said with a serious tone and stern expression.

"Thank you, Janette," he replied, quite startled and not sure of how to respond.

"But your hair is not very tidy," she then said. "Not at all like your friends. But perhaps he has a manservant."

"Perhaps he has," Guy said laughing, as he last cut Terold's hair.

She continued to wait and stare at Guy. He took another small bite of pie and looked at her as she continued to look at him.

He raised his eyebrows in encouragement to her.

"I am waiting for the cup and plate," she eventually said.

"Oh sorry, I didn't realise," Guy quickly responded and drank down the ale, spilling some from around the cup's edges to dribble down his chin.

He wiped his mouth again and passed the cup back to Janette. He then picked up the remaining pie and handed the plate back to her.

Janette then turned away and walked back to the tents. "Please pass on my thanks to Lady Felice," Guy said aloud, as he flicked his hand up in a wave and then walked across to Terold.

It took a while for the men and hounds to get ready for their hunt, but the riders eventually mounted their horses and then slowly cantered off into the trees, led by Sir Harold. The hounds, straining at their leads, were held by two servants who ran behind the horses.

The hound's barking softened as the forest gradually dampened out the noise, as Walter and Harry walked around the perimeter of the small field. They were on guard duty while Terold served drinks to Lady Elaine and Lady Edith.

Guy was standing at the edge of the meadow, still looking for ways to support his shield on the side of the horse without it rubbing against his leg.

"Is there a problem Guy?" Felice asked as she walked over with Janette.

Guy turned to greet Felice and looked over the lady's shoulders to see Father Cuthbert, who was a dozen paces behind and looking on. Guy smiled at the priest's attentiveness.

"Technical issue, my lady," Guy answered. "I am trying to support my shield to the side of my horse without interfering with my legs. However, I cannot firmly fix it, as I still need to allow for a quick release for when I need to use it in a fight." Guy pulled at the horse's neck reins and muttered aloud as he thought about it. "I need the shield to remain secure on the horse until I need to release it. But the release needs to be quick and easy."

"I am trying to picture a metal frame that I can construct out of iron strips that I can forge together. But it cannot be too heavy."

"You need to release it when you charge at an opponent?" Felice asked.

"Or to quickly dismount and join a shield wall, my lady. You saw the potency of such a wall at Anker Bridge."

"Also, my lady. Between you and me," Guy continued, looking at Felice with a mischievous smile, "as a surprise tactic in a melee."

"Oh, a novelty," Felice said smiling, "I am intrigued. Tell me more."

"Well, my lady, picture me with the sword in my right hand, riding against right-handed opponents. I just need to keep reeling right at the outskirts of the 'round table' and use the shield as a continuous ramming point."

"Riding around the edge like a scalloped fringe," Felice replied.

Guy pictured Felice's description in his mind.

"Exactly, my lady," Guy then said. "That is exactly what I will call the manoeuvre; 'The Scalloped Fringe'. I will try it out at the next opportunity." He smiled at Felice. "But I need to make a mechanism to allow it to work."

"I will also consider the matter," Felice said. "Perhaps your issue can be solved not in mechanics, but with simple belts and straps."

"I would be grateful, my lady. Any help will be most welcome."

"You would also need to train your horse to master this 'Scallop Manoeuvre'," she said.

"That would not be a problem, my lady. Bedivere can easily pick it up," Guy replied patting the horse's neck. "Like me, he enjoys a challenge."

"Is Bedivere your horse?" Felice asked.

"No, my lady. He belongs to your father's stable. But I always choose him above the others, if he is available, as I like his intelligence. Which, however, is becoming less frequent, as others also recognise his worth."

Then suddenly there was a squealing to the side of them, as a small farrow of piglets ran from out of the dark, dense undergrowth at the side of the forest.

"Ah, look at the babies," Janette said at the sight of the three young boars. But Guy instantly stepped in front of the ladies with his arms outstretched and moved slowly backwards, shepherding them away from the piglets.

"Be quiet, Janette," Felice whispered, when she also suddenly realised the danger.

"Felice, I need you to mount Bedivere," Guy stated. "You will be out of eye line."

"Janette, get on the horse," Felice commanded.

Janette was still confused at their actions but recognised the seriousness in the tone of Felice's voice, and quickly climbed on Bedivere.

Guy shook his head.

"Felice," Guy said again more firmly. "I need you to mount Bedivere and get out of harm's way." He emphasised the 'you'. "Once you have mounted, then slowly ride away to your mother and get everyone onto the cart and safely out of harm's way."

"What about you?" Felice asked with concern.

"Once you are away, I do not have to worry about you, and I can better protect myself."

"And warn Terold and Harry," Guy then said.

Felice nodded, and leapt across the horse's back, behind Janette. She then threw her leg over the horse's rump to sit behind the saddle and then reached around her maid to grab the reins.

"Go," Guy ordered, and Felice slowly walked the horse away, before then cantering into the middle of the field calling for the attention of others.

The noise, however, not only brought the sow into the field to protect its young but also a huge male boar. The massive beast ran out and abruptly stopped, snorting loudly as it assessed the threat to its family.

Guy continued to slowly back away, one small step at a time. His eyes were fixed on the male boar, with its long dark coarse fir, little beady eyes and large yellow tusks that curved upwards from the side of its mouth. The animal was both broad in the chest and across its back and showed its rage by squealing loudly at the threat.

The boar watched Guy's slow retreat, and aggressively charged at him for a couple of strides, before stopping short, snorting heavily, and then retreating.

Guy continued to purposefully move backwards, with his eyes focused on the male boar. But he constantly kept the mother in his peripheral vision, just in case it decided to charge at him.

Then a horse galloped up from behind, and Felice returned on her own mount and pulled up to a sliding halt to the side of Guy.

"Quick Guy," she said. "Get on."

Guy looked up at Felice, who was facing the boar with a large spear under her arm.

Guy sighed, and without a better option, leapt up onto the horse. But before he had a chance to bring his legs over to sit astride it, he was sent flying, as the male boar ploughed into the horse's legs.

Guy hit the ground but had the presence of mind to roll over to absorb the impact. He was winded slightly but was still totally aware of what was going on around him. He looked around for Felice and saw her lying on her back a few paces away with the spear pointing upwards, still in her grasp. The horse was thrashing around on the floor, crying in pain, and the boar, trapped within its legs, was throwing its head around and digging its tusks into anything that moved. Blood was splashing everywhere.

Guy heard Father Cuthbert faintly shouting 'my lady, my lady' repeatedly, in a strange high-pitched tone of panic. He then heard Terold calling, but his voice was away in the distance. So, without further thought, he sprang onto his feet and went to protect Felice.

"He grabbed Felice's arms and pulled her along the ground and away from the flailing horse's hoofs, and the rampaging boar.

He looked at the horse with sadness, as he backed away, but then noticed that it wasn't Bedivere, and he sighed slightly with relief.

"Felice!" He called. "Are you hurt?"

"I am alright," she said panting. "Let me get up."

Guy let go of her arms, and she quickly got to her feet, just as the female boar charged around from behind the thrashing horse. Its grunting and squealing, adding to the mayhem. The sow stopped when it saw them, lowered its head, and stamped its front foot.

"Stand still," he said and slowly crouched down to grab the end of the spear and dragged it back towards him. He then slowly passed it to Felice.

"Keep crouched and just use it to fend it off," Guy said and then slowly pulled his sword out of its scabbard.

"Keep very close to me Felice. If it attacks, then it needs to be in a position for a straight thrust. Anything to the side will not be enough."

"Guy, what can we do?" Terold suddenly called out from behind.

"Get spears from the cart, and then distract the female until I get Felice away," Guy said calmly. "And bring my bow and arrows."

Harry, who was twenty yards to their left, was suddenly shouting at the female pig and waving his arms in large arcs. The female boar now turned to face its tormentor and made aggressive short bursts towards him before retreating in a circle.

"Keep backing away slowly," Guy said.

"And then there was more squealing, as the male boar had finally untangled itself from the now dying horse and was now facing them. Blood dripped menacingly off the end of its tusks, and from the matted hair around its snout.

"Bugger," Guy said under his breath.

"Get behind me Felice and pass the spear under my arm, but keep it out in front," he calmly said, "and keep backing away slowly."

But then Terold started shouting, as he ran from behind them. The male boar then charged directly at Guy, who quickly fixed his stance to take the force of the impact.

The boar ran straight onto the spear and just pushed the shaft backwards, with no effect on the momentum of its charge. Guy felt the weight of Felice lift off him, as she was pushed backwards with the force of the blow. But then the boar charged onto Guy's sword, which he thrust out at the moment of impact, stabbing it straight in between the boar's eyes, as it lowered its head to bring its tusks down.

The thrust was true, and the blade went straight through its skull and into its brain. But the boar's weight and momentum crashed into Guy, who was pushed instantly backwards and over the top of Felice, who was trying to roll away to the side.

Guy crashed on his back, with the weight of the boar on top of him. He slid his hands off the sword hilt and grabbed both the beast's tusks, trying hard to hold its head away from him.

Felice also struggled to pull her legs away from under them.

The sword, which was embedded in the boar's head, caught underneath his left shoulder and levered him upwards, as the boar continued to thrash around in its death throes. Blood was splashing around all over him, both blinding and choking him and Guy could not tell if it was the boar's blood or his own. The boar's foul breath blew into his face and the smell made him turn his head sideways in revulsion, to expose the side of his neck to the boar's tusks. Then a spear thrust into the boar's side with a hollow thud, which Guy felt through his arms. It then took an arrow in the neck, then another spear and another arrow, until suddenly the boar's movements ceased. The stricken animal then fell limp on top of him, with shafts sticking out at all angles. "Get it off," Guy moaned aloud.

He then heard the twang of the bowstring as another arrow flew. Guy realised from the sound, that it was not aimed in his direction, and he suspected that the female boar was now the target. Guy struggled harder, as he started to panic. He knew that a single arrow would not deter the animal, but only enrage it further.

Then the weight as suddenly taken off him, to be replaced by more thrashing hooves. The female boar had charged past Terold, who had quickly jumped aside from its charge, and crashed into the dead body of its mate.

Guy rolled onto a ball and covered his head with his hands. He then rolled over and over, away from the carnage.

More arrows flew, as he heard their familiar whistle shoot over his body. He stopped rolling, to lie flat and still, with his face to the ground. Terold shouted and waved his arms to confuse the animal, Felice let loose more arrows, while Harry ran around and stabbed a long spear repeatedly into the sow as they forced it away from Guy. Then her squeals suddenly faded and stopped, as she slowly fell to the blood-stained ground and died. There was a sudden silence as everyone paused to take stock.

Felice then quickly hurried to Guy's side and fell to her knees beside him. He had rolled over again and was now lying flat on his back, with his eyes shut and his arms wrapped tightly around his chest.

"Guy, Guy." she cried. "Please, Lord."

"Don't fire an arrow into the pig, my lady. It will only make it angry," he said, both chuckling and coughing. He surprised himself by his laughing, as his situation did not seem to warrant any amusement. But he felt no pain, just a sense of exhilaration.

He then scraped his hand down his face to wipe away the boar's blood and opened his eyes. He looked up directly into Felice's eyes, which were directly above him and awash with tears that dripped down onto his cheek.

"Are you alright, my lady?" he said with sudden concern.

"Oh, Guy," she said. "Why is it always you?" and lightly cupped his cheek in her hand.

He smiled warmly at her.

"Just luck I suppose," he said, smiling, and then the pain hit him.

Guy was lying on a blanket under the awning, his head resting on a cushion. His upper armour had been removed and had been washed down and bandaged, as best as modesty allowed. There were a couple of small gashes in each forearm, and to the back of his right shoulder, but nothing life-threatening, unless there was a future infection. He felt, however, like he had fallen off the castle wall, and he ached everywhere. But he was lucky, as there were no broken bones. He had full use of his limbs and could bend his back with no breathing difficulties. His arms, however, were extremely sore from the thrust to the boar, and his elbows pained him whenever he bent them.

The Lady Elaine plied him with some more ale and Edith, with a bible in her hand, was praying her thanks at his side.

"I think that I have recovered well enough to get up and resume my duties, my lady," Guy said, and slowly pushed himself up and onto his feet. He flinched in pain from what seemed like his whole body and caught his breath to restrict the movement of his chest.

"Nonsense Guy," Elaine replied. "You need to lie down and just rest awhile."

"But, my lady, I need to be dressed and prepared for when your husband returns. I cannot be seen like this," Guy said with gravity.

Elaine looked at him for a while, and then nodded.

"But not without my help, and if it is too much, then you will lie back down and rest."

"Yes, my lady," he replied with a tone of gratitude.

She picked up his linen shirt and held it up to place an arm into a sleeve.

"There is no need, my lady. I am well able to dress myself. You should not be doing this."

"This is not the first time that you have come to the aid of my family," she said. "This is the least I can do." As she held up the shirt to allow him to put his other arm into the other sleeve.

He ached with every movement and an occasional sharp pain shot through an arm.

Lady Edith also put down her Bible and picked up the chain mail vest. She lifted Guy's arms upwards to allow her to pull it down over his raised arms. She then carefully moved it down past his head, to let it slide down over his torso as Elaine fastened the last tie of his shirt.

Then between them, they buckled his leather belt around his waist along with his empty scabbard.

"Thank you," Guy said and slowly bowed. "You have done me a great honour."

"I actually quite enjoyed it, Guy," Edith said. "I have never dressed a man before, never mind a knight in armour."

"Not quite a knight yet," Elaine said, smiling at Edith. "Except in spirit."

Guy carefully bowed towards the ladies in respect and with a grimace of pain, slowly limped out of the awning and back into the sun. He looked over to where the boars attacked and saw both Terold and Harry collecting arrows.

Terold looked up and noticed Guy. He waved at him extravagantly, before moving aside to allow a small group of guards to pull the dead horse into the trees.

Guy gingerly waved back, and then noticed the two boar's carcasses lying next to each other on the grass in front of Terold.

He then scanned the camp and saw Felice to his right.

Felice was sitting on a stool away from the awning, where she had watched him being dressed. But when he came towards her, she stood up and walked across to meet him, carrying his sword.

"All cleaned and polished," she said as they came together, and with the sword lying across both her outstretched hands, she handed it over to him.

"Thank you, my lady," he said and took the sword from her and ran it smoothly into the scabbard. "Are you hurt at all?" he asked.

"Lord no," she said and led him away by the arm into the middle of the field. "But my ears hurt from the battering my mother has given them," she said smiling. "I should not have got involved, I should have behaved more like a lady," she continued imitating her mother. "Although I do not know how a lady dies a horrible death on the tusks of a boar with both poise and grace."

Guy also smiled.

"Surely you must be at least bruised, my lady. You fell heavily onto the ground."

"There are some aspects of being a lady that I do recognise," she said, smiling, "and I will not discuss my bruises with you."

"It was also fortunate that my mother brought a change of clothes, and I will therefore not look too shabby in front of Athelstan when he returns."

Guy considered her words.

"Dare I ask if Athelstan is another suitor, my lady?"

"Who knows what's in my father's mind," she replied. "But I think not."

"But my reputation has to be established at court, and my mother concerns herself, in what that reputation will be." She sighed. "However, it is only my life that is being paraded around. But what will be, will be. I can only hope that any match will be favourable."

"So, Guy," she continued more buoyantly. "I believe you saved me this time, and I think my intended rescue of you only made matters worse."

"It made it more interesting Felice," he said with a slight nervousness as he used her name.

"The horse did however divert the boar," he continued. "And may have ultimately saved me. Who knows how it might have turned out if you had not bravely returned? I am just glad that we have survived to tell the tale." Guy then paused and looked at Felice. "Was the horse yours?" he asked with concern.

"I had ridden it a few times, but it was not as dear to me as Percy." She then smiled. "Do you remember him?"

"Oh yes, I think I still have the bite marks," he replied and then laughed. "He never did like me."

"He never liked anyone," Felice replied. "Only me."

"Then he had good taste, my lady."

She paused for a moment or two, as she took in his comment.

"I left your horse with Janette," she said, "and just jumped on mine as it was still saddled and ready."

"I hope you used the step and positioned your skirts and cloak accordingly," Guy said.

Felice laughed.

"She has not chided me over that yet. But I am sure she will," Felice replied. "I am sure she saw it."

Felice paused and held her head up. Guy also picked up the distant noise of the baying hounds, which signalled the return of the hunting party.

"This will be interesting, don't you think," Felice said. "I hope they caught a boar, and I hope it was bigger than ours, otherwise there will be hell to pay."

"I'll wager they didn't," Guy said, looking over at the bodies of the dead animals. "That is a monster of a beast."

Felice then sighed.

"I will need to be with my mother to greet my father and Athelstan," Felice said.

"Of course, my lady," Guy said.

She placed her hand on his arm and applied light pressure to her grip. She went to speak, but then held her words and just shook her head with a half-smile.

Guy stood there and watched her walk away.

"She is always in danger when she is around you," a deep voice said quietly from behind.

Guy turned around to see Father Cuthbert standing there, smiling at him.

"If it's not a gang of Warwick brigands out to harm her or a Viking war band out to capture her, then it's now dangerous beasts trying to kill her," Father Cuthbert continued lightly. "But I fear that her main danger is in herself, as it is obvious that she cares for you, Guy."

Guy looked closely at the priest who seemed sincere in his words and bore an expression of empathy.

"We have known each other for a long while, Father," Guy said, defensively.

"I know, and I can see how much you care for her," Cuthbert replied. "But all I can see is pain and unhappiness for you both, if you do not shield your young hearts from the reality of your situations."

"I do not want to cause Lady Felice any pain or unhappiness," Guy said.

"I know you don't, Guy. But I see no way of avoiding it, as there are no easy choices. So be careful and let the love of God and respect for Lady Felice guide you."

He also stepped forward and put his hand on Guy's arm in compassion and then hurried forward after Felice, with his usual small, rapid, steps.

Guy rode slowly back down the forest path alongside Felice, who had been provided with a replacement horse from one of the other ladies, as she did not want to be taken back on the cart. Sir Harold and Walter, who rode behind them, were discussing the schedule of events that occurred in the meadow.

They were lagging slightly behind the main party, but Guy found it painful to rise from the saddle, so he was unable to trot or canter. Felice who also complained of a sore back hung back to join him.

Father Cuthbert, who was riding in the cart was unable to accompany Felice and had to ride with the main party. Guy saw his unease as he watched them from the rear of the cart as it pulled ahead. Guy thought of his words about Felice, and he fully agreed with their sentiments. He knew the reality of the situation and recognised that there was only pain ahead for one or both of them. But he did not know what choice to make for the best, so as Father Cuthbert had advised, he just put his trust in God and followed his heart.

"Athelstan seemed amused by the day's events," Felice said, rousing Guy from his thoughts.

"More so than Sir Harold," Guy replied.

"That is because he missed all the fun," Felice said, amused.

"At least they caught a bore as well as a stag."

"Yes, but Sir Harold was not involved in the kill, as it was Athelstan's privilege. I suspect that he would have rather been on duty today and witnessed all our excitement."

Guy smiled and they continued in silence for a couple of minutes.

"Can I ask what you have planned over the spring and summer, my lady?" Guy then asked.

"My father's tournament is the big event, which we are all looking forward to. There are quite a few high-ranking people from both the nobility and the church who are attending, so my father is pleased. I will be expected to support my mother and father in making the event a success. There will also be parties from abroad, so we will be able to judge what the new fashions are."

"Excellent, my lady. New fashions, you say. I cannot wait," Guy said mockingly.

"I shall remember to discuss them with you," Felice replied with amusement. "In detail."

"After that, my plans are not fixed," she continued, happy to chat, but then moved her horse into Guy's to avoid a small cloud of gnats that were swarming above the path in front of her.

Guy moved his horse across slightly to accommodate her position on the track.

"My mother wants to be invited back to the King's court," Felice continued. "But such an invite is not certain. A lot will depend on the success of the tournament and gaining the King's favour."

"I understand Athelstan spoke with you," she then said. "Did he offer his congratulations for killing the boar?"

"No, my lady," Guy answered. "He did speak with me at length, and he was very enthusiastic about the boar, but he was giving me advice on how I should have killed it." Guy smiled. "He was adamant that a boar should have been killed with a spear, and that a sword thrust through the head was not very sporting?"

"What is the proper way of killing a charging boar, Sir Harold?" Felice called out loudly, but she continued to look forwards."

"How would I know, my lady?" Sir Harold answered, gruffly.

Felice smiled with amusement, as she knew that, like her father, Sir Harold was a keen boar hunter.

"But let's say that rare occasion occurred, Sir Harold, and you are faced with such sport. What would be the best way?" Felice continued calmly.

"I would first hold my hand up to stop it, and then have a word in its little piggy ear to direct it towards Guy, who would kill it for me."

"Excellent plan, Sir Harold," she replied, but then turned her head slightly and winked at Guy. "Although," she continued in a more exasperated tone, "is it best to use spear or sword?"

"I prefer to kill a boar with a knife, as in my mind the best way would be to get close and dirty. But you first must slow and tire the boar, which is where dogs, spears and hunting skills are required."

"But if you are not hunting for sport, my lady, and were faced with a charging boar, as you were today, then I would say that anyway would be acceptable in killing it." He paused. "Even throwing a horse on it."

Felice looked at Guy and smiled warmly at him.

Chapter Nine

The spring season was well upon Warwick, and the town and castle were now festooned with decorations. Banners and pennants were hung from poles that were attached to the roofs along each side of the main street. Most of them were in the colours and motif of the Earl of Warwick, but many other family emblems were present, that added to the spectacle.

For the last month, all the castle staff and hired tradesmen had been preparing tents and temporary accommodation in the castle grounds ready for the tournament. The town also had its normal accommodations cleaned, and made over, with their usual tenants being moved out to temporary shelters outside of the town walls or into specially prepared barns, provided by local farmers. The town's folk did not mind the disruption and change, as they were being handsomely rewarded through increased trade and revenue. They were also enjoying the increased community and carnival atmosphere that was building up towards the two-week event.

The weather had been exceptionally good throughout the early year and there was no sign that it was going to change. The increasing warmth and the growing number of people and livestock within the town made living conditions unpleasant and slightly unbearable at times, but this was compensated for with a more varied range of foodstuffs and ales. The town of Warwick was bustling with excitement, as the hard work was now nearly complete and its town folk were now in a party atmosphere, ready to enjoy the fruit of their labour.

Guy also enjoyed the town's display, but he had been extremely busy in its preparation. When he wasn't training, he was ensuring that the stables were able to support all the horses belonging to the tournament guests, with special attention to competitors. He also had to ensure that there was a range of spare horses available to either rent or buy. Although a lot of this would be usually sorted out between the competitors, who always had several spare animals, just in case they were needed. Guy also had to frequently help the blacksmiths in hurried alterations to metalwork within the town's building modifications and general preparations. He hoped that the number of smiths would eventually increase in the town, to support all the additional work that would accompany the arrival of all the horses and riders.

The policing of Warwick had been increased by raising some of the fyrd. The fyrd was the mechanism for the Anglo-Saxons to enlist numbers from the populace of the local towns and villages into the Earl's army in defence of the realm. The added numbers of traders and visitors increased the levels of criminality, and any misbehaviour was trodden on very quickly by both the castle guard and the newly created town guard. But the people's good spirits and enthusiasm for the festival brought about quite a lot of self-governance. The jails remained empty, mainly due to a new set of gallows that had been erected, and plainly visible, at the town's West Gate, to deter people from committing any serious offences.

Guy ate and slept when and where he could, as his parents were never around to provide any routine. When his father was at home, he was unable to hold any type of conversation without suddenly becoming diverted and dashing off to carry out some tasks that he had just remembered. His mother had been commandeered into the castle kitchens to start to prepare for the many feasts that would require cooking, so she was also absent. Although Guy was not forgotten, and there was often a pie or cake awaiting him on the table.

His mother had told him that the food was a gift from the cook, and especially made for him. This confused Guy, as he did not know the large and ferocious woman that well. Like all the other pages and squires, he was afraid of her lashing tongue, which was nearly always unleased at a time that caused most embarrassment to its victim. But lately, she seemed protective over Guy, and his mother said it was from the tales of his exploits, that reflected well on him. Guy was not too sure, he thought that it was perhaps due to the boar carcasses that he brought into the kitchen from the hunt.

It was now the eve of the tournament, and everything seemed to be in place. The town and castle had prepared well, it had sorted out the accommodation and built a large stock of livestock, fruit, vegetables, grain, and ale, ready to feed the visitors and guests. Nobles had already arrived, along with their entourages, including the royal party. Senior members of the clergy were already active, making outings to various churches and priories in small but grand processions. The opening feast was arranged for that night, but Guy would not be in attendance. On the day following the opening ceremony, there would be a newly arranged 'Squire's Melee' competition, as a light starter to the main events and Guy would be competing. The 'Squire's Melee' was Earl Rohand's idea and he had arranged it with his peers at the previous Easter festivities, to allow them to prepare their own squires for the Earl's tournament.

The 'Squire's Melee' proved to be a popular new event with the nobles, and the list was full, although a quarter of the entrants were from the Earl's staff.

The Warwick squires had been told about the Melee only two months previously. Earl Rohand had to wait until the number of competitors for the event had been confirmed before committing to it. The news had created great excitement amongst the young boys. Practise had intensified with greater focus and increased frequency, as did the number of injuries.

Guy had practised hard and was absorbed with 'Scalloping' which he had previously discussed with Felice. He practised this whenever he was alone, to get the horse used to his commands. Guy now owned his own horse, as Bedivere had been presented to him by Earl Rohand, as a reward for defending the ladies from the boar during the hunt. Felice had pressurised her father on the nature of the reward and Guy was very grateful to her for doing so. His partnership with the horse had thrived and had drastically improved his horsemanship.

He was also content in his swordplay. He knew the mannerisms of the other squires so well, that he was confident in how to beat them. So, it was only a matter of playing it out on the day. He did however feel slightly guilty for keeping the 'Scalloping' tactic from Terold. But he had told him that he was developing a surprise play, especially to counter Terold's knowledge of him. Terold laughed at the idea, but Guy was sure that his friend would now be doing the same and developing his own tactics.

Felice had also come back to him with a quick-release knot, for his 'scalloping' manoeuvre. The knot was a series of interwoven loops of a strong woollen twine that allowed for a single pull release while still holding the shield firm on the horse. Guy had to modify it to guard against any accidental release that might occur during battle. He also developed a small solid frame to angle the shield forwards. Overall, he was pleased with the result, as his previous fixed solutions were more cumbersome.

Guy returned to his home in the late afternoon on the eve of the tournament. He had been seconded into making a metal pin in the castle forge for one of the stable gates which had snapped. He, therefore, had missed his lunch, so had come home to see if there were any leftovers. There had been no training and therefore no canteen meal, so he had to fend for himself.

But as he came to the door, he heard men's voices from within, and he did not recognise any of them as his father. Guy opened the door cautiously to see who was inside.

To his surprise, Sir Harold was sitting at the table, facing the door, and eating a large wedge of pie.

"Good afternoon, Guy," he said jovially and filled his cup from a large skin of ale.

Another man with his back to Guy, turned swiftly around to greet Guy.

"Hello, Guy," the man said, and Guy was surprised to look upon the face of Sir Hector.

Guy just stood there aghast.

"Sit down boy," Sir Harold then said waving towards the third chair at the table. "Your father generously said it would be alright to come in and wait for you. And we thought we would bring some fare."

"Thank you, my lords," Guy said cautiously and sat down.

Sir Harold quickly filled Guy's cup with some ale and cut into the pie which he slid across the top of the table to rest in front of Guy.

"Eat up my Lad, you will need your strength for tomorrow?"

Guy took a bite and chewed slowly while he looked at the two knights in turn.

"There is nothing to worry about my lad, you are not in trouble, but we have a proposition for you," Sir Harold said. "Well Sir Hector has, and we do not want an answer from you today, so you will have some time to think about it."

But this just increased Guy's nervousness, as Sir Harold's last proposition was to make his father the Earl's Steward and that proposal was life changing.

"There is nothing to worry about, Guy," Sir Hector then said, also recognising Guy's concern. "The choice will be yours to accept the proposition or not. I have agreed on those conditions with Earl Rohand, and it will not reflect on you in any way on what you decide."

Guy however was still very worried, as their reassurances just made matters worse. The reference to the Earl made it all sound very ominous.

"But first, Guy," Sir Hector said lightly. "I was out walking the grounds this morning and I saw you riding at the far side of the training field within the elm trees."

"I did not see you, my lord," Guy replied.

"I do not walk in the open, Guy," he replied smiling. "I like to assess the opposition at every opportunity, so I generally just wander around discreetly and observe what is around me."

"And you were just riding in and out of the trees, but I could see that you had a purpose, and it has since intrigued me."

Guy looked at Sir Hector with slight apprehension.

"You had no weapons, but it was not just riding practice."

"No, my lord, although I did have my shield." Guy replied.

"Which was tied to your horse," Sir Hector stated with interest. "Do you consider your shield a weapon?"

"It can be, my lord," Guy answered, "I have fought in a shield wall."

Sir Hector looked across at Sir Harold.

"Oh yes. The Battle of Anker Bridge. What a day that was. A handful of the Earl's most trusted men against a hoard of Vikings. I must tell you about that sometime," Sir Harold said to Sir Hector with a grin.

Sir Hector smiled back.

"I will look forward to it," he said, and then looked back to Guy. "Was this practice in preparation for your melee?"

"It might be, my lord," Guy said with a mischievous tone and took another bite of pie.

"Would you like to tell me what it is for?"

Guy took a few moments to swallow some pie, "No, my lord," he then replied and waited in silence for Sir Hector to respond.

"And you are not going to tell me any more about it?" Sir Hector eventually said.

"No, my lord."

"But I will see it tomorrow."

"Yes, my lord."

Guy then smiled at Sir Hector.

Sir Hector paused and smiled back, obviously amused by the discussion.

"Talking about the Battle of Anker Bridge, Sir Hector," Sir Harold then said. "Do you know if Sir Roderick is attending the tournament?"

"Sorry I don't. But I have seen Otto."

"If you are not aware, Otto is Roderick's older brother," Sir Hector said as an aside to Guy.

"Any particular reason?" Sir Hector then asked Sir Harold.

"No, No," Sir Harold replied casually. "Just wondering if he would dare show his face."

"Anyway, Guy," Sir Harold then continued. "About this proposition."

"Sir Hector has approached the Earl and asked if it would be of benefit to your training if you accompany him after the tournament. He would like you to act as

154

his temporary squire for a month or so, while he gallivants around Europe."

"It will be mainly in Francia," Sir Hector cut in. "You will therefore gain valuable experience from other counties and cultures."

"His normal squire has had an accident and is no longer available," Sir Harold said looking carefully at Hector.

"The Earl has agreed to this, as long as you also agree," Sir Hector then said.

"As long as you retain your Warwick association and wear his livery," Sir Harold added.

"And can I also add an additional clause of using his Danish title of 'Guy of Warwick'?" Sir Harold then said smiling.

"'Guy of Warwick'?" Sir Hector asked.

"It is what Jarl Sitric calls him," Sir Harold said casually, swigging some ale.

"You have met Jarl Sitric, and he calls you 'Guy of Warwick'" Sir Hector asked Guy with an amazed tone.

"Yes, my lord," Guy answered wondering why Sir Harold was embellishing the event.

"I look forward to hearing these stories, Sir Harold," Sir Hector then said and picked up his cup.

"And many others, Sir Hector. I have lots of them."

"Well, Guy. You have until the end of the tournament to think about it and decide," Sir Harold said and got to his feet to depart. "You are very fortunate to get this offer, but it needs consideration, so do not be hasty in your answer."

"But I am aware that it means leaving your family for a while and to enter unfamiliar surroundings, so you need to be sure of your decision, as it will have to be for the duration. I would not be able to return you halfway through our adventure," Sir Hector smiled at Guy. "And I am sure that it will be an adventure."

"Oh!" Sir Harold said and held up a finger. "I nearly forgot. As I have said, Sir Hector has no squire at present, and a knight of his esteem cannot perform in a tournament without one. The Earl has kindly loaned you out for the next two weeks to act as his squire, regardless of your decision on Francia."

"However," Sir Harold continued. "This will be on top of your normal duties, so see that you plan them accordingly," and then turned and walked away to the door.

Guy also rose to his feet, followed by Sir Hector, who then placed his hand on Guy's shoulder.

"Do not worry, Guy," he said quietly. "I will only be competing in a single event, so it will not take up much of your time. I will come down later to discuss what I require from you." Sir Hector then smiled. "But your role is mainly for show, as I am very self-sufficient."

Sir Hector then followed Sir Harold out of the door.

"Oh, and good luck for tomorrow's event, Guy of Warwick," he finally said as he left. "And may the Lord's judgement be favourable."

The morning was warm and bright, and Guy had woken early with the calls of the birds, as they greeted the dawn. He quickly washed and dressed, before wandering over to the stables to clean out and water Bedivere. He then took the horse on a short leash and led it across the training field and down to the river.

The Avon flowed slowly and smoothly with a watery mist drifting across its surface. Swallows skimmed down into the mist to skirt the river's surface in erratic yet smooth displays. Bedivere's eyes were bright, and its ears pricked and twitched, as it took in the early morning chorus, and snorted a visible cloud of vapour out of its nostrils and up into the cool air. Guy stood close to the horse and stroked the side of its neck, as he looked over the river to the fields and woods beyond. Guy had not slept well, as his mind constantly switched between the excitement of the 'Squire's Melee' and the offer to accompany Sir Hector. He thought that indulging in his own company within the serene and natural beauty of the castle grounds might allow him to decide.

Guy had spoken with his father about Sir Hector's proposition to join him and his father understood the honour that it bestowed on Guy, but Guy could tell that he would prefer him not to go. But then his father casually threw in a comment that it might provide a better and quicker route to advancing himself in society than coming up through the regimented and structured training within the Earl's retainers.

For his father to consider social advancement was a surprise to Guy. It was not so long ago that they were only a family of peasant tradesmen, with no aspirations to better themselves. Now his father was looking to even further enhance their position as a family.

And as for Guy, that social advancement was to achieve the status of knighthood, and with Sir Hector's association, that status beckoned. Becoming a knight had always been a dream of Guy's and that dream had now intensified as it was quickly turning into a possibility. That possibility brought about the small chance of being able to be eligible as a suitable suitor to Felice and Guy would grasp at any small chance for that opportunity.

Guy sighed as he realised that he was no further forward in planning his future and patted Bedivere, before leading it away back towards the castle.

The field had a blanket of mist hanging over it, and Aethelflaed's mound reached upwards from the castle wall with an imposing majesty. Guy suddenly appreciated how lucky he was to be in his present situation and wondered why he would ever want to leave such magnificent splendour.

The tournament's opening ceremony was more like a large fair. There was an array of various entertainments from jesters, performing dwarfs, jugglers, bearbaiting, and wrestling contests. Musicians played in numerous places and food stalls lined the castle walls. There were many tents, dotted around the grounds, and several large canvas screens that were positioned alongside the river to serve as latrines. The 'round table' fighting arena had been marked off in the middle of the training field. However, for this occasion, earth mounds had been built all around the circumference of the large arena with tiered wooden planks that supplied seating. The eastern side of the round table had a wooden stage, built upon large wooden piles that raised the wooden platform several feet above the ground. The platform had rails all around its perimeter with shallow stairs constructed at each end. There were high poles that supported several large canvas awnings that then provided a canopy over the stage. These were decorated with many multi-coloured flags, banners and pennants that flapped wildly in the breeze. Cushioned benches were stretched across the stage on either side of six large chairs that were designated for the royal family. Large, heavy red banners, with the Earl's standard and motifs, were draped down from the floor of the platform to the ground. This added more grandeur to the grandstand for the Earl and his guests. Children ran everywhere, laughing, screaming, or crying. Old people shuffled around with sticks, being at liberty to strike out at the frolicking youths and complaining to anyone who would listen. Traders traded, singers sang, harpers played, and Warwick's townsfolk celebrated their Earl and his tournament.

Then cheers rose, as the royal party left the confines of the castle halls and walked through a guard lined avenue, towards the castle's 'round table'. King Edward the Elder was accompanied by the Earl, followed closely by their wives. The Archbishop of Canterbury and Lady Felice came next, followed by the lesser royals, including Athelstan and then the rest of the senior nobles and clergy. The remaining guests came behind in a more informal ordering.

As soon as the noble party passed along the pathway, the cheering crowds left their places and ran like a wave to get seats in the arena. When the royal party arrived at the stand, the seats all around the earthen mounds had been filled. Late arrivals were not accommodated with any kind of view and stood wherever they could. All around the arena, the people jostled and pushed to settle themselves into suitable positions, with the occasional angry skirmish, which caused a ripple of cheers from the other spectators around them.

When the Earl and his guests had seated, a horn sounded, and the squires entered on horseback in a blaze of colour. They shone with a bright gleam from the many pieces of polished metals of bronze, silver and gold that made up their armour. The horses rode around the large circular arena in a clockwise direction, with their riders holding tall wooden poles with pennants tied at the top, which showed the emblems of their sponsor.

Guy was one of the first into the field and he carried the usual red and black flag of the bear and ragged staff. His shield and top tunic also bore the Warwick symbol and his leather and chain body armour had been cleaned and polished. His armour glistened in the sunlight and, like the last time he fought in a competition, he wore Felice's satin token wrapped around his front shoulder strap.

The squires lined up in front of the royal stand and, in unison, they dipped their poles, as previously instructed, while bowing their heads towards the King in a show of respect. Pages then marched into the field and ran up to their appointed competitor, where they took charge of the standards, and quickly marched away again.

Guy breathed heavily, as he looked out from beneath the rim of his leather and steel helmet and searched for Felice amongst the ladies. She sat in the middle of the stand, alongside her mother, applauding politely and looking straight at him, smiling.

The herald then stood up at the side of the main stand and announced the rules. This time there would be no teams, just individual combat, but in the same format as Guy's previous melee, and it would commence at the sound of the next horn blow.

The squires turned their horses and rode away to find suitable positions while withdrawing their swords and accessing their nearest opponents. Guy just lightly walked Bedivere away to the edge of the arena and then slowly cantered in an anticlockwise direction around the perimeter of the field.

The horn blew and the crowd cheered in response. Guy gently kicked his horse on and, using his knees to encourage the horse, put his strategy into effect. He smoothly turned the horse inwards and then outwards in a series of small semicircles, while maintaining a canter around the perimeter. As he moved inwards, it brought different opponents into range, and Guy swung his sword to strike out at them as he passed.

The melee proceeded at a pace, and eventually Guy rode his horse to the side of the stand next to the entry gate. He quickly slid off the saddle, passing the reins to a page and releasing his shield, as was expected from the last competitor on horseback.

The 'Scalloping' had been a complete success. He had to waiver the manoeuvre, here and there, to suit the occasion, but he generally just cantered around the field in ever-decreasing circles, engaging available opponents as they presented themselves. He did not linger in any one exchange of swordplay, but just focused on operating his riding pattern. If he could not best an opponent in a couple of strokes, then he just rode by. In doing so, he selected no individual in one-to-one combat until the very end of the mounted section when he was one of the final two still left on horseback. At this point he just allowed his superior horsemanship to constantly position himself behind his opponent. He then waited until an opportunity arose where he could ride into his opponent's blind spot and backswing his sword to knock him off his horse.

But now he was faced with a different challenge as he was on foot with both sword and shield in hand and he looked around for an appropriate opponent.

Guy did not hear the cheering and cries of the crowd, he just focused on the opponents in front of him. Although he tried to avoid facing a fellow Warwick squire, he occasionally had to engage with them. But he instantly recognised each of them, changed his tactics to suit and then dispatched them to the ground. The melee quickly developed into two groups, which fought in separated parts of the arena with the spaces around them gradually cleared of fallen competitors and loose horses.

These two groups decreased in size and slowly rotated around the field as space was constantly sought to fight in. Guy however preferred the disorder in the middle of the group. He used the other beaten squires, who had fallen or were limping away, as obstacles to his opponents, but in which he could confidently fight around.

But eventually, the two groups became one, and four fighters became three and then there was just the remaining two. Guy stood there still fully armed, facing a bigger opponent who carried a much larger sword and a massive shield. Guy instantly recognised the strength that his opponent must possess, to have carried such weight throughout the melee. Guy also accessed the skills that were necessary to have progressed him to this final bout. Guy understood his disadvantage and then instantly realised the solution.

So, Guy stood up from his defensive posture and walked a few paces into the centre of the arena and unhooked his shield from his arm. The crowd was hushed as they watched with interest at the proceedings. Guy then turned to face his opponent and threw his shield to the side. He then swung his sword in a full arc on each side of him before adopting a crouched defensive stance. With both hands on the hilt of his sword and with the sword's point aimed directly at his opponent, he offered the challenge.

The crowd shouted in excitement at Guy's gesture, and then hushed as they awaited the other squire's response.

Guy's opponent was confused and unsure of what to do. Guy, however, just stood there, motionless, and waited.

The large squire then strode purposely forward and unhooked his own shield and threw it away, and with both hands on his hilt matched Guy's stance.

The crowd roared their approval. Guy just smiled to himself.

Guy stood in front of the royal stand and received his prize from the Herald. The crowd cheered loudly, and the royal party politely clapped their approval.

The King beckoned Guy forward and Guy walked up to stand in front of him, bowing his head low.

"So young man, I am told that you are 'Guy of Warwick'," he said. "You fought well, Guy, but why the arrogant show in the final encounter."

"A ruse, your Grace," Guy replied nervously. "I needed to remove his shield to gain the advantage."

"Really," The King said. "And what was the advantage?"

"Speed over strength, your Grace," Guy answered. "He was obviously good, to have performed so well carrying such bulk and weight and I have not previously seen him fight. So, I took away the unknown and fought him on my terms."

"So, you think as well as fight."

"It is what I have been taught, your Grace."

The King turned to the Earl. "My congratulations Rohand," he said. "You train your squires well."

"Thank you, my lord," the Earl said. "But Guy is an outstanding apprentice."

Guy then left the arena and went to look for Terold, who was sitting on a bench to the side of the field and smiling broadly.

"Well done, Guy," he said warmly. "It was that shield that did for me. He just ploughed into me with it. I thought that I had been hit by an Ox."

"He needed to be built like an Ox to carry it," Guy replied sitting next to him.

Small children massed around them just to look at Guy and his friend, while passers-by shouted their congratulations and good wishes. Guy tried to acknowledge them all, but there was so many.

"Here he comes," Terold then said quietly, as Sir Harold walked up across the field towards them.

The children moved away to allow him through. But he waved them away.

"Congratulations Guy," he said in a serious tone and slowly reached into his tunic to bring out an extremely large purse, which he then jangled at them with a broad smile on his face.

"You are going to make me rich," he said.

"And the Earl is ecstatic," he continued. "'It is what I have been taught, your Grace'," Sir Harold then said in a reasonable impersonation of Guy.

"That statement shone down well on me," he then said sitting down next to them.

"In fact, we all bask in your glory, Guy," Sir Harold said and then stood up.

"Well, I have other duties to perform, and you need to see to your horses and then to any other horses. After that, you may then have the afternoon off to enjoy yourselves."

Terold whooped and ran off to retrieve his mount.

"Before you go, Sir Harold," Guy said. "May I ask your advice?"

"Sir Hector's offer?" Sir Harold asked, with a serious tone.

"Yes," Guy replied. "What is your opinion?"

"I have only heard good reports of Sir Hector, and they have not changed with meeting him. I think you will learn a lot, and not just in knightly skills, but also in life skills. But Sir Hector operates in varied and colourful environments. Although the experience will be good for you, there also may be some hardship and perhaps even an element of danger."

Sir Harold paused and looked at him. "It may also enhance your reputation." He then smiled. "No," he continued. "Knowing you as I do, I can safely say that it will enhance your reputation."

"So, if I was in your shoes I would jump at the chance." Sir Harold then scuffed up Guy's hair. "And it will only be for a couple of months."

"You said that I was to retain the Earl's livery and emblems."

"Yes, Sir Hector has agreed to that condition."

"Can I also present your emblem, my lord?"

Sir Harold smiled warmly.

"I thank you Guy, but it is not appropriate as your allegiance is with the Earl," Sir Harold said. "But if you were to somewhere discretely display an oak tree, then we would both know, and I would be grateful for your regards."

"Thank you, my lord."

Sir Harold got up and walked away back to the castle. Guy also stood up and went behind the stand to retrieve his horse.

As he turned around the rear post to get to the horses, he was grabbed by his armour's shoulder guard and dragged into the large space under the stage's seating. The bright sunlight was suddenly replaced by a dry, humid, darkness and Guy blinked hard to allow his eyes to adjust. Shafts of sunlight from between the seating above picked up the floating specks of dust and created shards of dappled brilliance in front of him. Then Guy was suddenly faced by a tall man, holding a large wooden club, and Guy stepped quickly back as he recognised the threat in this man's stance. But then he was pushed back by a strong pair of hands from behind him. Guy then sidestepped to his left and turned so that the sloping roof was now at his back, and he could look on his assailants.

There were three of them. A tall man acted as if he was the leader of the group, one man stood slightly behind him and another man waited on the right. In the dark, with the light behind them, Guy could not see who they were or recognise anything in their looks or how they were dressed. But their silhouettes showed that they all carried large wooden cudgels.

The three of them stepped in to stop up any gaps for Guy to run through and they smiled when they realised that he was now cornered.

"So," The leader said, smacking the cudgel into the palm of his hand.

Guy looked at him in the dark. He was tall and thin with a dark thin moustache and a small beard, but Guy could not detect any other distinctive features in the dim light. He also looked across at his two young followers and tried to find anything in their appearances that would be recognisable, but he could not see any identifiable marks in their looks.

"We have been asked to pay our respects to you in a manner that you will not forget, and to repay a debt of honour," the man said.

"I do not know you," Guy calmly replied, "and I do not know of any payment of honour that I might owe." He looked around at his surroundings as he spoke, to access his options.

He saw none and decided that he would just have to react to their eventual attack. But he would need to be ready.

"But we know, and that will have to be good enough," the man replied and then nodded at the other two to begin the beating.

Guy prepared himself.

"However, I know you, Otto," a voice sounded from the shadows to the left of the men.

Guy seized his moment, as his attackers had all turned quickly around to see who had spoken. He sprung forward to his right, to roll forward over his shoulder to then regain his feet beyond the range of his assailants. The youth to the right waved his cudgel at the sudden movement in the dark, but he swung high and wide into free air as Guy rolled beyond him.

"Who's there?" the leader asked in alarm.

"Your sword, Guy," the voice said, and Guy instantly recognised it as Sir Hector. A sword was thrown out of shadows to land at Guy's feet."

Guy quickly glanced at his wooden sword and then picked it up without taking his eyes off his assailants. He then adopted a defensive stance with his sword held forward.

Sir Hector then walked forward out of the dark from behind a hanging clump of canvas and stood next to Guy. Guy glanced across to again access the situation and was surprised that Sir Hector was unarmed.

"However, what I don't know," Sir Hector said. "Is where you perceive any honour in attacking an unarmed young man, three against one, in the dark?"

"Sir Hector," the leader, who Guy took as Otto, spoke with a tone of apprehension.

Guy suddenly remembered Otto being mentioned as Sir Roderick's brother. Guy now understood that the ambush was retribution for embarrassing Roderick during the training session with Sir Hector, a few weeks earlier. But Guy also briefly considered Sir Roderick's possible involvement in the attack of the Earl's party near Polesworth, which resulted in the Battle of Anker Bridge. He wondered if that was perhaps the retribution Otto referred to.

"So, Otto," Sir Hector replied. "I have now reduced the odds against Guy by arming him, but it is still three against one and I would happily put my money on Guy at those odds." He smiled at Guy.

"However, I cannot guarantee that I would not get involved, as I like a good fight, and that will make it three against two, but I am now unarmed."

No one moved, and the silence hung around them.

"Or you can just leave without further ado, with no harm done," Sir Hector said, and gestured with his hand towards the far side of the enclosure.

"Come," Otto said quickly to his associates, and hurried away.

Both Guy and Sir Hector watched them go in silence.

"Thank you, Sir Hector," Guy then said turning to face his rescuer.

"Not a problem, Guy. Although I am disappointed that they chose to leave. It might have been interesting, as I am not sure what I could have done, unarmed. But it is heart-warming to note that the power of my reputation alone can win a fight."

"I would just have passed you my sword Sir Hector and then I would have sat down and watched," Guy replied.

Sir Hector smiled, as he gestured for Guy to leave the confines of the dark wooden enclosure.

"I will, however, look out for Otto in the melee," he answered, and then squinted as the bright light of the sun spread over him. "And pay him my regard," he then said with a hint of menace.

"How did you know I was in trouble?" Guy asked.

"As you know, Guy. I like to apply constant vigilance," Sir Hector replied. "Which includes the observation of people and their traits, especially rivals. Then after a while, you can smell trouble."

Sir Hector looked sideways at Guy.

"And you should be in no doubt, that I have been observing you closely."

Guy smiled at the compliment.

"I hope that I will not be in any more trouble. But thank you again, my lord, for looking after me."

"No thanks needed Guy," Sir Hector said. "If you join me in my little adventure abroad, then we will look after each other, both in needs and in deeds."

Sir Hector casually placed his hand on Guy's shoulder as he looked into the distance. "And I am confident that Otto will not bother you again."

Chapter Ten

Festivities continued throughout the next week, with contests being fought in the castle or at a village called Kite's Nest, which was situated a few miles north of Warwick. Both had purpose build 'round table' arenas, and the knights competed in many different disciplines. Guy accompanied Sir Hector to Kite's Nest and performed his squire duties with efficiency and, on Sir Hector's instructions, a large amount of show and veneration to please the crowd. Sir Hector was now dressed in his full tournament gear, with his armour fully polished and his shield showing his insignia of a black cross on a blue field with a small golden bunch of wheat in each quarter. The livery surprised Guy, as he was expecting a ferocious heraldic beast, and not the understated emblem as displayed, but Guy could not help but be impressed at the knight's skill and courage. But although the manoeuvres looked dangerous, Guy realised that Sir Hector was always fully in control and was never at any real risk. He controlled each bout and went about his business with style, proficiency and not without a small amount of exhibition. This was not the case for his opponents, who just struggled against him. Sir Hector won the 'Sword on Foot' contest easily and that was enough for him, as far as the Earl's tournament was concerned.

There was food and ale served at the Kite's Nest site, and when the contestants and guests had their fill, they joined a parade back to Warwick. They made a point of passing through the local villages, whose inhabitants celebrated their procession.

On their arrival back to the castle, Guy had to hurry to wash and dress ready for the evening feast. Guy had to carry out his cupbearer duties in both the Great Hall, which was just as boisterous as on the last occasions and in the lady's smaller hall on alternate days. The ladies' evenings were far more sedate than the men's dinners, which he un-expectantly now preferred, as the conversation was more considered, and he learned more about the happenings within the country. But he mainly liked being there because he was in the presence of Lady Felice.

But, as with every other occasion when he acted as cupbearer with the ladies, there was little contact with Felice. This did not concern him as he knew his role, but he was conscious of not staring at her when he was not serving others.

He did overhear Lady Elaine discuss their trip to Winchester as guests of the King's family, as Felice had eluded to, and it made him feel cold. He did not know why, because it was expected, but Guy did not want to be away from Felice.

Felice was watching Guy at that time, as she also overheard her mother's conversation and raised her cup for Guy to fill.

"So, Guy, what will you be doing when we are away for the summer, on the back of your tournament success?"

"Yes, Guy," Elaine cut in. "I hope you will get some reward."

"I have been asked to squire for Sir Hector, my lady. As he ventures around Europe," he replied.

The ladies all sat up in their chairs in surprise, as this must have been news to them. Felice spilt her drink and tried hard to let her shock dissipate unnoticed.

"My husband has not released you?" Elaine asked.

"No, my lady," Guy said, as he went to help Felice clean away the spilt wine from the table.

"It will be only for a couple of months, my lady. "I will still be in the Earl's service. I gather it is a sort of loan."

"Thank goodness for that," Elaine said. "What would we do without you?" She said.

"I have not accepted yet, my lady."

"Are you considering your options?" Felice asked relieved.

"Yes, my lady."

"You must go," Elaine added. "It will be an adventure Guy, and you can come back with tales of all your courageous deeds that will last us for the rest of the year."

"The adventures of 'Guy of Warwick'," Elaine then continued. "You will do us proud."

"It will probably be very mundane, my lady. Lots of cleaning and looking after the horses. But it would be an experience."

"I doubt that it will be mundane, Guy," Elaine said. "Trouble seems to single you out."

Felice was going to speak but suddenly went sullen and looked down into her cup.

"Is this young man, Guy of Warwick?" The lady to Elaine's right asked.

"Yes, my lady," Elaine replied and then smiled warmly at Guy.

"Guy, this is Lady Ecgwynn," Elaine said. "She is the wife of King Edward."

"My lady," Guy said and bowed his head.

"And you are the son of Rohand's steward, I hear."

"Yes, my lady."

"Yet, you are so accomplished."

"I believe I have been well trained, my lady," Guy replied.

"Yes, you must have. Your manners do not seem out of place for someone lowly born."

"Thank you, my lady."

"But that may not be the case when he is off guard," Elaine said laughing.

"I believe Guy is never off guard," Felice then said.

"Sir Harold may not agree," Guy responded. "His training in manners and etiquette can be robust."

It was not until the end of the evening that Felice caught Guy alone. She had left the room and returned later ensuring that she was able to pass by him. But when she did pass, she paused at his side.

"Will you join Sir Hector?" She asked quietly.

"I think so, my lady?" he answered and then sighed lightly. "There will not be much pleasure in Warwick if you are not here." He then swallowed hard at his boldness.

She looked at him, unsure of how to respond.

"Your manners may not be so guarded, after all, Guy," she said, raising her eyebrows.

"I have known you for a long time, Guy," she then said warmly. "I care about you, so please be watchful if you go with Sir Hector and do not put yourself in any danger. Make sure that you return home safely."

"Yes, my lady," he responded with resignation. He was saddened by her response, but his expectations were not high. But at the same time, he realised that he did not know what his expectations were.

Felice placed her hand lightly on his arm and then walked back to the table.

The next day found Guy lying awake in bed, with a sense of contentment. It was still dark in his bedroom, but it was always dark, as his room only had a small slit for a window. The birds were chirping loudly outside, as they called to each other, and Guy sensed that the sun would be rising.

He had gone to bed with a sense of embarrassment for revealing some of his feelings to Felice and disappointment at her reaction. But in the silence of the night, the embarrassment was replaced by a sense of fulfilment, on having said what he knew had to be said. The disappointment he had felt had been replaced with a sense of gratification because he knew that Felice cared for him. Considering his status in life, compared to hers, it was the best that he could hope for.

He also knew that he now wanted to accompany Sir Hector abroad, and that decision, which had been constantly preying on his mind, was settled and out of the way. So, a lot of his worries had now gone and all he had to do was to get up and find all the people he had to tell. This included Terold, who Guy was sure would be happy for him, but also a little bit jealous. But first, he had his chores to do, which for some reason he was looking forward to. A bit of routine was just what he wanted at that moment.

Guy, walked happily toward the stables to clean out Bedivere and prepare his feed. The castle and Warwick town was returning to normal, within the abnormality of the tournament activities. The townsfolk were becoming used to the festivities and in the numbers and privileged status of the many visitors. Guy was pleased with this; the Earl's tournament was an obvious success and he sensed that it may now bring a new life to the town. But he also hoped that it would not fundamentally change its character, as Guy was fond of Warwick and its inhabitants.

But as he approached the stable block, a woman dressed in a full grey cloak and scarf was waiting for him. She was standing in the doorway, huddled in her garments to protect her from the morning coolness. As he got nearer, Guy recognised Janette; Lady Felice's companion and he suddenly became more interested.

"Good morning, Guy," Janette said.

"Good morning, Janette," Guy replied.

"Are you always up this early?" She continued.

"Nearly always. It is the best part of the day," Guy answered. "And what brings you to the stables."

"My mistress would like to go riding today and she says that her normal guards are engaged on tournament business?"

"And what is she planning?" Guy asked smiling. "And who is to know? And what are they to know?"

Janette laughed.

"She is very determined," she said.

"I wager that 'determined' is not the description that her mother uses."

"No, probably not. However, she has asked her father for Sir Harold's assistance, or your assistance, in trying to arrange something."

"And has she asked Sir Harold?" Guy asked. Smiling again.

"Not yet," Janette said.

"And does the lady think that he will allow it, if she does ask?"

"I believe that she asked her father for Sir Harold's assistance or your assistance," Janette said with a coy expression.

"But of course she did," Guy said lightly.

"And who will be in her party?" He asked.

"Just, my lady, and me."

"No Father Cuthbert?" Guy asked.

"He will be at prayer with the Archbishop at that time," she said. "Lady Felice thought it inappropriate to mention her outing to him, in case it disturbed his meditations."

"That was considerate of her," Guy said smiling again.

"However, she does not believe that she will get away with leaving the castle with just a squire acting as a guard. Especially after the last outing to see Lady Edith, and the incident with the boar. Everyone here is mindful of her safety and the Earl's protection," Janette said in a serious tone. "My lady does not yet know how to bypass her father, or the guards without getting anyone in trouble. Especially you."

Guy looked back across the castle grounds, lost in his thoughts and then after only a few moments, an idea entered his mind. The idea then quickly grew into a plan and after a few more moments of further consideration, Guy knew what to do.

"Can you meet me back here in an hour?" Guy eagerly asked Janette.

"Of course," she replied. "My lady will be happy to release me from my duties."

Guy then looked into the stables and considered the tasks at hand.

"You couldn't muck out Bedivere, could you, while I am gone?" Guy asked mischievously.

Janette screwed up her face. "No, I couldn't," she replied haughtily.

Guy raised his eyebrows. "Then I will see you back here in an hour," Guy replied and walked off towards the castle halls.

Although it was early, Guy could not find Sir Hector in his chambers, and he had to make enquiries of the castle servant's. He was told that Sir Hector always woke early and usually went out of the castle towards the town. So, Guy went off to find him.

The taverns were still shut, and there was little activity around the centre of Warwick. Guy became concerned about where to find him, but with a flash of inspiration, he went to Warwick's church, and was surprised to find Sir Hector alone at prayer in the front stalls.

Guy did not want to disturb Sir Hector's peace, so he waited patiently outside the heavy wooden doors.

The knight finally came out and was surprised to see Guy standing there waiting for him.

"Good morning, Guy," he said, and Guy bowed his head in acknowledgement.

"My lord," Guy replied.

"Can I help in any way?" Sir Hector asked politely with an inquisitive look on his face.

Guy smiled.

"Hopefully," Guy replied. "Yesterday, you said that if I served you, we would have to look after each other in need and deed."

"I remember, Guy. But I do not believe I said 'serve'."

Guy nodded. "Then, my lord, it would be an honour to be your squire for your forthcoming travels."

Sir Hector smiled.

"Thank you, Guy. But it will also be my privilege to have you as my squire."

Guy smiled again.

"No thanks required, my lord," Guy said. "But I do have a need that requires a deed."

Sir Hector laughed. "Very well Guy, tell me all about it?"

Guy hurried back to the stables, as he was late for his meeting with Janette. She was already there waiting to meet him, although she stood several yards away from the stables, which was now filled with squires, pages and grooms, all going about their daily work.

Guy held up his hand to acknowledge her and then quickly stepped into the stables to groom and feed Bedivere.

He came back out straight away.

"You did see to my horse," he said to Janette, in gratitude.

"You must be joking," she replied. "And step into that disgusting place."

"Then who did?" Guy said confused.

Janette sighed.

"I mentioned it to 'my lady', and she made arrangements to have your horse looked after."

Guy raised his eyebrows.

"I believe she thinks highly of you," Janette said.

"That's because I can arrange for her to go riding," Guy said, with satisfaction.

The small party rode down Smith Street, and then out of the town.

Guy rode alongside Lady Felice with Sir Hector and Janette riding behind.

Both Sir Hector and Guy were dressed in armour and carried full swords and shields. Guy also had his bow tucked into his harness and his bag of arrows fastened to the back of his shield.

"And Sir Harold had nothing to say, my lady?" Guy asked.

"How could he," Felice responded. "As well you know Guy. Any refusal or offer of support would have cast an insult towards Sir Hector's competence."

"Reputation is everything, Guy," Sir Hector, who was listening to the conversation, called out from behind, laughing.

Felice turned backwards to smile at Sir Hector.

"So, Sir Hector. Guy tells me that he will be joining you as a squire," Felice said.

"He does me that honour, my lady."

"And your reputation goes before you wherever you go, and, if I may say, it is a great reputation, Sir Hector, even bordering on legend."

"Thank you, my lady. It has built up over many years."

"And it is enhanced with a fair amount of menace and mystery. I have heard that you are not a man to cross."

"As I said, my lady, Reputation is everything, and it is important how you nurture that reputation," Sir Hector said, amused at the conversation. "And I am happy that men do not want to cross me."

"I am also glad, Sir Hector. But I would also hope that they would not cross your squire for reprisal."

Sir Hector became more serious.

"I was very distressed at the death of my previous squire, my lady. The perpetrators were discovered, and retribution was made. And it was not made quietly.

Hopefully, my reputation will spread a protective cover over any future squires or companions."

"I am sure that you are right, Sir Hector, and forgive me for my comments, but I am just looking after Guy. My father has a special interest in Guy, and he would be very unhappy if he came to any harm."

Sir Hector remained quiet in thought, while Guy digested all this news.

"I hold your father in high regard, my lady. I also have high respect for you and in your concern for Guy," Sir Hector said, thoughtfully. "But I also have a high regard for Guy, and I will protect him with all my strength and guile."

Felice looked over her shoulder and smiled warmly at Sir Hector.

"I know you will, Sir Hector. Which is why I am pleased that he goes with you."

She then kicked the horse into a gallop and both Guy and Sir Hector spurred on their horses to catch up, leaving Janette to struggle behind.

After an hour of aimlessly riding through the leafy Warwickshire countryside, Felice decided to return to the castle. The small party ambled back along the banks of the River Leam towards its convergence with the River Avon and then back to Warwick. The party had been happy in each other's company and the conversation had been light and entertaining. Sir Hector told stories of his travels and the wonders that he had seen. But now, with Warwick insight, Felice took the opportunity to ride forward with Guy, leaving Sir Hector and Janette to, once again, follow behind.

"When do you depart, Guy?" Felice asked softly.

"It all depends on Sir Hector's plans, my lady, so it will be whenever he takes his leave of your father, but I suspect that it will be straight after the tournament's end."

for offering him the position of his squire, until he found a more permanent replacement. Sir Hector also conceded that Guy's capabilities also helped in the decision.

Sir Hector smiled whenever he discussed the timing of securing Guy's services from Earl Rohand. He was sure that the arrangement would have been less favourable towards him after Guy had become Champion of the 'Squire's Melee'. Although Sir Hector said that he would have still met any of the Earl's increased demands.

"What's Towcester like?" Guy asked casually. Sir Hector did not want any recognition of his title in private, but he still required that Guy was appropriately respectful in front of any other dignitaries that they met.

"It is like any other fortified Saxon town," Sir Hector replied. "But it is on the boundaries of Danelaw and therefore it is influenced by the Danes."

"What does that mean?" Guy asked.

"Burned and ransacked churches. Lots of bastard children and few maidens." He smiled. "Not all towns are like Warwick."

"But" Sir Hector continued, "there have been no raids for a while, since Ragnall made peace with Edward and that peace seems to be holding under Sitric's rule." Sir Hector then looked across at Guy. "Sir Harold said that you have met him?"

"Yes, and he was not what I expected," Guy said. "He was not barbaric at all, but circumspect and thoughtful."

"All great leaders are thoughtful. Battles are won in the mind, with planning and strategy, not by force," Sir Hector replied. "You demonstrated that in the melee."

"That was just luck," Guy responded. "He would have probably floored me with one push of that shield."

"We make our own luck, Guy. But I suspect that you weighed up the chances of your opponent falling for your trick. You then influenced it with your little display to improve your chances and then executed the plan without really thinking about it," Sir Hector said, and then smiled. "You can call it luck, but I call it natural ability. If you are ever in doubt of how to react to a situation, then just obey what your heart tells you and do not overthink it."

"And if in doubt follow your first option," Guy said remembering a tip Sir Hector had already told him.

"Absolutely," Sir Hector said. "Natural ability supported by trained instinct makes you very quick."

Guy thought about it, and they continued along the road in silence.

After a few more miles, they pulled off the road, as they observed a haze of smoke on the horizon. The smoke showed the location of the town ahead, so Sir Hector found a clearing where they could settle the horses, rest, eat and train. Guy enjoyed the training with Sir Hector, as he always pushed Guy, but never overstretched him. When mentoring, he always kept Guy on the edge of his capabilities, and as time went on, that edge kept increasing. But Sir Hector was good, and Guy never realised before, just how good he was. As Guy improved and started to work out his opponent, then Sir Hector would just move up a gear to maintain his superiority. Then just to confuse Guy, he would occasionally alter his style and sometimes swapped his sword arm.

Guy asked about Sir Hector's insignia and if it was a family emblem. He said that it was of his own design, and it represented his mother's philosophy. She had always told her son, that all you need in this world to be happy was to have the blue sky above, food in your stomach and God's protection. Guy had thought about that humble ideal and recognised, that although Sir Hector was all about show and confidence, there was no arrogance in him and a lot of humility. The more Guy got to know Sir Hector as a man, the more he appreciated and liked him.

Guy unpacked the horse and went to light a fire. The day had been fine, and the skies were clear so it was likely that they would sleep under a tree.

This had been a usual event for Sir Hector, which, at first, both surprised and dismayed Guy. He had thought that he would be staying in a selection of castles, manors or at worst local inns, and he had never slept out of doors before. But once he got used to making a bed out of dry bracken and eating well on both packed provisions and hunted game, he quite preferred it.

Guy worried about thieves and vagabonds, but Sir Hector said that it was rare that he was disturbed, and his horse was well trained to raise an alarm if it heard or sensed anything unusual. Sir Hector also said that he felt more threatened inside of towns, which provided a level of familiarity that favoured any would-be attackers. Whereas, in the open country, they would be at an equal advantage or disadvantage.

Guy recognised and understood both the detail and the deep thought that Sir Hector paid into how he lived his life, and it was all about advantage and disadvantage, and this was exactly how he fought. Continuous vigilance, with knowledge, detail, and planning, gave him an advantage that he made the most of.

"I fancy rabbit tonight, Guy," Sir Hector said, stretching his arms upwards.

Guy smiled and reached for his bow and arrows and started back towards the road, where he had already seen a brace of rabbits grazing in front of a hedgerow at the far side of a field.

"If you want stew then I will need some water," Guy replied warmly. "And if you fancy a roast then I need some more wood," Guy then stated as he walked away. He smiled as he thought of how Sir Harold would respond if spoken to with such familiarity.

Guy approached the field through a thicket of hazel bushes, careful with his steps to avoid any unnecessary noise and he crouched low as he approached the field boundary. He blinked his eyes to adjust his sight to the lighter aspect of the field in contrast to the dark shadows within the trees. He then scanned the base of the hedgerow on the right-hand side of the field, following it around the field's perimeter back to the road they had just ridden down.

He could see no rabbits, but in the twilight, he could see a group of men on the roadside and Guy observed them closely from his hide in the undergrowth. There were four men in total, and they had all un-mounted their horses. Three of them were standing together holding the horses, while the fourth man was examining the ground at the roadside.

Guy recognised their position as the place where he and Sir Hector had pulled off the road to search for a camp.

The single man then joined his companions and pointed at the small path that Sir Hector and Guy had taken into the small clump of woods. They all then led their horses down the same path.

Guy understood that they were being tracked and carefully backed off into the trees, before hurrying back to Sir Hector.

Guy and Sir Hector stood together in a small thicket of holly and rowan bushes that overlooked their camp and were well hidden from any observers. In their camp, which was about fifty yards away, they had laid their bags out on the ground each side of the smouldering fire and covered them with their blankets to look like sleeping travellers. They now waited to see what the four men's intentions were.

Sir Hector had no hesitation in creating this deception as soon as Guy had given his opinion that the men were acting suspiciously and did not appear friendly. Sir Hector had tied up the horses away from the campfire, at the opposite end to where the path entered the small clearing. Sir Hector did not like putting the horses at risk, but in the short time that they had, he could think of no better alternative.

Twilight was quickly gathering, and the fire started to cast shadows. Guy whispered an alert to Sir Hector as he detected movement at the right edge of the camp.

"Get ready Guy," Sir Hector whispered, as Guy slowly drew back his bow and held it tracking the leader of the four who was creeping forwards towards the campfire, "and protect the horses at all costs."

Sir Hector had insisted the Guy use bodkin arrows that would piece any chainmail. Guy wanted to use blunt heads, to disable the men. Sir Hector, however, had calmly shaken his head and said that their lives were at risk, so they must defend themselves by reducing their assailant's numbers, permanently. But, understanding Guy's unease, he allowed the compromise of waiting until they first showed their purpose, and if it was murderous, then killing them would be justified.

Another of the four men closely followed the first with the remaining two men keeping to the edge of the camp.

The two men in front crept slowly forward, picking their steps carefully and firelight suddenly glistened off steel indicating that they were armed with swords or large knives.

"Let them make their move," Sir Hector whispered.

And they did. The leader stepped past the first supposed sleeping figure and stood alongside the second blanketed form. He then raised the sword high and stabbed down hard with the point of the sword into the middle of the blanket. Guy released the arrow and watched it fly.

Confident that its flight was true, he reached for a second arrow. He effortlessly re-notched it and drew back the string. He aimed at the middle of the second attacker and fired again. Guy was confident that at 50 yards he would hit his target,

The first attacker, crashed forward as the arrow smacked into the middle of his back and he fell over the blanketed mound. The second figure instinctively crouched in defence, as he beheld his companion's death, which bought the arrow strike, which was aimed at his thigh, into the side of his head. He died instantly in a red mist of blood that exploded from his skull.

Guy had already reached down for a third arrow and sent it towards the two remaining figures who were standing in the dark within the trees.

The two attackers had realised their danger and turned to flee, but Guy's arrow whistled through the leaves and straight between the shoulders of one of them. The other ran on in panic and noisily stumbled through the undergrowth and deep into the cover of the trees.

Sir Hector grabbed Guy's arm, as the young squire stepped quickly forward to give chase. The knight shook his head.

"It is too dark Guy. It is best to let him go. He will not be back."

Sir Hector and Guy then left their hide and quickly retrieved their assailant's horses, which had been left tied up fifty yards along the path. They brought them back into their camp and tied them alongside their own horses.

After stripping the three dead men of their belongings, they threw their bodies over the back of one of their horses and took them into the increasing gloom of the wood. They then discarded the corpses far enough away from their camp to avoid them being disturbed in the night by any wildlife, who would smell the fresh blood. By the time they had finished and returned to the fire, it was dark, and they could no longer see into the trees.

Guy carefully gathered up his blanket and threw it into the trees as it was torn from the sword thrust and covered in blood from the body of Guy's first quarry. Guy felt disgusted by it, and he had no desire to keep it. Sir Hector had thrown him one of the attacker's blankets taken from their baggage, that they took from their horses, but Guy felt uncomfortable in using it.

After a cold meal of bread and cheese, they settled for the night.

"You did well Guy," Sir Hector said.

Hector was lying on his back, staring at the night sky above, with his blanket pulled up under his arms.

"I did not realise how deadly you are with a bow."

"I have just killed three men," Guy said quietly.

"You have just killed three murderers who were trying to kill you," Sir Hector said softly. "Would you prefer your own death, and all the sorrow that would cause to the people who love and care for you? And would you prefer these men to go away and murder other innocents and increase their spread of grief?"

"But killing a man is still a sin," Guy said.

"Evil is a sin," Sir Hector replied. "I have been involved with death for most of my life," he then continued, "and I believe that if a man's actions, although sinful, are carried out with good intentions, then there can be no evil. You should not condone yourself Guy; judgement of our sins will come upon us in heaven and what you did was not a sin."

Guy considered what Sir Hector said and wondered how Felice would have reacted to his death. He knew that it would have affected her, and he did not want Felice to experience any form of despair; not if he could prevent it.

"Anyway, your skills with the bow can only have been God sent," Sir Hector said in a less serious tone. "And you must keep practising Guy, as your skill is a differentiator, for nobility do not pull a bow."

Sir Hector then turned over onto his side with his back to Guy.

"And I believe that it will be most useful to me on this trip," he finally said and went to sleep, seemingly undisturbed by the evening's events.

The next morning, they awoke with the sunrise. The leaves of the trees rustled in the light breeze and birds chattered and chirped in a happy chorus. The horses were lightly stamping their feet and jostling each other as they waited to be untethered. The aroma of the dew enriched grass blew across them and invited them to graze.

"Can you see to the horses, Guy?" Sir Hector asked, as he lifted himself to his knees and carefully folded his blanket. "While I sort through the belongings of our visitors to see who they were, and perhaps why they were following us."

Guy slowly stood up and stretched his back, as he was both aching and stiff from lying on the rough ground. He did not remember going to sleep, or anything else from the night before. His remorse over his actions had not affected him as much as he thought they would, or at least they were not as important to him as the need to sleep. He then took a lead from Sir Hector in folding away his blanket before moving away from the remnants of the fire.

Guy led both Bedivere and Sir Hector's horse, which did not have a name, to the open field and let them loose, confident that they would not go far. He went back and took each of their attacker's horses in turn and tethered them on long leads so that they could graze comfortably. He would lead them down to the stream later, but he was conscious that the stream was where they left the bodies of their assailants.

He then went back to see Sir Hector.

"Have you discovered anything?" Guy asked when he entered their camp.

"Nothing to identify them," he replied. "But one of them had significant funds."

He handed Guy a purse that was full of coins. Guy weighed it in his hand and passed it back.

"No, Guy," Sir Hector said, holding up the palm of his hand. "I have already halved the sum and that is your share."

Guy looked at the bag feeling a sense of revulsion.

"Is this not theft?" Guy asked.

"Certainly not," Sir Hector answered happily. "I believe these men were paid to kill us and we wanted to stay alive. And through cunning and skill, we were victorious, so I regard this money and all their belongings as our winnings, and as we are a partnership, we share our earnings."

"How do you know they were paid to kill us?" Guy asked.

"Because I live in this world, Guy. One man amongst a gang of murderers does not carry a large purse unless he is paying for their upkeep. It will be for the first payment, with a larger sum of money due on delivery," Sir Hector answered in a 'matter-of-fact' tone.

"Otherwise, they would have slit his throat at the first opportunity, to rob him of his purse," he continued. "So, we now need to go and see if we recognise them, as I suspect they have followed us from Warwick."

They collected the tethered horses on the way to the stream so that they could be watered in the river. But they tied them up, downwind to where the dead bodies lay, so the expected smell of blood and slaughter would not disturb them. They then walked along the stream's bank until they came across the three bodies. A swarm of flies buzzed around the corpses and a couple of feeding crows hopped away as they approached.

Sir Hector turned one of the bodies onto its back, so it joined the other two in facing upwards towards the clear morning sky. He then looked down upon each of them. Fortunately, they had not yet been disfigured or eaten by the crows or any other animal from the woods.

"Do you recognise any of them Guy?" Sir Hector said.

"No," Guy said.

"I am surprised," Sir Hector said, lightly kicking the body of the man who led the assault on their camp. "He is one of the men who threatened you along with Sir Otto on the day the 'Squire's Melee'?"

"Are you sure?" Guy responded looking closely at the man. "It was dark under the Earl's stand."

"But it was not dark in the castle courtyard, which is where I followed them," Sir Hector said. "As I have told you many times, Guy. It is always good to know your opponents."

"Do you think that Sir Otto had a hand in this?"

"I cannot be certain. But on the face of it, it would seem likely," Sir Hector responded. "But we have a good foundation on which we can investigate further."

"What will we do with the bodies?" Guy asked.

"Nothing," Sir Hector replied. "We will stop in Towcester and report the attack to the town's reeve, who I happen to know. My reputation and standing are far above that of a handful of roadside thieves, and we will leave it to him to see if he can find the fourth assailant. He may also find the person who hired them, but I think that would be unlikely."

"We will also sell the horses to the reeve at a heavily discounted price to support our allegations, and no more will be said about it," Sir Hector continued.

"Will there not be a hearing to prove our innocence?" Guy asked.

"Of course not. I am Sir Hector, and my reputation carries the truth before me, and you are Guy of Warwick, a retainer of Earl Rohand and Champion of the Melee," Sir Hector smiled. "There can be no doubt on our word."

The pair arrived in the old Roman town and went straight to the reeve, who recognised Sir Hector straight away.

The reeve on hearing their story was deeply concerned for the attack on the two renowned travellers, and although he had not heard of Guy, his connection to the Earl of Warwick was enough of a reference. The reeve kept repeating his regrets for the scandal that might reflect on his town and promised to leave no stone unturned in finding the remaining culprit. He would not buy the horses at the discounted rate but insisted on taking the horses to the livery and selling them on their behalf at the going rate. Sir Hector accepted the offer but also insisted that half the sale should be donated to a town charity.

Sir Hector and Guy were then shown to the town's best inn where their horses were stabled, and they settled down for a late lunch. Guy was surprised and slightly overawed at the constant stream of the town's inhabitants who wandered into the bar just to look upon Sir Hector and his friend.

"You appear to be well known here in Towcester, Sir Hector," Guy said.

"The town is on the main route south, and I have passed through on numerous occasions," Sir Hector said. "And being on the boundary of Danelaw, it has had a few Danish issues which I have helped out with in the past."

"Danish Issues?" Guy asked.

Sir Hector smiled.

"The Danes, contrary to popular belief, are not barbarians but live their lives with their own laws and their own sense of justice which, although barbaric, are just different to ours. They are pagans, but only because they have not been introduced to our Lord's glory, and therefore are not aware of the constraints that are needed to curb their inbred behaviour. They still, however, hold up their own law and order, and have a sense of right and wrong which they commit to. That commitment means they fight with honour and will be loyal to any resolution of disputes that are decided through combat."

Sir Hector then shrugged his shoulders.

"I have helped the town out with the occasional resolution of disputes. Although, I was not involved in the siege that occurred a couple of years ago. But the burh fortress did its job and the town defended itself without me," Sir Hector said and smiled to himself.

Sir Hector accepted a cup of ale from a stranger who just walked into the bar and held it up to the man in appreciation.

"But there is a fine balance between fighting with honour to resolve a dispute, where the outcome is accepted by all, and engaging in a Viking blood feud. And take it from me that you do not want to get involved with a Viking blood feud."

"Your fights were to the death?" Guy asked.

"Yes," Sir Hector replied. "It is a requirement of their culture."

"I heard from Sir Harold that you have already fought a Dane," Sir Hector then asked.

"Yes. He was called Sven Blackheart," Guy replied.

"And you placed your opponent's axe into his hands before he died."

"Yes."

"May I ask why?"

"Because he was reaching for it, and I felt sorry for him."

"The Danes like to die in battle, as it represents honour to them. They believe that if they do die in battle, then they will fight on in their afterlife. It is therefore important to take their weapons with them, as it supports their transition as a warrior to the afterlife. So, what you did was give him honour in his death, and that will be remembered by the Danes. I suspect that your audience with Sitric was the result of that one action."

"I liked Sitric, he gave me an arm ring," Guy said.

"Then you are fortunate, and you have now gained a reputation with the Danes, and that will follow you."

After their meal, Sir Hector led Guy to a secluded spot on the eastern outskirts of the town to carry out their daily practise session. Sir Hector never neglected that duty, come rain or shine, but even this did not go unnoticed by the locals, and invited several onlookers.

During the sparring, there was a couple of good-humoured, but disparaging comments, from half a dozen of the town's, off duty, soldiers who watched from the side of the grassy meadow.

Sir Hector smiled and asked if any of them would like to pit themselves against his lowly squire. The crowd cheered the soldiers on in encouragement and one of the bigger men walked forward holding his arms up to show off his muscles. The crowd was suddenly boisterous, and Guy could see money change hands as wagers were placed.

Sir Hector picked up a spare padded jacket from the pile of training equipment that he always brought with him and casually threw it at the soldier. He then called out his odds for any bet takers. When all bets had been made, Sir Hector then gave both Guy and the soldier a light sparring sword. These swords were not as heavy as the large broadswords used in battle and had blunt edges and tips. But they could still break bones, or inflict mortal injury, if used to strike an opponent's head.

The opponents faced each other, and the noise of the crowd increased.

It took only two sequences of strokes for Guy to put the man onto the floor. He first let the man attack while he met each stroke with a parry. And, after measuring his opponent's capabilities, Guy efficiently executed his counterattack, to force the man onto the ground.

Guy, smiling warmly, pulled the man up and invited him to try again, while Sir Hector collected his winnings.

The other soldiers also tried their skills against Guy, who did no more than defend the attacks and lightly counter when appropriate. But he offered his opponents advice and instruction which they listened to, in earnest, even though Guy was just a youth. They recognised that his age did not restrain his capabilities.

Guy walked with Sir Hector back towards the inn. The knight was in good spirits at the performance of his squire. But, before they made the town, Sir Hector took a detour, as he wanted to quickly visit a local priory, which was a mile or so up the River Tove.

The Priory was a small, poor, establishment, and when they entered the small courtyard, the head monk came running out to greet them. Chickens were running around the yard and a young novice, holding his long cassock up to his thighs, was chasing them in unbridled pleasure. Guy could tell that he was not sane and made the sign of the cross on his chest to avert any evil.

"Sir Hector," the priest said, and warmly took the knight's hand between both of his. "You are very welcome."

"And welcome to you also, my friend," he said to Guy.

"Do not mind Jeffrey," he then said to Guy, noticing has aversion to the boy. "He gives no harm and is a constant joy to us."

"Thank you. Father," Guy replied.

"Guy, may I introduce Father Corey. He is an old friend and a good shepherd to the disadvantaged of this neighbourhood."

Father Corey beamed at both Sir Hector and Guy.

"We are only passing Father, so we cannot stay long, but I came to give you this offering for our penance."

Sir Hector handed over a purse full of coins.

"Thank you, my son," the priest said with great happiness. "You are always in my prayers."

"And for that, I thank you, Father."

"But you will not stay for some sustenance, meagre as it may be?"

"No, Father, we must depart. But I promise to stay longer next time."

"You are always welcome, Sir Hector," Father Corey said, his face still full of serenity and joy.

The priest shook Guy's hand and then embraced Sir Hector, before the two men walked back towards town.

"Do you always donate your winnings to the church?" Guy asked.

"No, only to a select number of establishments," Sir Hector answered.

"On the whole, I find most of the church corrupt," he continued. "But there are some pure soles who do God's service only for the glory of God and for the welfare of their fellow man. Not for the glory of gold and the benefit of themselves."

"So, I support these pure soles as best I can, and in return, they provide me with the occasional food and shelter. They also pray for my soul."

It was then that they noticed smoke above the town.

"That is not normal," Sir Hector said, nodding his head in the town's direction.

"There are multiple fires across the northern side of the town which probably means that it is being raided."

"Danes?" Guy asked.

"Probably," Sir Hector answered. "I can think of no other reason."

"Now follow me," he then said to Guy in a firm voice and turned back to the priory.

They left their training equipment with Father Corey and warned him of the possible attack, before running back towards the town. As they reached the main road into

Towcester, they met up with the handful of soldiers who had previously joined them on their training session.

They had also seen the smoke but were unsure of what actions to take.

Sir Hector quickly rallied them together and they instantly submitted to his orders as he led them towards the town.

They hurried down the main Northampton road, with the castle to their left, and then slowed to a halt as they approached the junction to Watling Street, as there were screams and shouts in the close vicinity.

Sir Hector held the group back and he crept forward to peer down the wide Roman road to his right. It was then that he saw the Danes. The road was clouded with heavy black smoke and flames shot up from the thatch of the roofs. The raiding party looked to be around twenty men. Some were astride horses, holding the middle of the road while others, on foot, ransacked houses at each side. They were slowly moving towards the fortress in the centre of the town. Bodies lay on the side of the road and the screams of women indicated their fate. There was no opposition from the town's guard and Sir Hector assumed that they had retreated into the burh's recently built fortress.

"Guy, I need you to take these men and get around to the enemy's rear and start killing them in the houses or side alleys. Do not get the attention of the main group, as I need them to stay where they are. They will not be expecting you, so try and keep it like that for as long as possible."

Guy just nodded.

"I will go and get help. I will then come at the main group head-on."

"Guy is in charge here, so you do as he says," he then told the soldiers sternly.

They nodded in unison.

"So, let's kill some Danes."

Guy led his small war band down the small alley that ran behind the row of houses that faced the Roman road. There were smoke and bright embers in the air and screams hung in the air from within the houses. They ducked under windows and crept past any open doors until the mayhem from within the houses died down. Guy then ordered four of the soldiers to the other side of the main street, under the cover of a particular dense smoke cloud.

"Split into two and enter each house alternatively. Keep screaming to mask our actions and hide our passage, but no calling out to each other in our Saxon tongue, it will alert the Danes."

Guy then waved them across the road, before turning to the two remaining men.

"I will lead and surprise them. My attacks will be swift and brief. You two will keep out of my way but mop up after me. But you need to be quick. We move between houses on my command."

Guy then turned and went back along the alley and moved into the first house.

There were two dead women in the single room of the house, although one was just a girl. Their clothes were ripped from them, and their throats cut. But there were no Danes to be seen or heard.

"Come," Guy said and moved along the buildings until they heard a woman squealing from the inside of a two-story warehouse. Without thought, Guy rushed straight in with sword raised. A large Dane was holding a woman face down onto the floor with a knee in the centre of her back and grasping her hair in one fist and holding a knife in the other. He looked up as Guy shouted out. He dropped the knife and tried to pull his sword from its sheath as he stood up, but Guy was straight on him, slashing his sword down across his neck. He felt it hit the leather of the tunic before deflecting into flesh.

Guy levered his sword to rip the blade across the Danish warrior's neck and pulled it away at the same time. He then quickly stepped away and turned to see another Dane, who was pulling clothes from a large wooden trunk in the corner of the room to try and find any hidden plunder. The man just looked at the chain mailed warrior in front of him with an open mouth. He was unable to move as Guy thrust his sword straight into his face, the point sliding deep into the eye socket. The man fell backwards, and Guy had to put his foot onto the bloodied mess that was the man's head, to help pull his blade free.

"Come," Guy said as moved on to the next building.

Two more Danes died at Guy's hands before he heard cries from outside, as the mounted Danes were calling to their companions.

Guy glanced down the road through the side of an open window and saw a shield wall that was slowly moving towards the mounted riders. The leader of the Danes was weighing up his options and working out if he could breach this wall when four mounted warriors galloped around from the side road and charged head-on at the Danes. The lead rider had his sword raised and the other three had spears pointed out to the front.

Guy instantly recognised Sir Hector at the front of the group and watched as he deftly moved his horse in between the two front Danes. With one deft stroke, he beheaded the lead Dane and drove his horse into the flank of the adjacent rider. Sir Hector's supporters ran each side of the group of Danes and thrust their spears forward and pieced leather and armour to bury their points into the chests of their assailants.

"To me," Guy called out and ran out into the road and waited for the other soldiers of his small war band to follow him.

"To me!" he shouted again, as the four men from the other side of the road ran out and stood alongside.

"Who can ride?" He quickly asked.

Three of the men acknowledged him.

"Get horses and gather this side of the Danes," Guy ordered the three men. "Now," he barked at them.

The men turned and went to catch the rider-less horses that were now running around in panic across the street.

"The rest make sure that any Danes on foot do not remount," Guy said to the other soldiers.

Guy then ran towards the nearest rider-less horse. "Quickly!" he shouted behind him.

It only took a minute or so for Guy and his three colleagues to gather in a line and start to ride towards the rest of the fighting. Guy watched the shield wall coming quicker down the road, although still holding formation. Sir Hector was still riding in and out of the Danes, slashing his sword to each side in deadly effect. Sir Hector then saw Guy and called to his other riders, and they all galloped to Guy's line.

"Well met, Guy," Sir Hector said, in good spirits.

"Do we wait or charge, my lord?" Guy asked smiling at Sir Hector.

"Oh charge, I think," Sir Hector said lightly. "Let's not give them time to gather themselves. You charge along their right flank, and I will take their left and that should leave a route down the middle for them to retreat through. Make sure nobody tries to follow them when they go."

Guy quickly passed on the instructions to his soldiers before Sir Hector bellowed, and they all charged forward.

Guy was with his war band of soldiers, who he had led in the fight with the Danes. They had remained close to Guy during the battle and now they did not want to leave him. They walked back alongside the ransacked houses and brought out the dead bodies, separating the Danes from the local town folk. The men were in good spirits and telling stories of their exploits, as they searched the corpses and removed any valuables, including their armour and weapons. This they shared amongst each other, as just reward for their efforts. Guy only took a gold torque and silver arm ring, as he did not want to take anything he could not carry, and he did not want to bother with trying to sell any of the items. The other men complained that he wasn't taking enough, as he did most of the killing, but he declined.

Sir Hector had ensured that the town gates were secured, and the locals were safe and accounted for. He also took his share of plunder from the Danes which amounted to several horses and weapons. He passed the booty to a trusted agent, recommended by the knights who rode with him, to sell the goods on, at a small commission. Guy thought that he should have done the same, but he had no real regrets, and he would learn from the experience. He had fought in another battle and came out alive. He had accounted himself with honour, and now felt relief at the outcome, along with a sense of pride in his achievements.

The town reeve insisted that Sir Hector and Guy stay on for another night as the town's guests and a feast was arranged to celebrate their victory and mourn the town's victims.

Sir Hector agreed to stay the extra night and with Guy, walked back towards the priory to recover their belongings.

"Well, that was interesting," Sir Hector said. "Did you learn anything?"

"The Danes were not as formidable as I thought," Guy said.

"This band were just raiding and not driven by honour or reputation. That makes a difference," Sir Hector replied.

"You never know how disciplined a Danish war band is and how well they are trained to fight together," Sir Hector then said. "But as individuals, they nearly always fight well in battle, and I have witnessed some mighty Danish warriors who fight alone and lead by example." Sir Hector then looked at Guy. "This you should recognise in yourself. You are also a natural leader, which was evident today and men will follow you."

They ate and drank long into the night and awoke the next morning, much later than they had planned and worse for wear from the ale.

Sir Hector retrieved his profit from his agent and bought Guy a blanket, to replace the one that was thrown away from the night in the woods, which now seemed a long time ago. The town's folk were taken back and amused when Sir Hector presented the blanket to Guy as a reward for his exploits in defeating the Danes and Guy accepted the blanket with due humility.

They then left Towcester accompanied by a guard of honour, made up of the soldiers and knights who fought alongside them. The streets were lined with well-wishers, who cheered their gratitude. The guard left them as they moved away from the town, with a lot of clasping of hands and promises to meet up again, before Guy and Sir Hector were suddenly alone again.

They walked their horses in silence along Watling Street and towards the town of St Albans, where their stay was uneventful. They then rode on to London.

Chapter Twelve

Guy leant over the wooden rail at the rear of the ship as it sailed down the River Thames, with the tide in its favour. He was standing on the raised steering platform of a large single sailed trading vessel, and he marvelled at its size and speed. Guy had never been on such a ship before, as the River Avon, which flowed through Warwick, only supported small rowing boats or coracles. Guy had spent many a happy hour with his father, fishing on a small boat on the tranquil, green, river, but this was something else completely. He felt happy for the first time in days, with the sun on his head, the wind in his face and clean air filling his lungs.

Sir Hector was sitting below on the lower deck, not trusting the concept of being afloat. He had said that he disliked not being in control, and Guy could understand that of him, but Guy loved it; it was living with nature. But whereas the woods of Warwick had a calm and serene beauty, the ocean was wild and uncontrollable. Sir Hector had told him that the sea could ease the soul in the peace of its calmest moments and then wrap you in abject terror, as you cursed the ferocity of its wild tempers. He described how you needed to fight with the last shard of your existence, as it tested your resolve on living. He also said it always reminded him to embrace life while you still lived it, to always sail towards calm waters and pray to God for your deliverance to a safe shore.

A large part of Guy's pleasure in being on board the ship was that it was a fast exit from London. He was excited when he arrived in the vast city, but his high expectations were shattered by the incessant noise, foul smells and unfriendly people. He found the city to be dark, damp, and putrid, with an underlining feeling of sickness and squalor wherever he went.

There were people of all races crowded in the town with beggars and thieves on every corner, and there were so many corners. The taverns were dangerous and violent, although Sir Hector frequented quite a few, to pick up gossip and information from across Britain and abroad. Guy would often accompany him, but always sat silently in a corner while Sir Hector renewed contacts and listened to their news.

Guy was twice involved in fights, which was a concern to him. Not because he could not handle himself, which he could, but in why the fights had started; over nothing. The first time was because a drunk had thought he had pulled a face at him. But Guy had only tried to hold in a sneeze caused by the heavy acrid smoke that hung in the tavern's air.

And there was smoke everywhere. Guy thought that working in a smithy was bad, but in London, it was ever present, and at times, Guy thought it was worse outside in the streets than inside the houses. Then there was the foul smell from the streams of excrement and offal that flowed down channels in the streets, down to the river. The rivulets of sewage and waste seemed to be always there in the background, along every road they travelled down. The foul discharge was created by the many butchers, fishmongers and tanners that worked within the great town. It was also from other filthy places that Guy did not want to think about.

Sir Hector thought this was all very amusing, but Guy could not wait to leave.

They only stayed for two nights, before Sir Hector found passage across the sea to Flanders and Francia. Sir Hector said that they were lucky to get places on a ship, with space for their horses, so quickly, and Guy held his hand over his breast, where he kept Felice's token. The short stay had pleased Guy, as he did not know how much longer he could have put up with the disgusting environment.

Sir Hector had met with his contacts to pick up the last of the information that he needed and settled the bill for the transport aboard the ship. He seemed quite satisfied with his business in London and boarded the ship in good spirits.

Guy had to work with the crew to securely tie up the horses, so that they would not hurt themselves or each other during the voyage. The horses had specially built planked stalls underneath the wooden steering platform at the rear of the ship. Guy tied large string feed bags in front of the horses so that they could eat during their journey and stayed with them until the boat was untied from its berth and its sails set.

Guy had then climbed up to the ship's upper deck as they left the town behind. They travelled east towards the river's estuary, and he watched the ever-changing countryside along the riverbanks. The gluttonous muddy marshes and thick swamps were all new to Guy. As were water birds that thrashed their wings and feet against the river's surface as they took fright from the ship's passage. There was also the many different types of trees, grasses and flowering plants that grew in sparse clumps along the banks, which Guy did not recognise.

They sailed for most of the day before they left the quiet waters of the Thames, and they were instantly buffeted by the strong winds and undulating waves of the sea. Guy climbed down the steps to the lower deck and sat alongside Sir Hector. The sea had been described to him by his father, but the vastness of the open water that stretched in front of them, as far as the eyes could see, unnerved him. It was cold, bleak, and uninviting and Guy, suddenly, felt very much out of place.

The ship started to roll as it carried the waves. The movement was unfamiliar to Guy, and he was starting to feel slightly nauseous because of it.

"First time at sea?" Sir Hector asked.

"Yes." Guy answered. "Its vastness makes me feel alone and insignificant."

"I know what you mean," Sir Hector said, thoughtfully. "It is like a representation of God. It can reward or kill you without knowing anything about you. Also, you must always bend to its ways and obey its rules and silent commands. Then you can feel at one with it."

Sir Hector smiled at Guy, as the young squire tried to comprehend what Sir Hector had said.

"Or so I have been told," he continued. "Personally, I hate it and cannot wait to get off this ship and put my feet on dry land."

"If you start feeling seasick, then go and talk with the ship's steersman and focus on the horizon. I find that helps."

"I may go and do that," Guy said. "But I thought that I would ask you where we are bound, and what I should expect?"

"We first land at a town called Boulogne, which is in a province called Flanders. We will then travel on through West Francia to a city called Soissons, which is to the north of Paris," Sir Hector replied. "I have an obligation to compete in a local tournament." He then took a deep breath. "I promised King Edward that I would attend as a favour to his brother-in-law. But with what I have heard in respect to the political unrest in Francia, it may not be a good idea, at this time, to hold favour with King Charles the Simple."

Guy had never heard of King Charles, but he thought that he should not show his ignorance in respect to royalty.

"It is not a significant tournament, and I will be only competing in the melee, so it should not stretch us too hard," Sir Hector continued offhand. But he then became more interested. "However, if I remember correctly, there is also a 'Spear on Horse' contest, which is an open invitation, and they are always interesting." He then looked at Guy and smiled. "Would you like to compete?" He asked mischievously.

Guy looked at Sir Hector, trying to understand what was behind the question.

"Why is it an open invitation?" Guy eventually asked.

"Because it is before the melee, and has less esteem," Sir Hector answered. "And people get hurt."

Guy wrinkled his nose. "I am OK with throwing a spear and I did have a bit of a play with one while on a hunt. But I have never fought or practised with a spear while riding on horseback."

"Well then," Sir Hector said, happily. "It's now a good time to give it a go. We will start training as soon as we can." He patted Guy on the shoulder. "In addition to your other training, you understand."

"If nothing else it will improve your horsemanship," he then added.

Guy smiled back, not fully grasping the situation, but he was determined and happy to take instruction from Sir Hector at every opportunity."

Sir Hector rubbed his hands together at the new challenge ahead.

"I think that I will go and see the steersman now," Guy then said as the ship dropped into the trough of a wave. He then stood up and, with a stagger, climbed back to the upper deck, leaving Sir Hector deep in thought.

Once again, Guy's association with Sir Hector allowed for special treatment from the ship's crew, and the Steersman instructed Guy in the workings of the sails and in steering the ship. He was shown how to catch the gusts of wind as they patterned the surface of the sea ahead and predict their movements. Guy leant against the heavy tiller, which moved the rudder and guided the ship forward, as he tried to read the surface of the water to tell the direction of the wind.

The activity took his mind away from any sickness, and by having control of the tiller, he could balance his body in expectation of the ship's movements. The wind blew in his face, as he controlled his way through the immense open water, with no certainty to arriving at his destination or in his ultimate survival from the dangers of the sea. All he had was hope and trust in others.

Sir Hector was right, he thought, the sea was like God. Sailing the ship through the waters was faith and the hope of arriving at his destination was prayer. He smiled as he realised that he was traversing the calm waters with assurance and skill, while being instructed by professionals. Perhaps his journey with Sir Hector was the same and he was being watched over by God. He pushed again at the tiller and the ship jumped forward as the sail suddenly bellowed. He started to enjoy himself.

They sailed into Boulogne harbour and pulled alongside a long wooden quay. Some of the crew jumped off, to tie the ship up against the wooden mooring posts, and Guy, who stayed underneath the upper platform, steadied the horses, as they sensed an end to their confinement. The cargo was first unloaded before ramps were laid down to give the horses an easy exit. Guy led them off one by one and tied them up on the quay. He then waited for Sir Hector to gather their belongings and say his farewell to the ship's captain.

Guy looked around to the mass of buildings at the end of the quay and was taken aback by the contrast of Boulogne to that of London. This town was vibrant, with a bustle of people and animals. It was not dark or oppressing like London and the inhabitants seemed happy, as displayed by the joy and laughter amongst the harbour's workers.

Guy enjoyed Boulogne with its Roman buildings and many inns, which were clean and friendly and served good food, along with interesting drinks. They could no longer get the watered-down ale, which was the staple drink in Britain, but had to buy wine by the jug. At first, Guy did not like the deep red acidic drink, but the more he drank the better it tasted. The food, however, was very good and very different to anything that he had ever eaten before. Sir Hector had said that the food had subtlety, because of the use of herbs and spices. He ordered different meals at every opportunity to acquaint Guy's pallet, but he would not translate the Flemish description of it to Guy and insisted that Guy used their local names. He also encouraged Guy, at every opportunity, to pronounce the names of everything in Flemish, or Frankish, if there was any profound difference in the dialects.

They also started preparing for the 'Spear on Horse' contest.

Sir Hector purchased a boar spear for Guy, although he insisted that Guy paid for half of its cost, on the assurance that they also split his winnings. The spear had two large lugs forged onto the spear blade, which was designed to stop a pierced boar from continuing its charge up the shaft and into the spearman. The lugs were also designed to stop the spear going too deep into a boar, or a man's, flesh. This would facilitate an easy withdrawal, but also allow it to pierce deep enough to kill or maim its victim.

But in battle, these lugs were also used to hook around shields and pull them away from an enemy. Guy, with his father in the smithy, had experimented with the size and length of these lugs, to optimise their best position from the tip and the best shape for a hook.

But Sir Hector's initial training was to get Guy to just ride past a row of long two metre poles, which were hammered into the ground. The objective was to knock off an apple, which was balanced on the top of each of the poles.

Guy did not think much of the training, but he rarely knocked an apple off.

They planned to stay for two nights in Boulogne, to let the horses recover from the sea journey and concentrate on Guy's training. Sir Hector was in no hurry to leave the town and again arranged meetings with more of his old friends and associates.

The inn where they stayed was comfortable and hospitable, and they enjoyed the company of other travellers, who passed on all the news of the area. Sir Hector constantly bought drinks and quizzed any of the inn's guests that came into the bar.

Guy was interested in the goings-on within this strange country. But he often got confused, and Sir Hector was very patient in trying to explain the politics when asked. There seemed to be a lot of disputes over who ruled where, and the locals discussed the nobility and royalty with what seemed a total lack of respect. The King of West Francia was Charles III of France, but he was often referred to as 'Charles the Simple'. There were other kings before Charles the Simple, called 'Charles the Bald' and 'Charles the Fat', and Guy even heard mention of 'Louis the Stammerer'. Guy found all this amusing and thought that it would be better to choose different names for your children rather than having to rely on their appearances, or impediments, to distinguish them. However, there was some discussion on whether Charles the Bald was actually bald.

However, Guy did pay attention to the questions that Sir Hector asked, the subjects of his discussions and any points that caught his mentor's attention. The people who interested Sir Hector the most were a man called Robert and a Dane called Rollo. Robert, who seemed to be a very rich and powerful noble, was both the Count of Poitiers and the Count of Paris, amongst his other titles. The other man was a renowned leader called Rollo, who was a Danish Viking, and held the title of the Duke of Normandy. This title and associated lands were given to Rollo by King Charles from the treaty of St Clair Sur Epte, after Charles had defeated him in battle. Charles had made Rollo the ruler of Normandy to protect his shores from Viking raids and then married his sister to him to secure the peace.

It seemed to Guy that signing a treaty with a famous Viking warrior and giving him a large swathe of land to defend against other Vikings was sensible. Especially when the alliance was sealed with the hand of his daughter. It all sounded strategically astute and not at all simple, as his name suggested.

However, the name of Hagano also kept cropping up, which seemed to unite all the people who they met in their dislike of him. Hagano seemed to be a favourite of King Charles, but of nobody else.

They left Boulogne early in the morning of the third day and took a straight road towards a town called Lens. The day was hot, but not uncomfortable, and the two men happily rode their horses at a slow walk. Sir Hector spent a lot of time teaching Guy the Frankish names for things they passed and then, with a lot of patience, getting him to wrap the correct grammar and accent around them.

It was a good way of teaching, and Guy enjoyed it. With Sir Hector's patience and Guy's determination, Guy became increasingly conversant with the language.

They also often stopped to practise Guy's tournament skills with both sword and spear.

They had moved on from target practise with the spear to absorbing and managing the shock of hitting an opponent. Guy already understood the force that came through the arm and the loss of grip on the spear handle from his recent experience with the boar. Sir Hector was explaining how you present the hit and then track the body in tangent with the force of impact and not to directly oppose it. Guy understood Sir Hector's instruction, but his mind was rushing ahead on how he could improve the mechanics of presenting the spear from horseback.

"Do you have an issue with any of this?" Sir Hector asked, observing Guy's lack of focus.

"No, not at all, Sir Hector," Guy replied, bringing his thoughts back to Sir Hector's instructions. "I understand fully what you are saying, and it has prompted me to consider the forces on the spear. But I am just thinking ahead of myself." Guy then thought for a while in silence before asking more questions."

"What are the rules of this contest?" He then asked.

"In what respect?" Sir Hector asked, suddenly interested.

"First of all, what constitutes a spear?"

"It is a standard boar spear. There is no specification I believe, except that the tip is capped."

"Capped?" Guy asked.

"A metal and leather sheath must be fixed over the spear blade and that sheath has a large rounded and padded end, which will not penetrate flesh. The sheaths are inspected before each bout to ensure that they are safe and secure."

"And what about the shaft? Does it need to be of any specific length or thickness?"

"I do not think so," Sir Hector answered, as his attention became more engrossed with Guy's line of questioning.

"And what of the lugs?" Guy asked.

"I have seen all shapes and sizes, as they do not affect a contest."

"And the weight and wood type?"

"They do not matter."

"And what about the shield and armour," Guy then asked, his mind racing.

"No specification. Again, I have seen all types of shapes and sizes," Sir Hector replied. "Why are you asking?"

"Oh, I have an idea," Guy then said, playfully raising his eyebrows.

"Are you going to tell me?" Sir Hector asked smiling, knowing full well that Guy would wait until he has firmed up his plan.

"I would like to make my own spear," Guy said. "And after it is made, I will then demonstrate it to you, and you can then tell me if it is appropriate."

"I will not approve of any cheating, Guy," Sir Hector said in a serious tone.

"No, I am not going to cheat," Guy replied in deep thought. "But I do intent to innovate."

Sir Hector laughed and patted Guy on the shoulder.

"I am sure you will," he said. "I do like a bit of innovation."

Guy cut various thick branches of wood from different types of trees and trimmed them into the same size staves, marking each so he knew where they came from. He also spent some time in the blacksmith's forge, wherever the town's blacksmith was found to be amenable or open to a small payment. Using his skills, he was able to form various blades and lugs for the spears. He also constructed an iron breastplate and strengthened a large helmet that he purchased by adding metal hinged plates to guard the neck and face. Sir Hector watched with interest when Guy sat with his knife and cut deep grooves into the tips of the staves. It also amused him when Guy rammed the staves into tree trunks only to see them splinter and snap on impact. He could tell that Guy was absorbed in modifying the spears, but he did not know to what end and hoped that Guy's efforts would not be a waste of time.

Guy's intentions for the breastplate were more obvious to Sir Hector, as he had shaped a single large vertical flute down the centre to deflect any spear blow along the sides of the plate and away from the body. The body was the main target area in a spear contest and Guy was developing tactics that would allow him to be hit but reduce the risk of becoming unseated from the horse. This was the innovation that Guy wanted to apply and give him an advantage over his opponents.

Sir Hector admired the design of the armour but also recognised that the breastplate still had to be presented to the oncoming spear at the correct angle. This had to be done while trying to score a hit with your own spear and that would require both skill and nerve. Guy also realised this, and he asked Sir Hector to include this element within the training sessions. This involved Guy standing stationary and allowing Sir Hector to run at him with a long stick to strike him in the chest before twisting his body slightly at the last minute to deflect it.

Guy was successful most of the time, although he was knocked backwards on more than one occasion, when he got it wrong. But when he was assured of his positioning and timing, he progressed the training to horseback. Although Sir Hector was never that confident to allow a real spear to be used.

Sir Hector indulged Guy in his additional training but included it as extra work to his own. He was conscious of the dangers that Guy had put himself in, especially in being hit in the undefended areas outside of his metal chest plate, especially in the eyes and face. Sir Hector was confident in his own capabilities to hit the target, but to ensure Guy's safety, he concentrated harder than usual, whenever he recognised any risks. Sir Hector even considered putting this extra training to use by entering the 'Spear on Horse' himself, but he did not want to go up against Guy and deferred it for another time.

Guy, however, was regularly sore and bruised. Sir Hector made up an ointment from a medicinal plant called Comfrey. He had found the small bush in the forest and used it to take away the pain and swelling. He also made up a compress, when he thought it necessary, and bound it tight around Guy's chest or limbs.

While they sat and talked, Guy carved away at the spear tips and Sir Hector, although intrigued by it, did not enquire of its purpose. He preferred to wait and either let Guy inform him of the reasoning behind it, or just try to work it out in the interim. Guy, however, was aware of Sir Hector's interest and enjoyed the secrecy. He was eager for the opportunity to demonstrate his design when it was completed. Although he would not know if it would fully work until he tried it for real within a contest. This risk he accepted, but there was a part of him that knew how foolish he would look in front of Sir Hector if it did not work.

The days remained warm, and they passed quickly. They mainly slept and ate in the open, as they passed through the towns of Lens, Arras, Saint Quentin and Laon. One night they stopped at an isolated priory close to Saint Quentin, which provided overnight lodgings and a sit-down meal. As in Britain, Sir Hector was known by the priory inhabitants and was warmly welcomed. The priests were both joyous at their arrival and grateful for their donations when they left. On Sir Hector's recommendation, Guy made his own donations and prayed alongside the priests, for what Sir Hector called future investment in his welfare and soul.

On the eighth day, the pair arrived in the city of Soissons, with two days in hand before the start of the tournament. Sir Hector, who was used to the protocol, went to the town's main tavern with Guy, and sat at a side table with cups of ale to refresh themselves. They left the horses in the tavern's livery but did not book any accommodation for themselves or the animals. As Sir Hector expected, they were eventually addressed by a servant from the palace, who invited Sir Hector to accept the hospitality of the Count of Soissons. Sir Hector introduced Guy and named him with his new title of 'Guy of Warwick' and the invite was instantly extended to him. Sir Hector happily accepted the invite, and arrangements were offered to attend to the horses and baggage. Sir Hector, however, insisted that they would personally tend to the horses and settle them in the Count's stables. He was also adamant that they unpack their own belongings.

"Sir Hector," Guy said, as they sat on a balcony bench, with their backs against a sun-warmed wall that overlooked the palace courtyard. "Am I your squire, guest or what? As it is no longer clear to me."

"What do you want to be?" Sir Hector asked back, amused.

"When we left Warwick Castle, I thought I was a squire and I felt like a squire," Guy replied. "But that feeling lasted a day, as you did not treat me as a squire and since then, I am not sure what I am. Guy paused and thought about it for a while. "I feel like a pupil, or an apprentice and I think that is what I would like to be."

"Then that is what you are," Sir Hector answered. "But as an apprentice, you now need to learn my trade, which as you know is all about respect." He paused for thought. "With not without a small amount of show and theatre," he then added. "So, when we are in front of nobility and with our peers, I will treat you with the respect that is due to 'Guy of Warwick'. You, however, will need to elevate the respect I know you hold me in, to that of reverence," Sir Hector said, smiling. "And I will not mind if it approaches a level of understated awe." He then placed his hands on his hips and puffed out his chest out in a staged pose of superiority.

"And so, my reputation increases, along with the respect and hospitality that is offered to me, and my way of life, is maintained."

Sir Hector watched closely as Guy reflected on his words with an air of sullenness.

"You have an issue with this, Guy?" He asked quietly.

"I understand about respect, Sir Hector," Guy said. "I witness it every day when I am around you, but you mentioned show and theatre. Are we nothing but mere entertainers?"

Sir Hector smiled as he understood Guy's thoughtfulness.

"You think entertaining the crowd conflicts with your principles of chivalry and honour?" He asked.

Guy shrugged his shoulders, "I have not thought about it before, but it does not sit right in my mind."

"Chivalry is a code of conduct between chivalrous people, and we demonstrate that in a show of deeds or behaviour," Sir Hector explained. "There is honour in demonstrating that behaviour, but it is only fully understood and recognised by people who share the same ideals. Wars, battles, fights and in some degree tournaments, are not governed by chivalry, although some of us strive to act within its rules." Sir Hector paused to let Guy take in what he said.

"In a battle, when there is time to fight one on one, then there can be a show of chivalry between foes. But if you show chivalry during battle when there are enemies all around trying to kill you, then you will die. A show of chivalry is then only a demonstration of foolishness or weakness, so you forget chivalry and fight back in any way possible to win."

"So, what are tournaments all about, if not a demonstration of chivalry?" Guy asked.

"For the crowd, it is all about entertainment, but for the competitors taking part, it is about gaining reputation," Sir Hector said. "A competitor in a tournament who is devious, ruthless, and opposed to the rules of chivalry, can still forge respect and reputation. This can be in equal measure to that of a more gallant competitor, as he equally entertains the crowd. You will meet with some unscrupulous contestants in tournaments, but in general, they are recognised as such by their peers and by the crowd," Sir Hector paused. "You could say that their unchivalrous reputation is also held in respect. But whatever the manner of that reputation, it needs not just to be demonstrated but also emphasised. This is so everyone understands its nature, which is why there needs to be show and theatre; to provide the emphasis."

"I have seen you over the last few days' strive to learn the arts and develop your skills and techniques, and also create new ones," Sir Hector then said. "What was the purpose of that, Guy, other than for an ultimate desire to win, and to be seen winning?"

Guy looked sullener at a sudden realisation of his strong desire to win.

Sir Hector laughed at him.

"Winning is not in conflict with chivalry, honour, or reputation Guy," Sir Hector said, laying a hand on his shoulder. "Although how you win and why you win, may be."

"And you need to win, Guy, or you will never have a reputation. Therefore, go and win and seek that reputation and let that reputation be a beacon of chivalry and honour. Let your efforts reflect the values of King Arthur and his knights, but do not forget that the real reverence for King Arthur was forged from his reputation born from victories."

Guy and Sir Hector dined that evening in the palace, as guests of the Count of Soissons. Guy was seated alongside Sir Hector, who tried to explain some more of the country's political landscape. Like Britain, the government was feudal based, with power being handed down from the king to the nobles and then maintained by inheritance within the families of the nobles. However, there seemed to be more distinct regions in Francia and far more nobles.

Their host that night was Herbert II, the Count of Soissons, the Count of Vermandois, and the Count of Meaux. It seemed quite an impressive list of titles to Guy, but not as impressive as Herbert being born of the Carolingian dynasty and a direct descendant of Charlemagne, whose life and deeds were well known to Guy. The Count's lands and titles were part of West Francia, and he was therefore allied to King Charles III. The Count of Soissons sat at the centre of the single top table that stretched across the width of the large stage on which it was built and was set back from the other guests in the hall. Sir Hector identified other nobles to Guy, such as Richard the Duke of Burgundy and his son Rudolf who sat to the right of Herbert. To the left of Herbert, there was a man that Sir Hector referred to as Ebles the Bastard, who was the Count of Poitou. Ebles looked detached from the others at the table and seemed to keep his own company. Guy commented to Sir Hector that Elbes looked quite miserable.

Away from the top table, there were the lesser nobility and important town folk and clergy. There were also some other tournament competitors present who, like Guy and Sir Hector, had also arrived early. They were, in the main, friendly, and respectful to Sir Hector and were also happy to make Guy's acquaintance. Guy thought that the evening was civilised and polite, without the drunken rowdiness that was usually exhibited at the many feasts that he had experienced in Warwick.

Sir Hector explained that Francia, overall, was like this, but he also said that everything was relative, and

Warwick was gentile compared to Danish feasts and celebrations.

"I believe you like the Danes, Sir Hector?" Guy said quietly, when Sir Hector finished a particular anecdote from his experiences with the Danes.

"They are uncomplicated," he replied. "And they are also generous to friends and allies."

"But they are pagan in their beliefs. Which is sad, but at the same time pure, as they hold their beliefs at a personal level, and they do not suffer the constraints of an ordered religion and its associated mandates. They are also not selfish over their gods."

"Selfish?" Guy asked.

"They do not hold my Christian beliefs against me, and they do not judge me as a man, because of them," Sir Hector replied. "Although some of the constraints that our Christian belief demands is considered as a weakness to the Danes."

"What weakness?" Guy again asked.

"Forgiveness, turning the other cheek, preaching that the meek will inherit the Earth," Sir Hector replied. "With the Danes, it is all about strength and honour."

"But what I do not like, is their wanton destruction, as they will burn and destroy anything in their way, and they will not discriminate people for their values. When raiding and pillaging, they will kill a good man as well as a bad one, with the same enjoyment and satisfaction."

The man on the other side of Guy, who had been listening to the conversation, leant forward, and smiled at Sir Hector.

"I disagree, Sir Hector," he whispered in English. "I think the Danes would have gained far more enjoyment in killing that bastard Ebles than they would in killing any good man."

Sir Hector leant forward and looked across Guy to smile at the man.

"You are probably right my friend. Do you know why he is here? I thought he was out of favour with the Carolingians."

"Who knows?" The man said. "But he would not be here if Charles or Rollo had attended."

Sir Hector laughed at the thought.

"Guy, this is Sir Terrel. He is a retainer to the King of West Francia and a formidable opponent in the melee," he said to Guy as an introduction.

Sir Terrel smiled at Guy.

"It was worth coming, just to hear you call me formidable, Sir Hector. As I doubt that there will be any tournament victories for me with you here."

"And you are Guy of Warwick," he then said to Guy. "How is the Earl?"

"He was in good health when we left him, my lord," Guy replied politely.

"I saw your name in the 'Spear on Horse'. But I have not seen you on the lists before. Is it your first tournament?"

"He has won a melee at a home tournament," Sir Hector cut in. "I deceitfully persuaded him not to enter this melee but to try out for the 'Sword on Horse' instead. It is a competition that I have never entered before, and I did not want to run the risk of him beating me in any of the other contests."

"Away with you Hector, he is but a boy," Terrel said smiling.

"Perhaps," Sir Hector said, inclining his head, and then looking across the room knowingly.

During the evening, a number of the other guests came up to greet either Sir Hector, Sir Terrel or both and they were all introduced to Guy. Guy thought it was all very cordial and pleasant. However, when Ebles came up, he ignored Sir Terrel and spoke directly to Sir Hector to request a private meeting.

Guy could detect the sudden tension in their company and Sir Hector quickly agreed to meet up, but not until the following day. Sir Hector did not introduce Guy to him.

"That Guy," Sir Hector said, when Ebles had returned to his seat, "was Elbes the Bastard, and the Count of Poitou. It will be interesting to see what he wants?"

"He wants trouble," Sir Terrel said curtly. "And he wants your services."

"Oh, no doubt. But knowledge is power, so it will be good to know exactly what he wants and why."

"He is a snake," Sir Terrel replied angrily. "And he lives in a barrel. He will allude and insinuate; drop hints and give false promises and you will gain nothing."

Sir Hector laughed.

"Oh yes, but all information leads to knowledge," he said quietly to Guy.

The next couple of days passed quickly. They ate, trained, and observed the people around them, as more contestants arrived in the town. Guy followed Sir Hector throughout the day, as he constantly looked at the livery of the horses and the many groups of retainers that bustled around the streets. A lot of this surveillance involved visits to taverns and hostelries, where they would sit for a while with a drink and occasionally eat a light meal. They would both look and listen to the people around them and pick up on any interesting conversation. They also regularly checked the tournament lists, which showed the entries in each competition.

Sir Hector would provide Guy with background information on the names that he recognised, which seemed to be most of them. But Guy found it difficult to remember them, apart from the odd few who Sir Hector especially highlighted for their reputations, both good and bad. His knowledge of the entries in the 'Spear on

Horse' was only second hand, as he was never interested in competing in that contest, as he thought it too dangerous, which did not fill Guy with any confidence. But, at the request of Guy, he reported back on their relative height and weight, which amused Sir Hector.

Sir Hector, like in all the other towns they visited, would often go off alone to meet up with his associates in private. Guy would just walk around the streets, to take in the atmosphere. Like the tournament at Warwick, all the town's main thoroughfares were decorated with bunting and flags. They were also lined with merchants, peddlers, and beggars, who constantly accosted Guy to sell their wares or services or just beg for his charity.

Sir Hector did not say who he had met or divulged any information on what he might have found out, and Guy did not ask any questions. He assumed that it was how he arranged his life on the road, concerning the planning of tournaments and other contracts in need of his skills. Guy, however, did enquire about his meeting with Elbes, but Sir Hector only said that it was interesting and would say no more of their conversation.

He did however tell Guy, some of Elbe's history and described a battle several years before. The battle was where Robert, the Count of Poitiers and Richard the Duke of Normandy defeated Rollo: the Dane, at the Battle of Chartres. Elbes had not arrived until after the battle had ended and was ridiculed because of his lateness. This in turn spread doubts about his bravery. To redeem himself, Elbes immediately left Chartres and chased after the retreating remnants of the Danish army. Elbe's troops, however, when confronting the Danes, were soundly defeated and Elbes, himself, fled from the Danes. To escape them, he hid in a barrel within a local fuller's workshop, bringing about more ridicule and derision for his cowardice.

In the evenings, Guy and Sir Hector continued to dine in the palace, as guests of the Count, and the atmosphere became livelier as more people attended. Guy got to meet more of the contestants and started to lose track of who anyone was. But the feasts remained cordial and well-mannered events.

Sir Hector also persuaded Guy to purchase some additional regalia for the tournament, including a full horse caparison. The large, bright red cape hung down each side of the horse and was shaped around its neck. It was trimmed with heavy gold-coloured scalloped edging and demonstrated the large black bear and ragged staff emblem of Warwick, which were sewn at each corner. The caparison was expensive, but Sir Hector convinced Guy that it was an investment to support his reputation. And reputation, Guy was learning, was everything.

Guy also purchased two shield covers in the same bright red livery, with the Warwick motif in their centre. They were a lot less expensive than the caparison but were equally well made and with the caparison and tunic, they made Guy feel more like a tournament knight.

Guy's contest was arranged for the afternoon of the tournament's first day, and the weather turned out warm, bright, and sunny. Guy had already prepared his equipment during the previous evening and had little to do that morning. So, he accompanied Sir Hector for the usual stroll around the main streets, to see who was there and what was occurring.

Sir Hector was in good spirits. He was full of stories and anecdotes, which Guy always enjoyed hearing, and time passed quickly as they strolled together. It was mid-morning as they returned to the town, after a brief walk around the training fields, when Sir Hector's attention became suddenly diverted.

"Well, well," he said to Guy and pointed to a couple of horses being groomed in a courtyard off the main street. "Recognise the livery?"

"Sir Roderick's," Guy answered.

"Or Otto's," Sir Hector replied. "They both use the same family colour and insignia." "Let us go and check what contest they are competing in."

They walked eagerly to the tournament lists and found that both brothers were enrolled in the tournament, with Otto competing in the Melee, and Roderick in the 'Sword on foot'.

"Excellent," Sir Hector said with enthusiasm. "I will look out for Otto. It will make the contest more interesting."

"In what way?" Guy asked.

"The melee is a way of repaying grudges and knowing Otto, he will still want revenge for my interference at Warwick, or for my treatment of him in the Earl's tournament," Sir Hector was smiling in what Guy thought was excited anticipation. "Otto will not want to do that in the later stages of the melee, as he will appreciate that I would hold the advantage. So, he will look to take me out at the beginning, either by himself or with the help of others."

"Can he enlist the help of others?" Guy asked again.

"Nothing is stopping him, and it is often done, but it cannot be too obvious, as it will damage his reputation and the reputation of his associates who help him," Sir Hector answered. "None of the top knights will want their reputation sullied, so you only ever need to address the possibility of opponents working together at the beginning of the melee. They will be removed sooner rather than later."

Sir Hector paused, and wrinkled his nose, as he thought.

"And I think with Otto, the possibility will be high, so we need to watch who he mixes with, and make careful notes," he then said.

Sir Hector then slapped his hands together and smiled broadly.

"Excellent," he said. "Come on Guy. Let's go to work."

Guy smiled as he watched Sir Hector. He had not seen the knight this happy and excited. It appeared that he liked anything that was out of the normal, especially if it held any risk or threat. Sir Hector suddenly came alive when there was any hint of danger, as if it was an environment that he thrived in.

It did not take long for Guy and Sir Hector to locate Sir Otto and Sir Roderick, who were sitting on benches outside of the main town's tavern, drinking wine from flagons.

Sir Hector and Guy remained in the shadows, under a low overhanging thatch roof. They casually leant against the rough plastered wall and looked closely at Otto's group of companions. Sir Hector only stayed there for a couple of minutes before moving away through the back alleys towards the tournament lists, where the contest entrants were displayed.

"Well, there are at least one of Sir Otto's companions in the melee and at least one in the 'Spear on Horse'. So, we both need to be on guard," Sir Hector said.

"Come on, Guy, I will show you which of Otto's friends you will be facing."

They went back into the shadows outside of the tavern and Sir Hector pointed out a tall thin man with neat, shoulder-length dark hair who was still drinking with Otto and Roderick.

"That is Sir Boden. He will be in a green and white livery with an emblem of a green field with a white diagonal cross and a black two-headed dragon badge," Sir Hector said. "I have seen him fight with sword and he is only barely competent. I do not think you should worry about him."

Sir Hector lightly slapped Guy on the shoulder.

"Anyway, I now know enough about our adversaries, and I think you should eat early, before you go into the contest," he then said, and led Guy away from the tavern.

"Oh, before we go," Sir Hector suddenly added, clasping Guy on the arm, to bring him with him as he turned around to walk back towards the tavern.

"Good day to you Otto," Sir Hector said, as he came alongside the group of men. "And to you also Roderick. What a fine day." He then took a deep breath and looked casually around at his surroundings.

"You already know, 'Guy of Warwick', I believe," he then continued casually. "We are here as guests of the Count. Are you competing today?"

"My regards, Hector," Otto replied with a scowl. "I believe I will see you in the Melee tomorrow."

"Excellent, I will look forward to our meeting," Sir Hector said. "But we can't linger as Guy needs to warm up and practise for the 'Spear on Horse' as it takes him a few bouts to get his eye in." He patted Guy on the shoulder and laughed.

"Good fortune to you in your endeavours," he then said, nodding to the men, and once again looked around at the surroundings. He then turned and walked away with Guy at his side.

"May I ask why?" Guy asked.

Sir Hector smiled.

"Knowledge is always an advantage," he said. "Otto knows that I will be looking out for him in the Melee. That increases my advantage. Otto's friend, Sir Boden, will now be wondering if I am telling the truth about you or not. However, Roderick will know full well that you are not trained with the spear, and he will advise Sir Boden accordingly. So, money will change hands in

bribes, and Sir Boden will be facing you in the first bout."
Sir Hector paused for a moment. "So, you now know who you are facing, and Boden believes, but is not completely sure, that you will not perform well in the first bout. However, he is wrong, as you are just as good from the start. And you also have your surprise which he does not know about. So, your advantage I think."
Guy smiled.

"My surprise?" Guy then asked knowingly.

"Oh, I am looking forward to seeing what it is," Sir Hector responded.

"I hope it works," Guy replied.

Chapter Thirteen

Sir Hector led Guy's horse through the crowd towards the main stand and tied it to the tethering rail on the outside of the fighting arena. The horse was fully protected with head and chest guards and draped with the new red livery of the Earl of Warwick, with its black bear and ragged staff. Bedivere was now fully used to his attire as well as the cheering crowds, so he was not overly agitated or excited about his surroundings. Guy looked across at Bedivere through the opening of his tent and noticed how his horse stood out among the rest and he was filled with sudden pride.

Guy had remained in the tent, as he tightened his harness and selected what he thought was the correct spear for the first bout. He fitted the large, protective, metal sheath to the tip of the spear and fitted the lugs. They were not attached to the front of the blade, as usual for a boar spear, but fixed at the back of the broad wooden shaft and acted like a swords cross guard. He then slipped the shaft through his hands and fingered the carved troughs at the tip of the shaft just before the blade and hoped that he had selected the right spear for Sir Boden. He then took a deep breath and walked out into the open.

The crowds had fully gathered, and the dignitaries were all seated in the stands. Horns were then blown to announce the start of the 'Spear on Horse' contest.

The contestants presented themselves in a line in front of the Count of Soissons, where a herald announced their names aloud.

The contest was a one-on-one fight with spear and shield, although the shield was optional depending on a contestant's horse skills. Guy was competent on a horse and could happily steer Bedivere just by the pressure of his knees on the horse's flanks. This allowed him to hold both shield and spear in each hand, but for this contest, he wanted to concentrate only on his spear and his body position. The shield would have been a distraction.

Guy was competing in the fifth bout of the contest, and, as Sir Hector had predicted, he was facing Sir Boden.

Being down the order allowed Guy to watch the first four contests and the more he saw, the more confident he became.

The contest involved the two opponents riding their horses from wooden rails that were sited at the opposite sides of the arena. The rails acted as the contestant's base and contained a rack of spare spears that they could collect at any time during the bout. The object of the contest was to push their opponent off their horse and onto the ground with a spear. Any rider dismounted for a defined period, determined from a simple sandglass, lost the contest. The rules were simple in that only the spear can be used to strike and push an opponent. Any strike on a horse will disqualify the offending contestant and a broken or dropped spear could be replaced by obtaining another from their rack of spares. Obtaining a spare spear, however, presents the opposing rider with an easy target and a high risk of injury. So dismounted riders were able to yield the fight to their opponent by lying still on the floor for the time duration.

"Well Guy, what do you think?" Sir Hector asked Guy, as he helped him to mount Bedivere at the holding rail.

"It is as I thought, Sir Hector," Guy replied. "It requires a degree of horsemanship, but mainly requires just determination, composure and an understanding of speed and force."

The horn sounded for the next bout and Guy picked up his selected spear and took hold of Bedivere's reins.

"Let's hope my understanding of forces aligns with my ability to apply them," Guy said and then pushed his helmet onto his head.

Guy then kicked his horse forward and entered the arena.

"What did they say?" Guy asked. But he could tell from Sir Hector's reaction that all was well.

"They just questioned the spear lugs, and I suggested that you usually impale your Boars with such force that they needed to be fixed further up the shaft," Sir Hector said. "They understood that they had no grounds to uphold any complaints, and at the same time they loved the spectacle."

"Thank you, Sir Hector," Guy said, smiling excitedly.

"Do not thank me, Guy," Sir Hector replied. "I did little. The Count, however, would like to meet up with us this evening to discuss your style and tactics. He was most entertained at your display and wondered if this was how we fought in our home tournaments."

"What did you tell him?" Guy asked.

"I said it was inspired from our travels across Francia and was an ongoing development from our daily training sessions," Sir Hector replied. "He was also most impressed that I was involved in your training."

He smiled warmly at Guy and helped him to unfasten the leather straps of his breastplate.

"I said that my training was only a minor influence. But of course, he took this as false modesty, and I didn't correct him."

"And your reputation increases," Guy said laughing.

"Of course, and with such little effort."

"But I cannot be this master instructor, if I do not know what was going on with your spears," Sir Hector added.

"It's all about forces," Guy replied, now eager to tell of his innovation.

"It seemed to me that when on a gallop you need to be the first to plant the spear point on your opponent with enough force to knock him backwards. This is before the force of impact pushes the spear backwards through your grip or your opponent's spear hits you. So, you need to increase the grip, hence bringing the lugs back to create a crossguard. This prevents the shaft sliding through your hand on impact."

Guy picked up a spear and gripped the shaft behind the lugs.

"A direct hit will, however, apply the full force of the charging horse through the shaft and then to the crossguard. This will then be applied to the rider's arm forcing him backwards."

Guy then held the spear forward and pulled his arm backwards to imitate the force of a hit.

"Therefore, you have to remove the force of impact by allowing the shaft to contract and then break."

Guy then rammed the spear into a large post, and it splintered and broke at the point where Guy had carved into the wooden shaft.

"The skill, however, is weakening the shaft enough to make sure that it breaks at a point where your opponent can not recover from the force of impact."

"But if it breaks and dismounts the rider, then there will still be time to retrieve another spear," Sir Hector said, nodding to show his comprehension.

"My advantage," Guy said.

"And if it doesn't break?" Sir Hector asked.

"Then the force of impact would not have been great enough to cause me any serious difficulty, or it will just unseat me."

Sir Hector considered Guy's tactics.

"So, you have a selection of spears from which you can choose, depending on your opponent's size and weight," Sir Hector said.

"Yes, but I also need to measure the speed at which my opponent charges at me and the speed which I attack my opponent. The spear will not break at anything other than a gallop towards a stationary target," Guy replied.

"But you have less chance of being knocked off at low speeds."

"Well done, Guy," Sir Hector then said smiling. "It was impressive, and you are now the champion of 'Spear on Horse'.

Guy smiled and thought back to the contest.

Guy had faced Sir Boden from across the arena and as soon as the horn blew to start the contest, he charged straight at Guy. Guy waited for a few moments to observe Boden's style of riding, kicked Bedivere and charged back at Sir Bolden.

They came together in the middle of the arena with a loud crash and cracking noise and the tip of Guy's spear flew up into the air. Sir Boden flew directly backwards off the horse and remained still on the ground.

Guy's other four bouts were not as quick as Sir Boden's. However, Guy only suffered a couple of hits, but with little force and they were deflected easily along with his fluted chest plate. He did, however, strike and push all his other opponents off their horses and break six of his spears in the process. The crowd roared every time Guy's spears broke on his opponent's bodies, sending shards of wood into the air. Two of the opponents remained on the floor, winded and they yielded the fight. Guy herded another opponent away from their base for the time duration. The contestant in the final bout was knocked off his horse unconscious and had to be carried out of the arena.

A complaint against the design of Guy's spears was made by Sir Boden, but with representation from Sir Hector, the spears were judged to be within the rules and the complaint was dismissed.

The spears did not cause any other of the contestants any issues and after the competition ended, most of them had come to congratulate Guy on his victory and to examine his spears.

Guy was awarded a gold medal and a purse of coin for his victory, which was worth the equivalent of Guy's annual upkeep as a squire for Earl Rohan. He gave Sir Hector half of his winnings, as promised, but then had to accept a return promise of half of the winnings if Sir Hector won the melee.

After the excitement and esteem of his victory, Guy quickly come down to earth, as he then had to carry out his groom's duties by seeing to Bedivere as well as Sir Hector's horse. He then had to hurry to get washed and dressed, ready for the night's entertainment.

Guy had to rush to get to the main hall, where a tournament official waited for him at the door and took him aside in preparation for the night's feast. As was the custom of the Soissons's tournament, Guy was brought into the hall, seated on a wooden throne, mounted on long poles. He was carried shoulder high by his fellow contestants, which, although it made him self-conscious, gave Guy a feeling of immense satisfaction.

"You see Guy. It is all about reputation," Sir Hector said as Guy eventually took his seat beside him and then applauded the competition winner of the 'Sword on Foot' contest, as he was also carried into the hall on a wooden throne.

"And on the whole, you have made a good start in creating yours," he continued and raised his glass to Guy.

Guy sat back in his chair and smiled to himself. He felt happy at his achievements, but he wondered if this newly gained reputation, really mattered, and in what new direction his life might take because of it.

The warm feeling of contentment was still with Guy, as he woke early the next morning. He lay on his bed and wondered what Felice would have thought of his recent accomplishments. Guy was always an early riser, and he spent the first few moments of the day reflecting on his life. That nearly always meant thinking of Felice and remembering the brief times that they had shared together. He would reflect closely on the individual moments and try and detect any hidden meanings that lay behind certain words or looks. He also pondered on what she might be doing at that moment in time, and if she ever lay in her bed and wondered what he was doing, in the same way. But, as always, he gave it up as fantasy, and shook the dreams from his mind, to focus on the reality of the present.

He arose from his bed and considered the tasks that were required of him. He was then hit with a sense of excited anticipation on the day ahead, as this was the day of the melee, the tournament's main event. Guy was looking forward to watching Sir Hector perform again. With a keen sense of expectation, he quickly dressed and swiftly left his room to prepare Sir Hector's horse.

It was later in the morning than Guy had thought and there was already a lot of palace workers and town's folk up and about. Guy could feel the heightened excitement in the bustle of the people, as they carried out their daily jobs with increased enthusiasm. Guy went straight to the palace stables and sought out both Bedivere and Sir Hector's horse.

Guy watered and fed them both, before focusing his attention on Sir Hector's horse. He meticulously brushed down his coat until it shone in the morning sun and then dressed it in light bridles before leading it out of the stables and across the town to exercise it.

The melee was the centrepiece event of any tournament and would always attract more spectators than the other contests. More spectators meant more trade and the street merchants were busy stocking their stalls with a wide array of products and goods for sale. As Guy walked down the main street, he could see small groups of people that were already hurrying towards the tournament arena to reserve good seats. Food and ale were at hand within most of the inns and taverns, as they had opened their houses early and money was already being gambled on the melee's winner.

The melee's other competitors were also preparing themselves and horses were being walked and groomed on every road. The day was warm but overcast, with little likelihood of rain. They were ideal conditions for the competition and Guy's anticipation was increasing by the minute.

Guy made his way to the training area and settled the horse at the edge of the first field. He folded a light blanket over the horse and jumped up across its back before swinging his legs over to sit astride it. He then lightly kicked the horse on and cantered it around the edge of the large rectangular grass field. There were other squires, who like Guy were also exercising their master's horses and they all nodded to him as they passed, to show their respect. Guy understood that this was all because of his victory in the 'Spear on Horse' contest, as they had not been so sociable over the last few days. Sir Hector's insistence that reputation was everything was becoming more evident every day.

Guy was halfway around the length of the field when there was a loud thud beneath him and the horse twitched heavily and then reared, throwing Guy backwards and onto the ground. The horse then rolled over sideward to the ground, before stumbling back to its feet, whinnying in pain. Guy, winded from the fall, gasped for breath. The pain in his chest made him bring his arms around to hug his body, as he rolled to his side, trying to protect himself from being kicked by the horse. The injured animal was still crying out in pain as it staggered on its feet, finding it difficult to remain upright. Guy tried to regain his composure and get to his feet to attend to the horse. But before he could get off his knees, the beast collapsed onto the floor in front of him with an arrow, that was buried deep into its flank, pointing upwards towards the sky.

Two other squires had ridden straight over to Guy to offer their help. One got down off his horse and hurried to Guy's side to see if he could assist.

"Are you alright, Guy of Warwick?" The lad said in a thick accent and held out his hand to Guy, who was kneeling upright.

Guy allowed himself to be pulled up and instantly regretted it as the pain shot through his chest. He looked down at the horse, which was now lying still on its side, breathing heavily.

"I am alright," Guy replied. "Thank you. But can you go and fetch Sir Hector, who is residing at the palace, as a guest of the Count and bring him back here straight away."

"I will go now," the lad said and got back on the horse and rode quickly away towards the town.

Guy then walked carefully over to the horse, which was now been examined by the other squire. He inspected the arrow in its side and cautiously looked over in the direction from where it was fired from. There was a wooded area at the far side of the field, but Guy could detect no movement.

Other riders had now gathered and as they saw the arrow and the direction of Guy's stare, they rode off quickly to see if they could find the perpetrator.

"It is no good," the squire stroking the horse's neck, said. "We need to put it out of its torment." He stood up and bowed his head to Guy. "I will go to the smith and fetch a hammer or axe," he said and ran away towards the town.

Guy, not knowing what else to do, sat on the floor in front of the horse's neck and continued stroking it from its ears downwards and waited. Its large brown eye stared up at him and Guy, looking into it, could recognise its fear.

It was not long before Sir Hector rode up, upon another horse, and quickly dismounted next to Guy.

"Are you alright Guy? Are not hurt?" He asked quickly with concern.

"No, I am not injured, my lord. But I do not think there is any hope for your horse."

Sir Hector examined the injury and unhappily shook his head, just as the squire returned with a large hammer.

"My lord," the squire said as he nodded to Sir Hector and handed him the hammer.

"Thank you," Sir Hector said. He then reached for the blanket that was on the horse's back and pulled it away from under the horse's body, before laying it gently across its face. He then swung the hammer straight down onto the horse's temple, killing it instantly. Sir Hector then went and snapped the arrow from the side of the horse and tucked it into his tunic.

"I am sorry Sir Hector," Guy said with deep regret.

"You could not have anticipated this, Guy. I am just glad you were not harmed."

All the squires had now gathered around the dead horse. One of the riders confirmed that they could find no one in the wood from where the arrow was fired.

Sir Hector was thanking the squires and pages for their assistance when more people ran up from the town to see what was happening. There were considerable murmurings and a few knights and nobles, who Sir Hector was acquainted with, came to have words with him. Their anger at the attack was evident.

Sir Hector quickly made arrangements with some of the local town's folk to have the horse removed. He did not want to know the details, but he suspected that it would end up with the local butcher. Sir Hector, however, was pragmatic about its final fate and just patted the dead horse on its flank, before walking back to the palace with Guy at his side.

When they entered the palace grounds, Sir Hector took out the broken arrow, with its white fletching, from beneath his tunic.

"What is your opinion on the arrow, Guy?" He said, handing it to Guy.

Guy looked at it closely.

"It is well made and of good quality," Guy replied.

"And I believe it hit its target," Sir Hector said. "I first thought that you were its intent, but I am now convinced that it was meant for my mount."

"Why?" Guy asked.

"Because of the quality of the arrow and the distance that it was fired from," Sir Hector answered. "If the bastard was less competent, then he would have waited until you were closer to him, but hitting you where you were, at the opposite side of the field gave him more time to retreat. He must have been confident on hitting his target."

Guy thought for a while.

"To force you to retire from the melee, or take away your chance of winning," Guy said.

"That's what I think. But there may be other reasons that I have not thought of yet." Sir Hector replied.

They both walked on in silence as they pondered the other reasons.

"Can I ask a favour from you, Guy?" Sir Hector then said.

"Certainly, Sir Hector."

"Can I borrow Bedivere for the melee? I could easily get a spare horse, but I have watched you many times in how you control him. I think I can replicate your touch and perhaps even repeat your last manoeuvre from Warwick. I know Bedivere is familiar with that."

"Of course, Sir Hector," Guy instantly replied.

"Thank you, but I now need to practise and become acquainted with Bedivere and adjust my style. So, I, therefore, need another favour."

"Anything," Guy replied.

"It is the archery contest this morning," Sir Hector said quietly. "Can you take the arrow and see if you can discover its match and who owns them."

"And you know where I would look first," Sir Hector added.

"Otto," Guy said.

Sir Hector nodded. "Or, more likely, one of his companions."

Guy was early to the archery range and there was little activity in the field, so he went into town to walk the streets. There was an atmosphere of great excitement in the town, and Guy could sense people looking at him, or he overheard his name whispered as he passed. But Sir Hector's name was also being bandied around in abundance, and as Guy listened, he could hear that it was mainly related to betting. The odds of Sir Hector winning had now been drastically reduced.

He discovered Otto and Roderick together in the Inn and they were happily talking together, but they had no weapons at hand and no other companions.

Guy went back to his room and picked up a large, hooded top that would hide his face and his archery equipment. He then went back towards the archery field to mull around the range, observe the bowmen and join in with the practice.

Guy came across Sir Hector in the training field, in which Guy was attacked that morning. Sir Hector was riding around on Bedivere and when he saw Guy, he rode over 'scalloping' the horse in a series of semi-circles.

"How does that look," Sir Hector said with delight.

"Looks good," Guy replied smiling.

"I have not felt this excited for a long time. It must be the challenge of something new."

"Did you find out anything?" He then asked.

"Blue and yellow stripes with a red border," Guy replied.

"The Dukedom of Burgundy," Sir Hector said. "Are you sure?"

"I am fairly confident," Guy said and passed Sir Hector the broken arrow that killed his horse and then a full arrow that he had taken from the archer at the practice ground.

"How did you get this?" Sir Hector said looking at the arrows closely.

"I was shooting nearly alongside him at practice and picked it up by mistake," Guy replied smiling.

"You are right. They are the same," Sir Hector said passing them back to Guy. "Was he better than you?"

"No," Guy said with good-humoured indignation.

"And did he recognise you?"

"I do not think so. I was wearing a hood, and I didn't stay long." Guy then patted Bedivere's neck.

Sir Hector stroked his chin as he considered Guy's news.

"So why does the Duke of Burgundy want me out of the melee? And does it have anything to do with Ebles, which is probable, as he has a finger in many a pie?" Sir Hector said. "And I do not know why they would act in support of Sir Otto." He tapped the side of his cheek in concentration. "So why would Richard or Ebles want me to lose the melee?" He thought aloud.

"Perhaps he has bet against you," Guy stated.

"I doubt that Ebles requires funds that badly, but it may be to support his offer of a contract," Sir Hector said and looked more serious. "If I lose at the melee then I am without funds and although that would not bother me, it may be beyond the understanding of Ebles and his greed. I may have to ask some more questions, but can you watch Ebles and Richard, the Duke of Burgundy at the melee, Guy, and see how they react when I win."

"If you are going to win, Sir Hector," Guy asked cautiously. "Am I allowed to put a bet on you? You are no longer a favourite, and I can get very good odds."

"I do not usually condone betting Guy," he replied with a look of seriousness. "But, as I am feeling very confident, I think it would be all right this once. Especially as you have promised to donate some of the winnings to a worthy cause," he said smirked.

"I always deliver on my promises, Sir Hector." Guy smiled and walked away.

Guy finished brushing Bedivere down and patted him on the hindquarters, before walking out of the stables. He left the palace and wandered down the main street and smiled at the reverie, as people celebrated what was an entertaining finale to the tournament. Drinks flowed, people sang happily, and Guy collected his winnings.

Sir Hector used his 'scalloping' to great effect until he worked out who was working with Sir Otto, before ruthlessly taking them out of the contest. He then, as he said he would, sought out Sir Otto and effortlessly danced around him and made him look slow and clumsy before grounding him with over excessive force. Guy smiled at the thought. He had seen Sir Hector fight on foot in a melee, but never on horseback, and it was impressive. He understood why he was renowned and why his reputation was so respected. Sir Hector constantly inspired Guy, every time he saw him fight.

After the melee, Sir Hector congratulated Guy on his horse. But when Guy's told him of both Ebles and

Richard of Burgundy's disappointment in Sir Hector winning the contest, he wanted to go and have a chat with a few people. Guy understood that these were his private affairs, so he contented himself with returning to his squire's duties in stabling Bedivere and then cleaning Sir Hector's armour and weapons. The town and stables were buzzing with analysis and appreciation of the fighting and Sir Hector's treatment of Otto did not go unnoticed. More than once, Guy heard comments that it must have been retribution for the killing of his horse. So, Sir Hector's reputation had increased, and Otto's was diminished.

"So, if it isn't 'Guy of Warwick'," a mocking voice called out from a doorway of a tavern to Guy's right.

Guy was walking down the town's main street, trying to find Sir Hector, as the evening feast was approaching, and the Duke's aides were seeking him to arrange the formalities that surrounded the tournament champion.

Guy looked to his side to see Sir Roderick standing there, with a skin of wine in his hand. He looked dishevelled and worse for the drink.

"As you see, my lord," Guy replied, with an equally mocking tone against Roderick's title.

"And how are the Earl and his precious daughter?" He asked, dropping the leather skin onto the floor, as he walked towards Guy.

"The Earl was in good spirits when I left," Guy answered. "And his daughter is still precious."

Roderick stood in front of Guy and stared hard into Guy's eyes.

Roderick's breath was stale and sour, but Guy remained calm and stared back with a confidence that surprised him. A few months ago, Guy would have backed away and acted subservient to Sir Roderick's bullying.

"So, you dare show your face away from the protection of Sir Hector," Sir Roderick said with slight anger in his voice.

"Sir Hector is not with me. As you see," Guy said. "But he was not with me at Atherstone when the Earl's party was attacked by mercenaries."

Guy's reply was full of insinuation, and he watched Sir Roderick closely to judge his reaction. Guy was not disappointed. Sir Roderick was caught off guard and could not hide his expression of guilt. Guy was now convinced that he had a hand in the attack.

"What have you found there, Roderick?" Another voice called from Guy's right.

"Nothing much," Sir Roderick replied to his brother, as Otto also strolled over to confront Guy.

"Two against one," Guy whispered to Roderick. "Better odds for you now, my lord."

Roderick pushed out at Guy with both hands, intending to force him backwards, but Guy was expecting it and turned his body to sidestep the attack. Roderick stumbled forward, and not being able to hold his balance, fell to the ground.

There were a few good-natured catcalls from the spectators that lined the streets, who were now paying attention to the confrontation. Guy smiled at them as he walked on as if nothing had happened. Then he heard the ring of steel as a sword was drawn from its scabbard and he quickly turned around to face his adversaries.

It was Otto who had drawn his sword and he held its point towards Guy. There was now a hush in the street, as the onlookers' sensed real trouble.

Guy smiled at Otto and then looked down over the front of his body. With an air of arrogance, he held the palm of his hands upwards to emphasise that he was unarmed. He then raised his eyebrows and smiled broadly at Sir Otto. Guy knew he should not provoke

Otto, but he did not feel frightened, and the crowd filled him with a certain sense of bravado.

Otto was then pushed aside by Roderick, who had regained his feet and had also drawn his sword.

"I will deal with him," Sir Roderick shouted angrily at his brother, as he pushed past Otto to approach Guy.

Guy again smiled and did not believe that even Roderick would attack an unarmed man in front of a crowd of witnesses.

But then a sword fell with a thud onto the ground in front of him, as someone had decided to aid Guy. But now Guy understood the seriousness of the situation. If he picked up the sword, it was then a legitimate duel. Guy looked at the weapon on the ground and knew that honour demanded that he picked it up.

Guy took a deep breath and bent down to grab the sword by its handle and as he did Roderick ran at him with his own sword raised above his head.

It was déjà vu for Guy, as Sir Roderick's actions were a repeat of the training fight in Warwick only a few months before. Guy waited until Roderick was upon him and then simply parried upwards, swivelled his body to his right, released the pressure on his sword and brought the pommel around and hard into Roderick's face. There was a crunching noise as bones broke and screaming as Roderick cried out in pain. He then fell to the floor holding his face as blood poured out from between his fingers. But Guy had turned again and readied himself for any attack from Otto, which he fully expected. But Otto was standing up straight with his sword hanging to his side and a knife held across his throat.

"Nice and easy, Otto," Sir Hector said, who was standing behind Otto and holding the knife. "Drop your sword."

Otto did as he was told.

"Kindly pick it up, Guy," he then said.

Guy casually picked up the sword and Sir Hector removed the blade from Otto's throat and calmly pushed him forward.

Sir Hector then took Otto's sword from Guy and threw it to the side.

"I am willing to account for you and your brother's behaviour as drunken stupidity," he then said to Otto. "And I will say no more about it. But any more threats to either Guy or myself will be considered as a vendetta and I will have more to say about that," the threat was heavy in his tone

Sir Hector then held his hand out towards Guy.

"Can I have my sword back please, Guy?"

Guy wiped each side of the blade across his trousers to clean it and then cleaned the blood off the pommel by rubbing it on the bottom of his tunic. He then handed it over to him hilt first and Sir Hector pushed it back into its scabbard.

"Shall we go now? We have a feast to attend," Sir Hector said, with an air of nonchalance and there was a ripple of applause from the gathered people and a few shouts of support followed them, as they walked away.

Guy tried to be casual as they walked, but he felt a weakness in his knees at what happened, and what might have happened.

"You were not concerned that I might have been killed?" Guy asked quietly.

"Not at all. I have seen you fight with a sword before and that move on Roderick was exactly as you described it would be when you practised at Warwick. I am most impressed how you can analyse and execute with conviction." He smiled and then continued. "You had also built up the tension nicely, and it would have been churlish to step in. Even though Otto is more competent with the sword than Roderick, you would have probably beaten him as well. But you might have had to wound or even kill him in the process, so I thought that enough was enough, and intervened. I hope you didn't mind?"

"Not at all," Guy replied.

"And it seems only fair that if I borrow your horse, then you should borrow my sword," Sir Hector then said light-heartedly. "I think that makes us even."

"I would think so," Guy answered

"God, it's good to have you around, Guy," Sir Hector said. "It makes life much more interesting; I don't think I have enjoyed myself so much for years." He rubbed his hands together and chuckled.

They attended the Count's end of tournament feast and Guy was amused when Sir Hector was carried in on the winner's platform. He did not look like he enjoyed the experience, and he held the side of the throne with clenched hands. Although he tried to put on a calm visage, Guy knew him well enough now to recognise his trepidation at not being in control. But he was eventually lowered down in front of the top table to a standing ovation. He lightly waved at the crowd's applause and took his seat next to the Count, where all the contest winners sat. As winner of the 'Spear on Horse', Guy was also sitting at that top table, but a couple of places away from Sir Hector. Guy had already made the acquaintance of the Count, who Guy thought was very polite and friendly, and had also managed to talk to other guests in a mix of languages.

Guy had already scanned the hall for Otto or Roderick and saw neither. He was therefore able to settle down to enjoy the evening, all the more for their absence. They ate and drank well and there were numerous entertainments in jugglers, acrobats, and storytellers

Guy had reasonable conversations with the contest winners that sat either side of him. Guy was pleased that his language skills were improving, although his neighbours spoke English very well and the feast passed quickly because of it.

Towards the end of the evening, Sir Hector came and sat alongside Guy, as the other guests had started to mingle with their own friends and the seats on either side of Guy had become vacant.

"All in all, an excellent tournament," Sir Hector said, looking quite content and happy.

"We have our tournament winnings, and we have increased our reputations, which was the prime objective. However, you also have your betting winnings and I have been given the pick of the Count's horses to replace the one killed, which the Count seems to feel responsible for. I will choose a horse of great worth, so there is also increased profit there." Sir Hector added.

Sir Hector then looked at Guy. "But away from profit, you have increased your fighting skills as well as your knowledge and experience in life. I believe that I may have done the same," he then said thoughtfully. "I think that we are quite good for each other. I will be sorry to take you back to Warwick."

He paused and then smiled to himself, as he sat back in his chair and placed his hands on his chest with intertwined fingers.

"Especially as we have both been invited back to compete in the Count's next tournament, and so, by proxy, to the King's tournament. That will be an extravagant and prodigious event, so all in all, it has been a good outing for us both."

"What we now need Guy, is to make you a Knight of the Realm, as soon as possible," Sir Hector said, thoughtfully.

"Is that possible," Guy asked with sudden excitement.

"Earl Rohan has the authority, so perhaps I should have a word with him on our return," Sir Hector replied.

"I would be very grateful if you would," Guy said.

"I know it means a lot to you for many reasons," Sir Hector said with a sly smile on his face. "But let us see how it goes, you need to be fully prepared and trained before you raise yourself to that level. But I think that you are well on your way. However, do not hold your hopes up too high Guy, as the Earl is a stickler for formality and likes his process and procedures, and you are still very young to be advanced to knighthood.

They sat in silence for a while, as Guy reflected on what Sir Hector had said, but then he put the dreams aside. He looked at Sir Hector and thought it might be a good time to risk asking a couple of questions that were on his mind.

"And how about all you're other businesses?" Guy asked. "Were they profitable?"

Sir Hector paused and looked at Guy.

"How much do you know about what I do?" He asked.

"Not much at all, Sir Hector," Guy quickly answered. "But needless to say, your reputation is very highly respected."

Sir Hector placed his hand on his chin and lightly stroked his cheek as he considered his response

"My fighting skills are not reserved only for tournaments. Although I would be able to make a good living out of it," Sir Hector said, thoughtfully.

"I also fulfil contracts of employment that make the most of my skills, and when I accept a contract, I will honour it. I also make it a rule not to discuss contracts, and I will remain impartial when I deliver the contract."

"This is also what adds to my reputation, and I may fulfil a contract to one party one week and fulfil another contract to an opposing party the next week, without bias."

"But I have total freedom to choose who I agree a contract with, and I try to choose wisely. With that choice, I trust in God."

"How is that?" Guy asked

"As you know I am constantly gathering knowledge, as it has great worth both in winning fights and judging who to fight for. I judge with my conscience and not for reward, and God, I hope, guides my judgement." Sir Hector became more thoughtful. "I am sure I have made mistakes, but I fulfil my contract and trust in God. God will have to weigh up the balance when I depart this mortal life."

"And you donate your winnings and payments to good causes," Guy said.

"Yes, to try and swing the balance my way," Sir Hector replied and then laughed. "But it is reward enough to help the good souls of this world, and I have many true friends amongst them. Hopefully, if they go to God before me, they will put in a good word."

"And may I ask about Ebles," Guy asked?

"On individual contracts, I will not discuss Guy. As I have already said, it is part of my reputation, and knowing my business will put you in danger. I would like to hold true to my promise to Earl Rohand and return you safely back to Warwick."

"However, Guy," he then continued. "On judging Count Elbes, with the little you know of him, what would you do in my position?"

"Does it mean taking sides?" Guy asked.

"In this case, yes," Sir Hector answered.

"I do not think that I have sufficient knowledge to answer, as I do not know the other side. But on face value, I do not trust Ebles, but then again, the other side may be worse," Guy answered. "How would you choose if it was a choice between Ebles or Otto?"

Sir Hector laughed.

"I would think that I had done something to upset God and that he was making it hard for me. But one may have the more righteous cause. Or I could just as easily decline both."

"Would someone hire you if they know they have an unrighteous cause?" Guy asked, keen for the conversation to continue.

"They have, and they will continue to try," Sir Hector replied. "But I find that most people think that they are in the right, and God is on their side. I rarely meet evil people, just misguided people."

"Not wanting to be discourteous, Sir Hector, but what gives you the right to judge."

"Well done Guy. That is the crux of it," he said smiling and he slapped his hand on the table. "And it is a question I constantly ask myself and the answer is simple. I believe God has given me the skills to do his work. God had given me the morals by which I live my life and God has guided me with the choices I have made and therefore God has moulded me for this position of judgement. I just need to put the effort in to gather enough information to provide an informed choice to make that judgement."

Sir Hector looked over at Guy for a reaction, but Guy sat in silence and mulled over Sir Hector's words. Sir Hector considered himself the tool of God and Guy tried to balance that with the positions of King's who also claimed that they acted with God's will.

"And I pray that I am justified in my actions," Sir Hector continued as he observed Guy's contemplation.

"And several good people in this world also pray for me and that my judgements are sound," he added.

"I will pray for you also," Guy said.

Sir Hector now laughed aloud.

"I believe that you have just judged yourself as a good person, Guy. Let's hope God is with you as well."

They then drank their wine and retired to their beds, bidding their host a good night.

Chapter Fourteen

Guy and Sir Hector planned to leave Soissons late the following morning, as Sir Hector wanted to get back onto the open road. He had commented that there had been too much excitement during their stay at Soissons and he looked forward to a more peaceful time. Guy, however, suspected that he had enough of the constant attention of the many strangers and just wanted to return to the more solitary life of travelling.

After securing their belongings onto their packhorse, Sir Hector went into the stables and selected a proud black destrier from the Count's personal stock. The warhorse was both battle-trained and battle experienced and had come with the recommendation of the Count's groom. The young boy seemed to be quite in awe of Sir Hector and went out of his way to help him. The groom, however, did ask for his involvement in the choice of the horse to be kept between the two of them and not disclosed to the Count. He was concerned that he might suffer the Count's displeasure at the loss of such a valuable horse. The groom also arranged for an exchange of saddles and bridles, as Sir Hector's old tack was a poor fit for the new horse and Sir Hector was pleased that the new equipment was of better quality.

They left the town quietly, without any recognition from the tournament administration, or from the people of the town, and once again they were content with their own company.

"Where are we heading to now?" Guy asked as they rode into woodland.

"I would like to travel to Normandy," Sir Hector said. "Which is back towards the coast, where we can arrange a voyage back to Britain. I did think of travelling through Paris, but I have had enough of large towns for the moment, so we will bypass it and keep to the country roads.

"What awaits us in Normandy?" Guy asked.

"I would like to meet up with a renowned Danish Jarl called Rollo, who is the Duke of Normandy. He is an old man now, but he is still formidable in both mind and body."

"Have you met him before?"

"Yes, but only in passing. He is allied to King Charles and defends the West Francia lands from any attacks from other Danes. My brief acquaintance with him, and my association with Charles, should provide me with an audience."

"Are you familiar with Charles?" Guy asked.

"Yes, I have met him many times and rode with him once when I was around your age, in the defence of Lotharingia against East Francia," Sir Hector said. "He is an interesting person, although very headstrong. But that makes him loyal to his friends and allies."

Sir Hector shook his head and smiled to himself. "Which is why I suspect he continues his association with his friend Hagano, who is not at all liked by the nobility of Francia," Sir Hector continued. "But Charles is not a stupid man, and I would like to know what hold, or influence, Hagano has over him to make Charles alienate his other supporters."

"I may not get to know it from Charles, but I might learn it from Rollo, who remains Charles's close ally," Sir Hector said.

The second day of their journey from Soissons started fair, but soon became cold and blustery. It did not take long for the sky to then turn dark and for the rain to hammer down. They were caught in the open when the deluge hit them, and it took an hour before they found shelter. It came in the form of an empty and disused barn that was half-hidden in a clump of small trees alongside the road. The barn roof was missing in places and other parts leaked heavily, but there were areas under which they could shelter and eventually light a fire to get warm and dry their clothes.

They sat close together around the fire trying to maximise its heat and they shivered incessantly, as the rain roared outside and splashed heavily on the barn floor around them. Guy made a drink of hot nettle tea, to try and take the cold away, which seemed to have spread into his bones.

But after the drink, Guy started to feel unwell and he started to shiver more violently, accompanied by beads of sweat on his forehead.

The coming of the rain seemed to have coincided with Guy catching a fever, which got progressively worse as the day passed. Come the night, Guy was burning up and complaining of severe headaches and pains in his joints.

Sir Hector was becoming concerned and piled as much wood on the fire, as he thought safe, to keep Guy warm without setting the remaining roof alight.

Sir Hector sat up throughout the night and constantly applied a wet cloth to Guy's forehead to try and stem the fever. Guy tossed and turned in his sleep and spoke nonsense as the fever showed no sign of abating.

As dawn broke, Sir Hector reluctantly left Guy alone in the barn to go in search of any herbs that might help in easing Guy's suffering, or to find any local farmers that might know of a healer. Overnight, Sir Hector had become increasingly concerned about Guy's condition, as he had seen many a man die from such fevers.

The rain had not stopped, and it fell from the sky in a vertical curtain. It once again drenched Sir Hector, as the rain ran down his neck to seep underneath his leather cape to soak his undergarments and chill his flesh. He struggled up the road, looking desperately along hedgerows and in the scattered woodland, constantly brushing away the rivulets of rain that ran down his forehead and into his eyes.

It was mid-morning when Sir Hector dashed back into the barn to check on Guy, who was barely lucid and not aware of his condition or surroundings. He was still hot to the touch and shivered incessantly.

But Sir Hector was relieved that he was still alive and banked the fire with wood and then went about mashing roots and berries on the inside of a large piece of bark. He boiled water on the fire and when it was bubbling, he infused small measures of the crushed plants into it. Once he was happy with the consistency and taste of the mixture, he held Guy's chin and poured small amounts into his mouth.

It took an hour for the effects of the remedy to start and Guy noticeably calmed. By late afternoon he was awake and conscious, although he complained of sickness, aches, and a banging headache. But Sir Hector was happy that he was over the worse, and mixed another concoction, that he made Guy drink. He banked the fire up again before lying on the ground, alongside Guy, to fall into a deep sleep. The rain outside continued its downpour.

The next day was also wet and windy, but the rain had diminished. When Sir Hector awoke, Guy was still asleep, but he seemed calm, and the colour had returned to his face. Sir Hector roused him at intervals and fed him a broth which was laced with more of the crushed herbs, although a combination of the mixture and the fever soon sent him back to sleep again. But Guy was now aware of his illness and his dependency on his friend. When he was conscious, he continually repeated his thanks to Sir Hector, who just smiled at him and encouraged him to eat more.

On the third morning of their stay in the barn, Sir Hector woke to the smell of cooking and found Guy sitting up with a rabbit spitted over the fire.

"How are you feeling today, Guy?" He quickly asked, as he sat up and stretched his back.

"On a par with how I felt after the 'Squire's Melee," Guy answered. "But I think I feel much better than yesterday and although I do not remember much about the day, I do recall thinking that I was going to die."

"You had quite a fever."

"Which you worked your magic on, my lord." Guy looked over at Sir Hector. "Thank you for your aid, Sir Hector. I am very grateful," he said with solemnity.

"No thanks required, Guy. It gave me something to do while it rained," he replied smiling and then looked around. "It seems to have abated."

"Yes, I think it will be a fine day. The rabbits were in abundance and pleased to get out of their burrows to feed. I fired my arrow from within the doorway."

Sir Hector looked closely at Guy.

"Now tell me how you are really feeling, as you still need to rest. We are in no hurry to leave, and you will need to build your strength up."

"I feel weak and nauseous," Guy replied in a more serious tone. "Especially after any exertion. I have a headache and my whole-body aches, so I would appreciate a rest, but I feel bad in delaying you, Sir Hector."

"I have no plans, Guy, which warrant any haste. The most important thing to me now is your health."

Guy improved throughout the day and after their evening meal, they both sat around the fire in their contemplations.

"Thank you again for healing me from the fever, Sir Hector," Guy stated. "I owe you my life."

"There is no need to keep thanking me, Guy. Just thank God for providing some Belladonna and Wolf's Bane. He must have been looking down on you." Sir Hector was thoughtful as he spoke.

"It was remiss of me not to carry a stock of these remedies and I did not know if I could find any of the plants at such short notice. I prayed that they might be growing in the vicinity, and it was God's will that they were," Sir Hector said in a serious tone as he remembered the sense of dread that he felt in not being able to find the medicinal herbs.

"Granted, you need to know where to look," Sir Hector continued. "And you then need to know how to mix the ingredients, because they are poisonous, as well as medicinal, and they can just as easily kill you, if you get the infusions wrong."

"But God decided long ago that I should learn the use of his plants and herbs, and perhaps it was all for this one moment, so that I could heal you. Perhaps there is a great purpose for you Guy, which has God's grace and protection."

"Or perhaps I am just lucky," Guy said, and he felt into the inside pocket of his tunic to touch Felice's silk token. "Where did you learn the use of plants?" Guy then asked.

"From my mother," Sir Hector replied. "She had a particular skill in understanding ailments and their remedies. People came from far and wide to get her help. She was always at hand in the town to assist in births and sometimes in deaths. The folk held her in a mixture of both awe and respect."

Sir Hector stared into the fire, as memories came back. " But even with the burden of all her patient's care, she did not neglect her role as my mother and made sure that I thrived and learned. She taught me her healing ways, using the different plants and herbs that grew in the woods and hedgerows. I learned which were poisonous and which weren't, how to collect them and understand their different parts and properties. How to dry them to store them and finally to prepare and mix them. And as you know, I am always keen to learn."

"But as her renown grew in the local community, the church felt that their power was being threatened by her skills and they suddenly decided to brandish her a witch."

He shook his head slowly.

"The bastards thought that only God could heal people and my mother's skills were considered heresy," Sir Hector said angrily. "She tried to tell them that her potions were accompanied by prayer, but it was an affront to their power, as people went to her first for comfort and healing and then afterwards to the church. The church wanted to burn her."

"But you said that she was still alive," Guy said.

"Ha!" Sir Hector muttered quietly. "Her supposed heresy coincided with the illness of the Archbishop. A deal was struck with my mother for her to provide a potion to cure the Archbishop and in return, he would spare her life. But she was banished from the town and told never to use her evil talents again."

Sir Hector shook his head again and he continued to look into the heart of the fire.

"However, priests still turned up if they ever needed a tonic or healing potion," he continued. "But they said that only their powers could ward off any evil intent from my mother."

"Hypocrisy at its finest," he said scowling.

"So that is why you do not like the church?" Guy stated more than asked.

"You are right, I do not like religion. Although I believe in both God and people's faith in God. I also have high respect for people with God-given skills, and for people who do God's work with dedication and compassion. But I find that these people are few and far between. But I despise the clergy who use the church for an easy route to power and wealth, by feeding off the fears and faith of others."

"So, most of the bishops and archbishops then," Guy said.

Sir Hector laughed.

"But watch them closely, Guy. If you understand their desires, then you can manipulate them to a better cause."

"And ultimately perform God's will," Guy said.

"Hopefully, Guy. Hopefully," Sir Hector said quietly. "Or we are both doomed."

They left the barn early the next morning, but not before Guy practised his swordplay. Sir Hector wanted to cancel the session to give Guy more time to recover, but Guy insisted that he was feeling better, and he needed the exercise. Although, after half an hour of the workout, Guy cut the training short, because a sudden fatigue crept over him, and he needed to rest for a while.

But while he was resting, he was considering his recent fever and Sir Hector's healing skills.

"As your apprentice," Guy asked smiling, "do you think that you could teach me some remedies for common sicknesses? Especially the ones that you made up for me over the last couple of days. The knowledge may be useful if you ever became ill and I had to return the favour."

"I used mainly Wolfs Bane, which is a plant mainly found in hilly regions and Belladonna, which is more widespread. You can find them in the wild but, as with most medicinal herbs, you find them more often in woodlands around towns, as the local healers will ensure their supply. Do you know these plants?"

"I know Belladonna," Guy said, "I was warned against it as a child."

"Yes, it is very poisonous, especially when mixed with certain other plants," Sir Hector said, and then looked over at Guy.

"I would not normally want to pass these skills on," he then continued, "as they can be dangerous in the wrong hands. Balancing the size, age and sex of the patient, the intensity of the illness and the mix of the ingredients require a lot of understanding and experience. But I think that you are well capable of appreciating the intricacies and complexities of the art, so I will teach you the rudiments. But you must treat this subject as serious as you treat your fighting, as mistakes can be just as costly."

"Thank you, Sir Hector," Guy then said. "I will be attentive and diligent in my learning."

"No thanks needed, it is as you said, I may need your help on our trip home. Understanding and recognising the plants is a good start, although mixing is more difficult. So, on our travels today, I will want you to find me some Belladonna and I will show you Wolf's Bane and Comfrey," Sir Hector said.

Sir Hector remained silent for a while as he thought over another idea.

"I think that I will instruct you in balancing the healing properties of these plants with their more poisonous attributes. These can be lethal in their application, and I will show you how they can be mixed to disguise their common symptoms. So, you will also find me some leaves of the Yew tree and Hemlock seeds."

"Not a problem," Guy replied, "I use Yew staves for my bows, and I can recognise Hemlock," Guy replied. But he then remained silent, as he suddenly understood the depth of knowledge Sir Hector processed, and how deadly he was as an adversary.

The weather had improved and although it was still cool and breezy, the skies were clear. The road they travelled along was wet and muddy, and they had to constantly pick their way through pools and deep ruts that were full of dirty rainwater. The going became easier when they rode through a large forest which allowed Guy plenty of hunting opportunities, allowing them to eat well throughout the day. Within the trees, Sir Hector allowed Guy to gather Belladonna and they also found more of the Wolf's Bane. Sir Hector also searched in an area of marshland and came back with the full plant and roots of Water Hemlock, which cured severe headaches, but was also extremely poisonous.

They stopped in the outskirts of the town of Beauvais and rested for a couple of nights, without bringing any attention to themselves. They then rode along the main road towards the distant town of Rouen, which was the centre of Normandy and where Rollo held court.

They passed many travellers on the road and occasionally, during the day, they invited strangers to eat with them so that they could gather news. It seemed that there was general unrest in the region and tensions were building between King Charles and Robert the Count of Poitiers, Paris and Orleans. On two occasions they had to pull off the road to allow a large band of mounted troops, who came quickly from behind them, to pass and move on westwards.

Sir Hector took careful note of their livery but did not comment.

Whenever they stopped to cook, Sir Hector instructed Guy in the mixing and dosage of the remedies, and in the increased measures that would be required to make them lethal.

They had been on the road for two weeks when they heard of a battle to the south of the region, where Robert had been reported to have defeated a small army of Danes in the Loire Valley.

This news concerned Sir Hector, who thought Danish raids in West Francia had been stemmed by Rollo's presence.

"I think we are seeing something bigger than a Viking incursion," Sir Hector said to Guy. "It may be the start of a rebellion against the rule of King Charles. There were some discrete meetings and private discussions at Soissons, trying to solicit support for a rebellion, which showed a high level of discontentment among the nobles. But there is always talk of a rebellion in Francia, and I did not think that it would escalate this quickly."

"Was Ebles involved?" Guy asked.

"He was one of them," Sir Hector admitted.

"I thought Charles was fairly secure in West Francia," Guy said, suddenly interested in Francia politics.

"He was, but his favouritism towards Hagano has upset both the nobles and the clergy, and they are dangerous parties to anger on their own, never mind together."

"I have heard Hagano's name mentioned on several occasions in the palace hall," Guy said. "Why has he upset the nobles?"

"He advises the King, and the King rewards him with land and religious institutes, which is taken from the nobles and the church."

"And taking away wealth from those greedy bodies is not a good strategy for any king."

"Does the King have any allies to help him?" Guy again asked, as he needed to understand the political landscape.

"A few nobles will still support him, but they will probably remain neutral in any call to arms. But he has an alliance with Rollo in Normandy, and I believe Duke Gilbert of Lotharingia remains loyal. I suspect our King Edward would put his support behind Charles, but Britain will not be able to provide any type of military aid in the short term."

"Does this impact our plans?" Guy then asked.

"I believe it probably will," Sir Hector replied. "If it is indeed a rebellion."

"What concerns you?" Guy asked, still aware of Sir Hectors continued apprehension.

"To be honest, it is you, Guy," Sir Hector said.

"Why?" Guy asked.

"Because of my promise to return you to Earl Rohan." Sir Hector paused and looked at Guy. "My instinct is to go and support the king, but that path is dangerous, and I cannot guarantee your safety when battles are involved, or when a king's security takes precedence."

"You have told me that you live your life by your instinct and that you believe that your instinct is guided by God," Guy said. "So, who am I to prevent you from carrying out your instinct and helping King Charles? It is my duty as your squire to follow you and support you."

"So, you are now a squire again," Sir Hector said, smiling warmly at Guy.

"Whenever it suits me," Guy said. "Do you know where Charles is?"

"I was told at Beauvais that he was in Paris, but I am not certain. However, loyalties in Paris will be divided between Charles and Robert, so we need to get to him as soon as possible."

"To do what?" Guy asked.

"Whatever we can. I am afraid we will not know until we find out exactly what is occurring."

"Then what are we waiting for?" Guy said, with a mix of both apprehension and excitement.

They travelled back on themselves towards Beauvais, along a main well-maintained road, before turning south towards Paris. They rode with an increased and more urgent pace.

It was into the late afternoon when they stopped and quickly pulled off the Paris road, on the north bank of the River Oise. In the distance, they had spotted the hazy dust cloud of cavalry, approaching them at a gallop from the south, and they did not want to be seen. They waited in a dense coppice of trees and watched the riders approach the bridge that crossed the river.

"It's King Charles," Sir Hector suddenly said. "What on earth is he doing on this road?"

"Stay here, Guy," he then said. "While I will try and see what's going on."

Sir Hector kicked his horse and galloped back towards the road, to cut off the soldiers.

Guy watched as Sir Hector took up a position along the road to block the column of riders. He held up his arms to slow them down and to

show his peaceful intent. Three men galloped quickly forward from the main group to investigate Sir Hector, while the rest of the troop slowed to a walk.

A rider broke off and returned to the main body before the whole group rallied forward to stop before Sir Hector.

Then Sir Hector and another rider came out of the group and rode towards Guy.

Sir Hector led his companion into the coppice and brought them to a halt in front of Guy.

"Guy, may I introduce Charles, King of West Francia."

Guy bowed his head to the king.

"You have my greetings Guy of Warwick. I wish it was under better circumstances," Charles said.

The King was a tall man with a manicured beard and a long sharp nose. He was dressed in polished armour of expensive chainmail and plate. He also wore a large, decorated helmet with engraved side plates.

"So, what is your advice, Sir Hector?" Charles said turning to face Sir Hector.

"The east is against you, and they will try and cut you off from Rollo," Sir Hector quickly said.

"Also, heading west to Rollo is the worst option for you if you want to resist the rebellion," Sir Hector continued. "You will be isolated in Normandy and the Counts can then cut you off and secure their governance of West Francia. If I was you, sire, I would go to Lotharingia to gather support to resist Robert from the east and hold Rollo in support to the west."

"And how do I get to Gilbert in Lotharingia?" Charles asked, after a moment's deliberation.

"You head towards East Lotharingia as soon as possible, but with a large amount of stealth; you cannot be detected. I suggest that you head for Lorraine, sire."

"But that means travelling back east, which you say is against me," Charles said.

"They will not expect it and that, I find, is always the best course of action, sire," Sir Hector said. "But you cannot take your personal guard, as that will attract too much attention. I suggest selecting a small body of trusted men that will not be challenged and then send your main troops to Normandy."

"As a diversion?" Charles asked.

"And also, for security." Sir Hector replied. "At present, I would not trust anyone, which is why I brought you here, sire, out of earshot."

Charles thought for a while and then nodded.

"Your advice and support have never let me down in the past, Sir Hector," Charles said. "But I will need trusted companions to attend me. Can I engage your services for this venture?"

Sir Hector thought for a moment and then looked at Guy, who simply shrugged his shoulders.

"I will be my honour, sire, for Guy and myself to escort you."

Charles returned to his generals and gave orders for them to take his guard towards Normandy. He also told them that he was going to Burgundy with Sir Hector to call on favours of the Count.

He then arranged for light baggage to be made ready and funds to be provided to Sir Hector, to support them on their journey to Burgundy.

Within an hour the King was ready to travel, and he parted company with his guard.

The King rode alongside Sir Hector at the front of their small band, with Guy and the packhorse riding behind. Guy was surprised at the ease at which the King travelled. It was as if he had not a care in the world.

Sir Hector, however, was constantly scanning the path ahead. He also kept looking over his shoulder and into the trees at both sides, as they travelled through the forest towards the town of Senlis. Guy was again surprised at Sir Harold's knowledge of the geography of Francia and when Guy asked him about it, he just said that knowledge was power. The King laughed at this and said that you do not keep power without wisdom and advised Guy to always use knowledge to attain wisdom.

They slept as rough as normal, with no consideration of the King's regal status, but the weather was both warm and dry, and Charles seemed to be enjoying the experience.

Charles sat and talked to Guy as they roasted a couple of rabbits over a small fire for their evening meal and Guy was surprised at how amiable he was. He asked Guy about his home and his adventures with Sir Hector. He was especially amused at his 'Spear on Horse' exploits in Soissons.

Charles also discussed his upbringing in comparison to Guy's. He seemed to appreciate Guy's endeavours and struggle to get to his position, as opposed to it being given by birthright.

"I admire a man who is driven to achieve a certain standing," Charles said. "Genuine reward inspires loyalty far more than the effort of retaining what you already have."

"Is Hagano driven?" Sir Hector asked, as he sat down alongside them after overhearing the King's last comment.

"Ah yes, Hagano," the King said thoughtfully. "Giving him such rewards might prove to be a big mistake on my part, but the rewards were minor compared to what I gave Rollo and I do not regret that decision."

"I believe Rollo is a man who is driven," Sir Hector said.

"Very true," the King said. "And he has driven all over us in the past," the King smiled. "Not only do I admire Rollo, but I also quite like him. He has always broken protocol and etiquette, without meaning offence, and it amuses me. However, he has compromised greatly in achieving his desires, but I trust his oaths."

"Did he really lift your foot to kiss it?" Sir Hector asked, already knowing the answer, but he thought Guy might like the reference.

Charles laughed aloud.

"Never fails to amuse me, every time I think back to it," Charles said.

The King then looked at Guy.

"After Chartres," Charles said, "I invited Rollo to negotiate a cessation of the fighting and offered him quite generous personal terms in the rule of Rouen and Normandy. He first had to accept me as his king, recognise Christ our saviour, and Christianity as the one true religion."

Charles smiled to himself as he remembered.

"This he did with his oath. In acceptance of my rule, it was customary to then kiss my foot, but instead of kneeling and bowing down to kiss it, he ordered one of his advisors to lift it to his mouth."

Charles laughed again.

"I was not expecting it and nearly went arse over tit, backwards."

Sir Hector laughed as he pictured the scene.

"Rollo was not at all embarrassed and laughed out loud. After recovering from the initial shock, I joined him in the amusement which I recognised as having no ill intent. Unlike my counsellors, who were horrified and took it as an insult bordering on assault." Charles then became more thoughtful. "I think however that we shared a common bond at that moment which has lasted for a decade."

"The nobles have never liked Rollo, and I believe they have never forgiven me for giving away land they think belongs to Francia or their own pockets. But the raids on our coast have stopped and we no longer pay ransoms to the Danes, which were at the time crippling our nation." He paused and thought. "Rollo is a good ally."

"Hagano, however, although not by any means from a poor background, has had to fight for what he has achieved. He also has a general dislike for the church that keeps me true on my duty to my people." Charles paused and considered his words. "And I also like him. But again, the nobles are against him. I think my favouritism towards him has finally driven them to protect their own interests and rebel against me."

"You, I also like, Sir Hector, because you have also risen from a humble beginning, and yet, are not orientated by greed."

"I thank you, sire, and on that basis, I think you will like Guy as well. In one moment, he will fight with a knight in the melee and in another, he will shoe their horse. He is also extremely competent in both," Sir Hector replied.

"I think that I like him, already," Charles said smiling at Guy.

They ate and then slept, rising at first light to continue their journey back towards Soissons.

They kept to small paths in the hills and made good time to gain a region south of Soissons, without being recognised.

They made an early camp in a hay barn, which was rented for the night from a local farmer. Charles wanted information on the rebellion and insisted that Sir Hector go into the local town to see what he could find out.

Guy saw to the horses with assistance from Charles, who seemed keen to pull his weight in sharing the chores, although he admitted to never grooming a horse before.

"I have never needed to perform this role, Guy," the King said. "Which is a shame, but I am conscious of how a king should act, even though I often fall short in what is expected of me. But here with you and Sir Hector, I am not a king. Neither of you are my subjects, so I feel a certain sense of freedom, and that freedom is sleeping in the open, telling stories around a fire and seeing to our horse's requirements." Charles sighed. "Are you surprised that I think of this as freedom?"

"I am not surprised, sire. I have never spoken openly with a king before, and I would not assume to understand what you think about."

"As a king, I do not think about what I would personally do, but what a king would do," Charles replied and then thought about what he just said. "But as a king, I would not have confessed such a lack of self-confidence. So, it must show this new sense of freedom that I feel that allows me to confide in a stranger."

"But you are still a king, sire," Guy replied.

"True, and I am God's appointed ruler over my kingdom, and with that there is a heavy burden to maintain its security and prosperity. Although Sir Hector says that my duty is only to ensure the happiness and well-being of the people I rule. Prosperity, he says, is irrelevant to a man's happiness, but I find that surprising coming from a mercenary."

Charles then smiled. "Don't get me wrong, Guy, I have the greatest respect for Sir Hector, and I know of all the good he does, but he could just become a monk to help the poor."

Guy remained silent and just listened to the King. He felt that Charles did suddenly feel free, and all this open talk was an expression of that freedom.

"But Sir Hector is an enigma. He is fastidious in everything he does and paints a picture of always being in control. However, underneath that façade, he just drifts along and goes with the flow, without any real care to where it takes him. He then accepts those eventual destinations as God's will."

Charles paused and thought for a while before continuing. "And with that, I like him and trust him and hopefully he will see me through this trial."

Sir Hector returned just before nightfall and reported on the local gossip.

He discovered that Herbert, the Count of Vermandois and Count of Soissons, and Richard, the Duke of Burgundy along with his son Rudolph were openly against Charles. Most of the local nobles and church dignitaries in the region were in support of Robert, the Count of Poitiers.

"What of Archbishop Herveus?" Charles asked. "He was always a loyal advisor to me."

"I have heard nothing of Herveus, sire. But I think that it is wise to travel towards Reims and away from Soissons as soon as possible," Sir Hector replied.

"What of their strength?" Charles continued.

"There are two hundred men in Soissons, but there are many more out in search of you. Your guard out of Paris was intercepted before they reached Normandy and they know you are in hiding. If they have any sense, they would be looking southwest for you, which I believe Ebles, the bastard is guarding as they will want to stop you getting to Rollo from the south. They would also be wise to guard the northern border to prevent you from seeking refuge with Gilbert in Lotharingia. But that border is wide."

"So, we continue towards Reims, at first light," Charles said.

They awoke with the dawn, and after a meagre breakfast they left the barn in silence, heading east into the heavy woodland.

The day was overcast with a hint of rain and the small group wrapped their cloaks around their shoulders, to protect them from the early morning chill.

They had just reached the cover of the woodland when they heard horses and men in the distance behind them.

"Guy, take the King and move on as quickly as possible, while I see what is going on," Sir Hector said and turned his horse to go back to the edge of the trees.

Guy kicked his horse on, down the narrow track and encouraged Charles to follow.

Sir Hector caught up with them after about ten minutes.

"We must hurry. The farmer must have recognised us and alerted the local landowner, who has sent a guard detail to find us. They will be tracking us, and I do not have time to cover our tracks."

Sir Hector kicked his horse past Guy and led the small party at a gallop towards the town of Reims.

They slowed at intervals to spare the horses but continued eastwards at a swift pace.

They reached the main Epernay road, and they spurred their horses along it for a couple of miles, before leaving it to the southwest of the town. They then made their way more slowly along a rough path that cut through a large area of marshland.

They saw no one, and began to feel safe, as they crossed the road to Troyes and then turned northward, to bypass Chalons to their left.

They safely crossed the River Coole at a ford and moved swiftly toward the River Marne, which would be their last obstacle before the town of Verdun and safety. They travelled across the flat land, when suddenly the tree covering ended and they were out in the open fields. In front of them was an old narrow stone bridge, with low walls that crossed the river. It was guarded by a handful of soldiers. The soldiers noticed them immediately and ran to a small thicket on the far side of the river to retrieve and mount their horses.

"We have a choice of fighting them or retreating and letting them chase us, but if we do retreat, then we may run directly into the other soldiers that are following."

"They have stopped on the bridge," Guy said as he watched the soldiers closely. "They do not yet know who we are."

"What are your thoughts?" Sir Hector asked.

"We casually walk down and hope they hold their positions. If they do, then one of us charges down the middle of the bridge and that should push two of them into the river and I think between us we can beat the four other guards."

"Agreed," Sir Hector said, after quickly evaluating the situation.

"You stay here with the packhorse, sire, and retreat if you need to." Sir Hector said to Charles.

"I am well able to join you," the King said.

"Of course, sire, but the two of us can happily manage this. However, please engage, if you feel it appropriate. But you must protect your sovereignty at all costs."

Sir Hector kicked his horse forward to walk towards the bridge, with Guy casually riding on his shoulder.

The two guards remained side by side on the bridge and waited for Sir Hector and Guy to approach.

"I will charge," Sir Hector whispered to Guy. "And veer left. You follow straight behind and take the right."

Guy could sense Sir Hector tensing his legs as they approached, but in all other ways, he appeared calm.

The guards adopted an official stance, as they sat upright on their horses, and awaited the two men. They let the two men approach right up to the beginning of the bridge when suddenly Sir Hector kicked the horse on. The horse instantly obeyed the spur and sprang forward towards the two guards. Sir Hector drew his sword as the guard's horses reared in panic from the unexpected onrush. As Guy had predicted, they had nowhere to go but to collapse sideward over the low walls of the bridge and into the river.

Guy kicked his horse on, and Bedivere galloped after Sir Hector running towards the men to the right, who had split evenly. Their melee experience came to the fore, and it did not take long for the remaining guards to be quickly dispatched with minimal effort.

They then quickly returned to the river to see if there were any survivors. The river, however, was deep and although the horses were struggling to get to the riverbank, the two soldiers, who were weighed down in armour, were nowhere to be seen.

Sir Hector brought his horse up to Guy and sheathed his sword. He was about to speak, when an arrow whistled past them and thudded into the ground in front of them. Sir Hector instantly leant forward and grabbed Guy's reins and pulled Bedivere behind him, turning his own horse to shield Guy. Another dull thud smacked out above the noise of the horses and Sir Hector fell forward over his horse's shoulder and onto the floor.

Guy saw the arrow in Sir Hector's back straight away and jumped off his horse to help his friend.

Sir Hector was trying to raise himself onto his hands and knees, but his left arm kept giving way beneath him.

"Go now, Guy, and get the King out of here. That is a command," Sir Hector hissed, through gritted teeth, as Guy bent down to examine the wound.

"Go," Sir Hector hissed again with a bubbling rattle to his voice and another arrow flew into his side, causing him to arch his back up in pain.

Guy quickly jumped back on his horse and tore across the bridge. He counted time in his mind and then swerved his horse in a random direction as another arrow whistled past him. He then galloped on straight again and shouted at the King to get into the trees.

Once into the woods, Guy shouted for the King to stop and then jumped down from his horse. He then retrieved his bow and arrows from the packhorse and ran back to the edge of the wood.

Three riders were galloping across the bridge and heading towards them. Guy nocked his first arrow and drew the cord to his ear.

He waited until they were halfway across the field before letting loose the arrow. The first rider flew back from his saddle directly into the horse behind causing it to trip and throw its own rider. Guy nocked his second arrow and fired again at the remaining rider, who was now at close range. Guy aimed directly for the rider's neck, and the arrow struck home. The rider died before his body hit the ground.

The remaining soldier had now regained his feet and was retrieving his own bow from his horse, which was lying still on the ground. Guy realised that this was the archer who had fired upon Sir Hector.

Guy took his third arrow put it on the string and drew it back. He then walked forward out of the trees and towards the man. The soldier had his arrow on the string but did not have time to draw the bow, as he looked up to see Guy walking slowly towards him with his bow at the ready.

The soldier just watched as Guy approached and then realising his dilemma raised his bow. Guy fired instantly and the guard had no way of avoiding the arrow, as it speared him through the throat.

Guy then ran back to the wood and jumped on his horse and galloped back towards the bridge.

Guy pulled Bedivere to a halt and slid straight off the saddle. He knelt alongside Sir Hector, who was lying on his front with his head to the side and grasped his hand between his.

"Have you noticed the arrows, Guy?" He said quietly, coughing at the effort and allowing blood to trickle from the corner of his mouth.

Guy looked across at the two arrow's white fletching's.

"They look familiar," Guy replied.

"Are they dead?" Sir Hector asked. His voice was weak, and his eyes were slowly closing.

"Yes, my Lord. But is there anything I can do for you?" Guy replied, his own voice shaking with emotion.

Sir Hector took a deep breath and grimaced. "No, Guy, the wounds are fatal." He then opened his eyes wide and looked at Guy. "I need you to gather my wealth and take it back to my mother, it is in my horse and also with Father Corey at Trowbridge, do you remember him, Guy?" Sir Hector then asked. He was obviously in pain but spoke clearly and serenely.

"Yes." Guy answered, quickly.

Sir Hector coughed again, and more blood welled up into his mouth and trickled down his cheeks.

"He has the rest of my monies and my will to dispose of it. He will provide you with a sum to take back to my mother. Will you do that for me, Guy?"

"On my oath, my lord."

"I don't need your oath, Guy. You have my trust."

Sir Hector grimaced as pain shot through him in spasms.

"So," He whispered. "I will now find out if my life had a purpose, and if God's hand was upon my actions. The prospect scares me."

"I will pray for your deliverance, my lord." Guy replied, with tears running down his cheeks.

A serene air suddenly came upon Sir Hector. "May God go with you, Guy," He then finally said.

He coughed once more and then, with closed eyes, he let out a final breath.

Guy brushed away the tears from his eyes and face before looking up at King Charles, who was standing above him, holding his horse.

"We need to go, sire. Can you get Sir Hector's body onto his horse, as I would like to bury him properly, while I will fetch our baggage?" Guy said, as he brushed more tears away with the back of his hands. Although stricken with grief, Guy knew that he must go on, as he was now in charge of a king.

"Certainly, Guy. You have my deepest sympathy," Charles replied with an obvious sorrow in his voice. "He was a great man, who will be long remembered."

Chapter Fifteen

Guy walked back over the bridge and passed the bodies of the guards, and with his knife, he dug into their dead flesh to remove his arrows. Under his leather tunic, the archer had the diagonal blue and yellow livery with red trim, showing his allegiance to the Duke of Burgundy. On recognising the uniform, Guy used his knife with more fervour than necessary, but he was now angry. He was still incensed when he reached the final body and turned it over. The anger was then quickly replaced with shock, as Guy found himself looking into the face of Sir Roderick, whose lifeless eyes stared back at him. Guy looked down at him, for a moment, mesmerised by the unexpected nature of the body lying there. He then decided that he felt nothing for the man's death; his involvement in Sir Hector's death made his presence on the field insignificant and not worthy of any attention. Guy then went on to remove his arrow from the body without any regard to who he was.

In doing so, Guy noticed that Sir Roderick also wore the Burgundy colours under his chainmail, and Guy swore to himself that Richard, the Duke of Burgundy, would pay for Sir Hector's death.

Guy then collected the packhorse and led it back over the bridge to re-join Charles. The King was already mounted and had already lifted Sir Hector's body across the saddle of his sleek black destrier, with a blanket draped over him.

"I am afraid it is the best dignity I can offer him," Charles said.

"Thank you, sire. It is better than leaving him in a field with those vermin."

They left the town of Chalons behind them and rode hard, until they found a small quiet wood situated within a loop of a meandering stream.

Here Guy stopped and tied up the horses and in the loose soil, he dug a grave. He carefully used Sir Hector's sword to break the soil and let Charles scrape the dirt into a pile with his own hands. When it was deep enough, Guy and Charles lifted the body carefully into the hole and Guy placed Sir Hector's sword on his chest, with his hands resting on the hilt. They then prayed over the body before filling it in and placing a large rock at its top to mark its site.

"I swear to remember this spot and revisit it in better times," Guy said. "I will also bestow it with a memorial that is worthy of his reputation and his nature," he then added.

"I ask that you come to me before you mark the grave, Guy, so that I can contribute to his memory," Charles added with solemnity. "I owe Sir Hector more than I would like to say."

They then left their friend's final place of rest and rode quickly towards Verdun and the security of Lorraine.

On arrival at Verdun, Charles instantly sought out the town's nobles and arranged a courier to immediately go to Gilbert and request a meeting.

They dined that evening, in the hill fort that overlooked the river, although Guy had little appetite. The court had been thrown into chaos at the arrival of the King, and Guy could not tell if Charles was welcome or not. After the meal, Guy was left on his own, and, in a daze, he constantly looked around the main hall. He stared at the crowd of dignitaries that bustled around the room, but he let the drone of their chatter wash over him. As with the food, Guy could find no interest in the people there and was numb to his surroundings. Sir Hector's death was constantly on his mind, and he felt a deep void within.

Charles eventually left the overbearing throng of the town's most important people, who had continually fawned to him for most of the night, and came to sit next to Guy. Guy saw him approach and rose from his chair and bowed his head.

"Sire," Guy said as the King stepped in front of him.

"Sit down, 'Guy of Warwick'," Charles said softly and waved at a servant, who was waiting at the side of the hall.

Charles waited until the servant attended him and handed over several rolls of parchment.

"Sir Hector told me a lot about you on our brief journey and I am glad to have met you, Guy. I now need to ride to Metz and gather an army to regain my kingdom. I suspect that, without the company of Sir Hector, you will want to return to your home. So, I have summarised my opinion of you, that I have gained from Sir Hector's reports and on my own experiences in your company. I have noted your courage and achievements during your stay in Francia and I have written my commendation of you in these scrolls."

He showed Guy the first one.

"This is for Rollo, as I strongly advise that you head for Normandy and seek his help. I have asked him to provide you with as much assistance as possible to get you home."

He then looked at the other parchments and rubbed his fingers over the wax seal.

"This one is for the Earl of Warwick, again reporting your bravery and valour. Sir Hector said that you sought knighthood, and this may help."

"The final document is for your king, and you must get it to Edward as quickly as possible. It describes wider events but also mentions your part."

Charles then held out his hand and the servant passed him a large leather pouch.

"This is gold that will enable you to get home without any difficulty. It also provides my tribute to Sir Hector that you should give to his mother."

"There is no need, sire, as I have my own funds, along with Sir Hector's winnings and the money gathered from the sale of his horse."

"It is my tribute to Sir Hector, Guy," Charles said. "It is for my benefit only, so please do me the honour and take it."

"Thank you, sire," Guy said.

"I leave tomorrow," the King then said. "I advise that you do the same while the country is still in disarray. I will therefore say my farewells and give you my thanks for getting me here safely. Your reputation is secure in my kingdom, and you will always be welcome when I once again rule."

The King then stood up and bowed his head to Guy, before leaving the hall.

Guy went back to his room in the fortress and packed his belongings, before climbing into the small wooden cot and falling asleep.

He woke the next morning and sought out the service of a castle servant to cut off his long flowing hair into a rough stubble, that barely covered his pale scalp, and to also clean shave his face. He then gathered up all his belongings and left the fortress halls to retrieve Bedivere from the stables. He packed his possessions tightly in his saddlebags and in a large leather backpack. He then slung his bow over his shoulder and left Verdun. His aim was to travel south towards Chalons, and then onwards towards the city of Troyes, in the region of Burgundy.

On the journey, he stopped at the small, wooded coppice in the loop of the stream, to pay his respects to

Sir Hector and to ensure that he remembered the site of his grave. The air was fresh, and birds sang in the trees as he stood over the still freshly dug soil. There was peace amongst the trees, as their leaves rustled lightly in the breeze, casting dappled rays of sunshine across the ground. Guy held his face upwards and closed his eyes to the warmth of the sun, as it bathed the land with life. But Guy knew that it would not last, and autumn was just around the corner, which would then herald the hardships of winter. Guy would make the most of the sustenance of the summer to ready himself for the hard times ahead, and like the trees and plants, he would quietly strengthen his resolve at the challenges ahead.

He travelled slowly on, and passed through many small villages, where he slept and ate in the comfort of the local inns. He occasionally left the main road during the day, to take small detours into the forest. Within the trees, he would catch game to eat, and collect herbs to flavour the food. He also searched for the medicinal and poisonous plants that Sir Hector had taught him. He was determined to fully familiarise himself with their uses and embed their recognition into his memory. He wanted to do this for Sir Hector and provide something material that he would always remember him by. He rested often, but when he cooked his meals, a sadness washed over him, as he reminisced on his travels with Sir Hector. The memories were not just on the events that they encountered together, but also on the quiet, peaceful times, just sharing each other's company. He now felt lonely for the first time in his life.

He reached Troyes on the fifth day of his travels, without experiencing any unusual occurrences on the way. He had met with the occasional traveller, who shared gossip, or he stood to the side of the road to give way to cavalry troops. Soldiers seemed to be moving around the region quite frequently, but they paid no attention to him, as they cantered past. There were times that he hoped to be waylaid by thieves or bandits, just for the chance to vent his anger and frustration on them. But none showed, and the hours and days merged into each other.

On his arrival at the town, he found, as expected, that Richard the Duke of Burgundy was in residence. He had received this information when he was at Verdun and planned his trip accordingly, with plenty of time to schedule his visit.

He went to the town's local inns and acquainted himself with the palace staff. With money exchanging hands in bribes, he arranged to be interviewed by the local Constable, for a position in the palace's guard and was accepted into the role straight away.

He joined the Duke's guard and was kitted out with the livery of the 'House of Burgundy', which was the same blue and yellow stripes as the men who killed Sir Hector. He was inconspicuous from the rest of the guards and with his hair cropped, no one recognised him from his exploits at Soissons.

He then, over the next few days, performed his duties as a guard. He then asked for, and was given, additional duties in serving food and drink in the hall, where he closely observed the patterns of behaviour and the traits of the Duke and his nobles.

When he was not on duty, he was busy in his small, rented room, situated on the outskirts of the town, experimenting with the plants that he had gathered from the woods. He was extending Sir Hector's methods in their preparations. He practised their distilling and disguise and while he was testing and experimenting, the town was left wondering why there was an epidemic of dead dogs lying around the streets.

It was not long before there was a celebratory feast at the palace, and although the guests were few, Guy knew that the Duke would be eating and drinking to excess, as was his accustomed manner.

Guy found that implementing his plans were very straightforward, in respect to the sudden absence of the Duke's cupbearer and his temporary promotion to the role as a replacement. His experience from performing similar duties at home paid dividends and allowed him to display his capabilities in the role to the head steward, with a high degree of competency.

So, all Guy had to do was wait until the Duke had drunk enough to be unaware of the different tastes of the wine and then pick his moment. This came when they played their usual drinking game that involved drinking the full content of their glasses if various words within a song were not sung out aloud.

The Duke noticed the change of flavour in the wine that Guy had served him and complained, allowing his glass to be filled with a second concoction. The Duke, tasting the difference in the new wine, then happily accepted it. Both drinks were from flagons that Guy had pre-prepared.

Guy smiled and knew that his plan had succeeded and within the days to come, the Duke's internal body functions would fail, and he would die a long, painful, and lingering death.

As soon as the Duke retired, Guy immediately left the palace and went back to his room in the town. He packed his few belongings by the flickering glow of a solitary candle and then closed his eyes to try and sleep.

He awoke with the first light of the morning, and he left his room to ready his horse. Satisfied that he was fully packed to go, he mounted Bedivere to leave the town.

He raised a skin of wine that he had kept with him from the night before and held it up towards the palace.

"For you, Sir Hector," Guy said, and took a drink.

He then threw it to the ground and rode away to the west, towards Paris.

Guy travelled in the same style as before, and just ambled along, sometimes riding Bedivere or sometimes walking beside his horse.

The days were unseasonably warm, although the nights were getting colder. Guy spent more time sleeping outdoors, as he travelled between towns, and only ate in the roadside inns.

He had long discarded his Burgundy regalia and had dressed back into his usual clothes, although he always wore his chain mail under his tunic, as he had no room for it in his backpack. His hair was growing long again, and his beard was filling out, as he moved away from adolescence.

Guy now felt the burden of manhood but could not recall the time when he had left his boyish ways behind. He thought about it for a while and decided that it was the moment that he put an arrow into the back of an attacker in the woods outside of Towcester. He had killed Danish attackers on his journey to Atherstone, but that was tempered by Sir Harold, who had celebrated the victory, yet still treated Guy as the inexperienced youth he was.

Killing the men who wanted to murder him and Sir Hector in their sleep, was a quite different experience and was treated as the serious nature in which it surely was. He believed that moment, in which he sent his arrows flying with the calm, planned, intent to end another person's life, had changed him forever.

Guy travelled well south of Paris, and he stayed for two days in the town of Chartres. It was here that he heard that Richard the Duke of Burgundy was gravely ill, and his son Rudolph was running the region's affairs. Guy was not sorry for his actions, but over the last few days, he had often wondered how far Sir Hector would have taken his personal retribution. He considered if Sir Hector would have gone beyond 'looking out' for an adversary in the next melee. But Guy was certain in his mind that if the roles were reversed, then the Duke of Burgundy would already be dead.

It took Guy another three days to reach Rouen, in Normandy, and Guy went straight to the castle, where he formally met with the gate commander. On the instructions of King Charles, he requested an audience with Lord Rollo, and then showed the seal on the roll of parchment that Charles had given him.

The commander, who was an obvious Dane, with blond plaited hair and a long unkempt beard kept Guy waiting at the gate, while he sought approval. When this was eventually given, he led Guy into the castle's grounds and up to the main hall.

Guy had to leave his weapons with Bedivere, outside the entrance to the hall, before following the commander through the doors. He strode purposefully along the centre aisle of the dark inner chamber, carrying the heavy saddle bags that held Sir Hector's wealth along with his own gathered fortune over his shoulder. Guy could see a man, who he assumed was Rollo, sitting on a large throne at the far end of the hall. As they walked closer and closer towards him, Guy saw the man's stature increase.

Rollo was an old man, who was well into his seventies, but Guy still detected a robustness and immensity about him that hinted that he must have been a powerfully built man in his youth. Rollo looked scornfully down at Guy as he drew near.

The commander stopped a couple of paces in front of Rollo and bowed. Guy also bowed.

"And you are?" Rollo asked in a deep booming voice.

"I am 'Guy of Warwick,'" Guy said, placing his bags on the floor in front of him. "And I have come from King Charles of West Francia, who is resisting the rebellion to his kingdom in Lorraine."

Guy, pleased with his practised announcement, stepped forward and handed over the letter that Charles had given him.

Rollo called over to a man who was standing in the shadows to his right. The man walked quickly to the throne and then took the letter that was handed to him by Rollo to examine the seal. He looked up and nodded at Rollo to acknowledge its authenticity.

The man then verbally translated the letter to Rollo.

Rollo did not take his eyes off Guy, as Charles's words heaped high praise on the young squire, and more than once referred to his knightly behaviour. Guy tried to remain fixed in his countenance and ignore the compliments, although it made him feel uncomfortable and embarrassed to have them said aloud in front of him. Sir Hector was also referenced several times.

"So, Guy of Warwick," Rollo said standing up from his seat and towering over Guy. "Being a friend of Sir Hector is recommendation enough, but you also saved King Charles's life. You are welcome in my house."

Rollo then slapped his hand down on lightly Guy's shoulder in friendship. It was a light tap, but Guy felt his knees buckle under the force, which was unexpected from such an old man.

"Thank you, my lord," Guy said.

"As requested, I will gladly assist you in returning to your homeland, and I will make one of my ships available to you as soon as I can get a crew ready. That will, however, take a couple of days, but while you wait, you must accept my hospitality. I will provide accommodation for you, and you are invited to dine with me and my family tonight. You can tell me your stories of what happened, and why Charles, who is not normally a man who lends himself to making recommendations, both trusted and befriended you in such a brief time."

"Gladly, my lord. I am grateful for your kindness." Guy said.

Rollo suddenly roared with laughter and the noise echoed around the empty hall.

"Do you see, Dag? I am a kind man," Rollo said to his Commander, who was still standing next to Guy.

"What is kindness, my lord?" Dag asked with no apparent emotion. "I do not believe I have experienced any of this 'kindness' in your company."

Rollo laughed aloud again and punched Dag on the shoulder. The warrior staggered sideward a couple of paces, before regaining his balance and rubbing his shoulder.

"Is there a translation for this 'kindness', Arnulf?" Dag asked of the translator, who was still standing next to the throne.

"There is no such word in Danish," Arnulf replied smiling.

Rollo, obviously amused by the conversation. Put his arm around Guy and led him back down the hall.

"But first, I will take you to Gisla; my wife, who will want to hear about her father's welfare."

"Of course, my lord," Guy said and walked with the mighty Dane.

Guy spoke at length with both Gisla and Rollo about Charles, his health, and plans. Gisla was only a girl and must have been a couple of years younger than Felice. But she was obviously happy with her marriage to Rollo, and she constantly smiled at him, who in turn, seemed very much attached to her.

They spoke for around an hour and Guy felt happy and content in their company. He had not spoken with anyone, in any depth, since he left Charles at Verdun. Guy, who always thought that he was happy with his own company, had not realised how much he missed shared conversation.

His audience came to an end and Guy was shown to his room within the castle keep. The chamber was comfortable, and he was also provided with a young slave girl, who saw to his needs. She did not speak but went about her tasks with little instruction. She brought Guy a change of clothes which, although plain, were functional, and she waited for Guy to undress so she could take his dirty clothes away for cleaning. Guy held the new clothes in his hand and looked at the girl, hoping that she would leave the room. But she just stood there impassively and looked straight back at him. So, with some embarrassment, he turned his back on her and quickly undressed, making sure that he exposed as little of himself as possible. The girl waited patiently for the dirty clothes to be passed to her and when she was satisfied with collecting all of Guy's meagre garments, she went to withdraw. Guy quickly stopped her and reached into the tunic pocket that was lying over her arm and withdrew the silk cloth which was Felice's token.

"For luck," he said, smiling. But again, she did not acknowledge him and just turned to leave the room.

She returned after a short while with a platter of food and a pitcher of ale, which she placed on a low table and left straight away, without acknowledging Guy or his thanks.

Guy ate the cheese, bread, and dried meat with gusto, not realising how hungry he was. He then, with a contented sigh, lay down on the large straw-filled cot in the corner of the room to rest.

Although he was tired, he could not sleep, so he decided to get up and find Bedivere, along with his weapons and belongings, and make sure the horse was being cared for.

Guy was able to find Dag easy enough, and the castle commander escorted him personally to the stables.

Bedivere was comfortable in a stall, and Guy looked through his belongings which were piled up alongside the wall.

"They have been perfectly safe here," Dag said. "No one would dare steal from Rollo or his guests."

"I can understand that," Guy said. "I would not like to offer any offence to Rollo."

"I do not believe that you could offend Rollo," Dag replied. "Old age has mellowed him, and although he comes across stern, he is very content to have settled in such a comfortable place. He no longer desires the life of a Viking, and his contentment brings a level of compliance and tolerance in others."

"His son however is a different story," Dag continued. "He is called William Longsword and he is formidable. You will meet him tonight, as he is in residence."

"Is he a renowned warrior like his father?" Guy asked.

"Oh, he can fight, but he takes more time to understand the rulers of this land. He is intrigued by the webs of lies and deceits that are used to maintain their power. He wants to fight them at their own games to achieve his ambitions."

Guy enjoyed the evening with Rollo and his family. He wore his newly cleaned dress robes, bearing the Warwick insignia, and was treated with respect and courtesy. He was asked about his upbringing and his life in Warwick and the people he knew and grew up with. They knew of their fellow Danes; Ragnall and Sitric, who had control of northern Northumberland and they were especially interested to hear that Guy had already met Sitric. They were amused that it was Sitric who gave him the title of 'Guy of Warwick'. Rollo and his son William probed for more details of the battles, fights, and tournament contests, in which they became engrossed. Gisla, however, would continually change the conversation, when she had enough of what she termed 'man's talk'.

They were especially interested in Soissons and William wanted details on everybody who was there and Sir Hector's thoughts on the attending lords.

"I think we will continue our support to Charles," Rollo said to Guy, although Guy thought by his tone, that his comments were directed more towards William. "He is the only person in this nest of vipers that I trust."

Rollo waited for a few moments to see if there was any response.

"You can relay that back to your King Edward, but for his ears only," Rollo said looking closely at Guy.

Guy nodded to show his understanding.

"But while we have the great 'Guy of Warwick'; apprentice to Sir Hector, the champion of the Earl of Warwick's melee and the winner of the Soissons 'Spear on Horse', we must show off his skills," Rollo then said aloud.

Guy suddenly blanched.

Rollo laughed at Guy's apprehension. "How about a quick impromptu tournament with my retainers, to put them through their paces," Rollo then said. "We Danes do not organise formal tournaments, but it will be interesting to have a little competition to test our abilities."

"Oh, I do love a tournament," Gisla said clapping her hands together in excitement.

"Best dresses on then, my dear," Rollo said, laughing at his wife.

"I think that I would also like to be involved," William said, also smiling.

"Good," Rollo replied. "Let us go for the day after tomorrow, and I would be grateful, Guy, if you help in its planning and in firming up the rules."

"Are there rules?" William asked in a serious tone, and he laughed in amusement when he saw Guy's expression.

Rollo laughed with his son.

"And we will dedicate it to the memory of Sir Hector," Rollo then said in a more solemn tone. "He would appreciate an exhibition of both skill and joyful celebration."

"I will order more ale then, father," William then said.

Guy spent most of the time with Rollo's commander, who was assigned to assist Guy in preparing for the improvised tournament, and although twice the age of Guy, Dag was becoming a good friend.

They had a small list of competitors, so they kept the contests down to just two; the melee and 'sword on foot'. Guy was happy that he had managed to convince Dag that axes did not play a part in organised tournaments.

Guy had the judges and contestants formally lined up in the courtyard and with the help of translators, he had the rules and etiquette fully explained to them. He was fortunate that half of the retainers were existing petit nobles from the region, who fully understood the tournament rules and requirements. They all supported Guy in educating the Danes, who were bemused by all the formality and protocol. This allowed Guy to spend some time organising the pageant side of the tournament, which was especially for Rollo's young wife, who was very much looking forward to the event. Seating was arranged, as well as heralds, entertainers, and suitable catering. Organising the food was less of a problem for Guy, as he found that the fare consisted mainly of bread, meat and ale, unlike the Soissons fare which was more refined.

Guy buried himself in this work and the two days passed very quickly.

On the day of the tournament, the castle household gathered around the temporary arena within the castle grounds. Rollo and his family were seated in a makeshift stand which was covered with flags, banners, and shields along with a canvas roof. Rollo's wife, Gisla, was very much enjoying herself and sitting on the edge of her seat, clapping her hands, and constantly looking around at all the activities and sights. Rollo happily sat back in his chair, with a look of contentment.

Guy started the tournament with the Melee, in which he spent most of the time chasing the same combatants, who refused to exit the arena after being eliminated and continued fighting. Even wearing his helmet, Guy could hear Rollo's laughter, as he pummelled these same fighters into a state where they were dragged from the arena in a condition of near unconsciousness. Guy controlled the melee and made it the exhibition of skill and bravery that Rollo wanted to see. At the end of the contest, Guy was the last man standing and the clear victor.

The 'sword on foot' was a different matter and the final two competitors left on the field were Guy and William Longsword.

William, like his father, was a giant of a man. He faced Guy with a large sword and shield, as well as a large confident smile that lit up his face.

Guy looked at him and straight away decided that he would use his speed to gain an advantage.

William was strong and although his strokes were hard, Guy could easily step away from them. William just continued to swing his training sword in large sweeping strokes and Guy continued to step aside. William soon became visibly tired, and he was noticeably slower in lifting his sword following his broad slashing strokes.

Guy, recognising his opponent's tiredness, feigned a step to the right and then waited for William to commit to his sword stroke. Guy then stepped back to the left and swung his sword around to slash into William's legs.

William, however, was waiting for this manoeuvre and brought his sword across with lightning speed, to parry Guy's stroke. He then brought the hilt back to smash into the side of Guy's helmet.

Guy went crashing to the floor, with the sound of ringing steel in his ears, along with a bleariness that fogged his vision, as he struggled to remain conscious.

Guy then just turned to lay on his back and breathed deeply, in an effort to recover his senses. The ringing sound in his ears eventually diminished, to be replaced by raucous laughing from both William and Rollo, who were now standing over him.

William held his hand out to Guy who grabbed hold of it, and he was then hauled effortlessly to his feet. Guy staggered a step sideward, before gaining his balance and then carefully pulled off his helmet. He brushed his hand over his head and then examined it for blood. Fortunately, there was none, but Guy knew from the pain that there would be a sizable lump in the morning.

"You need to understand Guy, that warriors of our stature are always considered to be slow and cumbersome and that we tire easily," Rollo said, still chuckling. "Sir Hector told me, on many occasions, that contests between individuals are fought mainly in the mind and that you only win by first controlling your opponent's moves. I therefore told William to fake weariness and present an opening."

Rollo then looked sternly, but warmly, at William. "But I did not tell him to hit you that hard."

"That was not hard," William said and patted Guy on the shoulder. "But the tap on the head will make you remember the lesson that we giants among men stand out as adversaries in the crowd, and we cannot hide in a battle." He then looked at his father and puffed out his chest in some shared humour. "We, therefore, have to fight hard against the best of the enemy's forces, and we do not live unless we are both strong and fast."

"But you are good, 'Guy of Warwick'" He then said. "Sir Hector would have been pleased with your performance."

"Thank you, my lords," Guy said, still rubbing his head. "It is a lesson that I will not forget."

"Come along, then," Rollo said and strode between the two men with his arms outstretched wide, embracing each of them around the shoulders and leading them towards the stand. "Gisla wants to present you with your prizes, and I thank you Guy for your efforts in planning this entertainment. I have not seen my wife this happy for a long time."

Guy stabled Bedivere and then went to the bathhouse to immerse himself in a large wooden tub of warm water. A young slave girl hurried around making sure that the bath was at the right temperature, by replenishing the tub with hot water from cauldrons heated on a large fire in the corner of the room. Guy was again embarrassed at his nakedness but tried to ignore the girl's presence. However, he could not ignore the girl when she then stripped off her clothes and stepped into the tub with him and reached down under the water and softly took hold of one of his legs.

Guy looked at her with open eyes, trying not to let his gaze wander down across her bare chest. She was unaware of his stare as she took a cloth from the side of the tub and started to wash his foot.

Guy sat nervously, wondering on the extent of the slave's washing, and felt stupid that he knew nothing of the protocols for such treatment and associated behaviour. This was a lesson that Sir Hector had not taught him.

That night, he ate his final meal in a crowded main hall, as they celebrated the tournament with the promised feast. This was the Danish feast that Sir Hector had told Guy about, where stories were told, songs were sung, and copious amounts of food and ale consumed.

Guy was given a place on the top table, as a guest of honour, and sat alongside Gisla. Guy, who spent a lot of time answering Gisla's questions, had to often lean right over to hear her voice over the noise in the room.

Rollo had told Guy at the beginning of the meal that a ship had been readied and the weather looked promising to start his voyage on the following day. Gisla had openly expressed her sadness at his departure.

Guy enjoyed the evening and the nature of Dane's feasting. There appeared to be few inhibitions in their enjoyment of good company, along with a love of life and life's pleasures. But he curtailed his drinking, as he did not want a sour stomach before his sea voyage, as he remembered his queasiness on the journey from Britain.

He rose from the table at the same time as Gisla. He considered it an appropriate time to leave, as he looked across at two of Rollo's men wrestling bare-chested in the middle of the hall.

He happily stepped outside into the cool summer night and walked across to the main entrance of the castle's keep and up to the stone flight of steps to his bedchamber. The room was kept warm from a fire that crackled in the middle of the large stone hearth. The fire, along with several lit candles, shone a warm orange light across the room and Guy took off his tunic and boots, before sitting down to remove his trousers.

At that moment, the door opened, and his attending slave girl entered. Guy stopped what he was doing and just looked at her expectantly to see what she wanted. She then pulled down the top of her heavy woollen dress, moving it over her shoulders and down over her arms, allowing it to fall in a heap at her ankles. She stood fully naked in front of Guy, who looked upon her with a gaping mouth. The temptation to take advantage of the situation and the hospitality of Rollo stirred within him. But thoughts of his love and respect for Felice entered his mind, and he felt sudden guilt at his improper thoughts towards this slave girl. To Guy, love and chastity went hand in hand and any submission to base desires would be a betrayal of his love for Felice.

He held up his hands and with a quiet and kind tone in his voice, he refused the girl's offer.

She just shrugged her shoulders, as if it did not matter either way, and pulled her dress back up her body. She then turned around and left.

Guy lay down on the bed and shook his head in disbelief at the girl's offer, but mainly at his refusal.

Guy led his horse onto a large sailing galley. A score of oarsmen sat ready at each side of the ship with their oars raised high as a salute to Rollo. The Duke of Normandy was standing on the river pier, looking over the ship with both his wife and his son William alongside.

A crew member took the rein from Guy and led Bedivere down into the bottom of the hull, where there was a purpose-built stall to retain the horse during the voyage. Although the ship was a trading vessel, Guy and his belongings were the only cargo, and the crew looked at him to gauge his worth. Guy returned to the ship's side and stood on the upper side strake to say his farewells.

"I thank you, my lords," he said and then nodded at Gisla, "and, my lady." He then returned his attention to Rollo. "For your kindness and hospitality."

Rollo laughed again.

"Twice in a week," he said. "It is confirmed. I am a kind man."

Gisla, smiling, nudged him with her elbow.

"You are more than welcome Guy," Rollo said. "And you have paid back our hospitality tenfold with your company and your entertainment," Rollo said.

"It is also only part payment for the service that King Charles and Sir Hector have done for us in the past," Rollo continued. "We will lend our support to King Charles, and we will not forget Sir Hector. And we will not forget you, Guy."

William Longsword then came to the side of the ship and grasped Guy's hand. "It was good to meet you, Guy. You must come back and see us again as soon as you are able, and may your Gods go with you," William said with an air of earnestness.

Guy said his final thanks and the ship was cast off. The oarsmen calmly fixed their oars in a practised efficiency and rowed down the River Seine towards the sea.

Chapter Sixteen

The ship rowed out of the Seine estuary and then hoisted its sails to steer north to travel up along the Francia and Flanders coast. They saw a couple of boats as they travelled along the shoreline and they gave their vessel a wide birth, as Guy's vessel bore the lines of a Viking raiding ship. They eventually entered the waters that lay off the town of Calais, at which point they then turned west and headed across the sea to Britain.

They arrived at the British coast without any mishaps. The weather, although blustery, did not develop into anything to concern the ship's captain and they pulled in the sails and rowed into the harbour of Sandwich.

The town was a regular trading stop for Danish and Frankish ships, and the flags of Normandy, that the Viking ship displayed, were known to the town's harbour master.

The harbour master, however, still walked over to the ship, as it was being tied to a convenient pier, to enquire of its business, examine its hold and collect mooring taxes.

Prompted by the ship's captain, Guy went to meet with the harbour master. He formally announced himself as an ambassador of the Earl of Warwick and an emissary from Charles, King of West Francia, to deliver a message to King Edward. Guy stated that he expected the appropriate overnight hospitality that was representative of his rank and mission. He also asked for the town reeve to be informed.

The harbour master said that there was no need, and he would arrange suitable accommodation for Guy and the ship's captain. He would also arrange for provisions to be sent to the ship to feed the crew.

Guy also asked for Bedivere to be fed, watered, and stabled overnight and then thanked the harbour master. He then handed over a silver coin in appreciation of his kindness.

Guy smiled to himself when he considered how much he had learned over the last couple of months. His gained experience, in constantly mixing with higher ranks who treated him as an equal, had both greatly improved his demeanour and increased his self-confidence. He wondered if he would still be recognised as the same man when he arrived home.

They left early the next morning, intending to sail north up the coast to the port of Hartlepool, where Guy would leave the ship and travel overland to the town of Durham.

He had considered his options and thought it best to fulfil his oath to Sir Hector and take all his immediate wealth to his mother and explain first-hand the details of her son's death.

He was in a certain amount of conflict in his duty to Earl Rohand and whether his responsibilities required him to return directly to Warwick. He still, however, considered himself under the instructions of Sir Hector, to carry out this mission to visit his mother. Those directions might have been countermanded if he had disembarked at London and travelled north, which would require him to stop off at Warwick. But sailing directly north to Sir Hector's mother seemed the best course of action in satisfying Guy's conscience.

The only outstanding issue would be to settle Sir Hector's affairs with Father Corey, at Towcester, and then deliver the remaining monies back to his mother, which would have to wait for another time.

It took three days to travel up the East coast, with overnight stops in small ports within East Anglia, and on the estuary of the River Humber. Neither Guy or the crew left the ship, and slept rough in the hull, but the stops did allow Bedivere to be exercised and to graze for short periods.

The weather was becoming noticeably colder, and the ship's captain constantly scanned the skies for any impending squalls or storms. He was becoming more impatient to drop Guy off, onshore, and sail back across the sea to his homeland, before any bad weather impeded him.

But the weather held, and the ship safely docked in Hartlepool. Guy was set off, onshore, with Bedivere and all his belongings and with a quick farewell from the captain, they cast off their ropes to row out of the port and back to sea. Guy led Bedivere along the wooden pier and into the town, as he searched for an appropriate inn where he could stable his horse and get a comfortable room for the night.

He found a billet with stables, close to the docks, and he settled Bedivere, before going to the local inn and paying for a hot meal and a cup of ale. The bar area was noisy, dark, and filled with fumes. The pie was greasy and wholesome, and the ale was sour. Guy smiled as it now felt like he had returned home.

On finishing his meal, he chatted with the local fishermen and asked questions about the local area to find out who was important and what the gossip was from across the country. Guy reflected slightly on his behaviour in that he was imitating Sir Hector's practises and gathering knowledge that might help him. The usual wave of sadness swept over him at the memories of his friend. But he shrugged the grief off and replaced it with a feeling of gratitude for the experiences they shared and continued to find out more information.

Guy did not recognise the names of any of the local dignitaries, but he was glad to hear that Sitric was still in charge of Northumbria. There were still some reports of minor skirmishes between the Danes and the Anglo-

Saxons along the border, but nothing to suggest any real conflict.

Guy spent a restless night, as the loss of the ship's movement affected him, but he woke refreshed and ate a hearty breakfast, before catching a ferry across the River Humber and then riding towards York.

He did not intend to stop off at York, but he had heard that Sitric was in residence in the town, and he thought that it would be polite to renew his acquaintance. He stopped at the town's gate and asked to see the commander of the guard. He waited until a large Dane appeared, who abruptly asked Guy of his business. Guy used Rollo's name to smooth the way and mentioned that he was an acquaintance of the Jarl Sitric.

The commander just nodded and went away, but it was Sitric himself who returned smiling broadly, as he walked up to Guy.

"Guy of Warwick," Sitric said, and then clasped Guy in a hard embrace.

"It is good to see you again."

Sitric then stood back a pace and looked at Guy.

"You have both grown and aged," Sitric said. "I suspect that you have stories to tell."

Sitric put his arm around Guy's shoulders and directed him through the gate and into the town.

"I have been in Francia and Normandy, my lord," Guy replied. As he tried to match the large strides of Sitric.

"And you met with Rollo. How is the old giant?"

"Old, but still a giant," Guy replied. "But I liked him. He seems quite content in Normandy."

"Don't believe it," Sitric replied. "If he is not planning to raid then his son is."

Guy smiled.

"Yes, I met with William Longsword as well," Guy then said. "But I believe their view of raiding has changed to political infighting."

They continued to chat as they crossed a square, and then passed through another gate that guarded the inner palisade.

"You will join me tonight, Guy, for a private meal. I would like to hear your stories, and I have a favour that I would ask of you."

Guy was now getting quite used to being a guest. It was no longer a novelty to have his horse stabled, getting his clothes washed, his boots repaired and then provided with lavish accommodation, supplemented with ample food. Guy was also comfortable in instructing the servants on his requirements and although polite, he was insistent on making sure his belongings were secure in his rooms.

Sitric met with Guy in a small room, off the main hall. There was plenty of light from a blazing fire and a handful of wall-hung torches. Although they were alone, Sitric had laid on a large table of food and drink.

Sitric asked if Sir Harold had found the organiser of the raid on the Earl's of Warwick's ladies at Polesworth. Guy told him of his suspicions about Sir Roderick and that he left him dead in a field in Francia.

"So, you put an arrow through him?" Sitric said.

"I did not know at the time that it was Sir Roderick who was attacking me," Guy replied. "But if it was him who was behind the attack on our party at Polesworth, then I would have rather had met him with sword and made it personal."

Sitric nodded his agreement.

"Please send my satisfaction to the Earl on this," Sitric said and then asked Guy to tell of his adventures since they last met.

"I think the Gods are with you, Guy," Sitric said, after hearing Guy's accounts. "But I am sorry for the death of Sir Hector. I knew him personally and was aware of his wider reputation; his death is a sad loss. Although in my world, he is now feasting with all the warriors he has fought and killed in the past. He will also be looking down, waiting for you to join him in his celebrations." Sitric took a large drink of ale. "But let us hope that it will be a long time to come, as I am sure that more adventures await you."

"But now of my favour, Guy," Sitric then said. "As I am eager to ask."

Guy nodded.

"Like Rollo, I feel the need to settle down," he said quietly. "I have fought many battles, both here and in Ireland, and I now just want to live in peace and look after my lands and my people, both Saxon and Dane alike."

Guy sat and listened, as Sitric chose his words carefully.

"There are still fights on the borders and there are still blood feuds to settle. Edward also looks to secure his kingdom and is a constant threat."

"He marries his children to the nobles of East and West Francia to secure political alliances. But I think it would be more advantageous for him to secure his position in his own country, now that he has expanded his reign to Mercia." Sitric paused and looked closely at Guy.

"So, I am suggesting that you might be able to support me to your Earl, in creating an alliance and see if he can then recommend it to Edward."

Sitric then smiled at Guy and sat back in his chair.

"I could always send emissaries to the King myself, but I think that I would like it to be his idea and therefore I would like to 'plant a seed' in his mind." Sitric looked at Guy for his understanding.

"Is that a correct use of the term, 'to plant a seed'?"

Guy smiled back. "Yes, my lord."

"And I have a few years to let that seed grow."

"Do you have anybody in mind, my lord?"

"Not particularly, as long as it will guarantee some kind of lasting peace, so that I do not have to constantly look over my shoulder and let me plan for my old age."

Sitric then laughed. "Listen to me Guy. Not the words of a feared Viking."

Guy laughed with him.

"I did however enjoy the company of Lady Edith, who I met when I was last with you in Mercia, and that, I feel, would be a good match."

"I will gladly 'plant the seed', my lord, and my recommendation will be truthful. I will tell of your support for me in all of the meetings I have had with you."

"Thank you, Guy. I think we Danes get accustomed to this comfortable life you lead in these fertile lands. Rollo has certainly found it and I think it changes your perspective on the joy of battle." He paused and thought for a moment. "Is Rollo really a Christian?"

"So it is said, but I saw no tangible evidence of it, my lord. There were no priests in Rollo's company, and I never saw him go to mass or prayers. But I am sure that his wife is Christian."

Sitric nodded and thought about it.

"I think that you should employ a priest, my lord," Guy added, smiling. "And have some deep theological arguments."

Sitric laughed. "I would like that, but I would think that I may be forced to kill any priest to prove a theological point."

Sitric then became more solemn. "I believe, Sir Hector was very religious," Sitric said. "How did you find the contradictions in his faith?"

"I didn't find any contradictions, my lord," Guy said defensively. "I think that Sir Hector did not believe in God so much as he had trust in God."

Sitric thought about what Guy had said and pursed his lips slightly.

"Sir Hector had faith that in this life, God has plans for his people," Guy added. "He believed that you must go with the flow, trust in your God-given instincts and hope that your actions prove virtuous."

Chapter Seventeen

Guy stayed overnight in the small settlement of Darlington on his way to Durham. He only managed to get rough lodgings and had to fend for himself for food and ale. Bedivere was however sheltered from the cold, as the evening was clear, and a hard ground frost provided the first hint to the approaching winter. Throughout the night, chill winds whispered an apprehensive threat over the surrounding countryside and a glaze of ice spread over the exposed windows of the inn's room.

At first light, Guy cast an extra blanket over Bedivere and wrapped his cloak hard around him, before he set off north. To keep warm, he wore his dress tunic, padded gambeson, and chainmail beneath his cloak. He also wore his full leather gauntlets but resisted putting his helmet on.

Guy travelled along a well-maintained road and arrived in Durham in mid-afternoon, where he crossed a wide stone bridge over a fast-running river. He then went straight to a large local inn to eat and get warm. He looked around for a pedlar, who might sell him some additional layers of clothes to protect him from the biting cold, but no one in the inn could provide him with any appropriate wares. Bedivere was tied outside, and he would need to find stables and secure his belongings, while he asked around to see if anyone knew of Sir Hector's mother.

It was not as difficult as he thought, as everyone seemed to know Sir Hector and the town looked on him and his reputation with a consolidated pride. His mother was also well known, and she lived north of the town along the River Wear on the road to a town called Chester-le-Street.

Guy thought that he would visit her the following day, as he was still chilled from his travels. However, once he agreed his accommodation and made sure Bedivere was settled, he went to look around the town to see if he could get hold of some more blankets or a warm coat.

Guy liked Durham, although he had to listen hard to the locals, as they spoke with a heavy accent and some words had merged between Danish and Anglo-Saxon. The town itself was built on a promontory within a tight loop of the river and the sturdy castle, which was built on top of the rocky outcrop, was therefore secure on three sides. There was also a large church dedicated to Saint Cuthbert, who was a great symbol of Christianity in Northumberland and well known to Guy. His body, which was reputed not to decay, had been carried around the kingdom to keep it from the ravaging Danes, and had inspired Alfred the Great's fight against the Norsemen.

Guy thought back to Felice's priest and whether he was named after Northumberland's Saint Cuthbert. Guy smiled at the thought, as he remembered that the priest was always, metaphorically speaking, being carried around by Felice's presence.

The people of Durham were friendly and hospitable. They provided Guy with a selection of winter coats and blankets. Guy chose one of each and although he wanted to buy more, he knew that they would be cumbersome to carry on the back of Bedivere.

Guy also found a tradesman, who was able to sew the emblem of Sir Hector's ears of wheat, onto the bottom edge of his tunic, alongside Sir Harold's oak tree, that he had added before he left Warwick. He fingered them both lightly and considered the impact that both Sir Harold and Sir Hector had on his life.

Eventually, he returned to his hostel and ate supper, as the night bristled in.

The following morning was just as cold as the night before. Guy shivered as he retrieved Bedivere from the stables and then made his way out of Durham, along an old Roman road to the town of Chester-Le-Street. The peasants, who he met on the road, were either suspicious of Guy or protective over Sir Hector's mother and were reticent to give Guy any directions. But he eventually found a boy who was happy to point Guy on the right way and with his guidance he came upon a small, thatched house. It was surrounded by a large garden that, despite the oncoming winter, was still well-stocked with various plants, some of which Guy recognised from Sir Hector's teachings.

The house, with its two smaller outbuildings, stood at the bottom of a slope at the base of an escarpment and was well maintained. Woods surrounded the house and garden and the River Wear slowly meandered past at the bottom of the valley.

Guy got down off Bedivere and led the horse the last few yards to the wooden fence that marked the house's boundary. He then tied the rein to a fence post and went to knock on the door.

An elderly woman answered and looked Guy up and down. She then focused on his face.

"You better come on in and tell what has happened to my son," she said, as she turned to go back into the building.

They stepped into a bright front room that had a large window that looked down over the wide valley.

"Does he still live?" She asked quietly.

"No," Guy answered softly. "He died in Francia several days ago."

"I am sorry," he then said.

Guy then reached inside his tunic and pulled out a large money pouch.

"His last words were to make sure that I brought you the remains of his wealth."

He laid the pouch down on a side table.

"There is more money that is in safekeeping at a Friary in Towcester. I will bring that to you at the next opportunity, but I thought it best to come here first and tell you about the news in person."

The woman slowly sat down and closed her eyes. She sat still for several seconds, breathing deeply, and the room was heavy with the silence.

"Thank you," she eventually said. "Now tell me who you are, and how you knew my son?"

Guy explained his relationship with Sir Hector, her son's support for King Charles and the events that led to his death.

Sir Hector's mother, who was called Elwine, was more interested in Guy's thoughts of her son, than in his exploits. She was happy that he had taken Guy under his wing and in his pride of his mother. She smiled as Guy described how Sir Hector seethed at the injustices of her past but then eulogised over her knowledge of plants, herbs, and remedies. She kept asking Guy questions about her son's character and interrogated him over certain points, as she tried to get more detail. She said that this was her last chance to fully get to know her son, as a man, and these were the memories that she would hold on to for the rest of her life. Guy, therefore, answered as honestly as he could. Her eyes watered when he discussed his own feelings towards Sir Hector, and his admiration of him as a man and not for his deeds. He described how his influence has already changed his life and that Sir Hector's personal legacy will remain with him forever in how he will lead his own life.

Guy spent all morning with Elwine, but eventually felt that it was time to leave and let her grieve alone over her son. He once again expressed his condolences as he stood to walk out of the house and into the garden.

Guy paused on the doorstep and turned to look at Elwine. She clasped Guy in a tight embrace and through tear-filled eyes, she thanked him for coming to see her. Guy promised to return as soon as he had a chance to visit Father Corey, but at that moment her expression changed, and she looked closely at Guy.

Guy sensing her change of mood looked down on her.

"I wish for you to have half of this remaining money or wealth," she said earnestly.

Guy just looked at her, confused.

"I do not need money and most of what I receive I use to help the poor and infirm," she continued.

"I thank you Elwine, but I cannot possibly take the money that Sir Hector left for you," Guy replied.

"I think my son would have wanted you to have support for the future," she said. "I can tell, from what you have told me, that in the brief time he knew you, he became very much attached to you. Perhaps even, in some way, like a son he never had."

"I never told Hector," she continued. "But when the Archbishop came to me for treatment, after I was banished from the town for witchcraft, he paid me handsomely for the remedy. The treatment lasted for several years, although I think, with the embarrassment of his ailment, he really paid for my silence. That money I used to give Hector the start in life that set him above his equals and, as it turned out, his betters."

She placed her hand on his arm.

"Take half the money and use it to make a difference for yourself in this life. Use it in the grace of God and, like my son, support the good people that bring light into this dark world."

She then gestured him towards his horse.

"And the other half I will use as an excuse for you to come back and see me again."

Guy jumped up onto his horse.

"I thank you, Elwine, and I swear that I will use the money for good. I will return with what is left of Sir Hector's estate as soon as I can, although I would have liked to have come anyway, just to share your company."

"You will always be welcome, Guy," she replied softly.

Guy walked Bedivere back down the road towards Durham with a sense of contentment. He had lived with the absence of Sir Hector for the last few months and now he felt his loss in a positive light. He felt that he could now return home, to Warwick, in a more gratified frame of mind, but he would look forward to coming back to Durham to see Elwine.

In her, he recognised all the good that was contained in Sir Hector. She was a reflection of his friend, and she was there to fill the hole of his loss, if and whenever it was needed in the future.

Guy returned to his lodgings, packed his belongings, and settled his bills. He rode Bedivere northwards out of the town and along the bend in the river to a wide ford which was his road south. He was now finally on his way home.

Guy's journey south was uneventful apart from being stopped by a band of Danes, who were travelling north. They halted their horses on all sides of Guy, who confidently dropped Sitric's name into the conversation, as his close friend and told them to pass on his regards if they passed York.

The Danes took heed of Guy's association with Sitric and decided that a single traveller who was dressed poor but at the same time, well-armed, would not be worth robbing. So, they left him in peace and Guy, just happily went on his way.

The weather remained cold, but dry, and Guy arrived in the large town of Derby late in the afternoon. He had slept rough on the previous night and decided to stay at an inn and have a warm room, if he could find one.

He came across a tavern and tied Bedivere to a post. He then went in to enquire of any available accommodation. The inn was warm and welcoming, and he sat next to the fire where he ordered food and ale. He removed his coat to reveal his tournament tunic which he still wore to keep warm. He had forgotten that he was wearing it and was slightly embarrassed by the looks from the other guests, as the bright red of the Warwick colours stood out in the darkened room.

"May I ask sir, if you are 'Guy of Warwick'?" A voice called out.

Guy turned quickly around at hearing his name. He looked towards a middle-aged man. He was standing in the centre of the room, alongside another man, with boyish looks, who was only a year or two younger than Guy. Both men were dressed in expensive-looking cloaks that hung back from fine tunics and trousers. They were both holding cups of ale in their hands and looked at him closely.

"May I ask who is asking?" Guy said politely, as he had repeated the same response that Sir Hector always said, whenever he was unexpectedly addressed in taverns.

"I am Sir Aldred," the older man said. "And this is my son, George. I was at Soissons, and I am quite sure that I recognise you."

Guy laid his coat on the wooden stool and walked across to greet the knight.

He bowed his head at Sir Aldred.

"My lord," Guy said, and then nodded his respect towards George. "I am 'Guy of Warwick', and I am flattered that you remembered me."

Sir Aldred smiled.

"Nonsense, my lad. You were the talking point of the tournament."

"In what way?" Guy asked with genuine interest.

"Oh, let me think," he said laughing towards his son. "Exploding spears, attacks in the training fields, sword fights in the streets and you managed to come out on top in most of them."

Guy smiled back, remembering the antics that surrounded him throughout the tournament.

Sir Aldred then became more serious.

"I heard about the death of Sir Hector. Is it true?"

"Yes, my lord," Guy answered, his levity suddenly disappearing. "I have just paid my respect to his mother in Durham."

The knight just nodded.

"Perhaps I can invite you to dine with us tonight, if you are not already engaged," he said. "We can exchange tales, although I think yours will be of more interest."

"I would be honoured, my lord," Guy replied.

"No, Guy. I think the honour will be all mine. I will send a page with the arrangements and allow you to rest after your journey."

Sir Aldred and his son both nodded to Guy and after quickly finishing their drinks, they left the tavern.

From the tavern keeper's sudden increase in courtesy and regard of his guest, Guy realised that Sir Aldred was clearly an important man in the area. From this newly formed association, he was now the centre of attention in the room.

'Reputation', Guy thought to himself. Sir Hector would be looking down from heaven with a broad smile on his face.

He then arranged for Bedivere to be stabled.

Guy sat quietly and finished his meal although he was constantly interrupted to answer several questions from the tavern keeper, who wanted to know more about his adventures. Guy did not mind the interest, as he had not spoken with anyone for quite a while, and he appreciated the new company.

As Sir Aldred had promised, a page entered the tavern and handed Guy a sealed letter which was the formal invite. The page looked nervous as he handed Guy the parchment, but Guy, with a genuine interest, asked his name and what he was up to. Guy could still remember being in the same position himself, only a few years ago, and was always grateful when a senior member of the castle household paid him any attention.

Guy then went to his room to bathe and dress and then waited for the page to come to escort him to Sir Aldred's residence.

There were a good two dozen guests gathered in the main hall, who Sir Aldred had managed to invite at short notice. Guy was impressed by how quickly he had arranged food, drink, and entertainment, and it was obvious to Guy that he was the attraction for the night.

Guy had to tell of how he had tailored his spears for his 'Spear on Horse' contest and Sir Aldred cut in to describe the sight of the wooden splinters flying around the arena. He also told of the arrow attack, as he exercised Sir Hector's horse. But he declined in telling about Sir Hector's death until later when he was alone with Sir Aldred and his son.

"So, he was killed by an arrow, from the same archer who shot at you in Soissons," Sir Aldred stated.

"Yes, my lord," Guy answered.

"And he was wearing Burgundy colours?"

"Yes, my lord," Guy answered again.

"Did you know that the Duke of Burgundy has died from a nasty illness?" He then said.

"No, my lord, although I knew that he was ill."

"And you killed the archer and mopped up all the remaining three assailants."

"Yes, my lord."

"And rescued, King Charles."

"I escorted him to Lorraine, my lord."

"Good on you Guy."

Sir Aldred then thought to himself for a while.

"I spoke with Sir Hector at the melee, after he wiped the floor with us all, and he said that you were also skilled with the sword. He said that you won a melee at Earl Rohand's tournament in Warwick."

Guy nodded.

"Could I ask you to put my son and some of my other retainers through their paces tomorrow morning? I would like to see what Sir Hector meant about lithesome."

Guy readily accepted the request, as it would have been impolite not to, but he was also slightly concerned that people constantly wanted to test their skills against him. He was starting to gain insight into what Sir Hector meant about providing entertainment and how it was aligned to reputation. In Guy's case, his reputation was associated with his fighting skills, and people wanted to witness it.

The weather was fine, and Guy met with Sir Aldred's retainers in a field alongside the river, which flowed through the eastern side of the town. Guy did not know what was happening, as the field was silent, and the retainers all looked to him with apprehension. He turned towards Sir Aldred, who watched from the side, but he remained impassive and looked back at Guy with raised eyebrows.

So, Guy took the organisation into his own hands and paired the retainers off and went through basic exercises. These routines were part of Sir Harold's training and ingrained in his own practises. He then swapped places with one trainee at a time and allowed them to attack him. For each opponent, he conducted a series of parries as he stepped backwards and then turned defence into attack as he walked forward with large slashing strokes allowing them to return the parries.

He was surprised at how limited they were in their fighting skills, compared to what he was used to at Warwick. He, therefore, had to reduce his own capabilities to match their limitations. When he eventually faced Sir Aldred's son; George, he called a halt and gathered the whole group in a large semi-circle. He had watched George, and although he was the best of the group, he was still very restricted in his manoeuvres. Guy asked George to accompany him as he went to talk with Sir Aldred.

"Their basic skills are sound, my lord, but their strokes and positioning are obvious. They can easily be manipulated, countered, and exposed. May I ask your permission to show them what they could do if they applied themselves with more imagination?"

"Certainly, Guy," Sir Aldred responded, with an air of anticipation.

Guy then turned and spoke to George quietly.

"I will fight you in a manner that you are used to for three sequences, so you can show your colleagues how good you are. But then I will change my style and fight using my own methods and see how you react," Guy said and smiled at George. "I am sure that you will think that I am showing off and you will be right. But my first lesson for you is in understanding that reputation is everything."

Guy patted him on the shoulder, and they faced each other and engaged.

For three sequences George moved forward and backwards with tight and extravagant strokes, which Guy easily matched and then Guy just danced around him. He twisted, turned, and continued to slap his sword flat at George's exposed body and arms. Guy then rolled over his shoulders to target George's legs and then leapt and swivelled in the air, ending up in front of

George, with his sword tip held to the middle of his chest.

There was silence around the group as the spectators were amazed at Guy's skills and then Sir Aldred clapped loudly. Guy removed his helmet and smiled broadly at George.

"You are good, George," Guy said and then placed his arm around his shoulders as he led him away. "But I think that you have limited training and limited opponents. You should pay us a visit to Warwick and stay for a while, as you would benefit from more varied training. I was tutored under Sir Harold of Arden, who is an accomplished knight and instructor."

"Thank you, Guy," George said with sincerity. "I will see if my father will arrange it. But I am happy, at the moment, just to boast that I have fought 'Guy of Warwick' and survived."

Guy stayed for another night, before packing his belongings at first light to prepare for the last leg of his journey, as he planned to reach Warwick by nightfall. He said his farewells to both Sir Aldred and his son, and once again invited George to Warwick, to participate in the Earl's training.

The homeward journey was uneventful, and it was cold as he crossed the River Avon, to the north of Warwick, and he rode Bedivere directly up to the castle gate. The sky was just holding on to the last light of the day and the town was quiet and peaceful as it settled for the night. Guy looked up at the castle palisades and he felt both tired and excited at the same time. He felt weary for his long travels but was overjoyed at arriving back home. He was hailed when he approached the gate, as a sentry asked his business.

"I am 'Guy of Warwick'" Guy said proudly, in response to the sentry. "And I have come home."

The castle was quiet as he led Bedivere towards the stables and then suddenly it wasn't, as Harry ran up to him, shouting his name and embracing him tightly in welcome. The sentry at the gate had alerted the other castle guards and Harry, who happened to be on duty, rushed down to meet his friend. Other castle guards also came up to slap him on the back and suddenly he was surrounded. Everyone was talking at the same time and Guy did not know which way to turn. Then some of the guards were pushed aside and Terold stood before Guy. They faced each other in silence and then smiled broadly in unison and wrapped their arms around each other.

"Move aside now and get back to your duties," a booming voice called out. The guards all stepped a pace or two backwards to let Sir Harold through.

"So, the wanderer returns," Sir Harold said smiling. "Welcome home Guy."

Sir Harold dispersed the crowd and Terold took Bedivere to the stables, while Guy went to see his parents. They had heard the noise in the courtyard and realised that their son had returned, and they stood in the doorway of their home with tears in their eyes. They hugged each other as a group, his mother unable to speak, until his father pulled himself away and looked at his son.

"You have changed Guy," Sigard said. "You look older."

"I feel older," Guy said.

Sigard remained silent and looked at his on, "We feared the worst when we heard of Sir Hector," he then said.

"I was fortunate," Guy responded with a heavy heart.

"Come in and sit down, son, and we will warm some stew," Sigard then said and hugged him again.

Guy had just finished his meal when there was a loud knock at the door.

Sigard opened it and then quickly stood aside as Earl Rohand stepped in, followed by Sir Harold.

Guy stood up and bowed his head in respect to his liege lord.

"I am sorry to disturb you Sigard, but I had to see for myself," the Earl said to his steward, and then looked at Guy. He smiled broadly.

"Thank God you have returned Guy," he said. "I have had constant updates but have not heard anything for a while. As usual, you seem to have been in the thick of things, but I am glad you are safe."

"Thank you, my lord. It is good to be home."

Sir Rohand then looked at Sigard and then back to Guy.

"I know you must be tired, Guy, and that you would like to spend time with your parents, but can I invite you to the hall for an hour or so. Your parents are also welcome, as my guests for dinner. I am afraid that I cannot wait to hear of your adventures."

"It will be our pleasure, my lord," Sigard quickly said, on behalf of his son.

"Excellent," Earl Rohand replied rubbing his hands together. "Come on up as soon as you are ready, and I will get things prepared."

"My lord," Guy then said with urgency. He went to his clothes bag and pulled out the parchments that King Charles had given him.

Guy formally presented the Earl with the letter which Charles had written for him.

"I was asked by King Charles of West Francia to give you this."

Earl Rohand looked at the seal and then back to Guy.

"I also have one for King Edward, my lord. I am tasked to give it to him as soon as possible."

The whole room was quiet as they looked at Guy in wonder.

"My word Guy," Earl Rohand said, breaking the silence "I am now looking forward to hearing what you have to tell even more."

The Earl left with Sir Harold and Guy's parents hurried around changing their clothes and getting themselves ready. Guy gave himself a quick wash from a small bowl and put on his dusty dress tunic. He also decided that the trousers he was wearing were the most presentable. He rubbed his unshaven cheeks and ran his fingers through his hair and wished that he could just go to bed.

Guy was not prepared for the greeting when he entered the hall. The Earl came over to the door himself and led Guy and his parents to a large table in the centre of the room, where his wife stood up to greet him. The Lady Elaine leant over to kiss Guy on the cheek and welcome him home. Guy looked down to the other Lady who remained seated next to Elaine and Felice looked up at him with tears in her eyes. Guy's breath was taken away at the sight of her. She had never seemed so beautiful, and Guy's heart was filled with joy, but all he could do was smile guardedly at her. She looked down to her feet, as her father turned Guy around and sat him down in his chair, before ordering drinks.

They ate their meal, and although Guy had already eaten his mother's stew, he still had an appetite for the fare presented to him. After the meal, Guy retold the stories of his adventures in Francia, although he did not tell of his trip to Troyes and the poisoning of the Count of Burgundy. He did tell of his visit to Elwine and asked Earl Rohand if this was the correct thing to have done. The Earl wholeheartedly supported Guy in discharging Sir Hector's remaining will as soon as practicable. But Guy was silent on the proportion of the money that Elwine had promised him, as he thought that it seemed too personal.

They were already aware of the Danish attack on Towcester, along with Sir Hector and Guy's involvement, but were unaware of the ambush on them, outside of the town. They were also interested in Sir Hector's assumption that they had been followed from Warwick.

They were amused at the antics of the Soissons tournament and laughed when he described the fight in the street with Sir Roderick and Sir Otto.

But the hall remained silent when he told of the fall of Sir Hector. They took a collective deep breath when he told them of how he discovered Sir Roderick's body amongst the dead, and that he was a party to the death of the renowned knight.

"My word, Guy," the Earl said. "I did not envisage that I would put you in so much danger when I agreed to you accompanying Sir Hector."

"And you got home all by yourself," Elaine said.

"I am sure, my dear, that if Guy killed so many enemies and avoided his own death in the process, he would have the capabilities to get home," the Earl replied.

"I have Rollo, the Duke of Normandy, to thank for that," Guy said and then went over his experiences in Rouen, including the impromptu melee and his fight with William Longsword.

"And you say he sent me his regards," the Earl said.

"Yes, my lord."

"And you do not know what was in Charles's letter to Rollo," the Earl continued.

"No, my lord, but I am sure that Rollo will support King Charles if he raises an army to recapture his throne."

"And you have this letter for King Edward?"

"Yes, my lord."

The Earl thought for several moments.

"I am sorry to inconvenience you further Guy, but I believe that we need to deliver this letter as soon as possible and I think your presence will be required," the Earl said thoughtfully. "What do you say, Sir Harold?"

"I agree, my lord," Sir Harold replied. "The situation in Francia will be of great interest to the King. Especially in respect to keeping his son-in-law on the throne."

"Do you not think he has been through enough?" Felice suddenly said with a wave of anger in her tone.

"Felice!" Her mother said, reprimanding her for her interruption.

"I do not think there will be any danger in Mercia or Wessex," the Earl said, taken aback by his daughter's outburst.

"Can you spare your son for a few more days, Sigard?" The Earl then asked Guy's father, knowing full well that his steward would not oppose his plan.

"Whatever you think is right, my lord," Sigard answered dutifully.

"Then that is settled. We will leave tomorrow after Guy has rested sufficiently," the Earl said in a tone of authority.

"Sir Harold. Can you and Sigard make arrangements, and plan to leave tomorrow afternoon with a minimal party?" The Earl commanded.

Sir Harold rose from his seat knowing that the arrangements will need to start straight away.

"Yes, my lord," Sir Harold said and gestured at Sigard to follow, as he left the hall.

"You will need your rest, Guy," Earl Rohand added. "So off to your bed. Ask for anything that you may need for the journey."

The Earl then also rose from his seat.

"We will therefore go and meet with the King."

Chapter Eighteen

Earl Rohand assembled only a small group of men to escort him south to the town of Winchester, where the King was in residence. It included Sir Harold, who insisted on attending, and three of his trusted household guards. Walter was also included to accompany Guy, in acting as squires to the two nobles. Guy was happy that after all his exploits over the last few months, he had now reverted to his old role as a squire. He could now relax, as all the responsibilities that he had assumed over the last few months were taken away from him. Terold, however, to Guy's great disappointment, was not included in the party, as he was needed to fill in for Sir Harold, in managing the training of the squires and pages.

They left early the next morning, even though Guy had still not fully recovered from the previous day. Guy, however, kept his weariness to himself, as they rode quickly down the old Roman road. Guy was asked to take a position between the Earl and Sir Harold so that they could question him further on his trip away. The Earl said it was important that they knew everything, as they would have to advise the King. They asked for Guy's opinions on the assembly of nobles at Soissons and the likely sides that they were taking. They were also intrigued by Charles's intentions and Rollo's subsequent support for Charles. They were also interested in William Longsword's views and standing, especially in his new political positioning. But to Guy's continual sadness, they constantly asked on Sir Hector's thoughts, although Guy could offer little insight because of his friend and tutor's reticence in discussing such affairs.

During their journey, they found accommodation or shelter easily enough to find, due to the Earl's status and in his ability to pay. This was fortunate, as winter had now laid down its pallet and painted the country with a grey tinged wash. Guy would not have wanted to live out in the forest, as on his travels with Sir Hector. Trees were now bare, and the landscape was bleak and inhospitable. The wind ripped across the grassy downs as they travelled through Wessex and the party were fully wrapped in a selection of hooded cloaks, heavy coats, fleeces, and woollen blankets to protect them from the cold.

They eventually arrived in Winchester, and they were taken directly to the palace, where the Earl, Sir Harold and Guy were taken directly for an audience to the King. Guy was aware of the grandness of the King's accommodation, but he still felt intimidated by its grandeur and stateliness.

They were shown directly into the King's private chamber, where Edward was seated at his large wooden desk. There was a handful of advisors from both the royal court and from the church, standing around the room.

The Earl's party walked up to the King and bowed in respect.

"Rohand," Edward said. "Your visit, although welcome, is unexpected, and I have brought you here to explain your presence which, I expect, is important. You are happy with our company?" He said, gesturing to his advisors in what was more a statement than a question.

"Your council is of course your own decree, sire," the Earl said politely, not looking away from the King. "But I have brought you a letter from King Charles of Francia who is at present in Lorraine and trying to assemble an army to recover his kingdom."

The Earl then placed the parchment that Guy had given him on top of Edward's desk.

"I have also brought you one of my retainers, who has just returned from Charles's company and also has a private message from Rollo of Normandy."

The King looked at Sir Harold.

"It is Guy, sire," Earl Rohand said and gestured towards his young squire. "He has just returned from a trip to Soissons with Sir Hector."

King Edward then sat up in his chair and reached for the letter.

Guy stood and watched Edward read the letter. The King appeared to be of a similar age as Earl Rohand, but his face was long and dark and shadowed behind well-groomed, long brown wavy hair. He had large inset eyes, a long nose, and a pointed beard. Although there was a fire in the room, he wore a heavy red cloak tied in front of his neck with a large gold clasp.

Guy also looked around the room at the King's advisors and noticed Athelstan standing next to the room's fire, which was crackling in a large stone hearth. Athelstan smiled at Guy from across the room and Guy nodded his head in both acknowledgement and respect.

The King finished reading the letter and rolled it carefully back up and placed it back on his desk.

"Charles has also sent me a letter, sire, which may also be of interest," Earl Rohand said and then took the roll of parchment from his coat and passed it to the King.

Edward then read that letter and handed it back to Rohand.

"And is this also your will, Earl Rohand?" the King said.

"He has my petition and support, sire."

Edward then looked at Guy.

"I wish to hear your account of your travels with Sir Hector," The King said to Guy. "But I would like you to do this as a trusted servant of your king and country. Your part in the defence of Towcester from a Danish incursion is already known to me, and I am thankful for your courage and valour in the protection of its people.

So, with the plea of your liege lord and with the recommendation of my brother-in-law, King Charles of West Francia, I would now raise you to a position of Knight of the Realm." He then stood up and walked away from his desk. "Do you have any objection in taking this position of service, 'Guy of Warwick'?"

Guy was taken aback by this shock of the King's words. Guy had not considered this possibility of such an offer and the shock rendered him speechless.

Guy looked to his side at Earl Rohand, who, with a serious expression, just nodded at Guy. He then returned his gaze to Edward, who was now standing in front of him.

"No, sire," Guy stuttered. "I would be greatly honoured."

"Then, in front of these witnesses, I would take your oath to faithfully serve both your liege lord and your king in support of this realm. You will swear to defend it to the best of your abilities and preserve its survival with your life, in the face of God."

Guy swallowed hard.

"I give you my oath, sire, and swear my loyalty."

The King held out his arm and Guy lightly took hold of his fingers and bowed his head to kiss the top of his hand

"With that oath and in front of these witnesses, I now make you Sir Guy, a Knight of the Realm."

"I will provide you with appropriate lands from within Mercia to support your position. Sir Guy," The King said.

Guy, still stunned at being awarded the title was further surprised at this presentation of lands, and suddenly wondered what such a knighthood meant.

"Thank you, sire," Guy said and bowed again to the King.

"But now I need to hear your accounts of Francia," he said to Guy.

"And, with your leave gentlemen," he then said to the others in the room. "I would like to do this alone with Sir Guy."

When the room had emptied, Edward gestured to Guy to sit opposite him in front of the fire and the King removed his cloak.

"Have you played the game of chess, Guy?" The King said.

"No, sire. But I heard Sir Hector discuss it a few times."

"It is an interesting game, and you should learn it, perhaps if we can make the time, I will teach you the basics."

"Thank you, sire," Guy said without any real understanding of what was been asked of him.

"It is a game of strategy, where you plan your moves and try to influence or predict your opponent's moves," the King then said, as he sat back in his chair.

"The game is remarkably similar to what is being played out in Francia and in our own kingdom. We move and sacrifice our pieces to a strategy that will win the overall contest. Part of those moves is to marry daughters to form alliances. Other moves are to instigate rebellions or wars, to remove other pieces," the King brought the fingers of his hands together and placed the tips to his chin.

"Some pieces are more valuable than others. Some I can afford to sacrifice, and others are key pieces which if lost, affect the strategy. Sir Hector was a key piece to me."

"Sir Hector was also a good friend," he then said. "So, if you describe your journey, with details, on who you and Sir Hector met, starting at Towcester, I would be grateful."

Guy was becoming well practised at telling his story. But this time he had to answer questions throughout the telling, as the King continually interrupted him to gather as much information as he could from his recollections.

Guy hesitated when he got to the part where he left Charles at Verdun to travel home. But he now considered his oath to the King.

"I have not told anybody else of this, sire. But I took a detour after leaving King Charles and went to Burgundy."

"The physicians suspected the Count's death as poisoning, but had no proof," The King said. "An unknown servant, who attended the Count, was new to the court and disappeared just before the Count's illness and mysteriously was never seen again."

"I am not proud of my actions, sire," Guy said unhappily. "But I have no regrets and I will answer for my sins to God."

"Did you know that Sir Hector was an assassin?" The King said quietly and watched Guy closely. "He was also called upon to ensure the death of many an adversary over the years, and he was an expert at providing such services. Your words could have come out of his own mouth."

Guy was taken aback by the revelation, but somehow, he was not surprised. Guy knew that Sir Hector, as well as mixing with royalty and nobility also worked in the dark underbelly of society and met with dishonest and unscrupulous people to gather information and perhaps provide services. Guy, however, had always ignored thinking about these aspects of Sir Hector's life, as it went against the high opinions and sentiments he held for his friend.

"But the Count was old and not long for this world, if you were under my service, I would have had you poison his son as well. As it is, I do not think Burgundy's position in support of Robert, the Count of Poitiers will change."

"However, it was still murder, Guy, and although outside my lawful jurisdiction, you will have to answer to God. But in your case, I suspect that he will be lenient," Edward then said.

"But I recommend that you follow Sir Hector's charitable works in providing for the needy, as penitence for your deed."

"I am already doing that, sire, but I was doing it in memory of Sir Hector."

"Then we will say no more of it," Edward finally said.

Guy then continued describing his time at Normandy with Rollo and William Longsword. King Edward thought their stance in supporting Charles very interesting.

When Guy finished and King Edward had learned enough, drinks were called for and Earl Rohand and Sir Harold were summoned to attend.

The King thanked the Earl for coming to Winchester at such short notice and sat them down for drinks.

"So, you went to see Sir Hector's mother," the King asked Guy.

"Yes, sire," Guy answered. "She was understanding of Sir Hector's death."

"I also had the pleasure of meeting with Sitric of Northumberland when I passed through York," Guy continued.

"Did you really, Guy," Edward said with interest, "and what did he have to say?"

"He was interested in Normandy, sire, and, as usual, on our Saxon way of life and our beliefs. He struggles to understand us, but I think if pushed he could be persuaded to settle down in a similar manner to Rollo. He may even convert to Christianity."

"What are his ambitions?" Edward asked with a greater interest.

"I think an alliance would suit him, sire. I believe he would give up territory for security."

"I think tomorrow I will teach you chess, Guy," Edward then said, smiling.

The Earl's party dined with the King and had rooms arranged for them within the palace.

Sir Harold alternated between amusement and embarrassment, as he came to terms with Guy's sudden elevation to that of equal rank. Guy matched his unease in equal measure. But they both walked down to the stables together to check on the horses, Sir Harold threatened Walter with a thrashing when Guy pretended to take offence at being ordered to blanket the horses for the night. Then, after seeing Walter's confusion, they heartily laughed about the situation which broke the ice.

Guy however fetched the blankets and made sure that the horses were warm enough and treated Walter as if nothing had changed.

"You are now a knight of the realm, Guy, and you must make the distinction to what was your previous standing as a squire. You can no longer behave like you used to," Sir Harold said to him as they walked back to the Royal Palace.

"But I have not changed," Guy answered.

"But you have changed," Sir Harold said. "And you are now a knight and lesser people both want and need to treat you like a knight. Otherwise, there is no point in aspiring to become a knight, and to make this world a better place," Sir Harold said.

"Remember how you dreamed of becoming a knight and the reverence that you hold for King Arthur and his own knights. You now have to personify that dream."

Guy slept uneasily, as he was excited at achieving his childhood wishes, but he was also apprehensive about what the responsibilities meant. However, in the cold darkness, he lay awake and thought of Felice. He considered his new status, and he knew that he could now socialise in different circles. He could also now look to marry into a noble line. But he wondered if his standing as a knight was anyway high enough to court not only an Earl's daughter but also an heiress to a great estate. Yesterday morning, his union with Felice was a pipe dream, but this morning, a slim chance of winning her hand had presented itself. But he still suspected that it was still only a dream, and that life was playing a cruel joke in taunting him with that faint possibility of happiness. He struggled with what the future may hold, but finally decided, that his position was no different to the time when he left being a blacksmith's apprentice, to become a page for the Earl in the castle. So, he would do what he did then, and just go with the flow. To carry on as normal until he was told differently.

He therefore got out of bed and went to do his daily tasks.

Walter was grateful to see him, as there was too much work for a single squire, but he was still apprehensive about how to treat Guy, and Guy could see his anxiety.

"Do not worry yourself, Walter, with this knighthood," Guy said. "I do not yet know what it means, although I had a similar experience with Sir Hector, when I journeyed with him as a squire. Our relationship ended up with a public acknowledgement in the deference of our positions, where I always addressed and served him in respect of his title and reputation. But in private we behaved as friends, although I always recognised his experience and greater knowledge."

"So, you are Sir Guy in front of others," Walter said.

"And just Guy in our own company," Guy responded. "You know too much about me to be in any doubt of my background and standing."

Walter smiled.

"So, you will still help with the horses?"

"I will help at the moment," Guy said, also smiling. "Until we return to Warwick, where I can order Terold to do all my old tasks."

"Can I be there when you do?" Walter replied, also smiling.

Guy returned to the Royal Palace and ate breakfast with Sir Harold before he was summoned to the King, who wanted to follow up on his promise of teaching Guy chess. Although he was initially nervous to informally socialise with the King, Guy quickly got to grips with the game, and he ended up enjoying its challenge. The King even presented him with an elaborately carved set of pieces, made from wood, and a polished game board. Edward cast aside Guy's thanks, although he was pleased that Guy promised that the next time they met, he would give the King more of a challenge with playing the game.

Guy decided to teach others this game on his return to Warwick, as playing against competent opponents might improve his skills. Guy also thought that being more of a challenge for the King might be advantageous in the future.

The King and Earl had between them negotiated property in the vicinity of Warwick, which included the land within Budbrooke, which his father had leased from the Earl before he rose to become his steward. The Earl had gained other lands as compensation and as a reward from the King for his loyalty. The Earl would remain Guy's liege lord, but he would be a Knight of the Realm and therefore also tied to the king.

Guy's land, which included tenants, were now his responsibility and he was their new overlord. His duties would be in their welfare and in the collection of taxes for the Earl, and ultimately the King. It was also in the provision of troops. Therefore, if the Earl raised the Warwick fyrd, which was a command for the local peasants to take up arms in support of the Earl or the King, then Guy would have to ensure that the peasants, under his governance, would be ready to fight in the defence of their land. The worth of this land made him, in effect, a Thegn, in the service of the Earl, which was a position of high social status in the Anglo-Saxon hierarchy.

Guy would need to design his personal standard, as his family had none, and this design would be recorded in the country's heraldic annuals.

Guy was not too concerned with the management of harvests, judging land disputes, or upholding the local laws that went with the position of a Thegn. He had seen his father perform these duties, as the Reeve of Warwick, for several years and the tasks did not seem beyond his capabilities. Sir Harold, however, said that he only had to employ a man to represent him in the day-to-day tasks and responsibilities. Guy would then only need to ensure that his administrator stayed both efficient and trustworthy.

"What about my training, my lord?" Guy asked Sir Harold.

Not for the first time, Sir Harold sat up in his chair and looked around him.

"Is your lord here?" Sir Harold replied, with raised eyebrows.

Guy sighed. After all the years that Sir Harold had chided him to adopt the use of his title as a sign of respect, he now wanted Guy to drop its use. Guy knew that he would find it equally as hard to get used to it.

"What about my training?" Guy asked again. "I am no longer a squire, and it feels that there is still so much more to learn."

"We both know that I have taught you all that I can, Guy. And I assume Sir Hector has taught you more," Sir Harold replied. "But perhaps you can help me in the training of the 'Earl's Terriers'. Unless the Earl has other plans for you, which I do not think he has had time to think about yet."

Guy thought about this for a while.

"When I stayed in Derby, I was the guest of Sir Aldred, who asked me to give a training session for his retainers. The standard of their training was far below what you provide Sir Harold." Guy then looked a bit sheepishly. "I sang your praises, Sir Harold, and invited Sir Aldred's son to visit Warwick, to witness how retainers should be trained for fighting."

"Thank you, Guy," Sir Harold replied with a satisfied tone. "And having Sir Aldred's son visit us would not be a problem. We had to put up with Sir Roderick staying at the castle for a couple of years."

"Then why not open your training to outside of Warwick and provide an elite school for people who are willing to pay for the privilege. It would increase the Earl's standing and forge new alliances. It will also make use of all the extra facilities that were built especially for the tournament."

Sir Harold thought over Guy's proposal.

"Not a bad idea, Guy," Sir Harold said, his mind still considering the possibilities of such a training establishment. "I will discuss it with the Earl."

Sir Harold continued to mull the idea over.

"Not a bad idea at all, Guy," he said again, nodding to himself.

The Earl had to stay in Winchester for two more days, as he attended further meetings with the King and other nobles. They had to agree on plans in the defence of the land from the Danes and in taking a position in Francia within the new political landscape.

Guy had spent some of his time with Athelstan, who took Guy hunting with him. The Prince picked up on their last meeting in the woods of Warwick and was determined to instruct Guy in the best way to kill a boar.

Although the hunt did not find a boar, they managed to run down a deer and Guy found himself enjoying the Prince's company. Guy heard from Athelstan that Robert, the Count of Poitiers had now declared himself the new King of West Francia. He was now consolidating his position with the support of the majority of the Francia barons and church dignitaries. Charles was still trying to raise support and manpower in Lorraine to retake the throne. Robert had also sent an emissary to Edward to see if an alliance of marriage could be negotiated, to place Robert on an equal footing to Charles, who was already married to one of Edward's daughters.

Guy wondered how Edward would move his chess pieces to meet this political manoeuvring.

The Earl's party left Winchester to return to Warwick. The skies were bright, and the air was crisp, but there was a light covering of snow on the ground, as the Earl took the group on a slight detour. The Earl wanted to show Guy the mysterious stone henge that grew out of the downs. Guy was fascinated by the giant stone rings, with their cold grey pillars and massive lintels that the Earl said had been built by the ancient tribes of Britain. Guy stared at the structure and wondered how it could have been built, never mind why. Earl Rohand could not explain its use, but he told Guy that the wizard Merlin, from Arthurian legend, was buried underneath. As he knew of Guy's interest in King Arthur, he thought that he might be curious at the monument. The Earl was right, as Guy spent a couple of hours just walking around looking at the structure and touching the stones. He felt a strange sense of energy emanating from their cold and stark solidity.

They then rode north across the downs until they joined the Fosse Way, which was the wide Roman road that would then take them north to Warwick. The Earl was in good spirits, as the snow brought his mind to planning the Christmas Epiphany and Nativity celebrations. This was the Christian reflective period that recognised the birth of their saviour, along with some more rowdy Yule feasts that the Earl provided for the Warwick townsfolk. These more raucous celebrations were more associated with the Pagan representation of the season and the mid-winter solstice. Although the distinction was blurred, it was not generally opposed by the church.

The Earl felt justified in making the trip to the royal court with such urgency, as his news was well received, and he had found favour with the King because of his prompt endeavours in providing the information. He had improved his prominence with the King and increased his powers in the kingdom with the reward of new lands. He was also happy with how well Guy was received by Edward, as the King was impressed with his adventures, conduct and commendations, which also reflected well on the Earl. And there was also the increased status in having another knight under his sponsorship. Overall, Earl Rohand was very satisfied with his decision to let Guy accompany Sir Hector on his travels.

It took just over a week for the Earl and his companions to arrive back at Warwick. They had to spend the night at the village of Wellesbourne, just south of Warwick, as the night closed in, preventing them making the final few miles. But this allowed for messengers to be sent to Warwick to announce the return of the Earl on the following morning. This meant that the townsfolk were forewarned and could line the main road into Warwick to welcome home the Earl and his party.

Word had also spread on Guy's advancement to a knight and, as he was both local to the town and a popular figure within the community, they celebrated his return with equal gusto. Shouts of 'Sir Guy' echoed in the thoroughfare of the tightly packed houses and Guy smiled at the people he knew. He also waved, playfully, at the young children, who ran between the bystanders as they followed the progress of the Earl through the town and into the castle fortress.

The castle commander had lined the path from the gate to the main hall with the castle guard and the Earl's family waited at the hall's doorway to greet the Earl.

Sir Harold slowed his horse to back away from Earl Rohand and quietly instructed Guy to do the same, while the rest of the party continued around to the stables and other quarters.

"Welcome home, my lord," Lady Elaine said and lightly curtsied in a formal greeting.

The Earl dismounted and bowed his head to his wife and then to Felice who had also curtsied.

"Father," she said.

"Thank you for this unexpected welcome," Earl Rohand said. "It has made the homecoming all the more gratifying."

Felice then turned to Sir Harold and Guy. She again curtsied, but this time with slow deliberation and a mischievous smile on her face.

"My lords," she said.

The Earl also smiled as he watched his daughter.

"So, you have heard of Guy's elevation?" The Earl said.

"Yes, my lord," Elaine replied and looked up at Guy. "Congratulations, Guy, I am sure it was well deserved."

"Thank you, my lady," Guy answered formally bowing his head.

He then turned to Felice and bowed in a more exaggerated manner, along with a haughty and serious expression. He then smiled warmly at her, before Sir Harold led him away to the stables.

Guy went home to his parents, who were overjoyed at his new title; his father especially so, for the honour it reflected on their family. It also meant that Guy would need to move out of their small house, and his father had just completed the arrangements for new living quarters for him in the main halls, alongside Sir Harold's apartment. The rent for which would be taken from his new allowance.

Guy told him of the land that was now given to him, and his father's eyes widened at the prospects. Sigard promptly offered his help in its management and administration.

Guy then went to find his friend, Terold, to quickly break the ice in respect to this new and awkward situation that they now found themselves in. Guy knew that Terold would not know how to react to Guy becoming a knight and the quicker they addressed the situation the better.

"So, all of this from spilling wine over a stranger," Terold said as they walked their horses around the training field. He smiled as he remembered when Guy first encountered Sir Hector, as a cupbearer to the Earl.

Guy suddenly became solemn at the mention of his friend.

"I am sorry for his death," Terold then said, recognising Guy's sadness.

"A lot has happened over a short time," Guy replied.

"But you will still be at the castle."

"I think so, but I am not sure what any of this means."

"Am I to be your squire?" Terold asked.

"Absolutely not," Guy answered. "I will want someone good."

Terold went to punch Guy in the arm, but then pulled it back as he suddenly realised that he could no longer do that to a person of Guy's new standing.

Guy laughed at Terold's reaction.

"I do not want things to change between us, Terold," Guy said. "Although I know that protocol will mean that it will have to for a short while."

"A short while?" Terold asked.

"We need to get you a knighthood as soon as possible," Guy answered. "Then you can punch me to your heart's desire."

Guy then looked at Terold.

"And I will help as much as possible," he said.

They walked on as Terold considered the possibilities.

"And you will still require a training partner?" Terold asked.

"Most definitely. I have a lot to show you from my time away."

"You also have a lot to tell me," Terold then continued.

Guy spent the rest of the day sorting out his new quarters and enlisted the help of the two pages, Edward and James. The boys were keen to renew their acquaintance with Guy, although they now treated him with a greater level of respect, which sometimes approached reverence. Guy however treated them the same and made sure that they had sufficient drink and food as a reward. He then felt a bit lost, as he had no further tasks, and wandered down to the stables to see Bedivere.

"Squire training in an hour, Guy," a voice called out from the doorway as he brushed Bedivere's coat with a handful of straw.

"And you really need to get a squire, to do that," Sir Harold then said.

"I need to do a lot of things, my lord. But I just do not know what."

"For years, I struggled in vain to get you to call me, lord and now when you haven't got to, you won't stop using the title."

"Sorry, Sir Harold," Guy said. "I will get used to it."

"The sooner, the better. But I would be grateful if you could put on a bit of a show for the boys, as they are keen to see the 'Champion of Soissons' in action."

"Champion of Spear on Horse, Sir Harold. Can you believe it?" Guy said laughing.

"No, I can't," Sir Harold said. "Where did you pull that one from? Sir Hector rarely used a spear."

"I believe that the ingenuity and innovation that I needed to win the title, was learned from you, Sir Harold. I just applied what you taught me to a new activity and picked up the niceties on the way."

Guy dropped the straw and brushed his hands clean of the dust as he walked towards Sir Harold.

"And of course, practise and hard work, which you also instilled in me," Guy then said.

"Thank you, Guy," Sir Harold said with humility. "It does me good to hear that from you."

"Oh, and I spoke with the Earl on your idea of opening up a school," Sir Harold continued. "He was all for it. In fact, he was quite excited at the possibilities, so we can start to plan for it straight away."

"That will be good. It will give me something to do," Guy said.

"Excellent," Sir Harold replied. "Would you mind putting on full armour and dress for this session, Guy?"

Guy turned up to the training field in full battle dress. He wore his newly polished mail over his bright red surcoat, along with his helmet, which glinted in the late afternoon sunlight. He came astride Bedivere, who was also adorned with its long red and gold-trimmed caparison, displaying the emblems of Warwick. Guy had his shield fastened to the side of the horse and his sword sheathed to his belt. He also carried a boar spear, held at the hip and pointing vertically into the air. He had quickly fashioned an old, polished spear into a rough copy of what he used at Soissons, although the lugs were not as strong as he would have liked and the groves at the tip too deep. He did however attach a small Warwick pennant that he found in the stable to its tip, which flapped in waves as the wind caught it.

The squires and pages numbered around twenty as they lined up in a rough square, with the squires in front and the pages behind. They looked on at Guy in wonder as he trotted Bedivere in a high gait in front of them, before bringing the horse to a sudden stop in front of Sir Harold. He then dismounted and led Bedivere around behind his friend, before bringing it back in a tight circle to stand alongside him."

"One thing that Sir Hector taught me, was to show off," Guy said quietly to Sir Harold, who was also impressed by Guy's entrance.

Sir Harold looked down at Guy's dress.

"You certainly look the part," he said.

He then reached down and ran his fingers over the emblem of the oak tree, which was Sir Harold's motif.

"Must have brought me luck," Guy said and smiled at Sir Harold.

"Would you mind addressing them?" Sir Harold asked, with a choked voice, as the emblem unexpectedly touched him.

"Not at all," Guy answered, surprised at how confident he felt in doing so.

He was about to speak, when there was a call from behind and they turned to find Earl Rohand hurrying down from the castle halls. Guy's heart leapt when he noticed Felice walking elegantly, several paces behind the Earl, with Father Cuthbert, in tow.

The Earl approached with a large smile on his face as he looked at Guy and Bedivere.

"And this is how you represented me in Soissons, Guy," he said with obvious pleasure.

"As well as in Rouen, and also in Derby, my lord."

"Felice came to fetch me as soon as she saw you leave the stables," the Earl said and looked behind him to his daughter. "And what did you say, Felice, when you saw him?"

Felice waited until she stood alongside her father and looked at Guy. "I said that Guy looked glorious in his armour and transcended the image of an Arthurian knight."

"That was it, and now that I have seen you myself, I can see that she was right."

Guy bowed to the Earl and smiled at Felice.

She wore a long light green cloak that was trimmed with a white fur collar and fastened with a silver broach. Her hair fell in waves down over the cloak, her eyes were bright, and her cheeks were kissed red by the winter chill and Guy's heart melted at the sight of her.

"So, Sir Harold what is happening?" The Earl asked.

"Guy was just about to address the boys, my lord and then he was going to help me put them through their training. He was also perhaps going to demonstrate some new techniques that he has picked up on his travels."

"That sounds good. I think I would like to see this. Will you be warm enough, Felice, or do you want to return to the castle?"

Guy caught his breath and waited on Felice's reply. He did not want her to leave.

"I think that I will stay for a while, Father," she replied.

"Over to you then Guy," the Earl then said.

Guy turned and faced the squires and then removed his helmet to hold it under his arm. He shook his head and combed his hair back with his fingers.

"As you all know, I have travelled to the far eastern boundaries of Francia, and I have fought in an official tournament at Soissons and a few unofficial tournaments elsewhere," Guy said slowly in a loud voice. "I also had to fight in a couple of skirmishes, where lives were at stake and lives were taken. I am here now, both as a tournament champion and as a

341

man who is glad to be alive. Those achievements were only won because of the training that I received here in Warwick under the care of Sir Harold."

There was an individual cheer from within the ranks and Guy thought it sounded like Ted.

"And I can say, that amongst all the many adversaries and enemies that I have fought against on my travels, the most capable fighters lie amongst this group of well-trained warriors that now stand in front of me."

More cheers rang up from the onlookers.

"And I fought those adversaries as a proud squire of Warwick." Guy then paused and looked at them. "Because that's what I was; a squire of Warwick." He paused again. "And I found that there was a great honour in that. The reputation of the 'Earl's Terriers' has now spread across foreign lands, and you now have to maintain and increase that reputation."

He paused again and looked across the boys.

"The hours of training and practise that we go through every day meant that I did not have to think about the basics of swordcraft or horse control. That all came naturally, which meant that I could concentrate on working my opponents out, with feints and deceptions, so that I could identify their weaknesses and then take advantage of them. This is what I learned here on this field against warriors such as Terold, and as you know, Terold has best me more times than I like to remember."

"Sir Hector, who you all met last summer, was a courageous and valiant man as well as a great knight, whose fame and reputation as a swordsman was recognised across the known world. He once told me that you do not make your reputation on the training field, here is where you grow and hone your skills to provide you with a platform to win fights and contests. He said that you never lose a fight when you are training, because it is never a fight, it is just a learning exercise. So do not be afraid to try things out on the training field and do not be afraid to lose a fight, as this will increase your knowledge and experience for when it matters."

"So, every time Terold thought he had beaten me in training, he was wrong." Guy then looked at Terold. "I wasn't beaten, I was just learning."

The boys all laughed.

"So," Guy then said and put his helmet back on. "Pick a partner and try something new and when it fails, learn from it, improve it and try it again."

Guy then curled his forefinger at Terold and invited him to face him and they sparred together like they used to. But Guy, straight away, knew that it was not the same as it used to be. Guy realised that he had fundamentally changed as a person and the joy of just play fighting had gone. Fighting to Guy had now become serious, and there was no longer any fun when you have fought to kill or be killed.

Guy encouraged a swift changing of partners and walked around the group facing different opponents and executing different manoeuvres.

Guy then halted the training and addressed the group again.

"Before we finish, Sir Harold asked me to show you something new." Guy then picked up his spear and jumped onto Bedivere. "So, as the Soissons's champion, I will demonstrate the strength needed to win such an illustrious tournament."

Guy then suddenly kicked Bedivere forward into a tight turn and lowered his spear as he charged the nearest tree. There was a flurry of black and bright red with flashes of gold and silver as Guy galloped forward.

Guy was a bit nervous as he had not practised for a while and concentrated all the harder on the target. But he hit the tree on the side of its trunk in the glancing blow that he intended. This caused the spear to explode in shards, allowing him to deflect the remnants of the spear away from the tree and retain a grip on the shaft while remaining in the saddle.

There was silence as the crowd, as he cantered back to the group. They were mystified at how Guy remained on his horse, after the force of such a hit.

Guy pulled Bedivere to a halt, dropped the broken spear shaft onto the floor and slid down from the saddle onto the grass.

Guy raised his eyebrows at Sir Harold as he walked by and then bowed to Earl Rohand.

"Well done, Guy," the Earl said. "I have never seen the like of that before."

"Practise, my lord," Guy said. "And a large bit of spectacle to please the crowd."

"Sir Hector would have been proud of you," Felice said softly, from behind her father.

"Thank you, my lady," Guy replied. "If you think more of me because of my little demonstration, then Sir Hector would have been satisfied. Reputation meant everything to Sir Hector."

"Then Sir Hector will be satisfied," Felice replied.

"I am now feeling a bit chilled, father. I think I will return to the castle after all," she then said.

"Perhaps, you could escort me, Sir Knight," Felice said to Guy.

"Certainly, my lady. With your leave, my lord," Guy said, asking permission of the Earl.

"Please do, Guy," the Earl replied.

Guy took hold of Bedivere's reins and brought him alongside Felice.

"Would you care to ride, my lady?" Guy asked.

Felice thought about it, but then shook her head.

"I think it would be better if I walked," she said and smiled. "But thank you, Guy."

Felice then turned and walked slowly towards the castle and Guy walked alongside her, leading Bedivere on a close rein. Father Cuthbert walked two paces behind them.

"Everyone is applauding you for your success Guy, but it must have been hard for you."

"I have grown up a lot, my lady and I understand myself far more than I did when we last talked together."

"And is that understanding gratifying?"

"Not in my grief of Sir Hector's death, my lady. And not in recognising some aspects of my own behaviour. But in my general capabilities and ambitions, I am satisfied, and I do not have any regrets in any of the choices that I have made."

"And have you now achieved your ambitions, Guy?" Felice asked.

"Not all of them, my lady," Guy replied. "I have one desire that I have borne for years, and it is like a chasm in my chest. But I continue to dream of what might be and I strive towards it. I hope that the emptiness will be filled, and my life will be complete."

Felice did not ask any more of Guy and they walked on in silence.

Guy had, again, opened the door to his feelings for Felice, and he struggled in reconciling what he wanted to do and say, against the reality of the situation.

Although he had improved his social standing, he was still a lowly knight and she was an Earl's daughter and heiress to great wealth, in both land and income.

But she was still unattached, and the dream could be sustained. But nothing was decided, nothing had been said.

He had hinted to his love for Felice, and she had deferred any response, but nothing had been fully disclosed and nothing had been rejected. This was the crux of Guy's dilemma. He knew that he desperately wanted to tell Felice of his feelings and wishes for the future, and he also knew that he would be rejected. But he wanted that certainty to allow them both to move on. So, Guy, rose early each morning and followed a routine of visiting Bedivere in the stables and then strolling around the castle gardens, which as a knight and a member of the Earl's household, he could now do. He then supported Sir Harold in schooling the pages and squires in fighting and battle training before eating lunch and then exercising Bedivere around the training field in the afternoon. He then practised with Terold in the late afternoon, before returning to the castle. All of this was in full view of the castle walls and the Earl's family chambers so if Felice wanted, she could plan to meet with him.

And this was something Felice did want, and she met Guy on the fifth morning of his routine by joining him in the castle garden. She was dressed for the cold and was accompanied by Janette, her lady-in-waiting. Janette however sat on a wooden bench at the garden's entrance, as instructed, allowing Felice to walk alone with Guy.

"I am glad you are back Guy," Felice said to him. "I worried about you going away with Sir Hector, and from the stories that you have told us, I was right to be concerned."

"It was far more dangerous than I imagined. But I managed to survive," Guy replied. "Since I have returned, the talk has all been about my exploits, but I have heard nothing about your trip to court. How was it?"

"Uneventful, I got paraded around a lot, but nothing came of it."

"So, no suitor?" Guy asked.

Felice smiled.

"No, but not from lack of effort from my mother."

They walked on in silence, but Guy's senses were captivated by Felice's presence, and he felt like he was going to either explode or break down if he did not speak.

"Felice," he said, taking a deep breath. "I have devoted my new life in the castle to become better than I was. I have trained and worked harder than anyone else, just to try and achieve status, so that I might be worthy of your attention." Guy then stopped and looked at Felice who stopped alongside him.

"The journey to Soissons and back was hard, my lady, and I faced death on many occasions. I only survived because of my feelings for you and the overwhelming desire for a dream that may be out of my reach." Guy paused, but Felice kept her head bowed and stared at her feet. "But I can no longer go on without telling you of my love for you. You are the reason why I wake in the morning, and you are my last thoughts at night. In between I am empty, except for the fleeting moments that I see you and behold your beauty or speak with you and share your grace."

Guy lightly took hold of her hand that rested at her side and held it by the tips of her fingers.

"I tell you this Felice because my soul demands it and I needed you to be in no doubt of my love for you."

"And my love for you should make me more worthy than any other man alive in gaining your hand in marriage. Although I am not high born, my devotion to you is my nobility and my love for you is my wealth."

Guy then remained silent.

Felice did not remove her hand from his, but just slowly raised her head.

Small delicate rivulets of tears ran lightly down her cheeks as she looked deep into Guy's eyes.

End of Book One